USA TODAY bestselling author **Jennie Lucas**'s parents owned a bookstore, and she grew up surrounded by books, dreaming about faraway lands. A fourth-generation Westerner, she went east at sixteen to boarding school on scholarship, wandered the world, got married, then finally worked her way through college before happily returning to her hometown. A 2010 RITA® Award finalist and 2005 Golden Heart® Award winner, she lives in Idaho with her husband and children.

USA TODAY bestselling and RITA® Award–nominated author **Caitlin Crews** loves writing romance. She teaches her favourite romance novels in creative writing classes at places like UCLA Extension's prestigious Writers' Programme, where she finally gets to utilise the MA and PhD in English Literature she received from the University of York in England. She currently lives in the Pacific Northwest, with her very own hero and too many pets. Visit her at caitlincrews.com.

THE SECRET THE ITALIAN CLAIMS

JENNIE LUCAS

THE BRIDE'S BABY OF SHAME

CAITLIN CREWS

MILLS & BOON

First Published in Great Britain 2018
by Mills & Boon, an imprint of HarperCollins*Publishers*
1 London Bridge Street, London, SE1 9GF

The Secret the Italian Claims © 2018 by Jennie Lucas

The Bride's Baby of Shame © 2018 by Caitlin Crews

ISBN: 978-0-263-93539-4

MIX
Paper from
responsible sources
FSC® C007454

Printed and bound in Spain
by CPI, Barcelona

THE SECRET THE ITALIAN CLAIMS

JENNIE LUCAS

To Julie Henke,
who flew all the way from St. Louis to Orlando
to meet me at a book signing.
Wonderful readers like you are why I do what I do.

CHAPTER ONE

FAMILY MEANT EVERYTHING to Hallie Hatfield.

Family meant home. It meant being safe and protected even when times were bad. Even when the money ran out at the end of the month. Even when the kitchen cupboards were bare. Family meant always having someone to watch your back, as you watched theirs.

As Hallie had grown up, in an old wooden house built by her great-grandfather, playing in the woods with her brother, learning songs from her mother, tinkering in the garage with her father, she'd known, even as a child, exactly how she wanted her life to be.

Someday she'd get married. She'd raise children, just as her own parents had, without much money but with lots of love. She and her future husband would grow old together, living close to her family, in a cottage with a view of the soft, green Appalachian hills where she'd been born. Their lives would be full of music and comfort. Because family meant everything.

Then, at nineteen, without warning, Hallie lost everything. Her family. Her home. All the meaning and security in her world.

Now, at twenty-four, the only family she had was the tiny newborn baby in her arms. Living in New York City, she had no job, no money and, as of today, nowhere to go.

But *this* as a solution?

No.

Hallie took a deep, furious breath. "No. Absolutely not."

"But Hallie—"

"Tell my ex-boss about his baby?" Keeping her voice low, not to waken the newborn baby sleeping in her arms,

Hallie glared at her friends. "After the way he treated me? Never!"

The other two women looked at each other. The three friends had been introduced months earlier at a single-moms support group, when a mutual acquaintance had realized that all three were pregnant with their first child, and, shockingly, none of them had yet told the fathers.

In Hallie's case, it was for good reason.

Her whole life, she'd tried to see the best in people. To be sympathetic and kind and good.

But she *hated* Cristiano Moretti. After what he'd done, he didn't deserve to know their three-month-old baby existed.

"But he's the father," Tess Foster said gently. A plump, kindly redhead who worked at her uncle's bakery, she cuddled her own tiny baby. "Hallie, you need help. It only makes sense to ask him."

"You're an idiot if you don't get child support," said Lola Price, who was blonde and fiery, and extra-irritable lately—which was saying something—as, unlike the others, she was still heavily pregnant. "Are you an idiot?"

Hallie ground her teeth. That question had already been asked and answered in her own heart. Yes, she'd been an idiot, letting her boss, a billionaire hotel tycoon, seduce her so easily into giving up her long-held dreams of a forever family, a forever home, for one night of passion.

One night? Ha! *Half* a night, since Cristiano had tossed her out of his bed at midnight and then had her fired from her housekeeping job the very next morning!

Who did that?

A selfish bastard with no heart, that was who. A man who'd ruthlessly thrown her into poverty and homelessness—since she'd also lost her company-paid housing—just because he'd wanted to avoid feeling awkward if he ran into her in the hallway of his hotel.

Hallie looked down at the sweet sleeping baby in her arms. Jack had been over nine pounds at birth, and he'd only gotten chubbier. She loved him with all the ferocious love in her heart. She'd always dreamed of having children. Now Jack was her only dream. Keeping him happy. Keeping him safe.

"You don't even have a place to stay tonight," Tess pointed out. "Unless you're going to call the police on your landlord."

"And you can't stay with me," Lola said, putting her hands over her huge belly. She didn't explain, but then Lola never explained anything.

"I wish you could stay with us, but my aunt and uncle would never allow it," Tess said mournfully. "They're already threatening to kick me out." She sighed. "If only you hadn't ripped up the check your boss stuck in the envelope with your severance pay."

Hallie lifted her chin. "I have my pride."

"But it was for a *hundred thousand dollars*," Tess said.

"And is pride going to feed your baby?" Lola said tartly.

Hallie's shoulders sagged. Lola wasn't sweet and comforting like Tess, but she sure had a way of forcing people to see hard truths.

After her supervisor had fired her, Hallie had stumbled out of the hotel in shock, then opened the severance envelope to discover a check signed by Cristiano personally. As if he thought paying her for taking her virginity would make it all right to toss her out like trash the next morning. Furious and heartbroken, she'd torn it into a million pieces.

Now Hallie realized painfully how that money would have changed her whole life—and Jack's. Because a year later, she had nothing.

But she hadn't known she would end up pregnant. She ran an unsteady hand over her forehead. So much for pride. She would have given anything to have that check back now.

"Come on." Lola stood up abruptly in the middle of the community-hall basement, surrounded by the folding chairs and a crowd of other single moms standing by a punch bowl and cookies that Tess complained constantly were stale. "We're going."

"Where?"

"To see your baby's father. Right now. It's your only option."

Hallie feared her friend was right. But thinking of facing Cristiano, her courage failed her. "I can't."

"Why?"

"I told you. I was just a notch on the bedpost. He was cruel—"

"Cruel?" Lola's eyes became fiercely protective. "You never said that. What did he do? Hit you? Threaten you?"

"Of course not," Hallie replied, taken aback.

"Then what?"

A lump rose in Hallie's throat. "He ignored me."

The blonde's shoulders relaxed slightly. "He's a jerk. But you're sure he's the father?"

"Yes, but I wish he wasn't!"

Lola's eyes were merciless. "Then make him pay. Child support, if nothing else."

Hallie thought of how desperately she needed money. The lump in her throat became a razor blade. "I can't."

"You don't have any choice. You have no family to help you. Are you seriously going to check into a homeless shelter while your ex lives at a luxury hotel, swilling champagne?"

Hallie sucked in her breath at her friend's frank words.

"And, you never know, he might be happy about the baby when you tell him," argued Tess, who was very tenderhearted. "There might be some perfectly good explanation why he kicked you out that night, then had you fired, then never returned your messages…"

Her voice trailed off. Even Tess couldn't quite overcome how ludicrous it sounded.

If only. Hallie gave her a wistful smile, then the smile slid away.

Tell Cristiano she'd had his baby?

Go back to the luxury hotel where she'd once worked as a housekeeper, to beg for the help of a selfish, ruthless tycoon, and this time give him the opportunity to reject both her and the baby in person? No way.

But looking down at her peacefully slumbering baby, his sweet little mouth pursing in his sleep, she knew Lola was right. Hallie had tried her best to survive on pride. But, after this latest disaster with her landlord today, she had nowhere else to go.

"All right," Hallie said in a small voice.

"You'll do it?" Lola's voice was tinged with relief. For all of the blonde's hard edges, Lola's protectiveness of her friends made Hallie suspect that on the inside she was every bit as kind as Tess but, for some reason, tried desperately to hide it.

"You're right," Hallie said glumly. "I have no choice."

The three of them, plus the two babies and Jack's folding stroller, all piled into a ride-share taxi. But by the time it dropped them off in front of the towering luxury hotel in Midtown, Hallie was already regretting her choice. Just half a night in Cristiano's arms had nearly destroyed her. How could she face him again?

Tess, with her own baby in a comfy sling against her chest, tilted her head back to look at the skyscraper that was the Campania Hotel. "He manages all this?"

"He owns it."

Both women turned to her sharply in the warm July night.

Lola wasn't easily impressed, but her eyes were wide as saucers. "Your ex is *Cristiano Moretti*?"

Hallie felt a little sick as she nodded.

"I thought it was the hotel manager," Tess said in awe.

"It doesn't matter who he is," Lola said fiercely. "Demand what is yours by right. For Jack."

Pushing the stroller, Hallie walked slowly past the neon sign of the Blue Hour glowing in the darkness. The hotel's jazz club had live music, and she'd once dreamed of performing there. Now, as she walked past the club, her failed singing career was the last thing on her mind.

What if Cristiano refused to see her? Or—worse—what if, when he found out about the baby, he demanded parental rights over Jack?

If only she could talk him into just blindly giving her that same big check she'd ripped up the year before!

She stopped, glancing back nervously when she saw her friends following her. "You're coming with me?"

"So you don't back out," Lola said.

"So you don't feel alone," Tess said.

With a deep breath, Hallie squared her shoulders and went through the enormous revolving door into the lobby.

The Campania's lobby was thirty feet high, gleaming with white marble floors and midcentury-modern furniture scattered around multiple fireplaces. One side held the long oak check-in desk, and at the very center of the lobby there was an elegant bar.

After going inside, Hallie stopped as well-dressed, wealthy guests passed them by on the busy summer evening.

"What's the problem?" Lola said.

"Can't you just go to his room?" Tess said.

"No," Hallie said. "There's security. You need a fingerprint on the elevator."

"Call him, then."

"I don't have his direct number. We never really talked before…" She hesitated.

Lola scowled. "You were just the hired help, huh?"

Hallie looked down, her cheeks hot. Even when she'd worked for him, there were about fifty levels of supervisors between a maid and the billionaire owner of an international hotel conglomerate. She said weakly, "I can try to leave a message with his secretary, or—"

Her voice cut off with a gasp.

Cristiano had just come out of the elevator on the second floor, open above the lobby.

The reaction was immediate, as if he were a movie star on the red carpet. Heads turned, people whispered and gasped. His entourage followed in his wake as he made his way down the stairs to the ground floor—a gorgeous, pouting model at his side, with two assistants and a bodyguard trailing behind.

But, for Hallie, everything else became a blur. Even her friends were forgotten.

All she could see was…him.

Cristiano Moretti was broad shouldered, dark and powerful, outwardly civilized in a perfectly cut tuxedo, but with a five-o'clock shadow on his hard jaw and glittering black eyes that hinted at a ruthless, brutal soul. Looking at him, Hallie shivered, caught between longing and fear, overwhelmed by memory of the night he'd seduced her. The night her whole world had changed.

As a trusted maid at the Campania Hotel New York, she'd occasionally been assigned the enviable task of cleaning and tidying the Italian tycoon's exclusive penthouse, used only when he was in town. Dusting pictures of Cristiano's gorgeous face as he stood beside famous politicians and celebrities, Hallie had developed a serious crush. She'd actually imagined that Cristiano wasn't just insanely handsome, he was also honorable and good.

Wrong.

She blinked now, looking at him. The way he smiled. So casual. As if he had not a care in the world. He was so arrogantly handsome, king of the world in his tuxedo, apparently off for a night on the town with a beautiful model. While she'd spent the last year struggling, looking for a new job when she was pregnant and trying to find a cheap place to stay in New York City.

For the last year, he'd been enjoying himself—swilling champagne, as Lola had said. He really had forgotten Hallie even existed.

As Cristiano turned to speak to the woman pouting beside him in a gold lamé minidress, Hallie breathlessly handed the stroller's handle to Lola.

"Keep an eye on Jack."

The blonde frowned. "The man will want to meet his own son."

Hallie set her jaw. "I will tell Cristiano in my own way."

"You're being irrational," Lola began, but Tess put her hand gently on Lola's arm.

"Let Hallie do it."

Hallie flashed the redhead a grateful look.

"Fine," Lola said, drawing back stiffly.

Swallowing hard, Hallie went toward Cristiano, planting herself in the middle of his path through the lobby. Her heart was pounding wildly.

It was funny, really. If she'd known when getting ready for the single-moms group that afternoon that she'd end up facing her old lover, she might have put on lipstick and worn something nicer than an old faded sundress that fit her post-pregnancy body. He'd probably take one look at her and wonder how she'd ever ended up in his bed in the first place. Well, there was no help for it now. And it wasn't like she would ever, ever, *ever* want to sleep with him again. Ever.

Putting her hands on her hips, she tried to hide her nervousness as she waited.

His bodyguard tried to smooth his way, holding out his arm. "Excuse us, miss."

Then, from behind him, Cristiano's eyes caught hers.

For a split second, he went completely still. Then his jaw tightened. "It's all right, Luther." He came forward. "What are you doing here, Hallie?"

He remembered her name. She was almost surprised. She hated the shiver that went through her at having him so close, towering over her in his tuxedo, nearly touching her. His dark gaze seared through her. She found herself wanting to blurt out everything, to tell him not just that she'd had his baby but that he'd broken her heart.

She forced herself to say, "I need to talk to you. In private."

His expression became distant. "That's not a good idea."

"I have something important to tell you."

"Tell me now."

"In the middle of the lobby?" Hallie's cheeks went hot. She could feel people watching them. Even the model, standing nearby in her high heels, was looking down at Hallie with scorn. They were all probably wondering why such a frumpy girl would dare talk to Cristiano Moretti. For a moment, Hallie's nerve faltered. She wanted to run away, to forget the whole thing.

Then she saw her friends watching from the other side of the lobby. Saw her sleeping baby cuddled in the stroller. That gave her courage. "It's important."

"Not interested." But as he turned to go, she stepped in front of him.

"Either you speak with me privately right now," she said, determined, "or I'll make a scene in this lobby you can't possibly imagine."

Cristiano stared at her for a long moment, as if assessing her. Then he held up his hand, halting the bodyguard's intervention.

"Go ahead to the gala, Natalia," he told his date. "My driver will take you. I'll see you later."

The woman's pout intensified. She glared at Hallie, then said, "All right, darling," and sashayed out of the lobby hips first, as if she were on a catwalk at New York Fashion Week. She was so obviously a model that even the sophisticated patrons of this luxurious hotel turned to watch her go. So did Hallie, a little wistfully. What would it be like to get that much attention wherever you went? *She* would be able to get an audition at the Blue Hour, for one.

"Follow me," Cristiano said, turning on his heel without waiting to see if Hallie followed.

She glanced nervously back at her baby and friends. Then, biting her lip, she went up the sweeping staircase, following the man she hated most on earth, to face him alone in his lair.

Cristiano Moretti's jaw was tight as he went to the wet bar in his private office on the second floor.

Lifting the lid off the crystal decanter, he glanced back at Hallie as she followed him hesitantly into the high-ceilinged room with its dark oak panels. "Scotch?"

Hallie shook her head, her beautiful brown eyes wide.

Turning back to the bar, he poured himself a short glass over ice. He could almost feel her vibrating with anxiety behind him. He put the lid back on the decanter, then drank the Scotch in one long, slow gulp. He realized he was playing for time.

But then, Hallie Hatfield had been Cristiano's biggest mistake. And at thirty-five years old, with his scandalous past, that was saying something.

He turned to face her. *"Va bene,"* he said shortly. "We are alone. What do you want?"

Hallie swallowed, blushed, hesitated. He could see her trying to formulate her words, but she didn't have to say anything. Cristiano already knew why she was here.

She'd come to demand money.

Silently he cursed himself. How could he have been so stupid?

He'd known this would happen. He was just surprised it had taken a year.

Hallie must have spoken with a lawyer who would have pointed out her excellent case for suing him for wrongful termination. His emotions had gotten the better of him the day he'd had her fired, because he'd never done anything so foolish, before or since.

Looking at her, he could almost understand why. Hallie had big, soulful eyes a man could drown in. And her curves! In a loose cotton sundress, her body was even more lush than he remembered. Her dark hair fell in waves over her full breasts, almost down to her tiny waist.

Cristiano could still remember how it had felt to have her in his arms, the sensation of her soft body sliding beneath his as their naked limbs tangled in the very bedsheets she'd made just an hour before.

He'd seduced her. There could be no doubt of that. Coming back to New York a day early, he'd heard her sweet, husky voice singing from the bedroom of his penthouse. Her wistful, heartbreaking melody had filled him with longing for things lost. Things he'd never had. Things he'd never dared even dream of.

Then he'd seen her, waving fresh sheets in the air with her arms spread wide. An incredibly beautiful, sensual brunette with an hourglass figure, leaning over to make his bed. Even that black housekeeping uniform had looked indescribably erotic on her.

A shocked sound had come from the back of his throat. She'd turned and looked at him. A tumble of emotions had cascaded across her beautiful face. Surprise, fear, delight. For a moment their eyes had locked, and he'd forgotten his own name.

Then he'd forced himself to give a casual smile. "You're not my usual housekeeper."

"Camille had to go home early today to be with her grandson, but she warned me not to let you catch me," she stammered. "I'm supposed to be invisible."

Coming forward, his eyes devouring every inch of her, he'd murmured, "You're anything but invisible. What were you singing?"

"Just an Appalachian folk song."

"It's beautiful." Coming close enough to touch her, he'd whispered, "So are you."

Her cheeks had gone rosy, her lips parting in unconscious invitation as she stood beside his enormous bed.

He'd reached for her.

Cristiano knew who was at fault. He'd wanted her. So he'd taken her. Without thinking of the consequences. If he had, he would have stopped himself. It was one of his rules: never sleep with employees.

But that wasn't the worst rule he'd broken. Hallie wasn't just an employee. She'd also been a virgin. Virgins were off-limits. He didn't toy with women who might mistake sex for love and become a problem later.

He'd known she was a virgin from the first time he'd kissed her, when he'd felt the tremble of her sweet lips. He felt her hesitation, her shyness, her inexperience. And he'd known. Somehow, this incredible woman was untouched.

It hadn't made him stop. He was a man who put few limits on his own behavior. But he had a code of honor. In Hallie Hatfield's case, he'd recklessly blown through his own rules like dynamite through a brick wall.

So it was no wonder he'd broken a third rule, afterward, and fired her for sleeping with him.

That wasn't the reason he'd given her supervisor, the head housekeeper, of course. But it had been obvious to Hallie. And clearly her lawyer, too.

But now, as Hallie stood across from him in his private office, biting her full, delectable lower lip, it was hard for him to think about lawyers when all he wanted to do was pull her back into his arms.

For a year, he'd done his best to forget her. He'd told himself he had. Now he knew that was a lie.

"Why are you here?" Cristiano demanded in a low voice.

"I came to…came to tell you…"

Her husky voice trembled, stopped. She looked at him.

Turning away, Cristiano set down the crystal lowball glass heavily on the dark wood bar. He clenched his hands at his sides to keep himself from the temptation of pulling her into his arms and kissing her to see if her lips were still as delicious as he remembered. He was drawn by the sweet sin of her mouth. Of her body. Of her deep brown eyes, luring him into their depths.

Possessing her once had not been enough. After he'd had her that night, he'd just wanted more. It didn't help that, naked and soft in his arms, she'd looked up at him in bed as if she were half in love with him already. She'd lured him like a siren to give him more than just his body. More than just his money.

But sex and money were all he could give any woman.

So he'd sent her away, tossing her from the warmth of his bed when his body was still aching for more. After she'd gone, he'd still longed for her, like a sweet, forbidden poison. First thing the next morning, he'd contacted her supervisor and arranged to have her fired. For her own good. And his.

But he had never stopped wanting her. And now, as he stepped toward her, his breathing was hard. And not just his breathing.

"Tell me what you want."

"I need to tell you something. Important."

"So you said." Cristiano's voice was low as he looked down at her. He came closer, almost close enough to touch her. His mind was scrambling for rationalizations as to why he should.

Perhaps if he slept with her just one more time…

Got her out of his system…

Stop, he told himself furiously.

Hesitating, Hallie licked her full, pink lips. He nearly groaned. Was she purposely taunting him?

"This…isn't easy to say," she whispered.

Gritting his teeth, he glared at her. "Let me say it for you, then. I already know why you're here."

Her caramel-brown eyes went wide.

"You know?"

He set his jaw. "You never cashed the check."

Hallie blinked, furrowing her forehead. "The check?"

"The morning after."

Her cheeks colored and she looked away.

"No," she said in a low voice. "I ripped it into a million pieces and threw it in the trash."

"Because you knew, even then, you could demand far more."

Hallie looked at him sharply.

"I can?" she whispered. "You'd give me money, just for asking? Why?"

"You want me to admit it aloud?" He pulled her roughly against him. She gasped as his hands suddenly moved over her waist, her hips.

"What are you doing?"

"Checking for a microphone." But even through the thin cotton of her sundress, touching her waist and hips without crushing her lips with his own felt like torture.

"Let me go," she breathed, not moving.

He released her. Stepping back, he leaned against the marble fireplace, folding his arms and keeping his voice very cold. "Who is your lawyer?"

"My lawyer?"

"Don't try to pretend you don't have one. You knew I'd want to keep this quiet. I'm not proud of it."

Her eyes widened. "Of—of what?"

"It would hardly improve the public image of my company if the CEO is sued for sexual harassment."

"Oh." Biting her lip, she looked away, staring for a long moment at the wall of leather-bound books he never read, and the leather reading chair he never sat in, both brought in by an interior designer to make his office look like a nineteenth-century gentleman's study. And all Cristiano could think right now was that he wanted to bend her back against the enormous dark wood desk, kiss her senseless, pull off her clothes and...

He had to get rid of her before he did something else he'd regret.

"Just tell me the amount," he said tightly.

"The amount?"

"How much?"

Licking her lips, Hallie said, "I want...the same amount as before."

"A hundred thousand dollars?" he said incredulously.

"I'll never bother you again. I give you my word."

Cristiano could hardly believe she'd ask for so little. Far less than he'd pay if they went to trial. Less than he paid his lawyers for a month. Was it some kind of trick? Or had she been given bad advice by the worst lawyer in the world?

Searching her face, he warned, "You'd have to sign a nondisclosure form."

"I'll sign anything you want," she said meekly, folding her hands in front of her like a nun at prayer.

Now Cristiano was really suspicious. "And a statement admitting that you were fired for cause."

"What does that mean?"

"You'd say it was your own fault you were fired." He gave a careless shrug, even as he watched her closely. "The reason can be anything you want. Tardiness. Stealing."

"Stealing!" Hallie repeated indignantly. Then her expression deliberately smoothed over and became meek again. "I will admit to being late. Yes. I was very, very late."

Something in Hallie's tone when she said *I was very, very late* rang true. And yet he knew it was not.

The morning Cristiano had decided to fire her, he'd asked the HR department to review her file, hoping to hear a legitimate reason she deserved to be let go. "Oh, no, sir," the HR head had chirped. "Miss Hatfield is one of our hardest-working employees. She works late and volunteers to work holidays instead of employees with kids. And she's never late!"

So he'd given the task of firing her to her supervisor, instead. Handing the head housekeeper a sealed envelope with a big check, he'd explained to the woman that he'd found Hallie intrusive and her singing annoying. The head housekeeper, whom Cristiano had never spoken to directly before, hadn't asked the same questions HR would have. She'd just followed his order.

So why would Hallie accept a hundred thousand dollars now, in lieu of a settlement that could have brought her millions? And want it so badly she was actually willing to defame her own character for it?

What kind of incompetent, useless lawyer would ever advise her to do such a thing?

Cristiano could barely restrain himself from telling her what a bad deal she was making. But his goal was to be rid of her before she caused him any more damage—personally or professionally.

"Fine." He turned to his enormous desk. Pulling out a standard nondisclosure agreement usually given to high-level executives, he pushed it across the desk toward her and scribbled something on a separate piece of paper.

"Might as well keep the lawyers out of it, and save us both time and trouble," he said carelessly. "Sign these and I'll write you a check."

Hallie looked at him sharply. "Give me the check first."

"What?" He gave a low laugh. "You don't trust me?"

"No." She looked at him with quiet determination. "Because I know what kind of man you really are."

His back snapped straight. "What kind is that?"

"You seduced me—" her dark eyes glittered in the shadows "—then had me fired. You took my job away, just to avoid the inconvenience of seeing me."

She was right. And he hated her for it.

"And now we both know what kind of woman *you* are," he said coldly. "The kind of woman who is willing to lie about herself for a hundred thousand dollars."

Her deep brown eyes held his, then dropped.

"Yes," she said in a low voice. "I suppose I am." She squared her shoulders. "But I'll still need the check before I sign."

"Fine." Turning away, he got his checkbook out of the safe. Scribbling the amount and signing it, he handed it to her.

Her hand trembled as she took the check. For a moment, she just looked down at it. Then she pressed it against her chest, looking almost near tears.

"Thank you," she whispered. "You don't know what this will mean to us."

"Us?"

"Me," she said quickly.

Obviously, she'd already found another lover. The thought bothered him. He pushed it aside. He had no claim on her, and she would have none on him once the deal was finished.

Setting his jaw, he held out the pen. "Now your side of the bargain."

"Of course." Taking the pen, she leaned over his desk to read the two documents—the nondisclosure agreement and an admission of fault. As she read, Cristiano's gaze traced unwillingly down her long throat to the dark hair tumbling down her back to the sweet fullness of her backside. Her breasts seemed fuller than he remembered.

He forced himself to look away.

Signing both papers with a flourish, she put the lid back on his pen, then handed it to him along with the signed papers. "Here."

She seemed strangely joyful, as if the weight of the world had just been lifted off her shoulders.

Cristiano barely restrained a scowl. His hand brushed hers as he took the papers and pen. Her cheeks went bright red, and she dropped her hand. "Thanks. Goodbye."

He watched incredulously as, without another word, she headed for the door.

"That's it?"

Hallie glanced back with a smile. "You wanted to be rid of me."

He couldn't believe it could be so easy for her to leave him when it was so hard for him to let her go. When it took all his self-control not to ask her to—

"Stay for a drink," he heard himself say. "Just one drink. To toast the future."

The corners of her lips curved into a humorless smile. "Isn't Natalia waiting for you?"

"Who?"

"Who?" She snorted. "The gorgeous supermodel you were taking out tonight."

"She's just a friend," he said impatiently. He knew the

Russian girl wanted more. But what did he care about her? Seeing Hallie today had brought back everything he'd tried to forget over the past year, everything he knew was forbidden but that he still wanted. "Share a drink with me."

For a second, Hallie hesitated. Then she straightened, glaring at him. "After the way you treated me, do you really think I would ever choose to spend more time with you?" She lifted her chin. "I never, ever want to see you again. Goodbye, Cristiano."

She turned away, clutching the check against her heart. She left him without looking back.

Cristiano stood in his private office, stunned.

Hallie would cause no legal trouble. The cost of his night with her had been minimal, one he'd been more than willing to pay. And now she was gone. For good.

His jaw tightened. It was what he'd wanted, wasn't it? He'd wanted to permanently rid himself of the temptation she offered. He'd never felt so attracted to anyone.

He'd slept with beautiful women before. The danger—the difference—was in Hallie's voice, so rich with heartbreak and longing. And in her deep brown eyes, which had looked at him with such frank joy. In her low, husky laugh that had melted him with her warmth and delight.

She'd made him feel things against his will.

Not with his body.

His soul.

So after he'd fired her he'd ordered his secretary to block Hallie's calls if she ever tried to contact him again.

Yet, tonight, he'd been the one who had asked her to stay. And Hallie, without any apparent difficulty or regret, had gotten what she'd wanted and easily walked away.

His pride was in shock.

As a matter of course, Cristiano always put his own selfish desires first. You had to look out for number one.

He'd just never imagined a kindhearted country girl like Hallie could do the same.

Rubbing the back of his head, he put his checkbook back in the safe. He told himself he'd go meet Natalia and spend the evening at yet another bland charity gala, but the thought seemed ridiculous.

Hallie had looked delicious, her body even more curvaceous than he remembered. She had a new maturity about her. Her dark eyes had become guarded, he realized. Not as honest and clear as he remembered. She'd held something back. Some mystery. Some secret.

Cristiano closed the safe, then stopped.

Something didn't make sense.

When Hallie had first met him in the lobby, she'd been nervous and tense. *I have something important to tell you*, she'd said. But what was it? Simply that she'd hired a lawyer?

Except she'd never actually said that. Cristiano had. She'd been slow to talk and so he'd filled in all the blanks. When he'd offered her money, she'd been surprised, even shocked. Surely that was why she'd asked to speak to him privately. Because her lawyer had told her to.

Unless she didn't actually have a lawyer.

Unless she'd come to him for some other reason. A reason she'd decided to forget once he'd offered her a check.

Cristiano's eyes widened.

He strode out of his private office and down the sweeping stairs that overlooked the huge, gleaming lobby with enormous chandeliers hanging from thirty-foot ceilings. His eyes scanned over the crowd of wealthy tycoons and beautiful starlets that filled the lobby and main bar of the Campania on a typical Thursday night.

He saw Hallie on the other side of the lobby, near the door, talking to two young women, a plump redhead and a pregnant blonde. Hallie smiled, her joy obvious even from this distance, as she reached out to take something from the blonde.

A baby stroller. Looking down at it, she smiled and cooed.

Cristiano's blood went cold.

A baby stroller.

A baby.

Later, he wouldn't even remember how he had reached her. His brain was blank, his body like ice as he walked through the faceless crowd toward Hallie Hatfield and the baby stroller she gripped by the handle. When he drew close, he heard her soft laughter as she turned to her friends. The other women's eyes went wide as Cristiano put his hand on her shoulder.

Hallie's face was still smiling as she turned. Then the blood drained from her face.

Cristiano looked from her guilt-stricken face down to the small, dark-haired, fat-cheeked baby drowsing in the stroller. He slowly lifted his eyes back to hers.

"Is this your baby, Hallie?"

The fear in her eyes told him everything he needed to know.

The other two women stared between them, wide-eyed.

"You didn't tell him?" the blonde said.

"Oh, Hallie," the redhead whispered.

"Please, just go," Hallie choked out to them. "I'll call you later."

The blonde looked like she intended to argue, until the redhead tugged on her arm and drew her away.

Standing alone with Cristiano in the crowded lobby of his flagship hotel, Hallie took a deep breath. "I can explain."

Cristiano looked back down at the baby. A baby with dark eyes exactly like his own. Suddenly he knew exactly why Hallie had come here today. And exactly why she'd changed her mind.

He controlled his voice with effort. "You have a baby."

She bit her lip. "Yes."

He lifted his cold gaze to hers. "Who is the father?"

Hallie said pleadingly, "Please, Cristiano, don't…"

"Who, damn you."

She flinched. When she spoke, her voice could barely be heard over the noise of the lobby. "You."

That single word exploded through him like a grenade. He had a child?

Heart pounding, Cristiano looked at the tiny, yawning baby. Emotions rose, choking him. Savagely repressing his feelings, he looked at her.

"You are sure?" he said flatly.

"Yes," Hallie replied in the same tone. "You know I was a virgin when—"

"I know," he bit out. "But perhaps after…"

"You think I rushed into bed with someone else after that?" Her expression tightened. "You are the only man I've ever been with. Jack is your son."

He had a child? A son?

His name was Jack?

Cristiano's throat tightened. "Why didn't you tell me you were pregnant?"

"I tried." Hallie's beautiful caramel-brown eyes narrowed. "I left two messages with your secretary."

Cristiano hadn't gotten those messages because he'd told his secretary never to tell him if Hallie called.

But he didn't want to hear reasons he might be at fault. He wanted to blame only her. "We used protection," he said accusingly. "How did this happen?"

She raised her eyebrows. "You are the one with all the experience. You tell me."

He ground his teeth. "You should have tried harder to contact me."

"After the way you treated me," she said, "I shouldn't

have tried at all. Why give you the chance to reject our baby like you rejected me?"

His shoulders tightened as her shot hit home.

"So you were just going to walk out of here tonight." His voice had a hard edge. His throat felt raw. "Once you had my check, you had no reason to tell me about my child. You were going to keep him a secret from me for the rest of my life, weren't you?"

Not meeting his eyes, Hallie gave an unsteady nod.

His hands clenched at his sides. "Why?"

"I've never known what it was to hate someone, Cristiano," she whispered. She lifted her gaze to his. "Not until you."

He was shocked by the fury and hurt he saw in her eyes. "I could not have hurt you that badly," he ground out. "We barely knew each other."

"You were so seductive. So tender. You made me think you cared, just a little." She ran an unsteady hand over her forehead. "But as soon as you got what you wanted, you showed me it was all a lie. You left me jobless, homeless. Pregnant and alone. I gave birth alone. I took care of him alone. Do you know how hard it is to look for a job when you have a newborn? I struggled to put a roof over Jack's head while you pretended we didn't exist." She looked around the luxurious lobby. "While you drank champagne and went to parties."

Her words made him feel oddly guilty. He didn't like it. "You never told me—"

"I came here to beg you for money, Cristiano." Her beautiful brown eyes were suddenly luminous. "To *beg*, so I wouldn't have to stay at a homeless shelter tonight. Can you imagine how that feels, asking someone you hate for help?"

No. Cristiano couldn't imagine lowering his pride to such an extent. Even when he'd been orphaned in Italy, desperately poor, he would have starved before he'd have done it.

But women were different, he told himself firmly. They didn't have the same fierce pride as a man.

"Then I offered you the check," he said, "and you decided to take the money and run."

"I'm doing you a favor," she said vehemently. "It's not like you'd want to be a father. So just forget I came here. Forget he was ever born."

Turning, Hallie started pushing the stroller away.

As he watched them go, the hotel's marble floor became suddenly unsteady beneath Cristiano's feet.

A flash went through him, memories of when he was six, when he was ten, of being dragged from one sagging apartment to the next, based on the preference of whichever useless new man his drunken mother had taken as her latest lover. He'd felt helpless as a child, lonely, never staying in one school long enough to make friends.

Most of the household's scant money had gone to alcohol. There had been very little for food and none for Cristiano's clothes, which the local priest quietly donated.

He'd never had a father, unless you counted Luigi Bennato, whom Cristiano assuredly did not. He'd never had a father to look out for him or protect him, even as a baby.

Without thinking, Cristiano stepped forward and grabbed Hallie's shoulder.

"I won't let you do this," he said hoarsely. "I won't let you take our baby away."

"Why?" she said scornfully. "Because you want to be a father?" Her eyes glittered. "Don't make me laugh. You're a selfish playboy, Cristiano. An indecent excuse for a man. You couldn't love someone if you tried, not even your own child. And now that I have enough money to support my baby, I don't want any part of you."

CHAPTER TWO

STANDING IN THE hotel's glamorous lobby with her arms folded, Hallie glared up at Cristiano as if she weren't in the least afraid. But the truth was her whole body was trembling with the effort it took to defy him.

She wished she'd followed her initial impulse when Cristiano had first come into the lobby, and turned and run.

But he'd have caught up with her before she'd even made it out the hotel's revolving door. A single glance at his supremely masculine, muscular body and the cold ruthlessness in his hard gaze was enough to tell her that.

Everything about Cristiano was dark, Hallie thought with a shiver. Dark hair. Dark eyes. Dark tuxedo. A five-o'clock shadow that stroked his hard cheekbones to the slash of his jawline and, most of all, his dark fury as he came closer to her, his hand still on her shoulder, his hulking body almost threatening.

"So this is what you think of me." His black eyes narrowed to slits. "That I'd coldly write you a check and abandon my child to your care."

She was quivering but refused to be cowed. "Money is all you could ever offer as a father. Why don't you just admit it?"

His grip on her shoulder tightened. "You lie to me, you take my money. Then you insult me to my face?"

He had a point, which made her want to throw the check back in that face. Her hand was already rising to do it when she remembered Lola's harsh words. *Is pride going to feed your baby?*

With an intake of breath, Hallie clutched the check more tightly. This money would be her baby's security and hope for the future. It would also give Hallie a chance to finally give up her stupid dream of becoming a singer and let her train for a real job, like an accountant or a nurse.

She wasn't going to let pride ruin her life. Not anymore.

Or Cristiano Moretti.

"You should thank me," she said.

He grew very still. "*Thank* you?"

"We both know, whatever you might say now, that you couldn't truly commit to anyone, even a child."

"How do you know?" he ground out.

"You, commit? For a lifetime?" She gave a choked laugh. "You couldn't even commit for a *night*." She tilted her head. "Were you that quickly bored, the night we were together? Or did you have another date afterward?"

His expression changed infinitesimally. "You think I sent you away because I was bored with you?"

Hallie thought of the glamorous supermodel she'd just seen on his arm. "What else?"

She couldn't let him see how badly that hurt her. When he'd first taken her in his arms that romantic night, she'd been so naive. She'd thought it was fate, an irresistible force drawing them together. She'd thought it was magic.

Hallie had been startled when he'd walked into his penthouse early that afternoon. She'd been warned to be invisible and that her cleaning must be spotless. After spending so much time dusting pictures of his handsome face, seeing Cristiano in the flesh had shocked her.

Cristiano Moretti was a dream come to life. A famous playboy, the self-made Italian hotel billionaire who dated princesses and heiresses.

And inexplicably, he'd wanted *her*.

One moment she and Cristiano had been talking by the bed; the next she'd been in his arms. After so many bleak years of anguish after losing her family and her home, when her handsome billionaire boss had lowered his lips to hers,

Hallie had imagined all the pain was behind her. She'd thought her life had just changed for the better.

And it had, in one way: her baby. Jack was all that mattered now.

"I'm leaving," Hallie said defiantly. "Once I cash your check, I promise you, we'll be gone for good."

Cristiano lowered his head until it was inches from hers. "And I promise you. You'll do nothing of the kind."

Her mouth went dry. As their eyes locked, her heart pounded in her throat as she realized her stupid, idiotic mistake.

She never should have openly defied Cristiano. Because he'd taken her words not just as a challenge but as an insult to his masculinity. To his honor, even.

All this time she'd been thinking about her pride. She hadn't considered his. And now he would make her pay for it.

"You don't want me," she whispered, her voice almost pleading. "You know you don't."

His dark eyes seemed like deep, fathomless pools as his gaze ripped into her soul. Then he straightened.

"You're wrong about that. I've wanted you for a year. And now I will have you."

"What are you talking about?"

His gaze fell to the stroller and his expression grew cold. "He's my child, Hallie. I'm not going to let him go." He focused on her. "Or you."

"I won't be your mistress, if that's what you mean," she said, struggling to keep her voice calm, not to show her rising fear.

"I know." Cristiano's black eyes suddenly glittered, and he smiled. "Because you're going to be my wife."

His wife.

Cristiano watched Hallie's eyes widen in shock.

It was strange, he thought. He hadn't known he was going to demand marriage until the words came out of his mouth. His whole life, he'd never once been tempted to marry. Of course he'd never imagined he'd be a father, either. And as he spoke the words, he suddenly realized he did want to marry her.

Call him an indecent excuse for a man?

Say he was incapable of committing for longer than a night?

Tell him he couldn't even love his child if he tried?

No.

Cristiano wouldn't abandon his newborn son to endure the same helpless childhood he'd known. Not when he himself had spent most of his adult life seeking vengeance on the father who'd abandoned him before he was born.

But he couldn't wrench his son away from Hallie, either. Mother and child were obviously bonded. Still, he needed to take control of the situation.

Marriage was the brutally simple solution.

"Marry you?" Hallie choked out, searching his gaze as if waiting for the punchline. "Are you crazy? I told you—I hate you!"

"And I'm none too fond of you." But as he put both hands on her shoulders and looked down at her, his nerve endings sizzled from the contact. He might be angry, but he'd told her the truth. He hadn't stopped wanting her for a year.

Her gaze fell unwillingly on his lips before she glared up defiantly. "Why would I marry you?"

Looking down at the baby, who was now awake and trying to grab his own feet in the stroller, he said quietly, "For our child."

"But…you can't seriously want to be a real father." There was a new nervousness in her voice. "If you want to see Jack, maybe we could talk about visitation—"

"No," he said coldly. Her expression looked relieved

until he continued grimly, "I will have full-time, permanent custody."

Hallie's beautiful face blanched. She whispered, "You'd try to take him from me?"

"No." He gave her a cold smile. "I want him to have two parents. Even though you didn't care about that."

Patrons and staff in the lobby had been staring at them for a while, but now they were coming closer, obviously trying to listen.

"I'm not having this conversation here," he said abruptly. "Come with me now."

She glanced around wildly, and he wondered if she was actually considering trying to flee. To help her avoid the temptation, he gently lifted the baby from the stroller.

"What are you doing?" she gasped.

"Holding my son," he said, and started walking. She immediately followed him to the elevator, as he'd known she would.

"Want me to come up with you, Mr. Moretti?" his bodyguard asked.

Cristiano shook his head. "Tell Natalia I won't be able to attend the gala after all. Give her my apologies."

"Sure, boss."

Cristiano continued into the elevator, with Hallie's stroller dogging his heels. Once inside, he pressed his fingerprint against the hidden button for the penthouse.

As they rode the elevator to the top floor, she watched him anxiously. He tried to act casual, as if he'd held a baby before, but he felt awkward. Even three-month-old Jack seemed to be looking up at him in disbelief, as if trying to decide whether to cry or not.

"You're doing it wrong. Hold his head like this," Hallie blurted out, positioning the baby differently in his arms. She shook her head impatiently. "Just give him to me."

"Forget it," he said crisply. Jack was his son and, in some

respects, until he secured her loyalty as his wife, Hallie was his enemy. There was no way he'd admit he didn't know what he was doing or give the baby back to her care in a sign of weakness and surrender.

The elevator door slid open onto a small hallway with a grand door and a smaller, inconspicuous one farther down. The top floor of the Campania Hotel was devoted exclusively to Cristiano's penthouse and terraces, with a small separate apartment for his bodyguard. He had a similar penthouse in his flagship hotel in Rome and smaller private suites in his hotels in Tokyo, Sydney, Rio, London and Berlin. He could have rented out the space to paying guests when he was away for an exorbitant amount, but he kept them to himself. Life was about little indulgences, or what was the point of being rich? A man, particularly a wealthy playboy, needed privacy.

Hallie followed him anxiously into the penthouse, as if she feared he might drop the baby. It was insulting. Especially as Jack gave a soft whimper in Cristiano's arms.

"Give him to me—now!" Hallie said.

Keeping his expression inscrutable and moving with deliberate slowness to show her that he was doing it as his own decision, not hers, he carefully handed her their son. Leaving the stroller in the foyer, she clung to the newborn as if they'd been separated for days.

"You bastard," she choked out. "Dragging us up here. It's practically kidnapping."

"Kidnapping?" He looked down at her coldly. "How about trying to steal my son from me for the rest of my life?"

Some of the anger in her gaze faded. "If you cared so much, you should have taken my calls when I was pregnant!"

He hated that she was right. With a low, bitter laugh, he turned away. "You remember your way around, I presume?"

She followed him into the enormous room with its starkly modern furniture and floor-to-ceiling windows that offered a magnificent view of the city's sparkling lights. To the left, an open-concept kitchen had all the latest appliances, none of which he'd ever used. There was a reason he chose to live in his own hotels.

He looked back at her. Hallie's cheeks were pink. He wondered if she was remembering when she'd cleaned here, as the maid. Or if she was remembering, instead, the night she'd helped him mess everything up again, tangling the bedsheets in a night of passion so hot it had burned past all barriers to create a child. A night he could never forget.

"Have a seat," he said coolly even as he fought the flash of heat at the memory. He indicated the white sofa that overlooked the spectacular view.

She tossed her head. "No, thanks. I don't intend to be here long enough to—"

"Sit down," he said more forcefully, and glaring at him, she obeyed, cradling the fussing baby in her arms.

Cristiano sat down in the white chair beside the sofa. He didn't need to see the city view; he knew it so well by now it bored him. He looked only at her.

"If Jack is truly my son, he belongs with me."

She set her jaw. "You're only saying that because I insulted your pride. You don't really care about him."

He narrowed his eyes. "Oh, you know that, do you? Because I'm an indecent excuse for a man? Because I couldn't love someone if I tried?"

She had the decency to blush. "I'm sorry if that was rude. But it's true."

He restrained himself from tossing a few insults back in her face, insults she richly deserved. "You don't trust me? Fine. I don't trust you, either." He looked down at the baby in her arms. "So from now on, my son is staying here."

"No."

"I will not allow him to disappear from my life just on your word that you'll take good care of him."

"And I won't let you turn our lives upside down, just because I injured your masculine pride!"

That was all she thought it was? Controlling his temper, he took a deep breath.

"I know from experience what it is like to grow up with no father and no name," he said slowly. "To live in poverty, with a mother too distracted by her own concerns to worry about mine. She moved us to a new town every time she took a new lover. Men who inevitably despised me as a burden, who thought I deserved to be screamed at, punched, starved."

The color drained from Hallie's face.

"What?" she whispered. "She didn't protect you?"

Cristiano shook his head. "She couldn't even protect herself. When I was eighteen, her last lover beat her almost to death. When I tried to intervene, she kicked me out." He gave a hard smile. "I learned my lesson. You can only look out for yourself."

Her soft eyes looked horrified, as if she'd never imagined any family could go so wrong. "I'm so sorry."

Cristiano hated the pity in her eyes. He regretted saying so much. He'd never spoken about his past to anyone. "I just wanted you to understand." He leaned forward in his chair. "I can't let you leave with him, then spend my life wondering if you're taking good care of my son, if you've taken lovers into your house who might hate him for crying, who might pick him up out of the crib and shake him hard until the crying stops—"

"I would never let that happen!"

"I know," he said grimly. "Because he's staying with me."

"But—"

"Did you give him my last name?" he interrupted.

"His last name is Hatfield, like mine."

"Something else that our marriage will rectify," he said.

Hallie looked down at her baby softly whimpering in her arms. Her voice was small as she said with visible reluctance, "I might be willing to talk about…about shared custody."

Why was she continuing to argue? Repressing his rising anger, he shook his head. "Marriage."

"But why?"

"I've given you the reasons." Suddenly he was finished trying to reason with her, trying to explain. He'd been far more patient and open with her than she deserved. For all the good it had done. He narrowed his eyes. "The discussion is over. We will wed. The decision is made."

"Made by *you*. But you're not my boss. Not anymore."

Cristiano tilted his head. He said in a deceptively casual voice, "You can refuse my proposal, of course."

"Then I refuse."

"Then our son stays with me."

Wide-eyed, she breathed, "Just because you're his biological father you think you have the right to take him from me? I'm his mother!"

"And I have an entire team of lawyers at my disposal. What do you have? Nothing. You've already indicated you're a liar and a flight risk. I'd request an immediate injunction from a judge to prevent you from ever leaving New York."

"Liar? When did I ever lie?"

"Just now. When you took a hundred thousand dollars from me under false pretenses, then tried to run away with my son without telling me he existed."

Hallie's face was deathly pale. The baby's whimpers rose to soft wails.

"I *am* a liar," she said suddenly. "You're not Jack's father, Cristiano. You never were. It was all a…a plot. To get money from you."

"You're the worst liar I've ever seen."

"I slept with five men right after you!" Her voice rose desperately. "Any of them could be his father. Here—take your money back!"

Pulling the folded check from the pocket of her sundress, she held it out to him.

Cristiano's lips curved.

"Why, Hallie," he said, without moving to take it, "are you trying to bribe me to give up my parental rights?"

Stuffing the check back in her pocket, she rose trembling to her feet. "I wish I'd never come here!"

His voice turned hard. "Sit down."

"And I don't care what you say." She lifted her chin. "Our justice system wouldn't take a baby from his mother!"

"So dramatic." He added with dark amusement, "You have a lot of faith in something you clearly know nothing about. How do you think judges and juries decide the truth? They believe the best lawyers with the best arguments. And what kind of lawyer would you find to represent you? An inexperienced pro bono attorney fresh out of law school? Some tired hack working on contingency? You'll have no chance. You will lose."

Cristiano watched the emotions struggle on Hallie's beautiful face. Remembering how she'd almost walked out with his child, he didn't feel sorry for her. At all.

He looked down at Jack, now loudly complaining in Hallie's arms. It had been so close. It scared him to think about it. If he hadn't been suspicious and followed her into the lobby, he never would have known. His son would have grown up believing his father had abandoned him. Rejected him.

Exactly as Cristiano's father had.

Hallie looked down at her wailing baby. "He's hungry," she said, avoiding his gaze. "Where can I go?"

"Right here."

"I'm not nursing him in front of you."

"I don't trust you not to run off."

"Fine," she bit out as the baby's wails increased. "At least turn around."

"Of course." He turned toward the wall of windows overlooking the city. The baby's crying ceased almost immediately, changing to soft, contented murmurs.

Cristiano's shoulders relaxed, and he realized that he'd been tense, feeling his son's unhappiness. He felt more sure than ever that his impulsive decision, demanding marriage, was right. It was the only way to ensure the baby's comfort and security.

His son's childhood would be completely different from his own. Jack wouldn't be abandoned by a father who cared only about his business empire, or left to the devices of a mother who cared only about her own selfish needs. He would never worry about getting beaten or having enough to eat. Jack would always have a stable home. And two loving parents.

Cristiano would do whatever it took, make any sacrifice, to make it so. And so would Hallie.

He would leave her no other choice.

Rising from the white chair, still with his back to her, he pulled out his phone, pressed a button and lifted it to his ear.

"Contact Dr. Garcia," he told his executive assistant, Marcia Lattimer, when she answered. "Tell him I'm bringing a woman and baby in twenty minutes for a checkup and paternity test."

"Yes, sir."

"What?" Hallie said in alarm behind him.

"Ask Matthews to pull the limo around," he continued.

He remembered the baby. "On second thought, the SUV. Have the concierge arrange a new baby seat to be sent down. Whatever is required for a three-month-old. I want it installed and ready by the time we're downstairs."

"Of course, Mr. Moretti," Marcia murmured. She was well paid to be on call around the clock. "Anything else?"

"I'll let you know," he said, and hung up.

"Paternity test?" Hallie's voice was low but enraged. "You don't even believe he's yours?"

"Can I turn around?"

"Yes."

He looked at her calmly. He was pleased to see the baby now sleeping contentedly in her arms. "You said he was mine. Then you said he wasn't."

She looked furious. "You know!"

"I believe he is mine, but I want proof."

She tossed her head. "What kind of quack doctor will do a paternity test in the middle of the night? It's after nine!"

Cristiano was amused that she thought of nine o'clock as the middle of the night. His own nights out often didn't start until eleven. "Dr. Garcia is my personal physician, one of the best in the city. He also appreciates that I fully fund his medical research."

She ground her teeth. "Is everyone in this city on your payroll? Do you always get what you want?"

"Yes," he said simply, to both.

Ten minutes later, they were seated in the back of a huge black SUV with tinted windows and a brand-new baby seat installed between them.

"Nice to meet you, ma'am," called Matthews from the driver's seat. "Cute little guy you've got there." He looked at Cristiano in the rearview mirror. "I understand congratulations are in order, sir?"

"Thank you," Cristiano said. He tenderly lifted a soft blue blanket against his sleeping baby's plump cheek. Feeling Hallie's gaze, Cristiano looked up. A current of electricity passed between them.

Biting her full, pink lower lip, she abruptly looked away. But his body was still aware of her. A new thought went through Cristiano.

He'd intended to marry her as a matter of honor and duty, but there would be compensations.

A year ago, he'd sent her away for her own good—and his. But fate had changed their lives. Now, through their child, they would always be connected.

Married.

And marriage would have other benefits. A wedding night. Endless sensual delights.

He wanted to kiss her. His gaze traced over the curve of her cheek, over the visible tremble of her pink lips as she stubbornly stared out the window into the dark city streets. He wondered how long it would take him to seduce her.

Would it be tomorrow?

Tonight?

Either way, Cristiano knew that nothing could now deny him the pleasure of taking Hallie to his bed. He would possess every inch of her. Every night. For as long as he desired.

Once they were wed, she would be his.

CHAPTER THREE

As THEY LEFT the doctor's private office downtown later
that night, Hallie was in despair.

She couldn't marry him. She *couldn't*.

But how could she not?

Closing her eyes, she leaned back in the seat of the SUV
and tried to picture herself as Cristiano's wife. She imagined Cristiano in a tuxedo, striding through his luxury
skyscraper while she trailed after him in a dumpy maid's
uniform.

How could the two of them ever marry? What did they
even have in common?

Just one thing. Her gaze fell upon the baby in the car
seat beside her.

What would it be like for Jack to be raised as a tycoon's
son, wealthy beyond belief? To go to all the best schools,
with the best tutors? To be proficient at all the sports of
the wealthy, like skiing, tennis, lacrosse? Every door in
the world would be open to Jack.

A lump rose in her throat. But would her son be happy?
Would he grow up to be a good, honorable man?

"Would you like me to take you home?" Cristiano said
in a low voice.

Hallie looked at him over the baby seat in the back seat
of the SUV. He'd taken off his tuxedo jacket and loosened
his tie. His dark good looks and smoldering gaze burned
through her.

"Home?" she whispered.

Cristiano lifted an eyebrow. "Whatever you might think
of me, I'm not a total bastard. Now that I have proof of paternity I want you to be comfortable."

He was willing to take Hallie home? He'd given up his ridiculous plan of forcing her to marry him?

A rush of relief flooded through Hallie; it was so great she almost cried.

"Thank you," she choked out.

"Give Matthews your address."

Her address. Remembering what had happened with her landlord that morning, she gulped. She didn't want to face that horrible man again. Plus, if Cristiano saw where she'd been living, he might change his mind and refuse to let the baby live there. Hallie barely wanted to go back herself.

"Um…in the East Village," she said vaguely.

Cristiano looked at her expectantly, dark eyebrows raised. Reluctantly she gave Matthews the address.

I just won't let Cristiano go in, she told herself. The apartment building looked respectable enough on the outside. Plus, maybe her landlord was very sorry for what he'd done. Maybe.

She looked down at her baby, who'd been fed and changed at the clinic and was now happily babbling. She stroked his downy dark hair, looking into the eyes that were exactly like his father's.

Then she suddenly remembered. Reaching into her diaper bag, she grabbed her phone. Just as she'd expected, she saw multiple messages from her friends.

Are you all right? Is he being nice?

From Tess.

Did he agree to pay child support? How much?

From Lola.

Why aren't you answering?

Are you being held hostage?

Should we call the police?

Quickly Hallie typed out a response to them both.

All well. Just got a paternity test. He says he wants to be a father to Jack. More later.

She tucked her phone away. Rolling down her car window, Hallie took a deep breath, looking out into the warm, humid July night as their SUV drove into the Lower East Side. She felt sick at the thought of seeing her landlord, who wasn't a proper landlord at all, just a guy who'd been willing to rent her a room in his apartment at a cut-rate price.

But the man had made it clear to her that morning that he expected her to pay in other, less tangible ways. She gulped. She never would have wanted to come back here, except she'd left behind all her most precious possessions. Her old family photos from West Virginia. Her grandmother's homemade quilt. Her father's watch. It was everything she had left of her family now.

Hallie took a deep breath. She'd just pay the landlord off, take all her stuff and then she and the baby could check into a hotel.

"Um…" Hallie bit her lip. "Do you think we could stop somewhere so I could cash my check?"

"You waste no time." The corners of Cristiano's lips twitched. "You think some check-cashing store is going to count you out a hundred thousand dollars in twenty-dollar bills?"

"Maybe a bank…"

"The banks are closed. Why do you need money?"

"I've been having a small problem with the landlord," she said quietly. He stared at her.

"Are you under the impression that I'm leaving you and Jack at your apartment?"

She drew back, bewildered. "Aren't you?"

"We're getting your things. Jack's things. Then we're going back to my penthouse."

"Oh," she whispered.

"Put that check away. Rip it up, invest it, cash it tomorrow, whatever you want. But I'll be providing you and my son with everything you could possibly need."

His voice was autocratic. Clearly he thought he was still the boss of her. She felt shaken.

"I thought, now that you have the results of the paternity test—now that you have some legal rights—you wouldn't need to get married."

"You thought wrong." The SUV pulled up at the curb in front of the five-story building. "Get what you need for tonight. Tomorrow, I'll arrange for your lease to be paid in full. That should take care of your landlord. My staff will return to collect anything big or heavy. Cribs, furniture. Or we can leave all that behind and buy new. Whichever you prefer."

"Um," said Hallie, who owned neither a crib for the baby nor any actual furniture.

"I'll wait here with the baby and give you your privacy. Don't be long." When she didn't move, his gaze sharpened. "Well?"

Turning, she blurted, "I don't need anything. Let's just go straight to your hotel."

"But you need clothes—"

"No, I'm fine."

He looked at her as if she'd lost her mind. "But we're already here."

"I don't want to go in!" Her voice was shrill.

Cristiano looked at her for a long moment. When he spoke, his voice was surprisingly gentle.

"What's really going on, Hallie?"

With an intake of breath, she looked away. Even at midnight the street was busy, and the neon lights of pizzerias and Laundromats littering First Avenue lit up the sultry summer night.

"After you fired me," she said softly, "it was hard to find a job. I finally worked as housekeeper for a couple on the Upper West Side. The job included room and board. But when I brought Jack home from the hospital they let me go."

His eyebrows lowered. "Why?"

She gave a humorless smile. "They said Jack's crying was causing psychic trauma to their two Chinese Crested show dogs."

"Are you serious?"

"With a newborn, I couldn't find a new job. I've lived off my savings for the last three months. Even the cheapest apartments were too much." She looked down at her hands. "So last month, I rented a room in a stranger's apartment. From an online site. I was amazed it was so cheap. Then…"

She stopped, biting her lip.

Eyes narrowing, Cristiano leaned forward in the back seat.

"Then?" he demanded.

"The man wasn't bad at first. But over the last few weeks, he started brushing up against me in the kitchen. Trying to catch me coming out of the shower. That sort of thing." She looked away. It was surprisingly hard to go on. "This morning, he…grabbed me."

Silence fell in the SUV.

"He attacked you." Cristiano's voice was toneless. It gave her the courage to meet his eyes.

"Maybe *attack* is too strong a word." She tried to smile, failed. "He tried to kiss me and reach his hand under my dress. When I pushed him away, he told me I wasn't paying my fair share of the rent so I should pay in other ways."

Trembling, she looked away. "I grabbed the baby and my diaper bag and ran. He yelled after me that I'd signed a lease and he'd be keeping all my things as payment. The only reason I have the stroller is because I'd left it downstairs." She whispered, "He has everything I own. But I'm not sure I can face him again."

Silence.

Slowly she looked up.

Then Hallie saw Cristiano's expression. The fire in his dark eyes. The cold fury that threatened imminent death for the man who'd scared her.

"I'm fine. Really." Putting her hands on his taut arm, she said hurriedly, "I hardly own anything. All my clothes would fit in a single duffel bag. It's just family photos and an old quilt…" She realized she was babbling and took a deep breath. "He didn't hurt me. He never threatened the baby…"

His voice was low and deadly. "He tried to force himself on you."

"I got away. Everything's fine, we're all fine—"

"*I'm* not fine," Cristiano bit out, and got out of the vehicle. He looked back at her, his handsome face as implacable as granite. "Which apartment number?"

"Promise you won't hurt him—"

"*His number,*" he ground out.

"Four C," she whispered.

His face was half-hidden in shadow in the gleam from the neon sign of a nearby bar. "Wait here."

He slammed the car door.

Hallie's wait seemed to last forever. She nervously watched the minutes pass by on the dashboard. She stroked her baby's cheek as he smiled up at her from the reverse-facing baby seat. "It's fine," she reassured Jack, who in response lifted his chubby arm to bat blindly at the giraffe toy dangling from the handle of his car seat.

Oh, she was being ridiculous. Most likely the two men were having a civilized chat, that was all. Cristiano was likely calmly writing a check—which was, after all, what he did best—and requesting that Mervin Smith, the man who possessed the rent-controlled apartment, would kindly pack up all her things and bring them down.

Right. Not even Tess would have believed that.

Nervously she looked up at Matthews, the driver, who was still sitting at the wheel. "I don't need to worry about what Cristiano might do, right? He wouldn't do anything violent. Right?"

Matthews peered up through his window at the building. "Luther's not here. That's a good sign."

"Luther?"

"His bodyguard."

Hallie brightened. "That's true."

"But Mr. Moretti was a brawler, back when he was young. He fought his way out of the streets of Naples."

"Oh." She swallowed. "But that was a long time ago. I'm sure Cristiano has changed—"

"And just last year—" Matthews stroked his beard thoughtfully "—two punks tried to jump him as he was jogging real early through Central Park. He put them in the hospital. And then there was the time—"

"That's good," Hallie said in a strangled voice, holding up her hand sharply. "You don't need to tell me more."

"Glad to help," the driver said, straightening his old-fashioned black cap. Then he sucked in his breath and got out of the vehicle.

Hallie jumped as her car door was suddenly wrenched open. She saw Mervin, with dried ketchup still on his chin and his too-tight T-shirt pulling up over his huge belly, on his knees on the sidewalk. He looked terrified.

"I'm sorry," he choked out. "I'm so sorry, Hallie—"

"Miss Hatfield," Cristiano corrected coldly, standing behind the man like a dark angel.

"Miss Hatfield," the man repeated desperately. "I brought down your stuff. Everything is there, totally perfect, I swear—"

"Thank you," she said anxiously. Her eyes lifted to Cristiano's. Even after what her landlord had done to her, she'd never wanted him humiliated like this. "It's all right now."

Cristiano looked down at the man with a sneer. "If I ever hear that you've attacked any woman ever again—"

"Never, ever, I swear," Mervin cried. Stumbling to his feet, he hurried into the building with one final terrified glance back.

As Matthews stacked the few boxes into the SUV's trunk, Cristiano calmly climbed into the back seat beside her and the baby. Matthews closed the trunk with a bang. Two minutes later, they were driving north through the streets of Manhattan.

Her heart was still pounding. "What did you do to him?"

Cristiano shrugged. "I asked him to apologize."

"You just…asked?"

"I asked nicely."

She thought about pushing the issue, then decided she didn't want to know. She hadn't seen visible signs of injury. That was the best she could hope for—and that the man had been sincere when he'd said he'd never try to force a kiss on any woman again. She took a deep breath.

"Thank you," she whispered. "I don't care about the clothes. But the pictures of my family mean the world to me."

He looked at her, then set his jaw. "I'm surprised you even care about your family after they turned their backs on you."

"What do you mean?"

"They left you and Jack to struggle alone."

Hallie blinked at him in surprise, and said gently, "They didn't have a choice. They died five years ago."

Cristiano's eyes widened. "Died?"

She swallowed over the lump in her throat. It was still hard to speak of it. "Back home, in West Virginia. I grew up in a tiny village in the mountains. I was nineteen, still living at home, working the overnight shift at a grocery store in a nearby town. A fire had burned much of the forest the previous summer. After a week of hard rain, one night a flash flood came down the mountain and ripped our cabin off its foundation. If I'd been sleeping in my bed, I would have died with my parents and brother." She looked down. "For a long time, I wished I had."

"I'm sorry," he said quietly.

Blinking back tears, Hallie looked blindly out her window. "I came home at dawn and found fire trucks where my house had been. It had floated down the river, knocked to one side, crushed into wood. They found my family later…"

She couldn't go on, remembering how she'd felt at nineteen when her whole world had fallen apart, when she'd lost her home and everyone she loved without warning.

Suddenly she felt Cristiano's hand over her own.

With an intake of breath, she looked up. His eyes were black as jet.

"My mother died when I was eighteen," he said quietly. "The night she kicked me out, I decided if she still wanted her lover even after he beat her, if she cared about him more than me, then fine, I'd go. But at three in the morning, I went back. I found the house on fire."

"Arson?" Hallie breathed.

He shook his head, his lips twisting. "Nothing so deliberate. Her lover had been smoking in bed. He passed out drunk, and they both burned to death." He gave her a crooked smile. "It's funny, really. Your family died of water. Mine of fire."

"Funny," she said over the lump in her throat. All this time she'd hated Cristiano, believing him arrogant and ruthless and cold. All of which he was. But she'd never stopped to ask why.

"I'm sorry." She twined her hand in his, trying in turn to offer comfort. "You know how it feels to lose family, too. To lose a home."

For a moment, he looked at her. Then he turned, pulling his hand away. Lights moved over them in patterns as they drove toward Midtown.

When the SUV pulled up to the grand porte cohere of the Campania Hotel, Cristiano lifted the baby's carrier from the back seat. Holding the handle with his powerful arm, he turned back to Hallie, extending his other hand to help her out of the car.

Nervously she put her hand in his. Just feeling his palm against hers as he helped her out made her shiver from her scalp to her toes.

He held her hand as they walked through the lobby with its soaring ceilings and elegant midcentury furniture. The space was filled with glamorous people, hotel guests and patrons of the lobby bar or the jazz club. She saw a sexy sheikh, pouting models and starlets.

All of them turned to stare at Cristiano as he passed. Then their gazes slid in confusion to Hallie, makeup-free and wearing a limp cotton sundress. Even more shocking was the baby carrier hanging from Cristiano's arm.

People stared and whispered as they passed. A few dared to approach Cristiano with questions in their eyes. He just nodded at them and kept walking.

He stopped only briefly to speak to Clarence Loggia, the hotel manager, as Matthews and a porter headed for the elevator with Hallie's boxes.

"Good evening, Mr. Moretti." Mr. Loggia was too well

trained to show even the slightest surprise at seeing either a baby or a former hotel maid on his employer's arm.

"How is it tonight, Clarence?"

"I am pleased to report the hotel is currently at ninety-six percent capacity. The Sultan of Bataar just arrived. He's taken the presidential suite for the entire summer, along with the rest of the floor for his entourage."

"Excellent. Please send him my regards and a collection of his favorite brandy and cigars with my personal compliments."

The man smiled. "Already done, sir." He hesitated, then lowered his voice. "Also, I thought you would want to know. Prince Stefano Zacco di Gioreale just checked in."

"Why does he insist on staying here?" A shadow crossed Cristiano's face, then he shrugged. "I suppose his money is as good as any other's."

"I thought you'd say that." The manager gave an impish smile. "But in light of your past history with the gentleman, I did take the liberty of adding a surcharge to his nightly rate."

"He deserves it, the Sicilian bastard. Nicely done, Loggia. Anything else?"

"Nothing that requires your attention."

"I see I'll be leaving the hotel in good hands when I depart. *Buonasera.*"

"Good night, sir."

Cristiano turned back to her. As they walked to the elevator, suddenly Hallie felt very tired. Without a word, he stepped ahead of her to press the elevator button.

"Hallie Hatfield!"

A woman's shrill voice behind her made her jump. Turning, she saw Audrey, who'd once been her supervisor. Not just that. She'd once been a trusted mentor and friend.

"What are you doing here, Hallie?" the other woman demanded. "Looking for another rich man to seduce? You're no longer employed here and not allowed to be loitering in the lobby with the guests. Get out before I call the—"

Audrey sucked in her breath as Cristiano suddenly turned around.

"Hallie's with me," he said mildly. "And I own the hotel, so that makes it all right, does it not, Ms.…." He looked at her name tag. "Ms. Johnson?"

Audrey's shocked face went white, then red.

"Yes, of course. I'm so sorry, Mr. Moretti," she stammered, backing away. She bowed her head repeatedly. "I didn't realize Hallie was with you. I'll, um, return to my duties—"

The woman fled. As Hallie and Cristiano got into the elevator with their baby, he frowned. "That was your old supervisor."

"Yes."

"Did she always treat you so poorly?"

She gave a brief smile. "No."

"Do you want me to fire her?"

Hallie gaped at him. She couldn't tell if he was joking, but just to be safe she quickly said, "No, of course not. I feel bad for her."

"Why?"

"When you ordered her to fire me directly, without going through HR, then gave her the mysterious severance envelope she wasn't allowed to read…" Hallie shrugged. "She's not stupid. She guessed we'd slept together."

"Why would she care?"

Did he really not know? "Because she's in love with you."

"Is she?" he said carelessly. Hallie gave him a wistful smile.

"Most women are, I imagine. Even I almost was, once."

Cristiano focused abruptly on her. She felt the intensity of his gaze burn through her soul. "You were in love with me?"

She swallowed.

"For a year, I often cleaned your penthouse—did you know that?"

He shook his head.

"Anytime your regular housekeeper, Camille, was sick or needed to take her grandchildren to school." She gave a wistful smile. "Dusting your pictures, I used to look at your face and wonder what it would be like to…"

"Yes?" he said, drawing closer, putting his hand on her bare shoulder above the straps of her sundress. A hard shiver went through her.

The elevator reached their floor, and the door slid open with a ding.

"But that was before I knew you," she said steadily. "Now nothing on earth could make me love you again."

She walked out of the elevator, head held high. Cristiano reached past her to unlock the penthouse door with his fingerprint, still holding their baby's carrier on his arm.

The city skyline, sparkling through floor-to-ceiling windows, was the only light in the penthouse.

The darkness was suggestive. Intimate. Setting down the baby carrier, Cristiano turned to face her.

"I don't know about love," he said in a low voice. "It's not something I've ever felt, or wanted to feel." Reaching out, he tucked a tendril of Hallie's hair behind her ear. "But from the moment I first heard you sing, I knew you were different from any woman I'd ever known."

"Thank you." Shivering from his brief touch, she tried to smile. "That's why I came to New York. Did you know? I dreamed of becoming a world-famous singer."

For all his praise, he looked surprised. "A singer?"

Hallie gave a low laugh. "Did you think I came all the

way from West Virginia because my big dream was to be a maid in your hotel?"

"No?" Cristiano smiled. "You certainly have the voice, *cara*. The heartbreak and longing of your song—you made me feel it. Your voice was the first thing I noticed about you." His eyes slid over her face, to her bare shoulders, down her curvy body beneath the cotton sundress. "Do you want to know the second thing?"

A wave of heat went through her. Her cheeks burned as she whispered, "No."

Maybe he wasn't doing it on purpose, she thought. Maybe he flirted without thinking, like breathing. He couldn't really still want her. But something in his eyes made her think—

He turned away, picking up the baby carrier. Beckoning Hallie to follow, he pushed open the first door down the hall.

"You can sleep here tonight."

Confused, she followed him into the pristine guest room that she'd cleaned many times long ago. "Who's in charge of cleaning this now?"

"Still Camille. I have no idea who her backup is." He gave her a crooked grin. "They're more careful than you were not to be seen."

With a snort, Hallie looked around the guest room. "Every time I changed these sheets, they seemed untouched. I used to wonder if the room was ever used."

He set the baby carrier gently on the floor. "It isn't."

Frowning, she turned to look at him. "Never?"

"You're my first guest."

"But surely you've invited family, friends—"

"I have no family," he said. "When friends visit, I give them their own suite downstairs."

"Oh." *No family*, she thought. And though he lived in a luxurious hotel, he had no real home. In some ways, they were the same. Strange. For a moment their eyes met. Then she saw the boxes stacked neatly in the corner. "My things!"

She rushed over and started digging through the boxes. Relief poured through her as she found the family pictures, her father's watch, her brother's old baseball trophy, her mother's music box. All the photos, still warped and faded, found on the banks of the river. Blinking away tears, she leaned back on her haunches and looked up at Cristiano.

"Everything is here. Thank you." Her voice choked. "You don't know what this means to me."

"So I'm not still an indecent excuse for a man?"

She blushed. "I never should have said—"

"It's all right." He turned away. "I'll leave you and the baby to rest."

"You're not afraid I'm going to try to run away with him in the middle of the night?"

He glanced back. "Are you planning to?"

Hallie thought of the fierce joy in Cristiano's face when he'd gotten the paternity test results that proved Jack was his son. How he'd been so protective of her. How he'd gotten her precious possessions back for her. He, too, had experienced the pain of losing family and home.

She could no longer imagine stealing Jack away when Cristiano wanted so clearly to be part of his life.

"You're Jack's father," she said in a small voice. "I wouldn't try to hurt you."

His shoulders relaxed. He motioned around the guest room and en suite bathroom. "It should be equipped with everything you require."

"And then some," she said, noticing the crib and a co-sleeper both set up on the other side of the king-size bed.

Following her gaze, Cristiano said awkwardly, "I didn't know how you and the baby prefer to sleep. My assistant said both of those were popular with new mothers."

"Thank you." She gave him a smile. "It'll be fun to use a co-sleeper that's new. The crib looks nice, too."

He gave a brief nod. "If you get hungry or need anything, just lift up the phone and dial one. It's an express line to the front desk and will be prioritized above all other calls. The staff pride themselves on answering on the first ring." Coming forward, he put his hand gently on Hallie's bare shoulder. She felt his touch race through her entire body, setting her nerves aflame.

"Until tomorrow," he said in a low voice.

After Cristiano left, closing the door behind him, Hallie took the baby carrier with her into the en suite bathroom. As Jack babbled contentedly from his carrier nearby, she took a quick, hot shower. She let all the sweat and anxiety of the long day wash off into steamy bliss. She washed her hair with the expensive shampoos and conditioners she'd once just stocked as a housekeeper. Afterward, she stepped into a soft, thick white terry-cloth robe from the heated stand. Her skin was pink and warm with steam as she came out and saw Jack was still happy in his baby carrier, cooing at the soft giraffe dangling from the handle.

"Now your turn, little one." Unbuckling him from the carrier, she cuddled him close, kissing his soft head and chubby cheeks. She gave him a warm bath in the baby bathtub she found in the bathroom cabinet along with baby shampoo. Drying him off, she put him in a new diaper and clean footie pajamas.

Cuddling her baby close, she went to the soft new glider chair by the bedroom window and took a deep breath, relishing Jack's sweet, clean baby smell. After reading him a short baby book from a collection on the shelf, she fed him and rocked him to sleep, then tucked him snugly into the co-sleeper.

Hearing her stomach growl, Hallie tried to remember the last time she'd eaten. A stale cookie at the single mothers support group? It seemed a year ago. Which reminded her. She grabbed her phone from her bag and messaged Tess and Lola.

I'm staying at his penthouse tonight. He got everything back from the landlord. I think everything's going to be fine.

Plugging her cell phone in to recharge, she turned to the bulky phone plugged in to the wall. Hungry though she was, she couldn't imagine calling room service, especially so late. She'd never ordered it herself, but her parents had told her about room service after they'd gone to a hotel in Cincinnati for their twenty-fifth anniversary.

"It was so expensive!" her father had exclaimed.

"With a required twenty-percent gratuity," her mother had breathed in shock, "and a delivery fee on top of that!"

"And the food arrived cold!" he'd added indignantly. "Room service is for suckers who want to burn money!"

Hallie smiled at the memory. Her smile faded as she felt all over again how much she missed them. Then she shook her head decisively. No room service. She'd just have to find something in Cristiano's kitchen.

Tightening the belt on her white terry-cloth robe, she peeked out into the penthouse's dark hallway, telling herself that Cristiano was already asleep in his own bedroom. But when she crept into the kitchen, she saw him sitting on the white sofa in the great room, his handsome, intent face shadowed by the glow of his laptop.

Looking up, he saw her, and the smile that lit up his hard, handsome features made her heart skip a beat.

"Can't you sleep?" Closing his laptop, he rose to his feet. He must have taken a shower, because his hair was wet. His chest was bare, revealing the defined curves of his muscled torso in the moonlight streaming through the windows. He wore only low-slung drawstring pajama pants. *Very* low-slung, clinging to edges of his hips, revealing the trail of dark hair on his taut belly.

Her mouth went dry. She had to force her eyes up.

"I'm, um, hungry," she croaked, praying he couldn't read her thoughts. Licking her lips, she gazed around the room, desperate to look anywhere but at his powerful bare chest, the flat plane of his stomach or the drawstring pants barely clinging to his hips.

"Did you call room service?"

What did room service have to do with anything? Oh, yes. She'd said she was hungry. Her eyes met his, and he gave her a sensual, heavy-lidded smile. She blushed to realize that he had caught her looking after all.

"It's not necessary. I'll just rummage in your fridge if that's all right."

Cristiano looked amused. "Go right ahead."

But as she opened the door of his sleek, commercial-grade refrigerator, she was disappointed to see only an expensive bottle of vodka and some martini olives.

She turned back with a frown. "Where is your food?"

"I don't cook."

Peeking in his freezer, she saw ice cubes. That was it. No ice cream or even frozen broccoli past its sell-by date.

She'd known from her time cleaning the penthouse that Cristiano Moretti wasn't exactly a chef, but the level of emptiness shocked her. Hallie looked through the cupboards with increasing desperation. They were empty except for a few items that belonged in a wet bar. Disappointed, she looked at him accusingly.

"Don't you even snack?"

He shrugged. "I lead a busy life. Why own a hotel if I don't use the amenities?"

"No one can hate cooking this much."

He gave her a sudden grin. "I prefer to think of it as quality assurance. What can I say? I'm a workaholic."

"I know," she sighed.

"Get room service."

She shook her head. "It's the middle of the night. And do you know how much it costs?"

He looked amused again. "You do know I own this hotel?"

She tried not to stare at the curve of his sensual lips. Then she realized she'd just licked her own. Her blush deepened. She croaked, "That's no excuse to—"

"I'll order it for you." He went to the kitchen phone on the marble counter. Picking it up, he looked at her in the shadowy kitchen. "What do you want?"

Want? What a suggestive question. Hallie's gaze lingered on his broad shoulders, his powerful arms, his muscular chest dusted with dark hair. She could see the outline of his powerful thighs beneath the thin knit fabric of his drawstring pants. He gave her a wicked smile. She realized he'd caught her looking again.

Quick, say something intelligent to distract him! she told herself desperately.

"Um…what do you recommend?"

No!

His eyes gleamed. "Shall I tell you?"

Her heart was pounding in her throat. "I'll have a cheeseburger and fries," she said quickly. "And a strawberry shake."

Cristiano's sensual lips curved, as if he knew exactly how her blood was racing and her heart was pounding. She was suddenly afraid to even meet his gaze. Turning to the phone, he gave the order swiftly, then hung up. "Your dinner will be here in nine minutes."

Hallie looked at him incredulously. "Nine minutes? That's impossible."

"Know all about room service, do you?" He sounded amused again.

"My parents told me horror stories. Cold food, small portions, no ketchup, then a big bill."

"Let's test out your theory." He lifted an eyebrow. "Care to place a friendly wager?"

"What kind of wager?"

Going back to the sofa, he sat down and patted the cushion beside him.

She sat down hesitantly beside him, perching awkwardly on the edge of the sofa. She was suddenly aware that she was naked beneath her bathrobe. Nervously she pulled it a little tighter around her. "What do you have in mind?"

"If your food arrives within—" he glanced at his platinum watch "—seven minutes and forty-eight seconds, I win. If it doesn't, you win."

"What do I win?"

His eyes flickered. "What if I cook breakfast for you tomorrow?"

She snorted. "Cereal?"

Cristiano shook his head. "Eggs and bacon. Belgian waffles. Anything you want."

She was impressed in spite of herself. "But you hate cooking."

"I won't have to do cook."

"You won't?"

"Because I'm not going to lose."

The man had confidence, she'd give him that. "And if you do win, what would you want from me?"

His dark eyes glinted wickedly.

"A kiss."

A rush of need crackled through her body as her lips tingled in anticipation. She croaked, "What?"

"You heard me."

She couldn't risk placing this bet. She hated him. Didn't

she? Not exactly. Not anymore. But she definitely didn't want him to kiss her. Did she? Okay, maybe she did, but she knew it would lead to disaster. On that, her body and brain and heart agreed. *She could not let him kiss her again.*

Yet Hallie was unable to look away from his hungry gaze. "Why would you want to kiss me?"

"Why not?" he said lazily.

Was he bored? Or just suggesting it to throw her off-kilter and make clear his power over her? "No, thanks. I'm not the gambling kind."

"I think you are. If you refuse my wager, then you're admitting that you might be wrong." He leaned toward her on the white sofa, almost close enough to touch. "And I might be right."

Her heart was in her throat. "About room service?"

"About everything," he whispered, his lips almost grazing her cheek.

She shivered at his closeness. Then she realized what he was saying and that he was talking about far more important issues than food.

"I admit no such thing." Still, as she drew back sharply, his gaze fell to her knee, and she realized that her robe had slipped open to reveal her crossed leg all the way to her thigh. Cheeks aflame, she covered her legs.

His eyebrow lifted. "Then take the bet."

"Fine," she snapped. "I'll enjoy watching you cook for me tomorrow." She lifted her chin. "But in addition to the food being delivered on time, to prove me wrong it also has to be the best cheeseburger, fries and shake I've ever had."

"It will be," he said without hesitation, and held out his hand. She stared at it for a moment, then shook it as quickly as she could, desperately ignoring her body's reaction at that brief touch.

And so it was that exactly five minutes and four seconds later, a full fifteen seconds before the deadline, she found herself looking despondently at the white linen-covered room-service tray resting on the coffee table. As Cristiano got up to chat with the smiling room-service waiter, she sighed. Even the incredible smell of hot French fries wafting through the air could offer no comfort. She knew she was about to lose their bet.

A kiss.

Hallie put her hands on her forehead. Why had she ever agreed to it? *Why?* How could she have been so stupid? Cristiano got room service all the time! He knew how long it took! He knew how good the food was!

Did she *want* him to kiss her?

But that was a question Hallie didn't want to answer, not even to herself, as the waiter left and Cristiano came back. Turning on a lamp, he looked down at her. His cruel, sensual lips curved. "Don't look so frightened."

She lied. "I'm not."

"You're terrified." Lifting the silver lid off the tray, he said idly, "Do you think I intend to take my kiss now, and ravish you against the wall?"

With a flash of heat, images came to her mind. Mouth dry, she croaked, "I—"

"Why don't you try it?" he murmured, sitting beside her on the sofa. "See if you like it?"

Her heart nearly stopped. She looked at him, lips parted. He held out a French fry.

"Decide," he said huskily, "if it's the best you've ever had."

She stared from the French fry to the challenge in his eyes. Snatching the fried potato from his fingers, she licked off the salt, then popped the whole length into her mouth. It was so hot, salty and delicious that she gave an involuntary groan of pleasure.

"So…good…" she breathed, briefly lost in ecstasy.

A strangled noise came from the back of his throat. Looking up, she saw his handsome face looked strained.

Clearing his throat, he rose from the sofa. "I'll leave you to enjoy it."

"Wait. I haven't tried the rest." Although she knew, even before she picked up the cheeseburger, that it would be the best she'd ever had. She took a big bite, licking a splash of ketchup and mustard off her lips, then washed it all down with a milkshake of fresh strawberries whirled into vanilla ice cream. The milkshake was so thick she had to suck hard on the straw.

Finally she looked up, defeated. "All right, you win—"

Her voice cut off when she saw his face. He looked hungry, ruthless. Something in his eyes was dark and wild. He took a step toward her, his hands gripped at his sides, and the memory of his words flashed in her mind.

Do you think I intend to ravish you against the wall?

She shrank back from the fire in his eyes. "No."

That one word, whispered soft as a breath, seemed tangible in the air, like a wall between them. He blinked. His expression changed as if a shutter had gone down. His civilized mask slid back into place.

"Good night," he said hoarsely. Turning, he hurried down the hall toward the master bedroom.

Hallie sat alone on the sofa, shivering from what had just happened. Except nothing had happened, she told herself, struggling to calm her breath. Nothing at all.

After turning off the lamp, she stared out blankly at the lights of the moonlit city. Woodenly she ate the rest of her meal. All she could think about was how badly she'd wanted him in that moment. But the word that had escaped from her lips was *no*. Because she was afraid.

Before her night with Cristiano, Hallie had barely been kissed. She'd had a few awkward kisses with her boyfriend in high school, who'd never tried to press the issue—with good reason, as it turned out, because as soon as he left for university he announced on Facebook that he was gay. And one time, Joe Larson, the mine owner's son, had tried to force his tongue down her throat at a company Christmas party. Before Cristiano, that had been the sum total of her sexual experience.

And now he wanted to kiss her?

Now he wanted to *marry* her?

She was way out of her league.

Rising from the sofa, she walked heavily back to the guest room, where she found Jack sleeping peacefully. Putting on underwear and pajamas, she brushed her teeth and crawled into the bed next to her baby, knowing she wouldn't sleep a wink.

But, somehow, she did. She rose only once in the night, to feed the baby. When Jack next woke her with a hungry whimper, she saw golden light flooding the window. She sat up in shock, realizing that she'd just had the best night's sleep in months. How was that possible?

"Good morning, sweetheart," she said, smiling at the baby, who gurgled and waved his arms at her.

When mother and baby came out into the main room some time later, both of them were dressed—Hallie in a soft pink sundress of eyelet cotton and sandals, the baby in a onesie and blue knit shorts. She stopped when she saw Cristiano sitting at the kitchen counter. Her cheeks went hot at the memory of last night. *But why?* she said to herself. Nothing had happened!

"Good morning." Cristiano's voice was gravelly as he set down his newspaper. "I trust you slept well?"

Hallie shifted her baby's weight on her hip as she stood uncertainly in the kitchen, beneath a shaft of golden light from the windows. His eyebrows lifted as he waited. His handsome face was courteous, his dark eyes civilized. Nothing like he'd looked last night...

She shivered.

"Hallie?"

She jumped. "I slept well. Thank you."

Hallie wondered when he would kiss her. She felt the weight of that debt between them. *It's just a kiss*, she told herself, but she couldn't quite believe it. She tried to tell herself that now that he'd had time to recover from the shock of learning he was a father, Cristiano probably wouldn't repeat his demand for marriage. But looking into his hard-edged face, she couldn't believe that, either. Cristiano Moretti was the kind of man who would stop at nothing to get what he wanted.

He wanted to secure possession of their child. She knew that. But now she knew he wanted more.

He wanted her.

Nodding toward the marble countertop and holding out a china cup edged with fourteen-karat gold, he said gruffly, "Have a seat."

"Thanks." Sitting down on one of the high barstools, keeping her baby securely in her lap, she watched in surprise as he poured her a cup of steaming hot coffee from a silver carafe. "You made coffee?"

"Room service." He nodded at the tray. "There's cream and sugar."

"Thanks." Too late, she saw the wheeled carts nearby and felt foolish. Adding copious amounts of cream and sugar to her coffee, she took a sip and sighed with pleasure. Glancing at him, she said shyly, "Would you like to hold the baby?"

Cristiano hesitated, looking down at the plump, babbling three-month-old. He shook his head. "Maybe later."

"All right." She was surprised anyone could resist holding Jack, with his adorably goofy smile and his fat little cheeks.

"I ordered you a breakfast tray. It's been here an hour, so it might be cold." Cristiano turned back to his newspaper.

"Thanks." She didn't feel hungry at all. She gave him a sideways glance. "You're reading in Italian."

He didn't look up. "Yes."

"And on paper rather than on a tablet."

"So?"

"It's very retro," she ventured.

He didn't answer. He seemed barely aware of her, while her hands were shaking from being this close to him. Had she somehow imagined the way he'd looked at her last night? Had he already forgotten that he'd demanded a kiss—and marriage?

Sitting at the marble counter that separated the sleek kitchen from the great room, Hallie looked slowly around his penthouse. Modern art was splashed across the walls. Strange, heavy sculptures were displayed on columns. Once Jack started to pull himself up and walk, those would be dangerous.

But such unimaginable luxury and style. So different from how she'd grown up. A flash of memory came to her of the cabin in the West Virginia hills, with its worn wood exterior, sagging furniture and peeling linoleum.

But so comfortable for all that. So full of love. Her beloved home. Her parents. Her older brother.

Gone. All gone.

They would never know her son.

A sudden pain, like a razor blade in her throat, made her gasp as fresh, unexpected grief ambushed her.

Setting down his newspaper, Cristiano looked at her sharply. "What is it?"

Blinking fast, she looked at him. She swallowed. "I was just remembering…"

"What?"

Jack fussed a little in her arms. She was grateful for the excuse to turn away. "Nothing."

Getting up, she set the baby down in his new play gym with a padded blanket on the floor, so he could bat at the brightly colored mobile overhead. She felt Cristiano's gaze on her as she went to the room-service carts and lifted a silver lid. Taking the plate of food and silverware, she returned to sit beside him at the counter. She forced herself to take a bite, then another. The waffles and bacon were indeed lukewarm, and all she could feel was sad.

"Can I ask you something?" Cristiano asked, setting his fork down on his own empty plate.

"What?"

"Why did you refuse my marriage proposal yesterday?" She glanced at him. "I told you—"

"That we hate each other. I remember." He took a drink of black coffee. The dainty china cup looked incongruous in his large, masculine hands. "It's just funny. I always thought if I ever asked a woman to marry me, the reaction would be very different."

"But you didn't ask. You told." Hallie looked at her limp waffles. "And I'm not convinced you know what commitment means."

"How can you say that?"

Setting down her fork, Hallie stared out at the view of the city and bright blue skies. "My parents married straight out of high school. They fought all the time, but never threatened to leave. We were a family. And family means sticking together, no matter what." Her voice choked, and she looked down at the marble floor. "After they died, it was all I dreamed about. Having a family again. A home."

"That's why you were still a virgin when we met," he said slowly. "You were waiting for the man you could give your life to. Not just your life. Your loyalty."

She nodded, unable to meet his eyes, bracing herself for his cynical, mocking response.

Instead, his voice was quiet. "I destroyed all your plans by seducing you."

Hallie's gaze lifted to his. Then she looked at their baby in his play gym. Jack was stretching out his chubby arms, waving them like a drunken sailor as he tried to reach the mobile hanging over his head. With a trembling smile, she shook her head.

"How can I blame you, when that night brought our baby? Besides." She stared down at her hands. "What happened wasn't just your fault. It was also mine." With a deep breath, she said, "If I had really wanted to wait for marriage, I wouldn't have let you or anyone else change my mind. No matter how badly I wanted you. Because I knew even then that I could never be more than a one-night stand to a man like you."

"You're wrong." His voice was low. "You were always more than a one-night stand to me."

"So that's why you had me fired and tossed out of the hotel?" Her lips lifted humorously. "Because you wanted to spend more time with me?"

"You were an employee. A virgin. But from the moment I first heard you sing, from the moment I saw you, floating my sheets softly through the air, I had to have you. I smashed every rule."

"You knew I was a virgin?" she breathed.

He gave a slow nod. "I could tell when I kissed you. But I still couldn't stop myself from taking you to my bed. And once I had you," he said softly, "I only wanted more."

"Then why did you send me away?" she said, trembling.

His eyes met hers evenly. "I was afraid you'd want a relationship. That you'd ask for a commitment."

His words burned her pride. "But I didn't."

"No," Cristiano agreed. He leaned toward her at the

counter. "But now I'm asking you. I want us to give our son a home. To be a family." Leaning forward, he took both her hands in his own, his eyes intense. "I'm asking you to marry me."

She sucked in her breath as all her childhood dreams clamored around her. Could it truly happen? Could a night of passion turn them unexpectedly into a family?

A home.

Loyalty.

Family.

He was offering her everything she'd ever wanted, and unimaginable wealth and luxury, too.

For a moment, Hallie was tempted. Then she shook her head slowly.

"Why?" he demanded.

She turned away from his arrogant gaze, busying herself with tackling a thick, salty slice of bacon. "A marriage of convenience? How would that even work?"

"I never said it would be a marriage of convenience." His black eyes pierced hers. "Our marriage would be very real, Hallie."

Beneath his gaze, she felt hot all over. She swallowed the bacon, barely tasting it. Her full breasts were suddenly heavy, her nipples aching and taut. Tension coiled, low and deep, in her belly.

Swallowing, she pushed the plate away. "You could have any woman for the asking." She looked at Cristiano's elegant penthouse, and the wide windows that showed all New York City at his feet. "Why not wait for someone you love? Someone—" her voice faltered "—who loves you?"

"I'm thirty-five years old, and I've never loved anyone. I never thought I had the ability." Cristiano looked at Jack, wriggling happily on the soft quilted mat of the baby gym. "Until the day I found out I had a son."

Hallie felt her heart constrict as she saw the way he

looked at Jack. In their intense love for their child, they were the same.

He turned back to her. "And now I know this. My duty is to protect you both. To provide for you. To give you a home. To give you my name. I offer you my loyalty, Hallie. For a lifetime."

"Your loyalty," she whispered.

Cristiano looked at her, his eyes black as night. "I will protect our son. No matter the cost."

His words sounded strangely like a warning. But that didn't make sense. Why would he warn Hallie that he intended to protect their son?

So much she'd thought about him was all wrong. He actually wanted to commit to her. To be a father to Jack.

Her son would have financial security, the best schools, the promise of a brilliant future.

And, even more importantly, Cristiano would always protect him and watch his back. If anything ever happened to Hallie, Jack would still be safe. She'd learned the hard way about loss.

Cristiano was offering her everything and, still, some part of her hesitated. "You're asking me to give up love—all hope of it forever."

"Have you ever been in love?"

"No," she was forced to admit.

"Then how can you miss what you've never had?"

His words were starting to make the impossible seem reasonable. "A marriage implies faithfulness…"

"Which I would be."

Her breath caught in her throat. She hadn't expected that. Cristiano Moretti, the famous billionaire playboy, was promising total fidelity. To her.

That thought was too outlandish to believe. She shook her head, her lips curving up at the edges. "Have you really thought this through? No more Russian supermodels?"

"You persist in underestimating me," he said softly. Reaching out, he tucked hair behind her ear. "When will you learn the truth?"

Hallie swallowed. "What's that?"

His gaze cut through her. "I want only you."

Her heart was pounding. A year ago, when he'd tossed her to the curb, she'd thought she'd made the worst mistake of her life. For the last year, she'd barely held on sometimes, trying to keep a roof over her baby's head. Security had seemed like a fairy tale.

Now Cristiano was offering her everything she'd dreamed of. She could secure her son's comfort and give him two parents and a stable home for a lifetime.

The only cost would be her heart. Their marriage would be about partnership and, yes, passion. But not love.

Could she accept that? For the rest of her life?

Or would her heart shrivel up and die?

Getting up from the barstool, Hallie crossed the great room uncertainly. She looked down at her sweet baby, cooing and playing happily. Holding her breath, she stared out the windows at the gray city and brilliant blue sky.

Silence fell in the penthouse. She felt the warm morning sun against her skin, the rise and fall of her own breath. Then she heard him cross the floor. Putting his hands on her shaking shoulders, he turned her to face him. His dark eyes burned like fire.

"One more thing," he said in a low voice. "Before you decide."

And pulling her roughly against his body, he lowered his mouth to kiss her.

CHAPTER FOUR

HIS LIPS WERE hot and yearning, burning through Hallie's body and soul. This kiss was different from the hungry, demanding passion of their first night. This time he tempted rather than took. He lured rather than ravished.

His hands tangled in her dark hair, stroking slowly down her bare shoulders and back. Shivers of need cascaded through Hallie's body. She could not resist his embrace, as wistful and tender as his whispered words, which still hung between them like mist.

When will you learn the truth?

What's that?

I want only you.

Her mind scattered in a million different directions, the penthouse whirling around her. She felt his desire for her through his low-slung pajama pants. She gripped his naked, powerful shoulders, feeling that Cristiano was the only solid thing in a world spinning out of control. His skin felt warm, his body solid and strong. This kiss, the sweet dream of his lips on hers, was all that felt real.

He deepened the embrace, pushing her back against the white sofa, his hands running over her body—over her naked arms, the spaghetti straps of her sundress. As the kiss intensified, hunger built between them until she kissed him back desperately, her whole body on fire. She gripped his shoulders, his mouth hot and demanding against hers. Feeling the sweet weight of his body over hers, the hard warmth of his muscular chest, she would have done anything—agreed to anything—to make this moment last...

"Say you'll marry me," he whispered against her skin. "Say it—"

"Yes," she choked out. She didn't realize she'd spoken until he pulled back, searching her gaze.

"You won't take it back? You won't change your mind?"

She shook her head. "It's what I want most. Loyalty. Family. Home."

"And this." And Cristiano kissed her, consuming her, until all that was left of her was fire and ash.

Cristiano had to take her to bed. Now.

If he didn't have her, now that he knew she was going to be his wife, he thought he might explode.

"You've made me so happy, *cara mia*," he whispered, kissing her forehead, her cheeks. The sweet intoxication of her lips. He started to lift her in his arms, intending to seal the deal immediately in his bedroom.

Then his baby son gave a low whimper.

"Jack," Hallie said immediately, and the sensual spell was broken. Looking at each other, they both gave a rueful laugh. Moving back, he let her get off the sofa.

After hurrying across the room, she scooped Jack up from his play gym. The baby immediately brightened in his mother's arms. "But I'm being greedy." Walking with him back to where Cristiano stood, she gave him a shy smile. "Do you want to hold him?"

He shook his head. To be honest, the baby seemed happier with his mother. And he couldn't blame Jack for preferring her. What experience did Cristiano have with children? He couldn't bear the thought of his son crying. What if he held him wrong again and Hallie scorned him for being a clumsy fool?

"Are you sure?" Hallie said, looking disappointed. But she didn't wait for an answer. She just smiled down at her son, crooning, "How are you, sweet boy?"

Cristiano's heart expanded as he looked at them, his tiny baby son with the chubby cheeks, held by his incredibly loving, sexy bride-to-be. Reaching out, he put his hand on his son's soft, downy hair. His eyes locked with Hallie's and he felt a current of emotion.

It was too much. Feeling his heart in his throat, he abruptly turned away. "We've been stuck in this penthouse long enough. I want to buy you an engagement ring."

"It's not necessary."

"But it is." He'd buy her the most obscenely huge diamond that the world had ever seen. "And our wedding must be arranged quickly, before I leave for Italy."

"You're going to Italy?"

"Tomorrow night."

"So soon!"

He turned to her with a frown. "I will visit my hotel in Rome. Also I'm building a new hotel on the Amalfi Coast and want to supervise the final preparations before the grand opening next month."

"How long will you be gone?"

"It doesn't matter, because you're both coming with me."

Hallie's eyes became round as saucers. "You want to take me and Jack to Italy?"

"Is that a problem?"

"I don't have a passport."

"Something we'll fix today, after we go to the jewelry store—and get our wedding license."

"You want us to be married in Italy?"

"That would take too long. The laws there are complicated."

Her lips parted. "You want us to be married before we leave?"

"Yes," he said roughly.

"A wedding? In *two days*?"

"Tomorrow," he said.

Hallie looked shocked. Coming forward, he took her in

his arms and kissed her. "Everything will be perfect," he whispered, cupping her cheek. "I swear to you."

"All right." Looking dazed, she gave him a crooked smile. "I'll take your word for it. After all, you were right about the room service."

He returned her grin. "I'll go get dressed." His body protested at the thought of putting on clothes instead of taking Hallie's clothes *off*. Still, he could wait the few hours until they were alone, until they weren't being watched so keenly by their three-month-old chaperone. Glancing down at his pajama pants, he turned toward his bedroom, intending to find a shirt and trousers. "We'll leave in five minutes."

Behind him, Hallie gave a laugh that came straight from her belly, deeper and more heartfelt than he'd ever heard from her before. "Oh, we will, will we?"

Frowning, he turned back.

"What's so funny?" he said suspiciously.

"Nothing." She gave him a grin. "Except you're used to people always being ready whenever you want them to be, aren't you?"

"I'm a busy man. Others wait for me. I don't wait for them."

"Not anymore." She giggled. "Now you have a baby."

She was right. It was, in fact, over an hour before they left the penthouse. In that time, the baby was fed, then he'd cried, and then they had to change his clothes when he spit up all over his onesie. He was burped a little more and cried some more. Then the real reason for Jack's earlier fussiness was revealed—a blowout needing a diaper change and yet another new outfit. Hallie calmly repacked everything in her diaper bag. Finally, just as they were about to leave, the baby let out a whimper and needed to be fed again.

Through it all, Cristiano was impressed with Hallie's infinite patience and skill. He wouldn't have had a clue what to do. When she'd looked up at him with a gentle smile and asked if he wanted to help burp or change the baby, he had been filled with alarm. He'd shaken his head. What did he know? Better to leave it to the expert. Patient and loving, Hallie was clearly born to be a mother.

Once again Cristiano congratulated himself on securing his possession of her.

By the time they were out of the hotel and on the street, he took a big breath of fresh air. Yellow taxi cabs raced down the avenue as backpack-carrying tourists fought for space on the sidewalk with lawyers in suits and food carts selling everything from hot dogs to cupcakes to falafel. The summer morning was warm and fresh, and the sunlight spilled gold on the streets of New York.

But the brightest glow of all came from Hallie's sparkling eyes as she snapped their baby's carrier into his expensive new stroller.

"Thank you for this, by the way," she said, nodding at the stroller.

He'd told Marcia to send the best one. "Does Jack like it?"

She turned it toward him. "See for yourself."

Peeking down, he saw that his baby, who'd spent the past hour causing a fuss, was nestled in the stroller cozily, smiling.

Cristiano's heart swelled in his chest as his son stretched up his chubby little hands, as if reaching for the towering hotel.

"All yours someday," he told Jack softly in Italian. Then he looked at Hallie's beautiful face as she pointed up at the top of the hotel in the clouds, talking tenderly to their son. Under his breath in the same language, he added, "All mine."

Hallie turned to him quizzically. "Did you say something?"

"Just that our first stop this morning is to get our marriage license." As they waited briefly outside the hotel, he took her hand. He felt it tremble at the intimacy of the gesture.

The black SUV with tinted windows pulled up. Matthews was at the wheel and Luther, the bodyguard, sat beside him in the front.

As Matthews folded the stroller into the trunk, Cristiano opened the door for Hallie. He snapped the baby carrier securely in the back seat, then followed her inside.

"Where to, sir?" Matthews said cheerfully as Hallie smiled down at the chattering baby.

"The city clerk's office downtown."

An hour later, they left with their marriage license. Cristiano exhaled deeply. *One step closer.* In twenty-four hours it would be permanent. He would give Jack his last name. And not just the baby…

His eyes lingered on Hallie as she climbed back into the waiting SUV, tucking their smiley baby into his car seat.

He could hardly wait to possess her in bed. Tonight. This afternoon. He paused. Or he could wait to make love until their wedding night, as Hallie had once wanted.

Could he give her that? Could he wait until she was legally his to bed her? Knowing that, after tomorrow, she would be his forever?

No. He couldn't.

"Now where, sir?"

Leaning forward in the SUV, Cristiano named the most exclusive jewelry store on Fifth Avenue. He glanced at Hallie to see if it met with her approval, but she was busy playing peekaboo with the baby.

When they arrived, Hallie stared out of the window, wide-eyed at the sight of the luxury jewelry store. "Here?"

"Here," he said firmly. He intended to woo her. Perhaps

he couldn't do love, but he knew about romance. Though he'd never shopped for an engagement ring before.

As Cristiano got out, he saw Hallie unbuckling their baby from the car seat. "You're bringing him with us?" he asked in surprise.

"Of course I am." As Matthews got the stroller from the back, she smiled down at her baby, tucking him inside it. "What would you expect me to do, leave him alone in the car?"

"He wouldn't be alone," Cristiano said, nonplussed. He'd intended to romance her, and even with his limited experience of babies, he'd already seen that they could be a distraction from romance. He'd told Luther to remain in the SUV, as bodyguards also could impinge on intimate moments. "Matthews and Luther could watch him."

She glanced back at the two burly men, and her lips curved. "Not exactly trained baby professionals. No offense."

"None taken, ma'am," Matthews said.

"None whatsoever," Luther said.

"Va bene." Cristiano gave in with grace. Perhaps Hallie was right, anyway. The engagement ring wasn't meant to cement just the two of them as a couple, but the three of them as a family. Still, he made a mental note that they should acquire a—what had she called it?—a *trained baby professional* as soon as possible. Because he had sensual plans for Hallie, and he knew she wouldn't be able to linger in his bed unless she was certain Jack was being well tended.

"We won't be here long," he said, as they pushed the stroller past the doorman and security guard into the gilded jewelry store. Smiling down at Hallie, he said huskily, "I already know what I want."

"I think you've made that clear," she said, her cheeks a charming shade of pink. So were her lips.

Cristiano stopped abruptly inside the entrance, beneath the stained-glass cupola high overhead. Not caring who might see, he pulled Hallie into his arms, her pink sundress fluttering behind her.

Ruthlessly he lowered his mouth to hers, kissing her long and lingeringly. The stained-glass cupola dappled them with colored light. He heard whispers and romantic sighs as some customers walked by, as well as the irritated grumbling of men as their partners hissed, "Why do you never kiss me in public like that?"

When Cristiano finally pulled away, he looked down, relishing the dazzled look in Hallie's brown eyes. Gently he traced her swollen bottom lip with his thumb.

"Soon," he whispered. "Very soon."

Hallie sucked in her breath as if still in a trance. Taking a step, she nearly stumbled. He felt a surge of supremely masculine satisfaction.

"Let me help." With a wicked grin, he took the stroller with one arm and her hand with the other. "Let's have some fun."

He already knew exactly the ring he wanted: the biggest diamond in the store. Maybe Hallie didn't care about luxuries like room service, but every woman wanted an amazing engagement ring. And Hallie would have the best.

The store manager's face lit up upon seeing Cristiano, who, though he'd never bought a ring, had purchased expensive bracelets and necklaces for various mistresses in the past. The man took them swiftly to a private room, where he spread out a selection of diamond engagement rings across a black velvet tray.

"Which would the lady like to see first?" purred the manager, who was short and sophisticated in a designer suit.

"Which is the best?" Cristiano said.

With an approving smile, the manager pointed at a middle ring, an enormous emerald-cut canary diamond set in platinum. Cristiano nodded. "That's the one."

He was surprised to see Hallie frown, her eyebrows furrowed. "But it's yellow."

"A special type of diamond, very rare and beautiful," the manager intoned, "for a rare and beautiful woman."

Staring at him, Hallie burst into a laugh. "And here I was thinking that since the color's off, we might get a discount."

The manager's smile froze in place. "It's the most luxurious diamond we possess, with a cost that is, of course, commensurate with its rare beauty."

"Try it on," Cristiano said.

Biting her lip, Hallie allowed him to slide it over her finger. Her eyes were huge as she stared down at the ring. The rectangular yellow diamond was so huge it extended over her ring finger to partially cover the two adjacent fingers.

"Twenty and a half carats," said the manager reverently.

Her hand shook visibly, and she yanked it off suddenly and placed it back on the black velvet tray.

"You don't like it?" Cristiano asked, confused.

Hallie shook her head. "It weighs like a billion pounds! It's cold! And the setting scratched my skin. What if I scratched the baby?"

"Hurt the baby?" he said incredulously. Any other woman he'd known would have grabbed the million-dollar ring with a fervent *thank you*.

Hallie shook her head. "I wouldn't want to worry about gouging out someone's eye with that thing." She tilted her head. "And since we're getting married tomorrow, why do we even need an engagement ring? It seems silly."

There was a suppressed scream from the other side of the counter. The manager looked as if he might have the vapors.

Cristiano turned back to her with a frown. "You don't want a ring?"

She put her hand in his.

"I'd rather just get a plain gold wedding band. For each of us."

Now he was really confused. "Doesn't a diamond symbolize forever? Exactly as you wanted?"

"It does," agreed the manager, nodding vigorously.

"Not for me." She entwined her smaller hand in his. "My parents just had gold bands. I don't need a big diamond or a big wedding. It's the commitment I care about. Knowing the baby's safe. That I am, too."

Her big, brown eyes were like pools to drown in. Cristiano could not argue with her. He turned to the manager.

"You heard the lady. Get her what she wants."

The manager's face fell at seeing his easy million-dollar sale slip through his fingers. Then he seemed to recall that a man such as Cristiano would be likely to buy other expensive trinkets for his wife over time, and he recovered.

"I know just the thing," the man said.

Ten minutes later, Cristiano walked out of the jewelry store into the sunshine with his beautiful bride-to-be pushing the stroller. From her wrist dangled a small red bag, which held two simple wedding bands in shining gold.

Calling an enormous diamond ring silly? Cristiano shook his head with wonder. Truly, Hallie was one in a million. But, seeing her smile, he was glad he'd let her have her way.

He had another surprise for her, too.

"Now we need to get you some clothes," he said after the SUV picked them up. He hid a smile. The surprise had taken some effort to arrange.

"Why?" Hallie looked puzzled. She looked down at her faded pink sundress and her slightly scuffed sandals. "What's wrong with this?"

"You'll need a wedding dress. We'll get the rest of your trousseau in Rome."

She gave a laugh. *"Trousseau?"*

Her expression made him feel old-fashioned, or at least *old*. "That is the word, is it not, for the traditional new wardrobe for a bride?"

Her grin widened. "That's the dumbest thing I ever heard. Why would I need new clothes to be a wife?"

"Because you're going to be *my* wife. There will be certain expectations."

"What expectations?"

She was blushing, as if she assumed he was speaking of sex. But he would hardly talk dirty with his driver, his bodyguard and their innocent baby all listening in. His lips quirked. "I am the owner of twenty-two luxury hotels around the world. That makes me the advocate for my brand. As my wife, you will be, as well."

"So?"

"So you need new clothes."

"You mean sexy? Expensive?"

"Sleek. Cosmopolitan." He ran his fingertips slowly down the side of her dress. The cotton fabric was rough and pilled from repeated washings. "I can't have my wife's clothes looking like they were bought at a discount shop. What would my shareholders think?"

"That I'm good with money and know how to get good value?" she replied archly.

He snorted. "In private, of course, you can wear whatever you want. I like the look of you in everything." Leaning forward, he whispered for her ears alone, "Or nothing."

He felt her shiver, felt his own body rise. He had to fight the urge to grab her and kiss her again. *Soon*, he promised himself hungrily. *Tonight*.

Cristiano leaned back against the SUV's soft leather seat. "You will need clothes that you can wear to events where you will be photographed and appear in newspapers as a symbol of the Campania brand."

"I didn't sign up for that."

"And yet it is so." He tilted his head curiously. "Most women would not object so strenuously to a new wardrobe."

"I'm remembering something I read in high school… that you should beware any relationship that requires new clothes."

His lips lifted. "You're talking about Thoreau. He didn't say beware the new relationship, he said beware the new enterprise."

"Marrying you, it doesn't sound like there's a difference," she said grumpily. The SUV stopped, and she frowned. "What are we—"

Then Hallie turned, and her jaw dropped when she saw Cristiano's surprise.

CHAPTER FIVE

HALLIE STOOD IN front of a full-length mirror, turning to look at herself from all angles. This wedding dress was deceptively simple, made of duchess satin with a bias cut. It made her post-pregnancy figure look amazing in a way that even she couldn't deny.

"That's it!" Lola yelled. "That's the one!"

"It's perfect," Tess said dreamily. "You look like a princess."

Hallie had been shocked to see Lola and Tess waiting for her on the curb in front of the luxury bridal shop on Fifth Avenue. Amazed, she'd stared back at Cristiano in shock. "What did you… How did you?"

He'd given her a wicked smile. "Your friends called the front desk of the hotel this morning, demanding to know if I'd kidnapped you, since you weren't responding to their messages."

"Oh," she'd said sheepishly. She had turned off her phone last night and forgotten to turn it back on.

"I told them to come see you for themselves. They're going to help you pick out a wedding dress. If you want."

"Are you serious?"

His smile widened. "Then you all have appointments for spa treatments next door."

She'd beamed at him, then her joy had faded. "But who will watch Jack?"

"He's coming back to the penthouse with me," Cristiano said gravely, "for a little father-son time."

He'd looked at her steadily, as if daring her to object. Hallie had felt it was some kind of test. "But," she said helplessly, "how will you know what to do?"

"I'll keep your diaper bag. Bottles, diapers. Everything I could need, right?"

"Right," she said doubtfully.

He lifted an eyebrow. "I run a billion-dollar company, Hallie. I think I can handle watching my own son while he sleeps for a few hours."

Put like that, she'd been forced, reluctantly, to agree. Giving Jack one last kiss on his plump cheek, she'd slowly gotten out of the SUV. Then she'd turned back anxiously. "I'll be back in two hours."

"Take all afternoon. Take as long as you want. Enjoy yourself. We'll be fine." Leaning forward, Cristiano had given her a goodbye kiss that had left her knees weak, and then he'd smiled. "Have fun."

And, somewhat to her surprise, Hallie had. For the last hour, she and her friends been pampered like royalty at the designer bridal store. Cristiano had already won the loyalty of both her friends.

Tess admired him for demanding marriage immediately. "It's so romantic, practically an elopement! And next he's whisking you off to Italy!" She'd sighed. "So romantic!"

Lola had liked that Cristiano had left them an open credit line and told her and Tess, as bridesmaids, to get new outfits, as well. "Even shoes!"

The bridesmaid dresses were already chosen. Looking at herself now in the mirror, Hallie knew that this wedding dress was the one. It fit her perfectly, no alterations required, and made her look, as Tess had said, like a princess.

Nervously she charged it to Cristiano's account, half expecting the manager to laugh in her face. Instead, the manager rang it up, then talked her into also buying demure white high heels, an elegant veil and bridal lingerie that made her blush. Once all her purchases had been packed and sent off to the penthouse, the three girls headed next door to spend a precious hour at the day spa.

"This is the life," sighed Tess, stretching out her legs as a pedicurist massaged her feet.

"Who's watching Esme, Tess?"

The redhead gave a guilty smile. "My cousin. Don't get me wrong, I love being with my baby. But a few hours to myself feels like a vacation."

"Yeah," Lola said, selecting a chocolate-covered strawberry from a nearby silver tray. "This fiancé of yours is not so bad."

Hallie snorted. "You're just saying that because he told you to spare no expense on the bridesmaid outfits."

"I want your wedding day to be perfect," Lola said demurely, rubbing her heavily pregnant belly as she smiled at the shopping bag that held her new thousand-dollar shoes.

"I just wish Lacey could be here," Tess sighed. "We tried to invite her."

"Lacey!" Hallie smiled at the memory of the energetic young woman who'd invited each of them to the single-moms group, then introduced them to one another. "I owe her a lot."

"Me, too. Because of her, I got to meet you losers." Lola's smile was fond. She held up her champagne glass for another refill of sparkling water from the hovering spa attendant. "Lacey's traveling the world happily with her husband and baby. She sends her love. And promised to send a wedding gift."

"I don't need a gift."

"Of course you don't," Lola said. "You're marrying one of the richest men in the world."

"She doesn't care about his money," Tess protested. She turned to Hallie, her eyes shining. "It's love that brought you together. Pure, perfect love. That's the only reason anyone would marry."

"Um," said Hallie, feeling awkward. Love had nothing to do with it. They were just getting married to give their baby a good home. But she didn't want to disillusion Tess, who was looking at her with dreamy, happy eyes. It made Hallie feel uneasy. She'd told herself that there was nothing wrong with a loveless marriage. Their arrangement would be both practical and sensible.

So why did her throat close at the thought of explaining that to her friends?

"Your baby's father reacted just like I said he would. As soon as he knew about Jack, he realized he loved you and begged you to marry him," Tess said joyfully. "So who knows? Maybe my baby's father will do the same."

"Give it up," Lola said, rolling her eyes. "He's never coming back, Tess."

The redhead sucked in her breath, looking like she was going to cry.

"We don't know that," Hallie said loyally, though she understood Lola's irritation. For as long as they'd known her, Tess had spoken constantly of the man who'd seduced her and disappeared. She'd spun out endless reasons why he might not have returned—ridiculous reasons, like his plane crashing on a desert island, or being kidnapped in Antarctica, or that he'd developed amnesia.

Privately, Hallie agreed with Lola. The guy was obviously a jerk and gone for good. But telling Tess that seemed like kicking a puppy.

Hallie gave the redhead a sympathetic smile. "It could happen, Tess. He could come back."

Her friend gave her a grateful smile. "You think so?"

"Stop encouraging her," Lola snapped. Unlike the other two, she'd never once spoken of the man who'd gotten her pregnant, no matter how many times they'd asked. "It'll just hurt her more in the end."

"Shush," Hallie told her, and turned to Tess. "He— What's his name again?"

"Stefano," Tess murmured. She blushed. "I never learned his last name."

"Stefano." Where had she heard that name recently? She tried to remember, then gave up. Hallie leaned back in her spa chair, closing her eyes. "He could be on his way to you already."

But as the facialist covered her eyelids with cool cucumber slices, a faint hint of memory teased her. Where had she heard that name?

"This is nice," Lola said, and sighed from the next chair. "You should put something about spa days in your prenup, Hallie."

"My what?" Hallie yawned.

"Your prenuptial agreement."

"Cristiano hasn't asked for one."

"He will. Trust me. Rich men always look out for themselves. He'll want a legal contract. Read your prenup carefully."

"A contract for marriage? That's silly," Hallie said, already half-asleep as the pedicurist massaged her feet. "Marriage is forever. We're going to take care of each other."

Two hours later, as Hallie walked back through the soaring lobby of the Campania Hotel, she felt so relaxed she glowed. For the first time since Cristiano had taken her virginity and kicked her out of the hotel, she felt...happy.

Cristiano had done that, she realized. He'd arranged everything.

He was so different from the selfish, arrogant bastard she'd once thought him to be. He'd gotten her the simple gold ring she wanted, instead of the enormous diamond. He'd invited her friends to join her for a spa afternoon. He hadn't once said the word *prenup*. And, even now, he was taking care of their baby.

"Hallie!"

She turned around, and all the relaxed, good feelings in her body fled.

Cristiano was sauntering through the lobby with a briefcase, Luther behind him. Coming up to her, he kissed her cheek softly. "Did you have an enjoyable afternoon?"

"Yes." *But where—where was—* Hallie looked all around with rising panic, her eyes wide. Her heart lifted to her throat. "Where's Jack?"

Cristiano gave a low laugh. "Upstairs in the penthouse. Safe. In the best of hands."

"Whose?" she choked out. "Why isn't he with you?"

Cristiano started walking toward the elevator, in no particular hurry. "I had to go to my lawyer's office, to collect the prenuptial agreement."

"The *what*?"

His handsome face looked down at her quizzically. "The prenuptial agreement, *cara*. Of course we must have one."

Hallie's jaw tightened. Turning away, she pushed the elevator button multiple times. When the elevator finally opened, she rushed inside. He followed her, frowning.

"Are you in a rush?"

"How can you ask me that?" She frantically tried to push the button for the penthouse floor, but it didn't work until he placed his finger against the keypad, after which the elevator door slid closed.

"Are you upset at the idea of a prenup? You surely cannot think I would marry you without one, exposing me to the risk of New York's divorce laws and the possibility of losing half my fortune."

She whirled on him. "You think I care about money?"

He looked at her evenly. "Everyone cares about money."

"You left our son with a stranger!"

Cristiano's shoulders relaxed. "He could hardly come with me to the lawyer's office. But you don't need to worry. I left him in the care of the best nanny in the city."

He didn't get it, Hallie realized. She'd been a fool to let herself be lulled into trusting him with her baby, even for an afternoon!

Her fears proved right. Even before the elevator opened on the top floor, she could hear her baby crying.

Wailing.

With no one apparently trying to comfort him.

Hallie rushed to the penthouse door. She was ready to kick it open, to scratch it with her hands. "What kind of home is this if I can't even open my own door?" she said furiously.

Wordlessly Cristiano opened the door with his fingerprint, and she rushed through it. Her baby's crying came from the guest room, but as Hallie rushed forward, a stern older woman in a uniform blocked her path.

"Get out of my way," Hallie thundered, pushing past her into the bedroom.

Picking up her tiny sobbing infant from the crib, she held him close to her heart, whispering and singing softly. The baby's wails subsided. Once she'd sat down in the glider and loosened her top, the baby was able to suckle, and his crying stopped abruptly and completely.

"You're making a mistake," the uniformed nanny said, watching dispassionately from the doorway. "It is a mistake I see with many of my ladies. If you give in to your baby's demands now, you'll be his slave. The only way to have a calm household is to get the child on a feeding schedule. You must let him cry it out, madam."

"Cry it out? Cry it out!" Hallie had never been much for swearing, but she suddenly let loose every curse she'd ever heard from her father, who'd been a coal miner and a serious overachiever in the field of swearing. "I'll cry *you* out!"

The woman blanched. "I was hired by Mr. Moretti himself," she said unfeelingly. "I have worked for princes and kings, and I am not going to be insulted by the likes of you."

"Get out," Hallie said, cuddling her baby.

"I'm not going to take orders—"

Her voice became shrill. "Get! Out!"

"Do as she says," Cristiano said in a low voice from behind the nanny, who whirled to face him. His dark eyes glittered in the shadows.

"Fine," she said stiffly. "But I expect to be fully paid for—"

"You'll be paid," Cristiano said. "But if you ask for a reference, don't expect any more princes or kings to hire you."

The woman left with a sniff. Cristiano went to Hallie, who was still sitting in the glider, trembling as she cuddled their baby. He put his hand on her shoulder.

"I'm sorry," he said quietly. "She came highly recommended."

Hallie took a deep breath. She had to force her voice to remain calm. "You have no experience with children."

His eyes flashed to hers, and his expression changed.

"No," he said finally.

She lifted her chin. "You have to learn."

His grip on her shoulder tightened infinitesimally.

"I was told she was the best in New York."

"The best? He was hungry and she was deliberately choosing not to give him a bottle!" She glared up at him. "How can I trust you after this? You convinced me to leave the baby in your care. *Yours*, Cristiano. Not some stranger's!"

For the first time, he looked uncertain. His arms fell to his sides as he muttered, "I told you. I had something to do."

"Yes—watching our son! The son you supposedly care about so much that sharing custody wasn't enough for you—you had to demand marriage! You insisted you wanted to be a father. Was that all just a lie?"

"No," he ground out.

"So why would you immediately desert him?"

"I did not desert him!"

"If you don't want to actually raise him, then what are we even doing?"

Folding his arms, he paced three steps. "You are being unreasonable."

Hallie took a deep breath. "No," she said steadily. "I'm not. If you want us to live with you…if you want me to be crazy enough to marry you tomorrow, then—" she lifted her chin "—I'm setting some rules."

He looked at her in disbelief. "*You're* setting rules?"

"Yes." She added coolly, "We'll even put them into that prenup of yours if you like. Just to make it all official."

He stared at her, clawing his hand through his dark hair. "Fine," he said, his eyes glittering. "Tell me these ridiculous rules."

"First. You will stop being so afraid of the baby."

"Afraid?" he said incredulously. "I'm not afraid!"

"You will learn to be a father to Jack," she continued, ignoring him. "You will learn how to hold him, change him, give him a bottle and bath and rock him to sleep."

His expression darkened. For a second she thought he would refuse. Then he said tightly, "Continue."

"Second. We will spend time as a family. You will join us for at least one meal every day—no matter how busy you are with your company."

"I don't intend to neglect you and Jack," he ground out. "Why would you want that in the prenup?"

Hallie looked at him evenly. "I don't intend to divorce you and steal half your fortune. But, strangely, you still want that written up in a contract."

His jaw looked so tight she wondered if he was hurting his teeth. "Fine."

"I prefer dinner, but if you have to work late, breakfast or lunch is all right, too."

"Anything else?"

Hallie glanced down at her tiny baby son, who had already fallen asleep in her arms. She thought of all her hopes, all her dreams. Only one really mattered.

"Third," she whispered. "You will love him and protect him with your life. As I do."

He stared down at her in the shadowy quiet of the guest bedroom.

"I accept your terms," he bit out. Going to his briefcase, he removed a legal document ten pages long. After turning to the last page, he scribbled something. He handed her the papers.

"Read," he said. "Then sign."

Hallie skimmed the document swiftly, elated to see he'd written all three of her rules exactly as she'd wanted, squeezing them in above the signature lines. As she read through the rest of the pages, the tiny font and legal jargon started to swim before her eyes.

Read your prenup carefully.

The memory of Lola's voice floated back to her, and Hallie wondered if she should get a lawyer to explain the details to her. But she didn't know any lawyers, and it all seemed like too much trouble when she just wanted to snuggle her sleeping baby and maybe take a nap herself, right here in the chair.

Besides, what was the point of getting married if she couldn't even trust Cristiano? He'd admitted his mistake. He intended to rectify it. She could forgive him. She wanted them to be a family. She wanted security for her son, and a home. Why else would she agree to a loveless marriage?

He'd agreed to her own rules. If he followed them, why would they ever divorce?

But, as she started to sign her name, she heard the echo of Tess's voice.

It's love that brought you together. Pure, perfect love. That's the only reason anyone would marry.

She hesitated, then gripped the pen. Her hand shook a little as she signed her name. She gave him back the document.

"Here," she said a little hoarsely.

"Thank you." His voice was clipped. Setting the papers down on the end table, he signed them without another word.

Hallie wondered what he was thinking. His handsome face seemed closed off, remote.

A rush of insecurity went through her. Were they making a mistake? In settling for a loveless marriage, were they just being practical—or were they selling their souls?

She swallowed and looked up at him. "Cristiano, are we doing the right thing?"

Straightening, he stood over the glider, looking down at her and the sleeping baby in her arms. His voice was cold. "What do you mean?"

"Settling for a loveless marriage..."

"Don't second-guess it," he said harshly. "The decision is made."

He turned away.

"Where are you going?" she said, astonished.

Cristiano stopped at the doorway, his handsome face in shadow. "I have work to do."

"Tonight?" Hallie yearned for him to give her reassurance—a kind word, a smile. "Can't you take the evening off? Tomorrow's our wedding."

"I have taken too much time off already. There are details to finalize before I leave New York."

"But—"

"Get some rest. After the wedding reception, we'll leave for Rome." His voice was brusque, as if she were one of his employees and he was giving her instructions. "You know how to order room service. I'll see you in the morning."

With that, he left, closing the door behind him.

Hallie shivered, looking out the window into the early-evening light, cradling her sleeping baby in her arms.

She should have been proud of herself for standing up to him over the prenuptial agreement and setting her own terms. Instead, she felt as if she'd just agreed to the terms of her employment.

Stop it, she told herself angrily. Once they were married, they'd be a family. Jack would have a secure home. His childhood would be happy, as Hallie's had been.

But something didn't feel right.

With a deep breath, Hallie pushed the feeling away. Tomorrow, she would leave the only country she'd ever known and set off into the unknown.

Tomorrow, she would be Cristiano Moretti's bride.

"Do you, Hallie Jane Hatfield," the judge intoned, "take this man to be your lawfully wedded husband?"

Cristiano looked down at Hallie as they stood in a quiet, elegant salon on the third floor of his hotel, with chandeliers, a frescoed ceiling and high windows that overlooked the wide avenue below.

"I do," she said, her face pale.

Cristiano's eyes traced over her voluptuous figure in the deceptively simple ivory satin wedding gown. Her dark hair was pulled back beneath a long, elegant veil. She held a bouquet of pink roses. Her beautiful brown eyes were emotionless.

"Do you, Cristiano Moretti, take this woman to be your lawfully wedded wife?"

"I do," he said, and marveled that he didn't have trouble speaking the words. He'd always thought making a lifetime commitment would feel like facing a firing squad. But he felt nothing.

Everything about this wedding had been easy. His executive assistant, Marcia, with the help of the Campania's stellar wedding planner, had pulled the ceremony together in twenty-four hours, so quickly and quietly that the paparazzi had no idea.

Just a few guests were there to mark the occasion. Hallie's two best friends were bridesmaids, each dressed simply in blue and holding a single rose, as requested by the bride. Two babies were also in attendance—tiny newborn Esme, the daughter of the redheaded bridesmaid, and Jack, who was dressed in a miniature tuxedo and held by the other bridesmaid, the pregnant blonde.

His own friend, Ares Kourakis, was there as best man. The Greek owed him that much, as Cristiano had once blindly supported him through a similar endeavor. His bodyguard, Luther, was there with his girlfriend, and Marcia was with her husband. Even Clarence Loggia, the manager of the hotel, had brought a date.

But looking down at his bride, Cristiano had eyes only for her. His gaze traced to her full breasts, pushed up against the bodice of the bias-cut satin, and his body stirred. Angry as he was, he still wanted her.

Last night, when she'd demanded he agree to her rules, he'd been astonished. His original prenuptial agreement had been entirely appropriate, standard among the wealthy. He'd assumed Hallie would sign it without demur. Instead, she'd demanded that he add clauses legally forcing him to learn to take care of their child and always come home for dinner. Seriously?

He didn't necessarily have a problem with either of those things. But he wanted them to be requested, not required. No man wanted to be blackmailed by his own wife the night before the wedding.

And then, as if that weren't enough, once he'd signed, she'd wanted emotional reassurance that their marriage was a good idea. With the wedding arrangements made and the gold rings bought, she'd wanted him to waste another night rehashing the reasons for their marriage!

Cristiano had seen many last-minute hardball negotiating tactics in the business world. He'd just never expected them from the mother of his child.

Hallie had gotten what she wanted. What more had she hoped to accomplish last night, asking for reassurance? Had she wanted to hear him beg?

Not in this lifetime. Cristiano glowered down at her.

"Then, by the power vested in me by the state of New York, you are now husband and wife. You may kiss the bride," the retired judge finished happily.

Hallie's emotionless gaze flashed up to his, the sweep of her dark eyelashes fluttering against her pale cheeks. She was breathing rapidly, and he noted the quick rise and fall of her breasts.

Cristiano was already hard for her. His hands tightened. There would be no more pleading, no more reasoning.

Hallie was his now. Forever.

After a year, his restraint could end. At last, he could claim his prize.

He pulled her into his arms. Lowering his head, he crushed his mouth to hers.

Their lips joined in a flash of heat that ripped through him like a fire. She gasped, then her resistance melted and she kissed him back, matching his desire with her own. As her hands reached up around his shoulders, he heard her bouquet fall to the floor.

The guests applauded and whistled. He took his time, relishing his possession.

When he finally let her go, Hallie's deep brown eyes were shocked and wide. She looked dizzy as they turned to face the cheers of their friends. Stepping forward, she stumbled and he grabbed her arm to steady her. The truth was, though he was better at hiding it, he felt exactly the same way. He wished they were alone so he could take her straight to bed. As it was, he had to adjust the coat of his morning suit to hide the blatant evidence of his desire.

While they accepted the congratulations of their well-meaning friends, Cristiano hummed with impatience. As they enjoyed lunch in a private room of his hotel's elegant restaurant, it was all he could do not to tell his friends to get the hell out.

Midway through their friends' champagne toasts, Cristiano could take it no longer. He cut them off, rising to his feet.

"You'll have to excuse us," he said perfunctorily. "My bride is tired, and needs time for a nap before our flight to Rome."

Everyone looked at Hallie, who appeared astonished.

"Thank you for coming," Cristiano said firmly. Rising to his feet, he reached his hand out to Hallie. "Please feel free to stay as long as you want and order whatever you like." He turned to the pregnant bridesmaid, who was holding Jack. The baby was happily smiling and clapping his hands. "Would you mind watching the baby for an hour?"

"Sure," she said, a glint of wicked amusement in her eyes.

As he pulled his new bride out of the private dining room, he saw the bridesmaids look at each other with a knowing grin, and even Ares Kourakis gave him a smug smile, as if to say, *See? It happened to you, too.*

Cristiano didn't give a damn. After all this time, Hallie was his wife. She was his by right.

He intended to make her so—in every way.

"You were rude," Hallie snapped once they were alone in the elevator. He pushed the button, then turned to her.

"Do you want to go back and make my excuses?" he said in a low voice, running his hand softly over her ivory satin wedding gown, up her arm, to her neck, to her sensitive earlobe and her cheek. He felt her shiver.

"You're a brute," she whispered.

"Yes," he growled. "And now you're mine."

"I'm not—"

Lowering his head, he cut her off with a rough kiss. Pressing her against the wall, he cupped her breasts, kissing down her throat. With a soft gasp, she surrendered, closing her eyes as her head fell back. With her in his arms, he was lost in a sensual haze. He'd almost forgotten they were in an elevator when he heard the bell ding and the door slide open on the top floor.

Lifting her in his arms, he carried her into the penthouse, kicking the door wide over the threshold. Once inside the bedroom, he set her down on her feet, letting her body slide slowly over his so she could feel how hard he was for her.

"Mrs. Moretti," he whispered, and felt her shiver at hearing her new name. In front of the windows revealing the shining New York skyline, with deliberate slowness Cristiano pulled out the pins holding her veil. Her lustrous dark hair fell tumbling down her shoulders.

"You're so beautiful," he said hoarsely.

Reaching up, she loosened his tie. Her brown eyes were soft and inviting. Tossing his black morning coat on the white sofa, he pulled her in his arms.

"You're mine now, Hallie," he said, fiercely searching her gaze. "You know that, don't you?"

"Only if you admit you're mine."

"Yes," he whispered. "Forever."

He lowered his mouth to hers, crushing her body against his own. Sensation and yearning and desire ripped through him, and in that moment he simply let go.

Let go of his anger. His self-control. His reason. He let go of his need to guard himself from everyone and everything.

All that mattered was her.

All that mattered was this.

He slowly unzipped her wedding dress, letting it drop to the floor. He took a ragged breath when he saw her in her wedding lingerie—a white lace bra and tiny panties that clung to her deliciously full hips.

Lifting her up with a growl, he lowered her reverently onto the bed.

Never taking his eyes off her, he loosened his platinum cuff links and unbuttoned his white shirt, then dropped it onto the floor. Pulling off his black trousers, he climbed beside her on the enormous bed, pulling her against his body.

"I've wanted you so long," he whispered.

Her eyes were luminous, and, like a miracle, she lifted her lips to his.

A rush of overwhelming need poured through him, and he crushed her violently against his hard body, plundering her mouth with his own. He yanked off his silk boxers, intending to roll her onto her back and push himself inside her, to impale with a single thrust.

Then he remembered that he had to be gentle. Even though his body was raging with the need to take her, she'd just had his baby three months before. A low curse escaped his lips. He might be a brute, but he wasn't a...a *brute*.

Gentling his embrace, he lingered, naked against her lingerie-clad body, kissing her slowly and thoroughly. Their tongues touched and intertwined in their kiss until he heard her soft sigh, until he felt her body rise. He stroked her face, lightly kissing her forehead, then caressing slowly down her cheek to suckle her ear. He gloried as he felt her shiver beneath him.

Moving down her body as she lay stretched on the bed, he cupped her breasts over the white lace, then with agonizing slowness, removed her bra. He nearly groaned at the sight of her magnificent breasts. He felt their naked weight, before he kissed down the sharp crevice between them, down to the sweet slope of her belly.

For a moment, he teased her with the warmth of his breath. Then he moved lower, and lower still. Finally, gripping her hips, he lowered his head between her legs, teasing her thighs with his breath.

Her hands gripped his shoulders, as if she were afraid of what he might do next, or afraid he might stop.

He ran his tongue along the edge of her white lace panties, letting the tension build in her. Then he ripped the lace off her body entirely.

Lowering his head, he tasted her, caressing her with the hot, slick pressure of his tongue. As she gasped beneath him, he spread her thighs wide with his hands. Ruthlessly, he pressed his mouth against her hot wet core, working the taut nub of her pleasure with his tongue. She gasped, then held her breath.

Then…she exploded.

Fierce joy filled him at seeing her ecstasy.

Moving quickly, he covered her naked body with his own. Lowering his head, he pressed his lips to hers, swaying his hips sensuously against hers. Still lost in pleasure, she accompanied him, her body rising anew. With deliberate slowness, he positioned himself between her legs. He watched her face, keeping himself under control as he finally pushed inside her, filling her inch by delicious inch. He heard her shocked gasp of pleasure. She wrapped her hands around his shoulders, pulling him down harder against her. And, with a groan, he obliged her, thrusting deeper until he was all the way inside her, all the way to her heart.

He was deep, so deep inside her.

Still dazzled by the pleasure he'd given her with his mouth, Hallie moaned softly as he entranced her anew, filling her so completely. She tried to remember when she'd ever felt such intense pleasure. Even their first night together, as incredible as it had been, hadn't been like this. What was the difference? Was it that they were wed, bonded together forever as man and wife?

Or was it something more, something she felt in the deepest corner of her soul—that he belonged to her, and she to him?

But, as he filled her so slowly and deeply, it wasn't just her body that ached desperately for release.

She wanted to love him.

That was the one thing she couldn't do. The one thing that could only lead to ruin: loving her husband.

For a moment, she looked up at his handsome face looming over hers, at his heartbreaking dark eyes. She closed her eyes, turning away as he kissed slowly down her throat.

Slowly, deliberately, he began to ride her. And all she wanted was more. She gasped, clutching at the white comforter beneath her, wrapping her legs around his hips. His thrusts seared her, hard and deep.

Gripping her shoulders, he pushed into her with increasing roughness until their bodies were sweaty, their limbs tangled. Her fingernails tightened into his shoulders, her back rising off the bed, until she exploded, flying even higher than before, higher than she'd ever imagined. Pleasure overwhelmed her in waves so intense she almost blacked out.

With a low growl, he thrust one last time, then roared as he exploded with her.

Gasping, they clutched each other, eyes closed. She struggled to catch her breath. He collapsed beside her, holding her as if she were the only thing that existed. They held each other, tangled in the shadowy bed, for what could have been minutes or hours.

When Hallie finally opened her eyes, she saw Cristiano was pulling away from her, sitting up.

"Don't leave," she pleaded, reaching for him. "We still have a few hours."

He smiled down at her, taking her hand and kissing it tenderly. "It would be good to arrive in Rome early. My jet is already waiting. We should go."

"But our friends…"

"Our friends will understand." Leaning down, he kissed her naked shoulder with a sudden wicked grin. "And there's a bedroom on my jet."

Shivering with need, exhausted with desire, Hallie grinned at him. She blushed, shocked at her own wantonness.

Lowering his head to kiss her one last time, he whispered, "You are magnificent, Mrs. Moretti." Getting up from the bed, he headed for the en suite shower.

Once he left her, she felt suddenly cold, bereft. She wanted him back in bed. Beside her. For always. And not just that.

With an intake of breath, Hallie realized how easy it would be to give her husband—the man who'd told her outright that he could never love her—not just her body, but her soul.

CHAPTER SIX

As the Rolls-Royce drove from the private airport into the crowded and winding streets of Rome, Hallie's head was twisting right and left. She knew she was gaping like a fish, but she didn't care.

After five years in New York, she'd thought no city could easily impress her; yet she'd never seen anything so beautiful, so decadent, so ancient, as the Eternal City.

She looked out the window at a red sports car zipping by, at a young girl in a scarf clinging to a smiling boy on the back of a cherry-colored moped. Down the street, she saw a passionate young couple gesticulating angrily at each other in front of a sidewalk café, before the man swept the woman up into a hungry kiss.

Roma. Hallie felt the city like a thunderbolt. It was like, she thought, a huge, sexy party, with food, wine and dancing—all on top of an ancient tomb. The city itself seemed to cry out: *Take every bit of joy today, for someday you will not be at the party, but below it.*

"What do you think?" Cristiano looked at her over the baby's seat in the back of the limo.

She shivered at the frank sensuality of his gaze. She could hardly believe that she was his wife. Cristiano was her husband. Good thing, too. What he'd done to her last night...

After their passionate interlude at the penthouse, they'd made good use of that bedroom on his private jet. Any time the baby slept, he drew her into his bed, into shockingly sensual delights so new she still shook at the memory.

He smiled, his eyes amused, as if he knew exactly what she was thinking about.

Blushing, she turned back toward her window, marveling as their Rolls-Royce sped down slender, crowded roads, following traffic laws she didn't understand. They'd been met at the airport that morning by their new Italian driver, who was called Marco, and new bodyguard, Salvatore. She gaped as they drove past one incredible ancient monument and cathedral after another. Finally, they arrived at the Campania Hotel Rome, a magnificent Mediterranean-style edifice near the top of the Spanish Steps.

Tilting back her head, she gaped when she got out of the Rolls, staring up at the glamorous hotel. She held her breath as she turned to see the view. All of Rome was at their feet.

"Like it?" Cristiano murmured lazily.

"I've never seen anything like it."

"Of course you have not." He grinned, looking pleased. "Campania is the best luxury hotel brand in the world. And the Campania Roma is the best of them all."

As Marco and Salvatore collected their bags, Hallie and Cristiano strolled hand in hand. Baby Jack, pushed by his father in the stroller, didn't seem nearly as impressed by their surroundings. He chewed on the stuffed giraffe clipped to his shirt.

Hallie looked down at the letters imprinted on a manhole cover near the sidewalk. "What is SPQR?"

"It's Latin. *Senatus populusque Romanus*—the Senate and People of Rome. You'll see the emblem everywhere in the city."

"Wow. This city is really old," she said in awe, and flashed him a grin. "Almost as old as you."

He lifted an eyebrow. "Am I old?"

She liked teasing him about the eleven-year difference between them. She countered, "You're teaching me Latin now?"

His dark eyes simmered. "Let me take you to our room, *cara*. And I'll teach you other things. All night long."

Her cheeks burned as a smiling, dark-eyed doorman held open the hotel door. Pushing the stroller ahead of them, they walked into the soaring lobby.

Hallie sucked in her breath. The opulence was unbelievable. Gilded Corinthian columns stretched up toward the Murano glass chandeliers high above.

"I didn't think it possible," she breathed. "This place is even more amazing than your hotel in New York."

He smiled at her. *"Grazie."*

She turned to stare as a chic fortysomething woman passed by, dressed to the nines in six-inch heels and a velvet skirt suit so well crafted the jacket was like a corset, and perfect scarlet lips. At the woman's side was a man in a well-cut suit who paused to let his eyes caress Hallie before he continued past. Hallie blinked in amazement, staring after them. "And the people..."

"What about them?"

"All the women look like movie stars. And the men like James Bond. Everyone dresses as if they're about to meet the love of their lives. What is this place?"

Cristiano gave her a sudden wicked grin. "Roma."

She shook her head in awe at a city where everyone, from teenagers to octogenarians, seemed to claim eternal sensuality as both a privilege and a duty. "You grew up here?"

"I lived here briefly."

She knew so little about his past. "You were born in Rome?"

His gaze shuttered, as if he could sense her probing.

"Naples," he said flatly. Clearly he wasn't interested in saying anything more.

Mr. Moretti was a brawler, back when he was young. He fought his way out of the streets of Naples.

His driver's words came back to her. Not for the first time, she wondered how a fatherless, penniless boy, neglected then orphaned by his mother, had made his fortune, turning himself into an international hotel tycoon.

"Look." Cristiano pointed at the lobby ceiling. She gasped, tilting back her head to look up.

On the ceiling, gold-painted stars decorated a midnight sky. Across the lobby, she saw huge vases filled with red flowers beside marble fireplaces carved with cherubs. The enormous sweeping staircase had an actual red carpet.

She'd never seen anything so incredible, not even in a movie. She stopped, feeling she was in a dream. "It's—it's—"

"I know," Cristiano replied. "The building was once a *palazzo* gone to ruin. I was only twenty-two when I convinced the *contessa* to sell it. It took two years to rebuild and restore it. I gambled everything I had—my reputation, my future. This place," he said softly, looking around them, "was the making of me."

His voice was deep with emotion. Hallie looked at him, her heart in her throat.

Coming back to himself, he smiled at her. "Come."

As they walked through the hotel lobby, everyone beamed at Cristiano, and not only him.

Somehow, weirdly, everyone in the hotel seemed to already know Hallie. As if, simply by marrying Cristiano Moretti, she'd suddenly become a celebrity in her own right—famous, beautiful and adored. They all beamed at her.

"Buongiorno."

"Buongiorno, signor e signora."

"Benvenuto, Signora Moretti."

After three different people of different ages greeted them, Hallie turned to Cristiano in bewilderment. "They know who I am?"

He gave her a crooked grin. "Of course they do. We were

married yesterday. By now everyone in Rome knows you are my wife. You're a celebrity here, *cara*."

"Why would I be a celebrity?" Then, looking at his face, she gave him a sheepish grin. "You're teasing me."

"I don't tease," Cristiano said. Taking her hand, he brought it to his lips for a brief, hot kiss, then whispered, "At least not that way."

She shivered until he released her hand.

"Be serious," she pleaded. She saw several people in the lobby covertly lifting cameras to take her picture. Why? Was something wrong with her? She looked down at the simple outfit that Cristiano's concierge had packed for her in New York. It was sleek and severe, less comfortable than her beloved sundresses: a black dress with a sweetheart neckline and black high heels.

Cristiano had assured her that the outfit would be appropriate in Rome. Now, her heart pounded at all the curious eyes staring at her. "Why is everyone looking at me?"

"Because many Italian women want to know your secret."

"What secret?"

His dark eyes flickered. "Of how you hooked me into marriage."

"Um, by letting you accidentally knock me up?"

With a snort, he said mildly, "In New York, I am not that unusual. There's a Sicilian tycoon in my hotel who is a well-known playboy, in addition to being a cold bastard. Even Ares Kourakis, my best man at the wedding, was called uncatchable before he fell for some little waitress from the West last year. But here, in Rome and Naples, everywhere in southern Italy, I am famous." He looked down at her, caressing her with his eyes. "And now, so are you."

Butterflies skimmed through Hallie. As he led her to the extravagantly gilded elevator, and they rode it to the top floor, the butterflies only increased. Marco and Salvatore went ahead of them, carrying their luggage.

Cristiano stopped at the penthouse door with the stroller. "Welcome to our home."

"Our home?"

He smiled. "For now."

Following him inside, Hallie saw a large suite of rooms, all decorated as lavishly as the lobby. The baby's blue-walled room was furnished with every luxury and comfort, with books and lavish toys. Next to that, she saw the enormous master bedroom, with a huge bed and walk-in closet.

Through sliding doors, she walked out onto a terrace. Purple flowers laced the edge of the railing and she felt the hot Italian sun beating down from the blue summer sky. Looking out, she gasped at the panoramic view, gaping in wonder at the old buildings, domed churches and Roman temples spread out across the seven hills.

Coming from behind, Cristiano wrapped his arms around her, pulling her back against his chest, nuzzling her neck.

"It's so beautiful," she whispered, and turned around in his arms, feeling she was in a dream.

He smiled. "You're beautiful, *cara mia*," he said huskily, lowering his head to hers. "And now that you're my wife, I intend to give you the world…"

For the next two weeks, whenever Cristiano wasn't working, checking every detail of this hotel—which had prepared strenuously for his inspection—he took Hallie and the baby to explore the city.

First, he insisted on taking Hallie shopping. With the new burly bodyguard at their side, they visited all the grand shopping streets of Rome, starting with the expensive boutiques near the Spanish Steps.

"More shopping?" she'd protested in dismay. "Is that really necessary?"

"One must be conscious of *la bella figura* in Rome. Even more than in New York. And it will help you relax, knowing you fit in."

"How would you know?" she grumbled. "You fit in everywhere."

Looking at her, he said quietly, "I came to Rome as a young Napolitano. I changed my clothes and changed my fate."

Hallie waited breathlessly for him to continue, to tell her more of his hard childhood and how he'd made his fortune. But he did not.

Sighing, she gave in, rolling her eyes. "Fine. Take me shopping."

She was relieved when the clothes were purchased and they could do what she really wanted—explore the city. They bought Jack a wooden sword and shield at the Colosseum and laughingly tossed coins in the Trevi Fountain. They drove past an enormous white-columned building that looked like a wedding cake, and the endless Roman ruins scattered around the city as casually as food carts in New York.

In the evenings, they had room service sent up to their penthouse for dinner, but once Cristiano took them out, to a simple outdoor trattoria with a private courtyard near the Piazza Navona. As the sun set, with flowers everywhere and fountains burbling, Hallie wistfully watched musicians sing and play guitar, remembering her old dream of a singing career. Cristiano had observed her, then had a quiet word with the trattoria's owner.

A moment later, the musicians spoke into the microphone and invited Hallie to come up on stage and sing. Embarrassed, she'd tried to refuse until Cristiano had said, "Please, do it for me."

Staring at his handsome face, she couldn't deny anything he asked of her. She'd gone up on stage and sung an old Appalachian folk song a capella.

Applause rang in her ears as she returned to their table. As she passed by, an American man claiming to be a record executive even gave her his card. Laughing, she showed it to Cristiano when she sat back down at the table.

"I told him thanks, but no thanks. My days of trying to get singing gigs are over."

"Are you sure?"

Remembering all the painful years of rejection, she nodded fervently.

"Good," he said huskily. "You'll sing only for me."

For the rest of the evening, Hallie ate pasta and drank wine and watched her new husband learn to be comfortable holding their baby. Seeing Jack tucked gently and tenderly in Cristiano's arms, she felt a rush of happiness, like everything was right with the world.

But once they left the trattoria's private courtyard, Salvatore had to hold back the rush of onlookers and paparazzi eager to take pictures of their family. It made her scared to go out on the street with the baby.

Each night, she sang lullabies to Jack, the same lullabies her mother had once sung to her, passed down from her grandmother and great-grandmother before. That night, when her baby finally slept, with his plump arms over his head, she turned and saw Cristiano silhouetted in the doorway, his face in shadow.

"Those songs you sing," he said in a low voice. "They break my heart."

Drawing her out of the nursery, he kissed her and pulled her to their bed. Then he made her heart break, too, with the purest happiness she'd ever known.

However, after living in a hotel for two weeks, she'd

started to feel trapped, unable to leave the penthouse without Cristiano and the bodyguard.

One afternoon while he was working, Hallie took her baby out onto the penthouse terrace to enjoy the warm summer sun. Watering the purple flowers that decorated the terrace railing, she tried to pretend she was back in West Virginia, in their old garden. Her mother had loved to spend hours taking care of their plants. As she watered the flowers, she would sing.

"Why did you never leave, Mama?" Hallie had asked her once in the garden, the year before she'd died. Hallie had just graduated from high school, and what the world was telling her she should want and what she actually wanted seemed to be two different things. "Why did you never go to New York and become a famous singer?"

"Oh, my dear." Turning to Hallie, her mother had caressed her cheek tenderly. "I did think of it once. Then I met your father and traded that dream for a better one."

"What?"

"Our family." Her mother's eyes had glowed with love. "Your whole life is ahead of you, Hallie. I know whatever you decide to do, you'll make us proud."

And so, after she'd lost everything—her mother and father and brother and home—Hallie had taken her father's meager life insurance and gone to New York. To try to make her family proud.

"Hallie?"

Lost in thought, standing on the terrace watering the flowers, Hallie jumped when she heard Cristiano's voice behind her.

Turning, she saw him, devastatingly handsome as always in a sleek suit. He wasn't alone. Behind Cristiano was an older woman, plump, white-haired and simply but perfectly dressed.

"*Cara*, I have someone I'd like you to meet." He looked

over Hallie's tank top and capri pants as she stood holding a glass pitcher from the kitchen. "Are you watering the flowers?"

She could hardly deny it, since he'd caught her red-handed. "Um, yes?"

"You must not. We have hotel staff who are paid very well to do it and who are supporting families. You would not wish them to be out of a job?"

"I suppose not," she said, crestfallen. With a sigh, she set down the glass pitcher on a nearby table. "I can't wait until we have a house of our own."

He frowned. "A house?"

"When we go back to New York."

"I thought you liked Rome."

"I do, but…" She thought of her friends with a pang. "Tess sent me a text that Lola had her baby yesterday. I miss my friends. I'm looking forward to when we can settle down and have a proper home."

A strange expression crossed Cristiano's face. "Well, we'll talk about that later." Clearing his throat, he motioned to the white-haired woman behind him. "I'd like you to meet Agata Manganiello. She lives in Rome and used to work for me. She was my first secretary, long ago."

"Hello…um…*buongiorno,*" Hallie said.

Smiling shyly, the woman said in careful English, "Hello, Mrs. Moretti. I am pleased to meet you."

"I'm pleased to meet you, too," Hallie said, then turned inquisitively to Cristiano.

"I have known Agata for almost fifteen years," he said. "She is careful, responsible. She's very good with children."

"I raised six of my own," Agata said proudly, "while working for Cristiano." She tilted her head thoughtfully. "I think caring for you was harder than the other six put together."

Cristiano gave a good-natured laugh. "You were a miracle worker," he said affectionately.

Hallie looked at him in amazement. He sounded so relaxed. And the Italian woman had called Cristiano by his first name. She'd never heard any of his other employees do that, not even Mr. Loggia, the manager.

Cristiano was treating this woman like…family.

"You're thinking of hiring her to watch Jack," Hallie said slowly. "Aren't you?"

His gaze met hers. "I'd like you to consider it."

"But I don't want a nanny."

"Not a nanny. A babysitter. Occasionally, I'd like to take you to dinner, just the two of us. And once my new hotel opens on the Amalfi Coast, there will be a grand ball to celebrate. We will sometimes need help. And I'd trust Agata with my life."

He waited, watching her. Biting her lip, Hallie considered. It felt very different from when he'd tried to force that last awful nanny on her by surprise.

Reluctantly she turned to the older woman. "You raised six children?"

Agata nodded. "And now I have five grandchildren."

She has kind eyes, Hallie thought. Cristiano said he trusted her with his life.

Slowly she asked, "Would you like to hold Jack?"

The woman smiled. *"Sì, naturalmente."*

Picking up the baby from the thick quilt on the terrace, Hallie placed him in the woman's capable arms and waited for him to fuss. He simply gurgled happily, reaching a flailing arm toward Agata's nose.

"I was thinking Agata and the baby could get to know each other this afternoon," Cristiano said. "If it goes well, I'll take you out to dinner tonight. Just the two of us."

Hallie opened her mouth to argue. Then she heard Agata crooning some Italian song as she snuggled Jack in her plump arms, to the baby's delight. She looked at them. Jack seemed happy and content.

"I'll think about it," she said grudgingly.

"Va bene." Cristiano kissed her lightly on the forehead. "I will be back in a few hours to spend time with Jack, then you and I will have dinner. As per your rules. Speaking of which—" he angled his head "—I've been thinking about making some new rules of my own."

She frowned. "What rules?"

His smile transformed into a grin. "Wait and see."

Hallie watched the Italian grandmother carefully that afternoon, telling herself she'd send Agata away the instant Jack seemed unhappy. But the baby seemed to love her, and Agata was easy to have in the penthouse, kindly and unobtrusive. It was almost, Hallie realized, like having…no, not her mother, but some kindly great-aunt come to watch the baby. Maybe it was the fact that Cristiano— who didn't trust anyone—seemed to trust her, for it made Hallie trust her, too.

Later that evening, with the baby safely fed and sleeping in his crib, she left capable Agata in charge and went out on a dinner date with her husband for the first time.

Hallie dressed carefully in a new, sexy black dress with a bare back that he'd bought her. Trying to match the drama of the dress, she pulled her long, dark hair into a high ponytail that hung down over her naked back. Going to the internet for makeup tips, she lined her eyes with black kohl and mascara to make them smoky and dramatic, then put on scarlet lipstick.

As she came out of the bedroom, she was nervous that Cristiano wouldn't like her new look.

But, when he saw her, his jaw dropped.

"You make me want to stay home," he growled, coming closer. In his own well-cut black button-down shirt and trousers, his dark hair rumpled and sexy, he looked amazing to her, as always.

"Please, take me out," she whispered.

"As you wish." Catching her hand in his own, he lifted it to his lips. His breath against her skin made her shiver all over. "I'll take you out." He gave her a sensual smile. "Then I'll take you in."

He never let go of her hand as they descended the elevator into the lobby. Past the crowds, she saw a bright red Ferrari waiting for them in front of the hotel.

"What about Salvatore?" she asked, looking at the two-seater car.

"I want to be alone with you tonight," he said, opening her door.

As Cristiano drove her through the streets in the fast sports car, she looked out her window at the sensuality of Rome at night. So mysterious and dangerous, the city seemed to whisper two words: *sex* and *death*. She felt his hot gaze on her. Then he punched down hard on the gas, racing over the hills of the city.

Eventually he parked in front of a nineteenth-century brick building tucked back on a quiet street. There was no sign it was a restaurant except for two valets standing mysteriously in front.

"What's this?" she asked as he helped her out of the car.

Cristiano smiled. "It's by invitation only."

Once inside, a maître d' escorted them through the building and out into a lush garden courtyard. Scattered at ten small tables, she saw people she recognized—famous performers, politicians and athletes. Her eyes widened as they walked past someone that Hallie knew had millions of social-media followers.

"What is this place?" Hallie whispered to Cristiano. His hand tightened on her arm as other patrons turned to look at them with similar interest.

"A Michelin-starred chef runs the restaurant as a hobby. He invites only friends, or friends of friends."

She looked at the ruined walls on the other side of the courtyard. They looked ancient. "How old are those?"

Cristiano glanced casually at the ruins. "Fifth century, I'd imagine."

They were escorted to the best table, beside an old stone fountain. She looked up. The only ceiling was the dark velvet of the Italian sky, twinkling with stars. Fairy lights were strewn against the rough, ruined walls, illuminating red flowers and greenery proliferating amid the cracks.

"Incredible," she breathed.

Cristiano reached for her hand over the table. His gaze was hungry. "You're incredible."

After fully enjoying each other every night over the last two weeks, she felt deliciously sore all over. And aware. So aware. Just his hand on hers made her body tighten and shiver. When the tattooed waiter spoke to Cristiano in Italian, she thought again how easy it would be to love her husband.

But she couldn't. It would be a horrible mistake. Because he would never love her back, and, eventually, that would make her love turn to hate.

Their meal started with a cocktail, the ubiquitous Aperol spritz, a light bubbly drink blending Prosecco, soda water and orange liqueur over ice and orange slices, but with an added twist of rosemary. Sipping the drink, Hallie felt the other celebrities staring at them. She glanced down at herself self-consciously. She whispered, "What's wrong with me?"

"Why do you think something's wrong?"

"Why would they—" she waved her arm toward the powerful, fascinating people at the other tables "—stare at me?" She bit her lip. "It's my makeup, isn't it? The bare back of my dress? I look weird, don't I?"

He leaned forward. "You are," he said huskily, "the sexiest woman in Rome."

She felt the weight of that compliment and saw, from the expression in his eyes, that he meant every word.

As their eyes locked, a pulse of heat rushed through her. Turning away, she took a sip of the light, bubbly cocktail to try to cool down. She cleared her throat. "But there are so many beautiful people here. Famous people. Why would they bother looking at me?"

"You're famous now, too. And unlike all of them—" he dismissed his fellow patrons with a glance "—no one knows anything about you."

Hallie gave an incredulous snort. "I'm just a regular girl from rural West Virginia."

Wordlessly Cristiano drew his phone from his pocket. Pressing a few buttons, he handed it to her.

Hallie stared down at the screen in amazement.

"See? You're a star," he said softly.

Looking at his phone, she realized it was true. Pictures and stories about her had exploded all over the internet. She was on news websites. Celebrity gossip pages. Someone had started a fashion blog in Italian, with a photo of her every time she'd come out of the hotel over the past two weeks, with a listing of each day's clothes, who'd designed them and where to buy them. There was even a page devoted to Jack's clothes. Her baby had somehow become a fashion icon.

It was jarring to see pictures of herself, taken without her knowledge, and pictures of her baby, too, all now online for the world to see.

She sucked in her breath when she saw a video of herself singing at the trattoria, posted on YouTube a few days before. It had already gotten over a hundred thousand hits. *A hundred thousand.*

Her mind boggled.

But not all the attention was positive. Some of the posts were downright mean. Strangers were calling her a gold-digger. And, apparently, Hallie's family tragedy made excellent news fodder. Many news stories breathlessly reported that Hallie was a failed folk singer from a poor Appalachian family who'd all died tragically in a flash flood, but then she'd gotten pregnant and was now married to an Italian billionaire, so wasn't she the luckiest girl in the world?

The words and pictures swam before Hallie's eyes. Her stomach clenched. Abruptly she gave him back his phone.

"You see why," he said quietly, "I want you always to take Salvatore with you when you're out on the street."

Hallie shivered. As a girl, she'd wistfully dreamed of growing up to be somehow special. Hadn't she even gone to New York hoping to become a star?

Now she found that being the center of attention just made her uncomfortable. Feeling the warm night breeze against the bare skin of her back, she tried to smile. "You didn't bring Salvatore with us tonight."

"This restaurant is exclusive. The patrons are mostly famous themselves." His eyebrow lifted. "Besides, I can protect you."

Remembering the night he'd forced her landlord to return her precious possessions, Hallie could well believe it. Biting her lip, she ventured, "Matthews said that you were a street fighter in Naples when you were young."

His expression closed up. "That is one way of saying it. I had no money. So I fought."

"And now you are a billionaire, with the most luxurious hotel chain in the world."

"So?"

"How did it happen? How did you build your fortune?"

Cristiano stared at her, his handsome face shadowed against the soft lighting of the garden.

"I was lucky," he said flatly. "I met a man who owned a small hotel chain in southern Italy. I convinced him to hire me and teach me everything he knew. Then I betrayed him."

Shocked, Hallie stared at him. With a cold smile, he took a sip of his drink, then looked up as the waiter arrived and, in both Italian and English, listed the five choices on the evening's menu.

Cristiano ordered the veal, Hallie the *spaghetti alla vongole*—pasta with clams in a light wine sauce. She added, "And could I get that with lots of Parmesan cheese, please?"

Both Cristiano and the waiter stared at her with identical horrified expressions.

"Clams...seafood...these you should not eat with cheese," the waiter said patiently, as if explaining to a toddler she shouldn't run into traffic.

Hallie smiled, but held her ground. "I still like them."

"But it is not done!" The waiter looked at Cristiano for support, but he just shrugged, as if to say, *Americans, what can you do?*

When the pasta arrived, Hallie covered it with Parmesan and thought it was delicious. She washed it all down with a glass of red wine, causing another shocked gasp from the waiter, at the thought that she'd drink red wine with seafood, not white. Hallie decided that maybe she enjoyed shocking people, because she didn't care.

As the evening lengthened, a pleasurable sensation seeped into her bones. Maybe it was the delicious dinner or the sensual wind against her bare skin. Maybe it was the fragrance of the flowers or sitting with Cristiano amid a fifth-century ruin beneath the starry sky. But she felt strangely like she was in a dream.

"When are we going back to New York?" she asked.

"I'm not sure." Cristiano watched her. "After I'm done in Rome, I'll need to go to the Amalfi Coast for a few weeks to oversee the finishing touches on the new hotel opening in Cavello. The grand opening gala is next month."

She brightened. "I've always wanted to see the Amalfi Coast."

"You and the baby will remain in Rome. I'll commute via helicopter."

"What? Why?" she said, dismayed. More weeks spent cooped up in the penthouse, afraid to go out alone on the streets of Rome didn't sound appealing. A prison was a prison, no matter how luxurious. "That's not what the rules say. What about our family time?"

"Rules are made to be broken."

"Not my rules. You gave your word."

He ground his teeth. "I cannot bring you with me. The Campania Cavello isn't yet ready for guests, and I can hardly let it be known that Cristiano Moretti's bride is staying in a rival's hotel."

"That would be bad," she agreed. She looked down at her empty plate. "Still, you must find a way," she said in a small voice. "I don't want to be separated from you."

"You won't be." His leg brushed hers beneath the table, and she looked up. The air between them changed.

Sitting across from Cristiano in the sexy black dress, defying the tattooed Italian waiter and even her own husband to enjoy her meal exactly as she pleased, Hallie realized she wasn't the same shy girl she'd once been. She felt stronger. Braver.

Becoming Cristiano's wife, living in Rome, wearing this sexy dress, with dark eyeliner and bright red lips, she felt bolder somehow. She didn't know why, but she suddenly felt powerful. Like his equal.

Maybe that was what gave her the courage.

"I need to know when we can go back to New York and buy our own house."

Taking a bite of veal, he frowned at her. "We have twenty-two houses."

She blinked, taken aback. "You mean your hotels?"

"Yes." He swirled his wineglass. "The hotels. All of them fully staffed in the most beautiful locations. The perfect way to live. We never need to settle. We'll never get bored. And I can run my company and build my empire."

"Your hotels are amazing, but…" How could she say it? "They're not home."

"A home, a home," he repeated irritably. "I'm tired of hearing you ask about it."

She looked at him in surprise. "I've barely mentioned it."

"For days now, all the lullabies you sing to Jack have been about finding home and losing home and longing for home."

She drew back, genuinely surprised. "Really?"

He scowled. "Plaintive, heartbreaking folk songs. Are you trying to wear me down?"

"I didn't realize…"

"From now on, sing happy songs to our baby," he ordered.

"Okay," she said, biting her lip. The songs she knew were mostly old Scottish-Irish ballads, a repertoire that didn't exactly specialize in "happy" songs. "Um… I'll try to think of some."

"And we don't need to buy a house. You should be happy living all over the world in penthouse suites with spectacular views, waited on hand and foot by staff. That should be enough."

She paused.

"It's…nice," she said carefully. "For a honeymoon. But we need a permanent place of our own. Maybe with a garden."

"A garden? In Manhattan?"

"They exist," she said defensively. "I worked once at

this amazing house on Bank Street. There was a garden tucked in back."

"By *garden*, do you mean a few pots on a stoop?"

"A real garden," she said indignantly. "My employers let me go because the owners lived overseas and were never there. They were going to put it up for sale."

"We would never be there, either," he said. "My work requires constant travel, and I want you with me."

"But soon Jack will go to school…"

"Truly you think our son is a prodigy if he needs to go to school when he has not yet learned to roll over."

Defiantly Hallie lifted her chin. "You talk about building an empire. I want to build a family." She hesitated. "I'd prefer New York, but I can compromise. If you want to live in Italy, I can make it work. I'll learn Italian and try to make friends—"

"We're not staying. After the new hotel is launched in Cavello, we'll spend a few weeks in Tokyo, then Seoul, Sydney and Mumbai."

"All those places," she said faintly. Beautiful places she'd only imagined. Normally she would have been thrilled at the thought of seeing them with her own eyes. But tonight, she thought longingly of her friends. Lola's baby, now one day old. "After that, we'll go back to New York?"

"Briefly. Then Paris, London and Berlin." He paused. "I have twenty-two hotels, and they all need my attention."

Her heart sank. Circling the world, she would barely see her friends. And forget about a garden. Her eyes fell forlornly to her plate. "Oh."

Cristiano scowled at her. "Surely you're not complaining about traveling around the world in a private jet, staying in luxury hotels."

But a life of luxury had never been Hallie's dream. Licking her lips, she said, "I'm sure all those places are amazing, but…"

"But?"

"How can we ever have a home if we never stay in one place for long?" Her voice was small. "How will I make friends? How will Jack?"

"Learn all the languages, as I have. Be a citizen of the world."

"A citizen of nowhere."

"Everywhere," he corrected coldly.

Angry tears lifted to Hallie's eyes, though she didn't want to fight, not on their first baby-free date. She tried to keep her voice calm.

"Traveling is fine, but eventually we need to stop and have a home!"

"What you call home I would describe as a prison. I'm not buying you a house, Hallie. It would be a waste of money."

The warm summer night suddenly felt cold.

"So you'll waste money on everything but the one thing I actually care about?" Folding her arms, she turned away stonily. By now, as the night grew late, many of the tables had emptied.

"Hallie." His voice changed, turned gentle. "Look at me."

Grudgingly she did and saw his dark eyes were tender.

"Tell me why a house means so much to you," he said. "Because I truly do not understand."

Hallie took a deep breath.

"The house I grew up in was built by my great-grandfather. By his own two hands." She tried to smile. "The songs I sing to Jack, the songs you love so much, they were the ones my mother once sang to me. My family lived for generations on the same mountain. I had close friends. A place in the world."

"If you loved it so much," he said quietly, "why did you leave?"

With an intake of breath, she looked away as a rush of pain filled her heart. Even after five years, grief often still caught her like this when she wasn't looking. "Everything was suddenly gone. My family. My home. I couldn't stay. I felt lost." Her hands twisted together in her lap. "My parents always said I should be a singer. Even my brother said it. So I tried. For five years."

"That's a long time."

She gave a choked laugh. "So many people try to break in as singers in New York. All so talented, better than I'll ever be."

"I doubt that very much."

"The harder I tried to succeed, the worse I felt." Looking down, she said softly, "And it didn't bring them back."

Silence fell across their table. She heard the clank of silver against china from a few remaining patrons and the distant sound of traffic and birds crying in the night.

"So why," Cristiano said slowly, "would you ever choose to leave yourself vulnerable to such pain? After losing so much, I'd think you'd never want a home again."

Hallie looked at him. "Is that why you live in hotels?" she said softly. "Never stopping. Never staying."

Cristiano's eyes widened slightly. Then he drew back, his jaw tightening. Rising to his feet, he held out his hand. "Come. The night is growing cold."

It was quiet in the sports car as he drove them back through the city after midnight.

How did you build your fortune?

I was lucky. I met a man who owned a small hotel chain in southern Italy. I convinced him to hire me and teach me everything he knew. Then I betrayed him.

Hallie looked at him sideways, wishing she had the courage to ask him who the man was and why Cristiano had betrayed him. She stayed silent.

Before their wedding, she'd convinced herself he was a good man, deep down. But now that they were married she was starting to see a darkness inside Cristiano she'd never glimpsed before.

She was suddenly afraid of learning things about him she didn't want to know.

When they arrived back at the hotel, they found Jack sleeping in his crib and Agata snoozing nearby on the sofa, her knitting folded neatly in her lap. After they'd thanked her and she'd left for the night, Hallie and Cristiano tiptoed into the darkened nursery. For a moment, they just stood together looking at their slumbering child.

Then Cristiano took her hand. Wordlessly he led her to their bedroom, and even though a corner of her heart was still angry, she could no more resist him than stop breathing.

Once in their bedroom, he pulled her against him. In the slanted moonlight coming through the blinds, his eyes burned through her. So did his fingertips, lightly stroking down the top of her sexy black dress, the bare skin of her back.

"I have followed all your rules, have I not?" he said in a low voice.

Confused, Hallie nodded.

"I've shared a meal with you both every day? Learned how to care for our son? Loved him?"

"You know you have."

"Now it is time for you to learn some lessons, also." Pulling her close, Cristiano nuzzled her throat, kissing the sensitive hollow at her shoulder before suckling the tender flesh of her earlobe. She shivered beneath his touch. Her heart was pounding.

"L-lessons?"

He stroked his hand along her cheek, rubbing his thumb against her lower lip. "How to truly please me."

Hallie's eyes went wide. "Have I not pleased you?"

He placed a single finger against her lips.

"You have, *cara*," he said huskily. "But I want more. Not for me. For you."

"There's more?" she whispered.

He smiled. "Even after two weeks of marriage, you are still so innocent." His hungry eyes met hers. "I will teach you how to know what you want and how to get it. I will teach you," he whispered, cupping her cheek, "how to experience a different level of pleasure entirely."

He kissed her, leaving her breathless and clinging to him. Reaching back, he pulled out the elastic of her ponytail, and her dark hair tumbled down her bare back. Roughly he yanked down her black sleeveless cocktail dress, dropping it to the floor. She stood shyly before him in only her tiny black lace panties, her naked breasts heavy and full.

With a low growl, he pushed her back against the window. Behind them was a vision of Rome, the sweep of cathedrals and Roman ruins spread across the hills, illuminating the darkness at their feet.

"The first rule is," he said in a low voice, "don't hold back."

He pushed his knee between her bare legs, gripping her wrists against the window as he kissed down her throat. She gasped with pleasure.

This is wrong, she thought, *so wrong*. Anyone could look up and see them through the window. She should put a stop to this. Be modest. Be...

Sensual kisses caused swirls of pleasure to cascade down her body. She wanted more. She wanted to wrap her arms around him, to feel him.

The first rule is don't hold back.

Yanking her wrists from his grasp, she folded her arms around his shoulders, drawing him against her. She kissed him back hungrily, matching his fire. But unlike her, Cristiano was still fully clothed. It didn't seem fair.

Grabbing the top of his shirt, she ripped it down the front, scattering buttons against the floor. She sighed in pleasure as her hands roamed the warm satin of his skin over the hard muscle of his chest, laced with dark hair. She squeezed his nipples and luxuriated in the sound of his gasp, followed by a low masculine growl.

He wrapped his hands over the back of her black lace panties, which had cost three hundred euros at a very nice lingerie shop on the Via Condotti. As she felt his hand move forward between her legs, she was wet and aching. Pulling him closer, she kissed him hard.

With a growl, he ripped off the black panties, leaving them a pile of crumpled lace on the floor.

"Please," she whispered. Amazed at her own boldness, she reached down to unzip his black trousers.

He gave a jagged intake of breath. With a single motion, he pushed down his silk boxer briefs. Using both hands, he lifted her backside, pushing her up against the window, as her legs wrapped around his hips.

Then he pushed inside her with a single, deep thrust.

Feeling him so thick and hard inside her, she moaned, closing her eyes and letting her head fall back against the glass. Her hair tumbled around them as she gripped his shoulders. As he moved, she didn't care anymore who might be watching. She didn't even pause to wonder if the window could break. She knew only she couldn't let him stop.

Her arms wrapped around his shoulders as he pumped inside her, hard and fast. Her full breasts pushed against his hard muscles, the hair of his chest rubbing against her sensitive nipples. She gasped with pleasure as, with each thrust, he filled her more deeply. Her legs tightened around his hips as she built higher and higher until, with a gasp, he exploded into her the moment she screamed his name.

Screamed quietly, of course, so as not to wake the baby. Even lost and frantic with abandon, though she might have been willing to risk shattering the window to fall to her death on the streets of Rome, she wasn't going to risk waking their sleeping infant. She was wanton, she was bold. But she wasn't insane.

For long moments afterward, sweaty and panting for breath, they held each other, collapsing against the enormous bed, their naked bodies intertwined.

"All right," Cristiano said in a low voice.

"What?" she said sleepily, lifting her head from his shoulder.

His expression was blank, his handsome features half-hidden in shadow. "I'll buy you a house."

Joy filled her heart. "You will?"

"But you must let me choose where."

"I don't even care where," she lied, pushing away her longing for her friends in New York. What difference did the location make? As long as their family had their own place with a garden, and they could live in one place long enough to make friends and really settle in, what did she care?

"You won't be sorry," she said tearfully. "We'll be so happy. You'll see. You won't regret it."

Cristiano looked at her, his eyes glittering in the shadows. "I regret it already."

CHAPTER SEVEN

CRISTIANO RARELY DID things for others, and he never did anything he did not want to do.

But perhaps there was something in do-gooding after all. Because the moment he decided to buy a house to please his wife, he'd discovered one for sale on the Amalfi Coast that was spectacularly satisfying for him to acquire. Especially at a cut-rate price.

Just weeks after he'd made his promise to her, their Rolls-Royce approached the magnificent estate on the rugged cliffs of the Amalfi Coast a short distance from the village of Cavello. A wave of euphoria went through Cristiano.

It was his.

He remembered the first time he'd passed through this same tall wrought-iron gate, surrounded by old stone walls. He'd been young then, newly orphaned, utterly penniless. And obsessed with revenge.

Luigi Bennato had been kind from the beginning. Strange for a man who'd ruthlessly rejected his infant son, in order to focus on building his small luxury hotel chain. But Cristiano had been coldly determined to impress him. And he had. Bennato had seen something in eighteen-year-old Cristiano, something no one else had.

But he didn't detect everything. He didn't see that Cristiano was his long-abandoned son.

Why would he? Even if he'd remembered Cristiano's mother, her name then had been Violetta Rossi. *Moretti* was the name of the man who'd been her husband when Cristiano was born. Her first husband. Her second husband had been an Englishman, her third an American. Both horrible stepfathers, whose only gift to Cristiano had been teaching him English. After a third screaming divorce, his mother had given up on marriage and focused on love affairs that were increasingly short, violent and toxic.

But Luigi Bennato was the man who'd destroyed her first. According to Violetta, before she'd met him, she'd been an innocent virgin who'd never tasted wine. Bennato had seduced her, then tossed her out of his life when she'd fallen pregnant and refused to have the abortion he demanded.

His mother had told Cristiano the story repeatedly when he was growing up. She'd always ended it the same way. "And Luigi was right," she'd say with a swill of bourbon and a raspy cough. "I should have done what he wanted. Then I'd be happy!"

After his mother's death, eighteen-year-old Cristiano had stood at her grave and felt nothing. What kind of man would feel nothing at the death of his own mother?

It was then that he knew himself for a monster.

But, standing in the rain, he'd had a new thought, one that lit a fire deep inside him. One that made him feel warm for the first time in his life.

Revenge. He had let the word settle against his lips, caressing it like a lover.

Vendetta. He'd loved the rhythm in his mouth.

Rivincita. He'd felt his tongue brush softly against his teeth.

He would have his revenge on the man who'd first made his mother a monster, so she in turn could make one of Cristiano.

And he'd had his revenge. In just three years, Cristiano got his vengeance. He'd claimed the ruined *palazzo* in Rome for himself, with Luigi's rival as his investor. He'd left Luigi's company in tatters.

Cristiano marked his adulthood from that moment. His revenge had been the act that had defined his life. The first step on a path that had made him richer than his wildest dreams.

The truth was it had been almost too easy. He still couldn't believe how quickly and completely Bennato had trusted him. It was almost, he thought sardonically, as if the man had *wanted* to be destroyed.

Now Cristiano was more powerful than Luigi Bennato had ever been. He was famous. Better in every way.

It still wasn't enough. Some part of him craved more, wanted to crush the ashes of the man's life smaller still. Which was why he'd chosen Cavello as the site of his newest Campania Hotel.

The old man's business had long since gone bankrupt, without enough capital to refurbish the hotels to satisfy the constant demands of perfection that a wealthy clientele required. Bennato's three small luxury hotels, once the jewels of Capri, Sardinia and Sorrento, had all long been demolished and replaced.

Several times over the years, Luigi had tried to contact him. Cristiano had never responded. He had no interest in listening to the man's angry recriminations. Let the man figure out for himself why Cristiano had destroyed him.

It was now seventeen years after he'd first entered the stately villa once owned by Bennato, and Cristiano had bought it for himself. The bankrupt, lonely old man was living in the former housekeeper's tiny house outside Cavello.

Life could be full of unexpected joys, Cristiano thought with satisfaction. As the Rolls-Royce pulled up in front of the grand courtyard of the elegant nineteenth-century villa, he smiled to himself, glancing at Hallie, waiting for her reaction.

Her eyes were huge as she looked from the villa to the terraced, manicured gardens overlooking the sea. *She's in shock*, he thought smugly. He was already keenly anticipating the sensual expressions of her gratitude later.

Their driver, Marco, opened the door and helped Hallie out of the car with the baby. Behind them parked an SUV carrying Agata, Salvatore and all the luggage.

Hallie's mouth was open as she looked out over the vastness of the estate, which had once been owned by the King of Naples.

"Welcome to your new home," Cristiano said. He waited for her cries of joy, for her to fling her arms around him and kiss him with the intensity of her delight.

She simply held their baby, looking up blankly at the palatial villa.

"Our home," he said encouragingly. "Just like you wanted."

Looking at him, Hallie shook her head. "This wasn't what I had in mind at all."

"It's the grandest house on the Amalfi Coast. What can you possibly dislike?"

"It's too big."

"Too big?" he said incredulously. How could anything be too big?

Hallie looked at him. "It's like a hotel."

"We'll be the only ones living here."

"We'll need a megaphone to find each other."

He frowned. "And the gardens—what do you find wrong with those?"

Slowly she looked around the manicured gardens, from the formal hedge maze to the perfectly arranged flowers and palm trees overlooking the blue Tyrrhenian Sea.

"It's…like a park," she said. Turning back to face him, she shook her head. "How can I possibly take care of it all?"

"We'll have staff, of course."

"Oh." She looked oddly dejected. Not exactly the reaction he'd been hoping for.

"Would you prefer a sad, broken-down apartment?" he said shortly. "Where you can hear neighbors screaming and your windows get smashed by thieves? Where the electricity is often out and even your few, most precious possessions can disappear at any moment to pay for—"

For your mother's whiskey, he'd almost said. He caught himself just in time.

"No. Of course not." Putting her hand on his arm, Hallie gave him an apologetic smile. "You're right. I'm being a jerk."

He didn't respond. He was suddenly picturing his mother the last time he'd seen her. Violetta's face had been bruised and bleeding from her lover's fists, and she'd been screaming at Cristiano for trying to defend her. That was his last memory of her face. He'd returned hours later to find her house ablaze.

He could still feel the searing pain of the flames when he'd nearly died trying to get inside to save her. He could hear the crackle of the fire and the furious howl of grief that rose to the dark sky when they brought her body out of the embers and ash.

"I'm so sorry." Feeling Hallie's hand against his cheek, he focused on her again. "I've made you upset, haven't I?"

"No," he bit out.

"I can see I have. I'm sorry for sounding so ungrateful. The house is beautiful. Thank you."

Reaching up on her tiptoes, she kissed him. Taking her roughly in his arms, he kissed her back hungrily until their baby, still held on Hallie's hip, complained about the close quarters, and they both pulled away with rueful laughs.

Tilting her head back to look at the palatial villa, she said, "I'll try to get used to it."

Cristiano took her hand. "Come see inside."

As they walked through the long hallways, over the tiled floors and past the antique furniture and tapestries, Hallie obligingly oohed and aahed over every detail he pointed out. Having gotten over the initial shock, she seemed determined to be pleased.

He'd arranged for new furniture to be put in the master bedroom and the baby's nursery next door. Finally they walked out onto the villa's wide terrace and Hallie approached the railing. Beneath the hot August sun, hungrily she drank in the incredible view as soft sea breezes lazily blew tendrils of her hair.

"Wow. Maybe this place isn't so bad." With a laugh, she glanced back at him with sparkling eyes.

But Cristiano didn't return her smile. As he looked out at the magnificent view of the sea and the village clinging precipitously to the rugged cliffs on the other side of the bay, he was overwhelmed by the memory of the last time he'd stood on this terrace. He could still see Luigi's bright eyes, the man's chubby cheeks smiling as he'd said, "My boy, this *palazzo* in Rome, this is going to be the thing for us! It will take our company global!"

Our company, Luigi had said. *Our.* The memory was like a rough piece of cut glass on Cristiano's soul because, after three years of working for the man, Cristiano had started to like him, even respect him. Bennato had been generous, kind. He'd treated Cristiano almost like a son.

He shook the memory away angrily. If Bennato had wanted a son, he shouldn't have thrown Violetta and Cristiano away like trash. The old man deserved what he'd gotten. Bennato was the one who'd taught Cristiano the lesson: Life meant every man for himself.

And yet, suddenly, Cristiano didn't enjoy owning the villa as much as he'd thought he would. Thinking of the times he'd ignored Luigi's calls over the years, he wondered what the old man would have said.

"The view is incredible," Hallie whispered. She wiped her eyes surreptitiously. "Thank you. You don't know what this means to me. You don't know how I've longed to have a real home where we can stay forever and ever."

He opened his mouth to inform her that after the Cavello hotel opened in two weeks, they would still be traveling to Asia on schedule. He'd bought this house as a temporary amusement, perhaps a long-term investment. But he doubted they'd return to Italy for another six months, or perhaps even a year.

As he looked down at her, though, the happiness in Hallie's face made him change his mind. Her caramel-brown eyes glowed at him.

He didn't want her to stop looking at him that way.

"You're welcome," he said softly, taking her hand. Together they looked out at the picturesque rocky coastline plummeting into the blue sea.

Later that night, as they slept together in the palatial master bedroom, with the windows open to salty sea breezes scented with tropical flowers, Hallie made him very, very glad that he'd made her so happy.

But he could make her happy anywhere, Cristiano told himself afterward, as she slept so contentedly in his arms. He had nothing to feel guilty about. Yes, he'd bought her a house. He'd never promised they would stay.

Cristiano looked toward the terrace, toward the moonlit sea. His arms tightened around his wife. He had promised himself long ago never to sacrifice his own needs for another's. And he never would.

Life meant every man for himself, he thought. Even in marriage.

After just two weeks of living in her new home on the Amalfi Coast, Hallie felt she had fallen into sunshine and joy.

She sang all the time. Songs about dreaming of love and falling in love and being in love.

For no particular reason, of course.

Hallie was thrilled to have a home at last. A place, as she'd told her husband, where they could stay forever and ever. Even as formal as the villa was, with its endless gardens, the view was breathtaking from every window, looking out with a sharp drop to the sea. And when she went outside the villa's gate, no one bothered her here. No paparazzi. No fashion bloggers sneaking pictures of Jack. Here, Hallie could just be herself.

It was true that Cristiano hadn't been around much. He often worked eighteen-hour days, personally overseeing the final touches of the lavish new hotel in Cavello, on the opposite cliff, while still running his worldwide empire.

And if he'd broken her dinner rules a few times, disappearing from the house before dawn and not returning until well after midnight when she and Jack were asleep, well, she'd decided to bend the rules. He was busy. Hallie could understand. He'd given her what she wanted most— a home, and she'd tried to be flexible. She hadn't even complained.

But she was relieved it was almost over. Tonight, the Campania Hotel Cavello would have its grand opening gala, and then Cristiano would be able to spend more time in their new home. They could finally be together as a family.

His constant absence had to be why, in spite of the beauty and comfort, this villa still didn't feel quite like home to her. Maybe it would just take time. But she still didn't have the feeling of home she'd had as a child, living with her family in the rickety wooden house in the mountains.

True, there was a staff of four to oversee the house and gardens. It sometimes made her uncomfortable having servants cook and clean and pull weeds for her, but she'd told herself she'd get used to it. She should be grateful. All she had to do was care for her baby, decorate her home as she pleased, bake cookies if she felt like it, and water any flowers she wished.

Still, in spite of being surrounded by servants and having Jack with her, sometimes her days felt lonely.

Since they'd arrived on the Amalfi Coast, she'd seen Cristiano only at night, in the dark, when he woke her up to set her body on fire with bliss. Then, in the morning, when she woke, he was always gone. Like some tantalizingly sweet dream.

Strange she should feel lonely when she was never alone. Even when she walked to the village with the baby, Cristiano insisted she take Salvatore with them. It bewildered her because there were no paparazzi here, and it was hard enough trying to make new friends, given her lack of Italian, without also having a hulking bodyguard standing behind her, scowling behind his sunglasses.

But the villagers were friendly and interested in meeting the wife of the man who'd brought so much new employment to the area. And baby Jack, with his bright smile and chubby cheeks, charmed everyone he met, even on the rare occasions when he cried.

Hallie was slowly learning Italian from Agata, who was very patient with her. Living in a brand-new country where she didn't speak the language, she was trying her best to settle in, make friends, to find a dentist and doctor and grocery store, and do everything she could to make the Amalfi Coast feel like home.

Except for the wistful memory of her childhood home, Hallie didn't miss West Virginia. She missed New York. But she tried to push that feeling away. Hadn't she told Cristiano that their home could be anywhere? If Italy was the place he loved most, then she would be happy here. She would try to forget New York, especially since every time she tried to text or phone Tess and Lola lately, they seemed distracted. No wonder, with newborns.

But she missed their friendship.

The afternoon before the gala, Hallie played with Jack in the huge formal salon, kissing his fat baby feet as he lay stretched out on a blanket beneath a flood of afternoon sunshine. Soon, Cristiano would come home and they'd get ready to go to the gala together. As she sang yet another song about true love, she knew tonight would be magical. After tonight, their lives could truly begin.

Her voice suddenly choked off as she realized she did know happy songs after all. Love songs.

Wide-eyed, Hallie looked out the wide windows at the palm trees and blue sky. She stared down at her cooing baby, his dark eyes exactly like Cristiano's.

And she gasped aloud, covering her mouth with her hand.

There was a reason she'd been singing only happy love songs lately.

Because she felt them.

She was in love with Cristiano.

Her husband. Her ex-boss. The man she'd once hated. The man she'd never thought she could trust.

She trusted him now. He'd become a real father, a real husband. He'd brought her home. He'd given her what she'd dreamed of most: *a family*.

She loved him for everything he'd done for her. For the way he'd made her feel. For the person he'd encouraged her to be. Bold. Fearless.

Was she fearless enough to tell him she loved him?

Hallie gulped.

If she did, would his handsome face light up? Would he say, "And I love you, *cara mia*," then kiss her senseless?

Or would he just look at her coldly, and say nothing?

Love had never been part of the deal. Cristiano had told her outright he didn't think he was capable of it.

Yet, he treated her as if he did love her. Marrying her. Buying her this magnificent home. Giving up his lifestyle of constantly traveling in order to remain here, in one place. Just to make her happy.

She put her hand on her forehead. What should she do? Should she remain silent and keep things safely as they were?

Or should she take the chance and risk everything in their marriage to tell him she loved him?

"It's just arrived from Rome, *signora*," said Agata, coming into the salon with a designer garment bag in her arms.

"The dress," Hallie said, rising unsteadily to her feet. "Cristiano told me he'd called in a favor with a designer, to send me a special dress to wear tonight."

"Sì." The Italian woman didn't meet her eyes, but Agata had been acting strangely all day. Taking the garment bag from her, Hallie laid it across the elegant sofa. Unzipping the bag, she discovered a breathtaking strapless red ball gown with a sweetheart bodice and full skirts. It was a dream dress. A Cinderella dress.

Hallie touched the fabric in awe.

"Maybe he does love me," she whispered.

Agata made a strange noise.

"What?"

The Italian woman cleared her throat. "Cristiano told me not to say anything. He intends to tell you himself."

"Tell me what?" Hallie said, holding up the beautiful red gown and looking at herself dreamily in the mirror. Maybe she'd tell him she loved him tonight, while they were dancing at the gala. If she could just be brave enough, maybe she'd be rewarded. Maybe against all odds, he'd pull her closer in his arms and—

"You are a good woman, *signora*. What he is doing is not right, keeping it from you."

Hallie turned in bewilderment. "What are you talking about?"

"Then again, I understand why he hates this house and wants to be away as soon as he can."

Hallie sucked in her breath. "Cristiano doesn't hate this house!"

The older woman looked at her sadly. "He does, *signora*. Because of the man who used to own it." She turned away. "And that is why, while you are at the ball tonight, he has ordered me to pack all your things. Tomorrow, you leave for Asia. Me, I have refused to go. I will return to Rome, close to my grandchildren."

"Leaving?" Hallie drew back. "But we just got here! It's our home! We're not leaving our home. And I don't want you to leave us!" Agata had started to feel like family.

"I'm sorry, *signora*. He said to pack everything," she said quietly. "I doubt you're ever coming back."

Anguish went through Hallie. It couldn't be true.

And, in a flash, she knew it was.

She'd thought Cristiano had changed, that he'd been willing to sacrifice his restless travel for her and actually settle down in one place.

But he hadn't changed at all. This so-called home was temporary, like everything else in his life.

And Cristiano had told Agata first. Before his own wife.

Hallie's hands clenched at her sides. While she'd been trying to compromise, to make this place her home, he'd been lying to her. He'd never intended to settle down at all.

Hallie looked around the villa. This antique furniture wasn't to her taste. It was too big, too fancy, but since they'd arrived, she'd convinced herself to overlook that, so badly had she wanted a home.

Now he wanted to drag her and the baby back to his empty lifestyle of moving from hotel to hotel to hotel?

All she wanted, all she'd ever wanted since her parents and brother had died, was a home. A family. A place in the world.

Hallie choked out, "If he hates this villa, why did he buy it?"

Agata looked at her sadly, her wrinkled eyes mournful. "He bought it for the same reason he hates it. Because the man who once owned it was his friend, then his enemy. Luigi Bennato was the first to give him a real job. He taught him how to run a hotel. Then Cristiano turned on him. Ruined him."

Hallie shivered as she heard the echo of Cristiano's voice. *I met a man who owned a small hotel chain in southern Italy. I convinced him to hire me and teach me everything he knew. Then I betrayed him.*

She wasn't sure she wanted to know more. In a small voice, she said, "What happened?"

"I worked for Luigi," Agata said. "Before I worked for Cristiano. I still don't understand. For three years, they worked together, as close as father and son. Cristiano used his charm and Luigi's money to convince a widowed countess to sell her *palazzo* in Rome. Then, instead of developing the hotel together as they'd planned, at the last minute Cristiano took the information to one of the international hotel chains. He cut Luigi out of the deal. Left him bankrupt."

Hallie stared at the older woman, cold with shock. "But why?"

"I still do not know. Yet, even after Cristiano betrayed him, Luigi tried to protect him. He even convinced me to accept Cristiano's job offer in Rome. 'The boy's still so young,' Luigi told me. 'He'll need someone he can trust.' So I left Luigi's hotel for Cristiano's. And now he's a broken man. He has no family, no money. He lives in an old shack. I feel badly for him."

"Why are you telling me all this?" Hallie whispered.

Agata looked at her. "He wants to talk to you."

"Who?"

"Luigi Bennato."

Hallie stared at her in shock. "Why would he want to talk to me?"

"I do not know." The white-haired woman looked at her steadily. "All I know is your husband owes him a debt."

Meet the old man Cristiano had betrayed? Hallie felt caught between fear, curiosity and loyalty to Cristiano. "I couldn't. Besides," she said hesitantly, "how do I know he wouldn't attack me or something?"

"Luigi?" Agata gave a low laugh. "He has a good heart. Better than Cristiano's. Luigi is no risk to you. He's waiting in the forest on the other side of the gate."

A trickle of fear went down the back of her neck. "He's here? Now?"

"Tomorrow you leave Cavello, possibly never to return. He might not live until your next visit. I told him I would ask you. If you wish to see him, it is your choice."

Hallie stared at her, a lump in her throat.

"I'll leave you to get ready for the gala. I need to pack for your trip." She sighed. "And my own back to Rome. Tonight will be my last time watching Jack, while you're at the gala." Agata smiled sadly. "I will miss you both."

"Won't you come with us?"

"I'm sorry." The older woman's eyes lifted apologetically. "I do not want to leave Italy. It's my home. My place is here."

Hallie hugged her hard. After Agata left her in the salon, she was still blinking back tears, but she couldn't blame the older woman for not wanting to endlessly circle the globe. Hallie didn't want to do it, either.

She wanted a real home. She wanted to be surrounded by the people she cared about and who cared about her.

She wanted to love her husband, and she wanted him to love her back.

Hallie sucked in her breath. What would she do about Luigi Bennato?

Her eyes fell on her baby, playing happily on his blanket. She couldn't go behind Cristiano's back to talk to the man he'd betrayed. He wouldn't like it. At all.

But then—Hallie's face suddenly hardened—he'd done a few things lately that she didn't like, either.

She picked up her cooing baby. Crossing to the foyer, she grabbed the stroller in quick decision. If Cristiano wouldn't explain anything to her, if he wouldn't tell her about his past or open his heart, she would find out without his help.

If she loved him, she had to try to understand.

"Going somewhere?" Her bodyguard, Salvatore, stood in the doorway, looking at the stroller.

Blushing, she said quickly, "Oh, no, I just wanted to clean the stroller."

"All right. I'm going to lunch."

Hallie waited until the bodyguard had gone into the kitchen to have his usual lunch and flirtation with one of the maids. Quickly she tucked Jack into the stroller, along with a pacifier, a blanket and an extra diaper just in case, and crept quietly out of the villa.

It felt scary and exhilarating to go by herself. She realized that this was the first time she'd gone out alone since the day she'd told Cristiano about the baby, back at his hotel in New York.

Jack cooed happily in the sunshine as she walked swiftly toward the rough stone walls leading to the gate. Around the side, some distance up the hill, she saw an old man peeking through the trees. She stopped, wondering if she was making a mistake.

Gathering her courage, she took a deep breath and pushed the stroller forward.

"Signora Moretti—you are she, yes?" said the old man anxiously as she came forward. He was plump, and his hair was gray, and there was something about him that seemed oddly familiar.

Hallie took a deep breath. "You wanted to talk to me?"

She was startled to see tears in the old man's rheumy eyes. "Cristiano's wife," he whispered. "I have seen pictures of you." His gaze fell to Jack, who was waving his fat arms, as he whispered, "And his son?"

He'd seen pictures of them? Oh, yes, right—she was famous. "I'm so sorry, Mr. Bennato. I don't know the whole story between you. But I know my husband betrayed you. You must hate him for what he did to you."

"Hate him?" The old man's dark eyes looked strangely familiar. She tried to think who they reminded her of. He shook his head. "I am proud of him for doing so well. I am glad for him to have my villa."

Her lips parted. Surely no one could be *that* kind, no matter what Agata had said. "That is very generous…"

"An old man like me, I don't need a big house." He looked at the baby with longing, then lifted his tearful gaze. "I'm so happy to meet you both."

"But why? After the way Cristiano betrayed you, why would you…?"

Then she looked more closely at the old man's eyes. Black, like obsidian. Like her baby's.

Like her husband's.

"Cristiano's your son," she whispered. "You're the father who abandoned him."

Luigi gave her a tearful smile. "I saw a picture of Violetta in the paper after she died in the fire. Her last name had changed, but I recognized her. When I read she was survived by an eighteen-year-old son, I was desperate to find him. Before I could—" he took a deep breath "—Cristiano himself showed up at my hotel, asking for a job."

"You knew he was your son?"

"I thought...maybe. He looked like I did when I was young. And Violetta had told me she was pregnant with my child. But sometimes she lied to me, especially when she was drinking. One day, I could take it no longer and told her we were through. She said she was pregnant, so I tried to make it work. I made her stop drinking. But she screamed I was making her a prisoner. When she was six months pregnant, she disappeared. I never saw her again."

"Why didn't you tell Cristiano? He thinks his father abandoned him!"

"I did abandon him." The old man's voice trembled. "I tried so hard to find them. But I should have tried harder. I never should have given up. What I read about the life Violetta was living before she died..." He shuddered. "I cannot imagine what that boy went through as a child. When Cristiano showed up at my door asking for a job, he seemed to have no idea I might be his father. He said he just wanted to work at the best boutique hotel in Italy. I thought it was a miraculous coincidence."

"Why didn't you tell him?"

"I decided I couldn't reveal myself as his father, not until I was sure it was true. But I kept putting off the test. I think I was afraid," he said quietly. "By the time I finally stole a hair off his brush and sent it in for the test, it was too late. The day he betrayed me..." His voice trailed off as he looked out at the sea. "That was the same day I got proof he was my son."

"So why didn't you say something?" Hallie cried. He gave her a small smile.

"It was too late. I didn't want to cause him pain. He had no idea I was his father when he betrayed me. And I thought...perhaps I deserved it. So I let him go."

Closing her eyes, Hallie took a deep breath, pain filling her heart. She looked down at her happy baby. She couldn't imagine the pain of losing him. "Why are you telling me all this?"

Luigi gave a wistful smile. "He has done well, my boy. He's built his own hotel empire over the last fifteen years. He's been more successful than I ever was." He blinked fast. "He is my only family. When he refused to answer my phone calls, I tried to accept it. But then I read about him having a wife and child…" More tears filled his rheumy eyes as he gently stroked Jack's head. "He's my grandson. You're my daughter-in-law. But my son…" He lifted his gaze. "Please. You must convince him to speak to me."

Hallie hugged the old man tightly, wiping away her own tears. "I'll make this right," she said softly. "I swear to you."

When she finally returned to the villa, the afternoon was growing late. Hallie was still shivering with emotion and regret. How would she tell her husband that the man he'd betrayed had been his own father?

Her baby had fallen asleep in his stroller so she left him in the foyer when she heard Cristiano calling her from the salon. Nervously she went to see him.

She found Cristiano pacing angrily. When she entered the salon, he turned to her, his expression furious.

"Where have you been?" he said tersely.

She stopped. "On a walk."

"I told you to always take Salvatore!"

"I wanted to be alone." She bit her lip, trying to think of how to break the news to him. She wanted to do it gently and couldn't. Her brain was exploding. "I met your father."

"What?" Eyes wide, Cristiano stumbled back. "What are you talking about?"

"I got a message that a man wanted to meet me. So I went to talk to him." She looked at her husband anxiously. "Perhaps you should sit down…"

He didn't move. "You met my father?"

"I'm afraid this is going to be a big shock." She took a deep breath, then said very gently, "Cristiano, your father is Luigi Bennato."

For a long moment, he stared at her. Then he turned away, his shoulders shaking. At first, she thought he was crying. Then she realized he was laughing. His laugh was harsh and strange.

Hallie stared at him, wondering if the shock of the news had disjointed her husband's mind.

"Don't you understand, Cristiano?" she said in a low voice. Reaching out, she put her hand on his shoulder. "The man you betrayed—he's your father. I'm so sorry. Such a horrible coincidence—"

"Coincidence?" He whirled on her, silhouetted in front of the windows overlooking the sea. His dark eyes glittered. "I knew Bennato was my father. Of course I knew! And from the moment my mother died, I vowed to make him pay!"

Hallie drew back, astonished. She whispered, "You knew?"

"My mother told me how he ruined her life. She was just an innocent girl when he seduced her. He gave her her first drink, and when she got pregnant, he told her to go to hell!"

Hallie thought of Luigi's heartsick face, at the tears in his wrinkled eyes when he said, "I tried so hard to find them. But I should have tried harder. I never should have given up."

"Luigi told me, after Violetta got pregnant," she said slowly, "he tried to make her stop drinking. But she hated that, and she ran away. He said he tried so hard to find you—"

"He was lying," Cristiano said coldly.

She shook her head. "I believed him."

"Of course you did." His lips twisted in a sneer. "A

man as devious as Bennato could easily twist your innocent little heart."

His scorn made her shiver. She lifted her chin. "You're wrong. If you'd only speak to him—"

"What else did he say?" He came closer to her, his face like stone. His powerful body left her in shadow.

Hallie saw the cloud of darkness around him, and for the first time she was afraid.

This was the darkness she'd feared. The darkness she hadn't wanted to see.

"You'll never talk to him, will you?" she whispered. "You hate him beyond all reason. You'll never be free."

Cristiano's black eyes narrowed into slits as he repeated dangerously, "What did he say?"

"He regrets not protecting you when you were a child. He's all alone now. He wants to make amends. He wants a family."

"He wants money."

"No." She shook her head eagerly. "If you'd seen his expression when he touched Jack's head—"

"Jack?" His expression changed, then his folded hands dropped to his sides as he roared, "You let him touch our son?"

"Of course I did. He's Jack's grandfather!"

"Don't call him that!" Furious, he turned away. "Where is Jack?"

"Sleeping in his stroller. In the foyer—"

Cristiano strode out of the salon. When she caught up with him in the foyer, she found him cradling their sleeping baby tenderly against his powerful chest. When he looked up at Hallie, his dark eyes glittered.

"You will never," he said in a low voice, "talk to that man again. Or allow our son anywhere near him."

His voice frightened her. "You're being ridiculous!"

"You will give your word," he ground out. "Or I'll never

allow you to leave my sight again without six bodyguards at your side."

"You won't *allow* me?" she cried.

His jaw clenched. "It's a dangerous world. I have enemies. Luigi has good cause to hate me and he could choose to take it out on you. Or our child."

"How can you think of the world like that?"

"Because that's how it is," he said grimly.

Hallie stared at him in horror. He was refusing to even consider that he might be wrong about Luigi. Justifying his own selfish actions by trying to punish a sweet old man who hadn't done anything wrong.

"It's not true." The lump in her throat became a razor blade as she whispered, "The world is full of second chances. It's full of love if you only—"

Still cradling their sleeping baby, Cristiano turned away. "I'm done talking." He looked at his platinum watch. "I'll take Jack upstairs to Agata. Go get ready for the gala."

"Why are you acting like this?" she whispered.

"It's my responsibility to protect my family."

"But not to tell us anything." Anger filled her. "Agata told me that we're leaving Italy tomorrow."

He looked off-kilter. "She told you?"

"Did you think I wouldn't notice when she started packing all our clothes?"

"Yes. We're leaving for Tokyo." He lifted a dark eyebrow. "So?"

Swallowing over the pain in her throat, she choked out, "You said this was our home."

"And the next place will be, as well. And the place after that."

Hallie stared at him. "You spent millions on this villa, just for us to live here a few weeks?"

"And if I did?" he said coolly. "I can buy you ten more

houses anywhere around the world. I can always sell them again. What does it matter?"

Hallie looked at him, stricken. "You said we'd have a home. You said we'd be a family."

"And we are. But we're doing it my way."

"And your way is to drag us around the world at your beck and call, and tell me who I can and cannot speak with?"

Holding their baby against his chest, Cristiano set his jaw. "Either you're with me, or against me. Either you're my partner—"

"Your prisoner!" she cried.

"Or you're my enemy." His eyes glittered. "Decide carefully, *cara mia*, who you want to be. Now get ready." He gave her an icy smile. "You must sparkle like a star tonight."

And he left her.

Numb with shock, Hallie went back into the salon. She collected the red Cinderella dress. But as she carried it upstairs, it felt heavy in her arms.

As she got ready that night, putting on exquisite lingerie and the gorgeous designer ball gown, she felt cold inside. She brushed her dark hair until it shone, then stopped, looking at herself in the mirror.

When she tried to defy him, to fight for their happiness, he saw her as an enemy instead of recognizing it for what it was—love.

How could it be otherwise, when he'd never known what it was to be really, truly loved by another?

Either you're with me, or against me.

How could she get through his darkness, the pain of his childhood that still enveloped him like a shroud?

How could she show him that the world was more than danger and betrayal and cruelty and regret? Could she show him that she wasn't his enemy, but that she was fighting for his happiness, as well as her own?

Cristiano had given them his name, his wealth, his status. But Hallie and their son would never be more than possessions to him. He would never give them a home. Unless…

She took a deep breath.

There was only one way to break through. One risk she had to take, to win or lose it all.

Putting on lipstick, Hallie met her own scared eyes in the mirror.

Tonight she would tell him she loved him.

CHAPTER EIGHT

WEARING HIS TUXEDO, Cristiano paced furiously at the bottom of the villa's sweeping stairs. They were already five minutes late to his own hotel's grand opening gala.

Another transgression to add to the list. A low curse escaped his lips.

He could not believe Hallie had gone behind his back to speak to his father, his mortal enemy.

He'd thought he could trust her. Their marriage had been going so well. Living in this lavish villa overlooking the sea, as he'd been busy overseeing the Campania Cavello's final preparations, Hallie had been the perfect wife: beautiful, patient, supportive and uncomplaining. She'd been an excellent mother to their son by day and a hot temptress in Cristiano's bed by night. In his opinion, it was the perfect relationship.

Then she'd snuck out to meet Luigi Bennato behind his back.

Cristiano ground his teeth. He would send Salvatore to visit the man and warn him off. No, better yet, he'd send a lawyer. Send a cease-and-desist letter. Get a restraining order. Yes. Then he'd take Hallie, leave Italy and never return.

But the world was a small place. What would stop Bennato from contacting Hallie again if she wanted it? Pacing, he clawed his hand through his dark hair.

If Hallie wouldn't obey his rules, how could he protect her? How could he keep Hallie and the baby safe? How could he make sure he never lost them?

His eyes narrowed. He hoped she now realized the error

of her ways. He expected her to apologize tonight. He would try to forgive her.

He would also make sure she never had the chance to betray him again.

"Am I late?" He heard her sweet voice from behind him.

Turning, Cristiano looked up and sucked in his breath.

Hallie was at the top of the stairs, her glossy hair pulled up in an elegant bun. Her red ball gown fit perfectly, from the tight bodice to the full skirts. He held his breath as he watched her come down the stairs, in awe at her beauty.

"You are magnificent," he said in a low voice. She smiled, her cheeks turning a pretty shade of pink.

"You are too kind." But she gave him a troubled glance from beneath her dark lashes. Her lips were full and red. His eyes widened, then fell lower to the round curve of her breasts, plump and ripe beneath the corset-style bodice.

Even as angry as he was, he was tempted to grab her and take her back upstairs. He'd already started to reach for her when he caught himself. He couldn't miss the gala tonight. He was the host. He took a deep breath and forced himself to pretend he was civilized.

"I have something for you, *cara*. The perfect addition to your dress."

Reaching into his tuxedo jacket pocket, he pulled out a flat black velvet box. Inside it was a sparkling diamond necklace. As she gasped, he put it gently around her neck, attaching the clasp at the back.

Hallie looked down at the glittering stones. "They're beautiful."

"Nothing compared to you, my beautiful wife," he whispered, kissing her. Feeling her lips against his was pure heaven, making him tremble with the power of her unconscious sensuality. When he finally drew back, he was more determined than ever to make her submit to his will, to keep their perfect marriage exactly as it was.

He held out his arm. "Shall we go?"

She hesitated, then took his arm, wrapping her hands around the sleeve of his black tuxedo jacket.

After helping her into his red sports car, he drove the short distance to the new Campania Hotel Cavello, clinging to a rocky cliff overlooking the village across the bay. A uniformed valet took their car, and they walked into the hotel on a red carpet. She clung to his arm as photographers flashed pictures of them. "Look over here!"

"Signora!"

"Mrs. Moretti!"

Hallie didn't exhale until they were inside. Then her eyes widened as she breathed, "Wow."

She looked around the lobby of his new hotel. The Campania Cavello made up for its boutique size by the lavishness of its furnishings and incredible view. Seeing the awe on Hallie's face, Cristiano felt his heart swell with pride.

"And this is just the lobby," he said, putting his hand over hers. "Wait until you see the ballroom."

Joining the other illustrious, glamorous guests, he led her into the gilded ballroom. She stared up at the high ceilings, the bright mirrors, the chandeliers. Multiple French doors opened straight onto an expansive terrace, decked with bright pink flowers, and, beyond that, the moonlit sea.

Whirling back to face him, she breathed, "This place is amazing." Her head suddenly craned. "Is that Nadia Cruz?"

Cristiano shrugged as the famous Spanish actress, now married to a duke, walked by in a tight dress. He had eyes for only one woman. He wanted her in his arms. Against his body. In his bed.

But the object of the evening was to celebrate the grand opening of the hotel with the celebrities who would be his future guests. Any hotel, no matter how exquisite, depended upon publicity from a certain type of clientele to make the property popular amongst the glitterati.

So for the next hour, he forced himself to greet powerful guests with all the force of his charm. He gave them his complete attention, until the new hotel's manager privately informed him they were already booked up through Christmas, and the red-carpet arrivals had drawn attention from the press worldwide.

The Campania Cavello was a smashing success.

As soon as the music began, Cristiano took Hallie's hand. "Dance with me."

She looked around nervously at all the famous people in the ballroom. "We should let someone else go first."

"No one," he said arrogantly, "would dare."

Holding her hand tightly, he led her to the center of the ballroom floor. He felt the eyes of all the guests on him, heard their whispered comments, and he knew that every man here envied him tonight. Not for his money or power—for the beautiful woman in his arms.

He'd been envied before, as a well-known playboy, a free-spirited billionaire who traveled the world, never settling down in any place or with any person.

This was different. Successful beyond imagination, he was now also married to a beautiful woman who'd been untouched by any other man. She'd not only given him the best sex of his life, she'd given him a son, an heir to carry on his line. Cristiano's future was secure.

He deserved to be envied.

As they danced, Cristiano looked around the gilded ballroom of the lavish Amalfi Coast hotel. This was his. Cristiano's hands tightened on Hallie. And so was she.

He'd come a long way from hardscrabble poverty in Naples, when he'd been unwanted, unloved and often hungry and dirty. His parents hadn't wanted him. His mother had resented him; his father had abandoned him.

Now he had a new family.

From the beginning, when he'd first charmed that rich

widow in Rome into selling her *palazzo* for a song, Cristiano's charm had been his second-greatest asset.

The first, of course, was his ruthlessness.

I've conquered the past completely, he thought. *I've won.*

Dancing with Hallie, he couldn't take his eyes off her.

"You are so beautiful," he said huskily, swaying her in his arms. "Every man here wishes he could be in my place."

"To own this hotel."

"To be in your bed."

She glanced around shyly. "Don't be silly."

"You have no idea how desirable you are," he whispered against her cheek, leaning forward. "Later tonight, you can apologize for that foolishness with Bennato," he murmured lazily, running his hand down her back. "And I will forgive you. Because I can deny you nothing."

"I'm not sorry," she said.

With an intake of breath, Cristiano looked down at her.

"Because I did it for a good reason." Her caramel-brown eyes were feverishly bright.

"What is that?" he said coldly.

Her red, luscious lips curved in a tremulous smile.

"Because I love you," she whispered.

For a few seconds, frozen on the dance floor, he stared at her as couples continued to whirl around them.

"You love me," he said slowly.

"Yes." Hallie's face was deliriously happy. "I know it wasn't supposed to happen. But it has. I love you, Cristiano. For the boy you were. The man you are. The man you'll be."

The boy you were.

Hallie's words felt like ice in his heart. She saw past his defenses? Past all his wealth and power, to see the helpless boy he'd once been?

His hands tightened on her.

"I love you," she choked out, searching his gaze desperately. "I'm not your enemy. And I'm not your servant. I'm your wife. I'm fighting for our family. For our home. I'm fighting for you…because I love you."

Music swelled around them in the ballroom. A warm sea breeze blew in from doors opened wide to the moonlit terrace.

Hallie *loved* him.

How could she?

Then he got it.

A low, fierce laugh bubbled up from inside him as he realized what she was doing. He relaxed instantly.

"What's so funny?"

"Nothing," he said, still laughing. He shook his head admiringly. "I just respect you."

"You *respect* me?"

"Yes." He sometimes thought that women didn't realize how valuable it was, respect. Most men he knew could tolerate a lack of love far better than any lack of respect. But the women he'd known in his life, starting with his mother, seemed to feel the opposite, willing to put up with a total lack of respect from their lovers, finding it acceptable to be taken for granted and talked down to, as long as they were loved. He'd never understood that.

Hallie clearly didn't see his perspective, either. Her deep brown eyes looked hurt. "That's all you have to say?"

"I don't blame you for trying. You thought that angle might work. But it will take more than that to manipulate me."

Her beautiful face was pale. "You think that's what I was trying to do? Manipulate you?"

"Of course it is." Leaning down, he confided, "You're wasting your time. That emotional stuff doesn't work on me, but—" reaching down, he twisted a tendril of her hair "—you're welcome to try to convince me in bed. Not that it will work, but we'll both enjoy it."

Angrily she pulled her head away. "I'm telling you the truth!"

"Fine." He rolled his eyes. She seemed determined to stick with her story. "But there will be no more complaining. We will never stop traveling. We will never settle in just one place. And if you ever speak to Bennato again—" he looked at her evenly "—I will divorce you."

Her brown eyes were cold. "You would divorce me? Just for talking to someone?"

Cristiano would have thought it obvious. "For talking to my enemy."

Men in tuxedos and women in bright, sparkling gowns continued to dance around them, in a ballroom lit by gilded chandeliers and flooded with silvery moonlight.

"That's how the world is to you, isn't it?" Hallie said slowly. "Either a person is your enemy or your slave." Her eyes were huge as she whispered, "You're never going to change, are you?"

His expression hardened. "Hallie—"

"No!"

She ripped her arm away, leaving him alone on the ballroom floor. His illustrious guests were now staring at him with big eyes and rising glee. Of course. The only thing people liked better than heroes with enviable lives was seeing those lives fall apart spectacularly.

Turning, he followed his wife out of the hotel.

She was already halfway up the twisting street, climbing the hill. She meant to walk the mile back to the villa, he realized. Even in that impractical red ball gown and high heels. Most of the paparazzi had gone, but a scruffy-looking photographer was following a few feet behind her, peppering her with questions.

Cristiano's whole body felt tight as he turned to the valet. "My Ferrari."

The young valet got his car back in thirty seconds. Jumping into the sports car, Cristiano roared along the street and quickly caught up with her. He rolled down the window.

"Get in the car," he barked. "Now."

Hallie didn't even look in his direction. She just kept climbing up the steep road in her high heels and red ball gown.

By now, the photographer had backed off and was simply taking pictures of them both. Cristiano ground his teeth. He had no doubt that the celebrity gossip sites would be full of stories about "Trouble in Paradise" tomorrow.

"Now," he ordered.

She tripped on a rock, nearly twisting her ankle. Muttering under his breath, he pulled over, blocking her path with his car. Still not looking at him, she climbed in, slamming the door behind her. Without a word, he pressed on the gas, and the powerful engine leaped forward with a roar.

Everything seemed to have changed between them. She remained silent, seeming fragile, brittle. A side of her he'd never seen before.

The pleasurable night, which had seemed so bright and delicious, was suddenly lost. Entering the security code at the gate, he drove up the sweeping drive. The villa was frosted by the opalescent moon in the dark, velvety sky.

After pulling the car into the separate six-car garage, he turned off the engine. They both sat for a moment in silence. Then Hallie turned to him with sudden desperation.

"Could you ever love me? Could you?"

It was a serious question. He looked at her across the car. She hadn't been trying to manipulate him, after all. She actually believed she loved him.

The thought chilled him to the bone. He had the sudden memory of himself as a boy, hungry and cold and pathetically desperate for love. Crying for it.

He'd never feel that way again.

"No," he said quietly. "I will never love you. Or anyone."

Her face became a sickly green. She turned to open her door. Stumbling out of the car, she rushed from the garage and onto the driveway, red skirts flying behind her.

"Hallie, wait," he said tersely, slamming the car door behind him.

She didn't slow down. She fled toward the villa's gardens overlooking the sea, the skirt of her red dress flying behind her, a slash of scarlet in the moonlight.

He followed, reaching her at the hedge maze, with the eight-foot-tall, sharply cut hedges towering above them, luring them into the shadows of the green labyrinth.

"Hallie, damn you! Stop!"

Grasping her arm, he twisted her around, pressing her back against the hedge.

"Let me go," she panted, struggling. "You—are a *liar*!"

Her breath came in hot, quick gasps. His lips parted to argue, but as he looked from the fury in her eyes to the quick pant of her full breasts, pushing up against the strapless bodice of her dress, desire overwhelmed him. He tried to kiss her.

For the first time, Hallie turned her head away so he could not.

Cristiano stared down at her with narrowed eyes, his own heart suddenly pounding with anger at her rejection.

"I never asked for your love," he ground out. "I never wanted it."

She lifted her chin, and her eyes glittered in the moonlight. "No. You just want to possess me. You want my body. Not my heart."

Silence fell, with the only sound the angry pant of her breath. His gaze again fell to her sweetly seductive mouth. Her pink tongue licked the corners of her red lips.

"Love me if you want. I don't care." He looked down at her. "But you will obey me."

"*Obey* you?" She gave a harsh laugh. "This isn't the Middle Ages. I am not your property. And I never will be."

"Aren't you?" He breathed in the scent of her, like vanilla and summer flowers. Her skin beneath his grasp felt hot to the touch. Her dark eyes sucked him into fury and despair, all tangled up in wanton, desperate desire.

Gripping her wrists against the hedge, Cristiano lowered his head roughly to hers.

He did it to prove a point. To master her. But as he kissed her, as her struggles ended and he felt her surrender, when he felt her desire rise against him like a tide, he too was suddenly lost.

I love you, she'd said. *I am not your property.*

Kissing her, he was dizzy with need. He wanted to take her right here, right now, in the moonlight and shadows of the labyrinth.

Hallie wrenched away. "Don't touch me," she whispered harshly.

He stared down at her in shock. Without her in his arms, he felt suddenly bereft. Rejected. *Vulnerable.*

The one feeling he'd vowed he'd never feel again.

Rage exploded inside him. He let it build until it was all encompassing, blocking out any other emotion.

Looking down at his wife, he narrowed his eyes and spoke the words he knew would hurt her more than any others.

"You want me to tell you I love you, Hallie? Fine," Cristiano said coldly. "I love you."

Hallie stared up at him, her heart in her throat.

He loved her?

Trembling, she stumbled back a step into the shadows of the hedge maze. She whispered, "You do?"

"Want me to be more convincing?" Coming closer, he

kissed her cheek, her lips, her throat. "I love you, *cara mia*," he whispered. "I love you. *Ti amo*."

And she heard the mockery behind his words.

Tearfully she said, "I didn't know you had such cruelty in you!"

"Did you not?" he said, looking devastatingly handsome and cold as marble in his perfectly cut tuxedo. "Then you chose to be blind."

Hallie felt like crying. The way he'd looked at her at the gala had made her bold. It had made her brave. All her instincts had told her that if she took the risk, if she told him she loved him, she could rescue him from his dark past.

Her instincts had been wrong.

Now, standing in her red dress in the shadowy hedge maze, she felt like she was in a Gothic Victorian nightmare. Knowing he didn't love her back was heartbreaking, but she might have been able to endure it as long as she had hope that, someday, perhaps he could.

Cristiano had taken even that hope away from her, and then used her own words of love to mock her. He'd made it clear that their marriage would be on his terms alone.

She was to fill his bed and raise his child, and he would give her nothing in return. Not his heart. Not his love.

Not even a home.

She wiped her eyes. "You heartless bastard," she whispered. "What have you done to me?"

"Now it's my fault, because I cannot return the love I never asked you to feel?" He looked down at her icily. "I do not have the ability to produce feelings on command. What you want from me, I cannot give."

Pain ripped through her and, along with it, the humiliating realization that for all his coldness and cruelty, she loved him. Still.

"What will we do?" she whispered.

"Our marriage will continue as always."

Her eyes widened. "Are you serious?"

"Nothing has changed between us. We leave for Tokyo in the morning."

Hallie didn't realize her knees had buckled beneath her until he was beside her, supporting her arm.

"It's late, Hallie," he said quietly. "You're tired. Come inside."

She looked up at him wordlessly as he half carried her into the villa. Inside, it was dark and quiet. The rooms were elegant and empty. They seemed to go on forever.

On the second floor, they found Agata sitting outside the nursery, knitting. The older woman looked between them, then said only, "The baby had a good night. He just fell asleep."

In the darkened nursery, Hallie looked down at her sleeping baby. Jack's fat arms stretched back above his head. His chubby cheeks moved as his mouth pursed in his sleep.

Coming behind her, Cristiano put his hands heavily on her shoulders, his voice firm. "Let's put our quarrel behind us, Hallie. This is what's important." He looked down at the crib. "Our son. Our family."

A lump rose in Hallie's throat.

He was right. Family was the most important thing to her. For years, all she'd tried to do was recapture what she'd lost. To have a family again. A home.

How had it all gone so wrong? A lifetime in a loveless marriage stretched ahead of her. Instead of having a home, surrounded by friends, at her husband's command she would be forced to travel from hotel to hotel.

Her hands tightened at her sides. And her son would be raised to think this was *normal*. He'd see the cold relationship between his parents and think it was what marriage was. What *family* was. He'd never know what a family was meant to be—a rowdy, chaotic life of give and take, of arguing and joking and kisses, filled with love.

Her tiny baby's soul would be warped by this, just as Cristiano's had once been.

With an intake of breath, Hallie looked up.

Cristiano frowned when he saw her expression. "What is it?"

She'd thought commitment made a home. That was why she'd married him. She'd thought, if she took his name, if they lived under the same roof, under his protection, they'd be a family.

But there was a reason that, in spite of all his money and lavish gifts, Hallie hadn't felt as happy and secure as she had as a child. A reason, even in this amazing, luxurious villa, she'd never truly felt at home.

"Love makes a family," she breathed. "Love makes a home."

Certainty rushed through her, clanging like a bell. Her husband had said he would never love her. He would never take that risk. He would never give up anything he couldn't afford to lose. He would never give himself.

Hallie's heart tightened. Her back snapped straight.

Turning on her heel, she went to the enormous master bedroom. She took a suitcase from the shelf of the walk-in closet.

Cristiano's voice came from the doorway. "What do you think you're doing?"

There wasn't much to take. She didn't need all the expensive designer clothes, not anymore. And she'd left her family treasures back in New York. Along with her friends.

She looked at him.

"I'm going home."

"Home," he scoffed.

"New York." Saying the name aloud made her realize how desperate she was to return. "I'm going home to the people who love me."

She turned back to the closet, then stopped. He'd bought

her so much, but what did she actually need? Nothing. She didn't want anything he'd bought her. Because he hadn't been buying her clothes. He'd been buying her soul. Telling her how she had to behave and where she would live and who she would be.

Looking down at herself, she couldn't bear for the beautiful red ball gown to be touching her skin. It reminded her of how naive she'd been, to believe she could just tell him she loved him and magically change him, like some fairy tale!

Reaching back, she savagely yanked on the zipper, pulling off the dress and kicking it away from her body. She stood in front of him, wearing only a white lace bra and panties and the cold diamond necklace on her throat.

"Hallie, don't do anything foolish."

"You don't believe in love. You don't believe in home." Reaching up, she pulled off the glittering diamond necklace and held it out, a hard heap of metal and stone. "Take it back."

When he didn't move, she opened her hand, letting it drop heavily to the floor. Turning away, she dug through the closet until she found one of her old cotton sundresses. Pulling it over her body, she left the closet, carrying the empty suitcase.

"Go, then," he growled.

Stopping by the enormous bed where he'd once given her such joy, she whirled to face him. His eyes were black.

"Go off in search of this imaginary man who will feel whatever you want him to feel, whenever you want it, trained on your command like a barking dog."

She took a deep breath, her heart full of anguish. "That's not what I—"

"*You* can go," he interrupted. He paused. "My son stays."

Hallie's mouth went dry.

"What?" she croaked.

Her husband's dark eyes glittered as his cruel, sensual lips curved. "You heard me."

"You would take him from me?" she whispered. "From his own mother?"

"You are the one abandoning him, if you leave. And, as I warned you from the beginning, he is my priority. Not you."

His words stabbed her in the heart. "But—but you're hardly ever home! You spend all your time working. You'd rather see Jack raised by some paid nanny?" She lifted her chin. "I don't care what you say, no judge would agree to that!"

Cristiano tilted his head. "It seems you didn't read our prenuptial agreement carefully, *cara*. In the event of a divorce, unless I am in breach of our agreement, primary custody goes to me." He smiled. "You are, of course, welcome to visit Jack whenever you wish."

His voice was silky, as if he knew he'd just beaten her. And he had. She staggered back, unable to believe that the man she loved could be so cold and unforgiving.

"You bastard," she whispered.

"Me?" His eyes suddenly blazed. "I've done everything for you, Hallie," he ground out. "Everything. I've given you everything any woman could possibly desire. I bought you this house—"

"Because you wanted revenge against your father! Nothing to do with me!"

"This house was for you. Hurting Bennato was just a bonus. And yet you still decided to go behind my back and try to help him infiltrate our family."

"He never meant to abandon you! Why won't you even talk to him?"

"Because he would say anything to try to hurt me. And, at the moment, so would you."

That made Hallie gasp. "Do you really believe that?"

"You're either with me or against me."

Searching his gaze, she choked out, "Are you trying to make me hate you?"

"Perhaps. At least hate," Cristiano said softly, tucking back a tendril of her hair, "is an emotion I believe in."

They were so close, facing each other in the luxurious bedroom, next to the enormous four-poster bed. Beyond that, the French doors opened to the terrace on the edge of the sea.

Hallie looked up at her husband. The powerful, sexy billionaire that every other woman wanted. To the outside world, she knew it seemed as if she had everything any woman could ever want.

But he was so damaged inside, the truth was she had nothing at all.

She said, "I won't let you take my baby away."

"I won't have to." He gave her a hard smile. "Because you're not going anywhere. We will remain one big happy family. You will remain at my side. In my bed. Bearing my children."

"Children?" Her voice was strangled.

He lifted an eyebrow. "We will have other children," he said mildly. "Surely you would not want Jack to be alone?"

It was the final straw. Closing her eyes, Hallie took a deep breath.

She knew what she had to do. The thought turned her heart to ice. It wasn't what she wanted.

But he'd left her no choice.

"I'm done arguing about this," Cristiano said. "You will be happy, as you were before. You will appreciate what I can give you and ignore what I cannot." Reaching out, he cupped her cheek.

Opening her eyes, she spoke, her voice clear and un-flinching. "You missed dinner with us this week."

He frowned. "What?"

"Twice. You were gone from dawn till midnight. You

didn't share a single meal with us on those days, as Agata and other staff members can attest."

His shoulders were suddenly tense. He knew what she meant. Dropping his hand, he said defensively, "I was working at the hotel—"

"It doesn't matter. You failed to uphold my rules. So you're in breach of our agreement," she said, stepping back.

Her husband stared at her, his dark eyes wide. His lips parted to speak and closed again.

He looked vulnerable. Shaken.

Hallie forced herself not to care, to treat him exactly as he'd treated her.

"As you're in breach of the prenup, I will get primary custody. So I'm taking Jack with me to New York. Please feel free," she added lightly, in the same tone he'd used, "to visit whenever you want."

Cristiano stared at her in shock, not moving.

No. Hallie blocked the pain from her heart. She wasn't going to feel anything. She wasn't going to let him push her around ever again.

She turned away, dragging the suitcase behind her. Stopping at the door, she faced him one last time across the shadowy bedroom where they'd once set the world on fire.

"Thank you, Cristiano." Her voice echoed between them as she said flatly, "Thank you for teaching me how the world really is."

And she left.

CHAPTER NINE

"SIGNOR." LOOKING UP from where he'd been pacing the hotel's terrace just after dawn, Cristiano saw Luca Pizzati, the new manager. The young man gave him an apologetic smile. "Sir, you are acting crazy. The entire staff is threatening to quit."

Cristiano's mouth fell open. How could the man say such a thing?

The day after his wife and child left him, Cristiano had planned to leave for Tokyo. And after that, Seoul. And after that... Cristiano couldn't remember. But he'd been forced to stay in Cavello. Something wasn't right here, and until he could find the source of the problem, he couldn't leave. He could barely eat or sleep. All he could do was pace the halls of the hotel, checking every detail, trying to find the problem that haunted him, taunted him, just out of his reach.

"Look at this," Cristiano ground out. He yanked a purple flower from a bougainvillea bush that was a slightly different shade from the rest. "A disgrace! Do I have to fix everything?"

The young manager looked at the flower, then Cristiano.

"Signor Moretti," he said gently, "when was the last time you slept?"

He bit out furiously, "How can I sleep, until the hotel is perfect?"

"It will never be perfect," the manager said. "Because people are living in it."

Cristiano took a deep breath. Blinking hard, he looked up at the beautiful new hotel. It was already full of guests and getting nothing but praise. He looked down at the flower in his hand. He'd been about to scream at the gardening staff because the bougainvillea flowers were not all the exact same shade of purple.

Pizzati was right. He *was* acting crazy.

Crushing the bloom in his fingers, Cristiano tossed it to the ground.

"You're right," he said in a low voice. "Please give the staff my apologies. I... I will stop."

The manager came closer, a look of concern in his eyes. "Shall I send for your driver? Or would you like Esposito to take you home?"

The empty villa was the last place Cristiano wanted to be. There, he heard only the echoes of his baby son's laughter in the nursery, of his wife's sweet singing in the garden. And in the bedroom, the haunting echo of her soft moans from the times he'd made love to her.

Lost, all lost.

And he was tired. So tired. Thinking of his wife and child, a strange ice spread slowly through Cristiano's body, down his neck, to his spine, until his fingers and toes felt numb. At that point he felt nothing, absolutely nothing.

"Sir?"

He focused with effort. Then he nodded heavily. "Thank you, Mr. Pizzati. I leave the hotel in good hands. Please order my pilot to ready the plane for Tokyo."

"Of course, sir." The manager sounded relieved. Cristiano could only imagine how many problems he'd caused the man over the last ten days.

He tried to remember what his scheduled meetings in Asia were about. Marcia had left him multiple messages, as had various board members, all of which he'd ignored. He took a deep breath. He pictured the Campania Hotel Tokyo, ultramodern and gleaming in the Shinjuku district.

But when he tried to recall the details, all he could remember was the darkness in his wife's eyes the night she'd left him.

Thank you for teaching me how the world really is.

"Have a pleasant trip, sir," the manager said.

Turning, Cristiano left the terrace without a word. When he came out of the lobby into the bright Italian sunshine, Marco was waiting to take him back home.

Home. The word tasted bitter on his tongue. There was no such thing. It was a lie. A dream. Like love.

As the Rolls-Royce passed through the gate one last time, he looked up at the magnificent nineteenth-century villa. He wished he'd never come here. He'd done it to prove that he'd triumphed over his past.

Instead, it had triumphed over him.

When Hallie had told him she loved him, he should have said the words back to her and made her believe them. Why hadn't he tried? It would have been a lie, but at least their marriage would have endured. She would never have known the difference.

Why, instead, had he mocked her, then told her the truth—that he didn't have the ability to love her or anyone? Was it pride?

Or had he just wanted one person on earth to really, truly know who he was deep inside? A man so flawed that he didn't know what love was, or home?

But he did know one thing.

He looked at Luigi Bennato's spectacular villa, clinging to the cliffs above the bright blue sea.

He was done with this place. He would put it on the market at once.

An hour later, after the staff had packed his clothes, he was on the way to a private airport twenty minutes inland.

Cristiano stared out of the sedan's back seat window, not noticing the palm trees or tiny stone churches or lush groves of lemon trees.

He wondered how Hallie was enjoying New York. Was she happy? How was the baby?

Was Hallie already looking for a new home? A new love? His stomach twisted.

He'd heard she'd signed some kind of record deal with a top executive at an independent label in New York, the man who'd casually given her that card in Rome. Life could be like that. One chance meeting could change your life.

Like coming home early to find a beautiful maid singing in his penthouse while she changed the sheets of his bed.

Clarence Loggia, the manager of the Campania New York, had called Cristiano last night to tell him that Hallie's agent had arranged for her to make her big debut tonight at the Blue Hour, the hotel's jazz club.

"I assume you approve," Clarence had said delicately.

His wife? Appearing on stage, singing for strangers, while Cristiano was on the other side of the ocean? No way. He wanted her to sing only for him, like a songbird in a cage.

Closing her eyes, he'd thought of Hallie's sweet, haunting voice. Her songs of longing and heartbreak. Love. Home. Family.

"No…" Cristiano had started, but he forced himself to finish, "No problem. Tell the club's manager to give her everything she needs. The best time slot, good lighting, advertising. Everything."

"Of course, Signor Moretti." He'd paused. "You will be there, no?"

"No," Cristiano had replied, and he'd hung up.

He wondered how Hallie was feeling right before her New York debut. Was she scared? Would the audience appreciate her, as she deserved? Would they realize what a gift she was to them?

Staring out the window, he saw they were passing an old shack he knew, even though he'd never been there.

There was only one way to put the past behind him. Only

one way to truly triumph over it, once and for all. And it had nothing to do with money.

You'll never talk to him, will you? You hate him beyond all reason. You'll never be free.

"Stop," he said.

His driver looked confused but obligingly pulled over into a gravel drive on the side of the road.

"Wait here," he told Marco and Salvatore.

Outside, as he shut the sedan door behind him, he could hear the roar of the sea beneath the cliff, hear the soft sway of palm trees in the hot summer wind, scented with sea salt and spices from across the Mediterranean.

His heart was pounding as he slowly went to the front door. *I'm afraid of nothing*, he told himself. He pounded on the door with his fist. He heard footsteps. Then it opened.

And Cristiano saw Luigi Bennato for the first time in fifteen years.

The man looked bowed, gray. A shadow of the boisterous, vital man he remembered. Had time done this? he wondered. Or had it been his betrayal?

Seeing him, Luigi's dark eyes widened. Suddenly life and color came back into the old man's pale cheeks. "Cristiano?"

"I'm giving you back your villa," he said tersely. "It's yours. Keep it. Just never contact me or my family again."

Hands clenching at his sides, he turned away.

"No," the old man said.

Cristiano stopped, turning around in shock. "What?"

The gray-haired man looked at him. "I don't need a villa. What I need," he whispered, "is a son."

"You should have thought of that before you tried to force my mother to get rid of me when she was pregnant," he said, "then tossed her out on the street."

"All I did was keep her from drinking while she was pregnant. And she hated me for it."

"Why would you do that?"

"Because from the moment Violetta told me she was pregnant, I loved you."

The wind blew softly against Cristiano's face. From a distance, he could hear traffic on the road, the cry of seagulls.

"That's a lie," he said in a low voice.

"You know how she was. You know better than anyone," he said sadly. "Violetta was beautiful. Charming. But so broken. She accused me of keeping her prisoner. A few months before you were born, she disappeared without a trace."

Cristiano thought of his mother's fury if anyone tried to take her alcohol away. Once, when he was nine, he'd dared to pour out her bottles of whiskey while she was passed out. She'd slapped him so hard his ears rang for weeks.

"You made her a drunk."

"I did?" Luigi slowly shook his head. "We met in a bar, when she offered to buy me a drink. I'd never seen any woman hold her liquor so well. Stupidly, I was impressed."

That made sense to Cristiano, too. Agata had told him that when she worked for Bennato, the man had rarely touched alcohol. He took a deep breath.

"If you knew I existed, and you claim to care," he said slowly, "why didn't you keep trying to find me?"

"I did. For years," the old man choked out. He blinked fast, shaking his head. Tears streamed down his wrinkled cheeks. "But you're right," he whispered. "I should have looked harder. It wasn't until I saw her picture in the paper, a few days after she died, that I knew where you were. But before I could leave for Naples, you showed up at my hotel in Capri, asking for a job. I thought it was a miracle. I thought it was my chance."

"Why didn't you say anything?"

"I told myself I needed proof first. But the truth was... I

was afraid." He swallowed. "After the way Violetta raised you, why would you ever forgive me? I was a coward. And I waited too long. By the time I had proof you were my son, you'd already left. And I didn't want to cause you more pain."

"I betrayed you."

"I didn't see it as a betrayal."

"How did you see it?"

The elderly man whispered, "Justice."

A tear slid down his wrinkled cheek.

Cristiano stared down at him in shock. Everything was different than he'd imagined. Everything.

"Can you ever forgive me?" Luigi choked out. He reached his shaking hand to Cristiano's shoulder. "I loved you so much. But I could not protect you. I failed."

Cristiano stood frozen in front of the old wooden shack. The sun felt too bright on his face. Clenching his jaw, he looked out at the sea.

Hallie had tried to tell him. She'd tried to save him from his own darkness.

"So you just let me destroy you," Cristiano said slowly. "You let me take everything from you, and make it mine."

"Of course I did," Luigi said quietly. "You're my son. Your happiness means more to me than my own. I love you."

Cristiano heard the echo of Hallie's voice.

Love makes a family. Love makes a home.

"My mother said you abandoned us," he said. "After she died, I wanted to make you suffer."

"It's not your fault, my son," Luigi said hoarsely. "I should have taken you into my arms the day you walked into my hotel. I should have—"

With a sob, Luigi pulled him into his arms.

For a moment, Cristiano stiffened.

"So much time has been lost," Luigi whispered, hugging

him. "Because I was afraid. Because I was ashamed. Years we can never get back. Oh, my son. Can you forgive me?"

So much time has been lost.

Still held in his father's arms, Cristiano thought of the ten days he'd been separated from his wife and child. Ten days had felt like eternity, driving him half-mad.

What if they were separated for a lifetime? Until he, too, was apologizing for his cowardice and shame?

He gasped, and suddenly realized he was hugging his father back. Hearing Luigi's sobs of joy, Cristiano's heart cracked in his chest.

Emotions suddenly poured through him. Grief and anguish and every other feeling he'd blocked for years. Everything he hadn't let himself feel.

And love.

Love so big it seemed to be exploding out of his body with light brighter than the sun.

As he stood in a little village on the edge of the Amalfi Coast, hugged by his father for the very first time, Cristiano took a deep breath. Even the air seemed different in his lungs.

"Thank you for that," Luigi said, finally releasing him. He wiped his eyes. "You've made an old man so happy."

As Cristiano stared down at his father, everything became crystal clear.

Hallie.

Oh, God, how could he not have realized it before?

She was the one who'd tried to convince him to forgive his father. She'd loved Cristiano, even when he didn't deserve it. She'd seen the hurt and darkness inside him, and, instead of scorning him, she'd tried to heal it. She'd been brave enough to love him, flawed as he was.

He'd tossed it back in her face.

His spine snapped straight as he looked across the sea

and realized, for the first time, exactly what love meant. What *family* meant.

Love didn't consume, like fire.

It gave, like the sun.

Cristiano took a deep breath and felt his shoulders expand as he sucked all the world into his lungs. His eyes narrowed in a private vow.

If she forgave him, he would show her that her faith in him hadn't been wrong.

He would give his wife, every single day on earth, a reason to sing.

"Cristiano?"

Eyes wide, Cristiano stumbled back from his father.

"I have to go find Hallie," he said. "I have to tell her... tell her..."

"Go." His father smiled at him through his tears. "And when you see her, please tell her something more. Tell her *thank you.*"

"I can't do this," Hallie whispered.

"You can," Lola told her firmly. "I didn't go to all the trouble of getting dressed and leaving the house with a newborn just for you to back out at the last minute. You can do it."

From behind the Blue Hour's curtain, Hallie glanced out at the audience. "There are so many people."

"They'll love you. Look," Tess said. "I've got your biggest fan right here!"

Hallie smiled down at Jack, who was in a stroller next to Esme's, trying to grab his own chubby feet.

Hallie bit her lip as she looked out again from the wings of the jazz club's small stage. She would have preferred some out-of-the-way coffeehouse, with only five or six people in the audience. But her agent was no fool. He'd argued for Hallie to make her debut at the Blue Hour. "Why would you go anywhere else? You're married to Cristiano Moretti!"

Even for someone with half a million hits, the number of people who'd watched the YouTube video of her singing in Rome, it wasn't easy to perform in such an exclusive venue. So she'd told her agent to ask the manager, confident that when Cristiano heard about it he'd tell them all to go to hell.

But, apparently, he'd agreed.

Why was Cristiano being supportive of her career, when he'd made it clear he didn't give a damn about her?

It was a mystery.

Even after ten days, Hallie still couldn't believe he'd let them go so easily. Cristiano wasn't the kind of man to let himself be defeated, certainly not by some legal technicality. Why hadn't he come after her? Why hadn't he fought?

The answer had to be that he was secretly relieved to be rid of them.

She took a deep breath, looking down at the short black dress the music label's stylist had found for her. Tomorrow she was supposed to start work on an album, followed by a publicity tour. Once, this would have felt like a dream come true.

Now, it just felt like a job. A way to support her child so she wouldn't have to depend on a man who didn't love her.

The truth was that she didn't want to sing for strangers. She wanted to sing for the people she loved. For Cristiano. And she would have given it all up in a second if he'd come for her, to fight for her. For their family.

But he hadn't.

A jagged pain filled her throat. *Bad for singing*, she thought, and tried to think of happier things. She'd used some of that hundred-thousand-dollar check, which she'd tucked away in her savings account, to lease a one-bedroom walk-up apartment in the Lower East Side. But she was trying not to spend that. She wanted to save it for Jack's future, so she never had to ask Cristiano for anything ever again. Not even the alimony required by the prenuptial agreement. She hadn't filed for divorce. The mere thought of divorce filled her with blinding pain.

At the moment it felt like she was barely putting one foot ahead of the other. She didn't know how she would have survived without her friends.

"Stop that," Tess said, as she caught Lola yawning behind Hallie.

"I can't help it," the blonde said. "I only got four hours of sleep last night. Thanks to you," she said to her tiny baby with mock severity.

"Four hours isn't so bad," Tess said encouragingly. Lola rolled her eyes.

"One hour. Four times."

"Oh," Tess said, because there wasn't much good to say about that. Then she brightened. "But before you know it, your baby will be as big as Esme." She looked down at her five-month-old daughter, a dark-haired baby with adorable fat rolls on her thighs and bright emerald-green eyes.

"It's time," the stage manager called, and Hallie sucked in her breath.

Lola squeezed Hallie's shoulder. "I know you'll be great."

Tess gave her a sideways hug. "We'll be cheering for you!"

Then they left with the babies, and Hallie was alone. She heard the club's host announce, "And let's have a big Blue Hour welcome for debut artist… Hallie Hatfield!"

She'd left the Moretti name behind. The glamorous bride celebrated in the fashion blogs, the woman who'd brought the famous Cristiano Moretti to his knees—that obviously wasn't her. She was just Hallie, plain and simple.

Trembling, she went out on stage, in front of the house band. Beneath the spotlight, she couldn't see anyone in the audience, not even Tess or Lola or the babies. She gulped. She wasn't sure she could do this.

Then…

Closing her eyes, she focused on the music. The songs her mother and father had once sung to her, and her grandparents before.

Hallie's lips parted, and against her will she saw Cristiano's face. She sang directly to the man she loved. The man she'd lost.

Tears streamed down her cheeks as she sang of longing and heartbreak and regret. When she finally sang her last note, silence fell across the club.

Opening her eyes, Hallie looked out into the darkness beyond the spotlight. Had everyone left? Had they hated her songs and just gone home?

Then she heard it, sweeping across the club like a low roll of thunder.

A rush of applause built to shouts and cheers, lifting her sad heart. She smiled, overwhelmed with gratitude. She hadn't failed the audience who'd come to hear her, but still she felt sad.

"Thank you," she choked out. Wiping her tears, she stepped back from the microphone. As she turned away, she heard one man's voice above the rest.

"Hallie."

There was a collective intake of breath across the club. Turning back, she narrowed her eyes, trying to see who was calling to her. It sounded like…but it couldn't be…

The spotlight moved, and she saw him.

Her husband stood in the middle of the crowded jazz club, amid all the tables, his dark suit more rumpled than she'd ever seen it.

"Cristiano?" she breathed.

His dark eyes cut through her soul. Turning to the crowd, he held out his arm toward her. "Hallie is my wife."

He spread his arms wide. "Have you ever heard such a voice?"

The audience applauded and hooted, stomping their feet. But Hallie had eyes only for him.

"What are you doing here?"

Cristiano's voice carried across the room as he turned to face her. "I don't need you, Hallie."

She sucked in her breath.

"At least that's what I told myself." He started walking past the crowded tables, toward the stage. "The truth was, I was afraid to need you." He stopped in front of the stage, staring up at her. "Because I was dead inside."

The club was so quiet you could have heard a pin drop.

"But you brought me to life." Cristiano smiled at her, his dark eyes shining. "It was your voice that caused the first crack in the wall around my heart. The first time I heard you sing. Do you remember?"

She nodded, a lump in her throat. How could she forget?

"I saw you, so vibrant and sexy and alive, and I knew from that moment that I had to have you. But it wasn't just your incredible voice that drew me. Not even your beautiful face and body. It was your soul, Hallie," he whispered. "Your heart."

By now, camera phones had appeared at every table, lighting up the club like candle flames, recording the moment as the famous billionaire Cristiano Moretti went onstage to join his wife.

"No." She struggled to speak. "I can't believe it."

"I spoke with my father," he said humbly. "And you were right. Everything you said. You were right."

Her heart was in her throat as she looked up at him.

"I know what love means now," he whispered. Then, to her shock, he fell to his knees on the stage in front of her. There was a gasp across the club.

Cristiano looked up at her. His eyes were vulnerable and

raw. For the first time, the darkness was gone. For the first time, she truly saw his soul.

"Let me try to win back your heart. Let me show you I can be the man I was always meant to be." He took her hand in both of his. "I need you, Hallie," he whispered. "I love you."

Reaching down, she put her hand to his rough cheek in amazement. "You love me?"

He nodded, blinking back tears. "Tell me I'm not too late." His voice broke. "Tell me I still have the chance to be the man you deserve."

She pulled him to his feet. "The chance? No. You don't have a chance to win back my love." Hallie smiled at him through her tears. "Because I never stopped loving you, Cristiano."

His handsome face filled with joy. Cupping her face in both his hands, he kissed her, long and hard. Hallie felt the flame spark between them, as always.

But something was different. Something was new. They knew each other now, really and truly. The fire burned bright and clear between them, in a blaze she knew would last forever.

Ignoring the applause and hoots from the audience, Cristiano looked down at her. "And you were right about something else."

"What?"

He gave her an impish grin. "The house you loved on Bank Street. The one you told me about. It does have a garden. And it was for sale, just like you said. I told my broker to put in an offer."

"What!"

"If you still want it," he amended. He searched her gaze. "Do you, *cara*?"

"Oh, Cristiano." Happy tears filled Hallie's eyes at the

thought of having the home she'd dreamed of for all her life. "Do you really mean it? We can stay?"

"Forever, if you want." He cupped her cheek. "Because you're not just my wife. You're my love song," he whispered. "My happiness, my heartbreak and joy. You're my everything."

Looking down at her hand wrapped in his larger one, Hallie felt her heart in her throat.

"And you're mine." She looked up at him, blinking back tears. "From the moment you said you loved me, all my childhood dreams came true. We can live in New York, or anywhere in the world. Because now I know, for the rest of our lives," she breathed, her eyes shining with joy, "wherever we live, we're home."

* * * * *

THE BRIDE'S
BABY OF SHAME

CAITLIN CREWS

This book is dedicated to the memory
of the best Christmas afternoon tea ever with
our editors Megan Haslam and Flo Nicoll in London,
when Jane and I came up with the idea for this duet.
And then had so much fun writing it!

CHAPTER ONE

RENZO CRISANTI LOATHED ENGLAND.

He was no fan of great, sprawling London, choking on commuters and tourists and lumbering red buses wherever he turned. He disliked the countryside, oppressively green and ever damp. He preferred his native Sicily, its mountains and sweeping Mediterranean views. England was too dour and grim for a man who had gone from the colorful streets of his hometown to a career racing impossibly fast cars all over the planet.

He might have retired from racing, but that didn't change the fact that he was a Sicilian. In his opinion, that made him the best of Italy plus that little bit extra—and it meant he was fundamentally unsuited to what the English called their summer.

Even on an evening like tonight in late June, the English sky was wringing itself out, much colder and rainier than it ought to have been in Renzo's estimation.

He preferred his own small village in the mountains outside Taormina at this time of year. A warmer sea in the distance and a happier sun to go along with the sweep of all that history, with Mount Etna rising in all her glory above it all.

Instead, he found himself just outside Winchester, England, winding in and around rolling hills so far out into the countryside that there was hardly any light. There had been a towering cathedral rising up over the medieval city, but still, Renzo preferred the battered, ageless wilderness of the Sicilian countryside to all this manicured charm. He'd felt hemmed in as he'd driven through the Winchester city center before heading out to the surrounding fields.

He wished he'd followed his initial knee-jerk reaction to this whole situation weeks ago.

Because Renzo had known Sophie Carmichael-Jones was nothing but trouble the moment he'd laid eyes on her.

Steer clear, something had whispered inside him the moment he'd seen her, like a kick in the gut.

But he'd paid that foreboding voice no mind.

Renzo had been in Monaco for the annual motor race, though not as a driver. He'd stopped racing while he was ahead and still in one piece several years back, and had channeled his notoriety into a line of clubs, a few select hotels dotted around Europe, and a vineyard back in Sicily. And where better than Monaco to advertise to the very high-class, European clientele he hoped to serve? He'd been enjoying a drink with some friends when he'd happened to look up and see her.

She had glowed. That was the first thing he'd noticed, as if she'd walloped him with all that shine. She'd worn a metallic gown that had been perfectly demure on its own, but that hadn't been the source of all that *light*. That had come straight from her.

Renzo was no stranger to beautiful women. They flocked to him and he, in turn, considered himself something of a connoisseur. But this one... Her dark hair had been pulled back with a certain insouciance, only a few tendrils escaping and showing the faintest hint of a deep copper beneath the lights. Her lips had been painted siren red, her brows were dark, and she'd worn large, gleaming earrings that Renzo had known in an instant were real despite their size. She'd looked elegant. Chic. Endless legs that suggested a certain coltishness and that lovely, inescapably aristocratic face.

But her eyes, brown and shot through with gold, had been so sad.

Their gazes had collided, there on the floor of the Casino de Monte Carlo. Renzo had lost his train of thought. Not something that often happened to a man who'd made his name and his first fortune thanks to his singular focus and steady hands.

He'd stood up from his table, crossed the floor, and found himself standing before her without knowing he'd meant to move.

He had been aware of everything about her, there in the middle of a crowd that he'd hardly noticed. She'd caught her breath. He'd seen color high on her cheeks. And he'd known that the chemistry he could feel, electric and intense, was affecting her, too.

It was insanity.

"You must tell me two things," he'd told her, feeling as if they were all alone when he knew full well that they were not. That half of Europe stood arrayed around them. He couldn't seem to bring himself to care. "One, your name. And two, why you are so sad. This is Monte Carlo, *cara*. Nothing but joy is permitted."

"I'm not sad at all," she'd said after a moment, and somehow, he hadn't been surprised that she was English, though she'd spoken to him in the same Italian he'd used. Just with that unmistakable accent. "That would require far more emotion than the situation warrants. A better description is *resigned*."

"You are far too young and much too beautiful for resignation."

Her lovely lips had curved, and Renzo had wanted nothing more than to taste that red-slicked smile. Then, there. He wasn't fussy.

"While you strike me as far too sophisticated for such idle flattery," she'd replied.

Renzo had been in the grip of a fever. Looking back, that was the only explanation. He'd reached over and taken her hand in his—

And they'd both breathed a little heavily at the contact.

He'd been aware of his own heartbeat, intense and demanding. He'd seen her pulse, there in the column of her neck, drumming out the same insistent rhythm. He would never know how he had restrained himself from leaning over and covering it with his mouth.

It had been as if they'd made lightning between them, such wild electricity he marveled the whole of Monaco didn't burst into flames. It was as if their skin could scarcely contain it.

Renzo had known then and there that he would be inside this beautiful stranger within the hour.

Or die trying.

"Let me try this, then," he had said, casting aside his customary charm for the urgency the moment appeared to warrant. "I need you, *cara*. I don't care who you are or what you had planned tonight. I want you. I want to taste every part of you again and again, until I would know you in the blackest night. I want to taste you in my mouth. I want everything—and then I want to do it again. And again. Until there's nothing left of either one of us."

"I don't believe in immolation," she'd said, though her voice was hoarse.

"You will."

She had shuddered. She had swayed slightly on her feet. She shot a look over her shoulder, somewhere through the crowd, then had returned her attention to him.

He could read her need and better yet, her surrender, all over her face.

Renzo had wasted no time. He took her hand in his and

led her to the private exit, where he could retrieve his car without any interference from fans or photographers. In moments, they'd been speeding away, up into the hills toward the villa he maintained far above glittering Monaco and the Côte d'Azur spread out below.

"I am Renzo Crisanti," he had told her, because there was something in him that needed her to know him, whatever that meant. Whatever came next. "And, *bellissima*, you still haven't told me your name."

She had shifted beside him, all sleek lines and the quiet, humming intensity of her considerable beauty—so much like the cars he loved and handled the same way he intended to handle her.

With all his skill and focus. With all the acute ferocity that had propelled him to the top of his profession.

There was a reason Renzo had never had a crash. And he didn't plan to change his record that night, not even for this mysterious woman who'd already had him tight and hard and greedy when all he'd had of her was a brief touch of her hand.

It was as if he'd never had another woman in his life.

"You can call me Elizabeth," she'd said.

It was the first lie she'd told him, Renzo thought now, trying to tamp down his temper. But it was nowhere near the last.

He pulled his car over to the side of the road, near what looked like an abandoned old croft—or whatever it was they called their falling-down sheds in this part of England. He cut the engine and unfolded himself from the low-slung sports car, adjusting the ends of the driving gloves he wore out of habit as he stood there beside the vehicle and attempted to access his usual, legendary calm. The motor made its noises, as if protesting that he'd cut the drive short. The summer rain had let off, but the night was still cool. Renzo flipped up the collar of his leather jacket against the pervasive damp and checked his watch, impatient.

And perhaps something a good deal more intense than merely impatient, if he was honest.

Because he had a score to settle with the woman he was meeting here, off in the middle of nowhere, so late at night in a foreign country.

As if he was answering a summons. As if he, Renzo Crisanti, were so malleable and easily led he would travel across the whole of Europe for a woman he had already bedded.

His fingers stung and he released them, unaware he'd clenched his hands into fists at his sides.

At first he thought it was just a shadow, moving rapidly down the hill from one of England's grand old houses in the distance. The directions she'd sent had been explicit. This country lane to that little byway, skirting around the edges of stately manors and rolling fields lined in hedgerows. But the more he watched, his eyes adjusting to the inky dark, the more he recognized the figure approaching him as Sophie.

Sophie, who'd given Renzo her innocence without thinking to warn him.

Sophie, who had called herself Elizabeth on that long, hot, and impossibly carnal night in Monaco.

Sophie, who had lied to him. To *him*.

Sophie, who had sneaked away while he slept, leaving him with nothing—not even her real name—until she'd chosen to reveal it in the most humiliating way possible, in a hastily mailed newspaper clipping.

Of Sophie Elizabeth Carmichael-Jones, daughter of a wealthy and titled British family, who was engaged to marry an earl.

Sophie, *his* Sophie, who would be another man's wife in the morning.

Renzo's jaw ached. He forced himself to unclench his teeth, and his fists again, while he was at it. He was a man known far and wide for the boneless, lazy manner with which he conducted both his business and his pleasure. It was his trademark.

It was a mask he had carefully cultivated to hide the truth—that he was a true Sicilian in every sense of the term, especially when it came to the volcanic temper he'd spent his life learning to keep under strict control.

This woman made him a stranger to himself.

She skidded a bit on the wet grass at the bottom of the hill, then righted herself. And her swift, indrawn breath as she started toward him seemed to crack through him like thunder.

There were no lights out here, lost somewhere in England's greenest hills, for his sins—but Renzo could see her perfectly. He'd meant what he'd told her in Monte Carlo.

He would know her if he was blind.

Her stride. Her scent. The particular way she held her head. The little sound of erotic distress she made in the back of her throat when he—

But this was not the time for such things. Not when there was so much to discuss, and her with the wedding of the year in the morning.

She was wearing a simple pair of leggings tucked into high boots and what looked like long-sleeved shirts, layered one on top of the other. Her clothes molded themselves to her trim figure and showed off the sleek, sweet curve of her behind and those long, long legs he'd had wrapped around his shoulders while he'd thrust deep inside her and made them both groan. Her dark chestnut hair fell down all around her, looking like a soft black curtain in the darkness.

She stopped before him, and for a moment, all he could think about was that night. She'd been sitting naked in his bed, laughing at something he'd said while she'd piled her hair on the top of her head and had tied it in a knot.

So simple. So unconsciously alluring. Then, and now when he knew better.

So devious, he reminded himself harshly.

But what he remembered most was that he'd had her three times by then.

It was a hunger he couldn't contain, couldn't reason away, couldn't even douse afterward when he'd wanted to think of other things. It had been weeks and yet here it was again, as voracious and as greedy as it had been that night in Monaco.

Worse, perhaps, because he had tasted her. Because he knew exactly what he was missing.

Renzo thought he likely vibrated with his need for her, only now it made him as darkly furious as it did hard.

"Renzo…"

She said his name quietly, tipping her head back so she could look him in the eye.

And if her eyes were sad, or resigned, or anything else at all, he told himself he didn't care.

"How nice to see you again, Sophie," he said in English, a language they had never spoken to each other.

He saw her shudder at the sound, but he forged on, unwilling to permit himself to do anything but what he'd come here to do.

Which was make her pay.

"Please accept my deepest congratulations on your upcoming wedding. I read all about it in the papers," he drawled, flint and rage and no mask to hide it. "Tomorrow, is it not?"

Sophie felt sick.

She wanted to blame it on the shocking news she'd gotten two days ago at her doctor's office, but she knew better.

It wasn't the mistake she'd made or the person she now had to accept she was because of it.

It wasn't the miraculous little accident that was growing inside her, whether she believed it or not. The accident that was proof that those stolen hours in Monaco hadn't been a dream, after all—that what had happened between her and this startlingly handsome stranger had been real. It was something she could cling to no matter how much of a mess she found herself in now.

But that wasn't what had her stomach in knots tonight.

No. It was the way Renzo was looking at her.

As if he hated her.

Which was fair enough. Sophie wasn't too fond of herself at the moment, now she knew the truth about the headaches she'd been having the past week or so, and that oddly *thick* sensation that wasn't quite nausea—

But Sophie wasn't sure she could bear it. Not from him.

Her distant father, more calculator than human, was one thing. Her even more remote and disinterested fiancé another.

But Renzo was the only thing in her life that had never been a part of this grim little march toward fulfilling the sacred duty that she'd been told was her responsibility since her birth. Every single part of her life had been orchestrated to lead directly and triumphantly toward her wedding tomorrow. She had been raised on dire warnings about the perils of shirking her obligations to her family and endless stories about the many ancestors who would rise from their vaults in protest should any hint of a scandal taint their name.

There had never been any light. Or hope. Or anything like heat.

Sophie was so *cold*. Always and forever frozen solid, no matter the weather.

Because she'd been aware since she was very small that

the sorts of things that warmed a body—strong spirits, wild passion, scandalously revealing garments of any kind—were not permitted for the Carmichael-Jones heiress.

She was to be without stain. Virginal and pure until she handed herself over to her husband, a man chosen by her father before she could walk.

Because the world kept turning ever closer to a marvelous future, but Sophie had been raised in the past. The deep, dark past, where her father didn't condescend to ignore her wishes—Sophie had been raised to know better than to express one. Even to herself.

Everything had been ice, always.

So Sophie had made herself its queen.

But Renzo had been all the light and hope and heat she'd given up believing was possible, packed into that one long, glorious night.

Every wild, impetuous summer Sophie had ever missed out on. Every burning hot streak of strong drink she'd never permitted herself to taste. Every dessert she'd refused, lest her figure be seen as anything but perfectly trim while clad in the finest couture, the better to reflect both wealthy families of which she was the unwilling emblem.

Renzo had been lazy laughter and impossible fire, intense and overwhelming, vast and uncontainable and so much *more* than she'd been ready for that she still woke in the night in a rush, her heart pounding, as if he was touching her again—

"Why am I here?"

He sounded impatient. Bored, even. Something in her recoiled instantly, because she knew that particular tone of voice. Her father used it. So did her fiancé. They were busy, serious men with no time for the frothy, insubstantial concerns of the woman they traded between them like so much chattel.

She wasn't a *person*, that tone of voice told her. She was

made of contracts and property, the distribution of wealth and the expectations of others. Hers wasn't a *life*, it was a list of obligations and hefty consequences if she failed to meet each one.

The old Sophie would have slunk off, duly chastened. She would never have come out here in the first place.

But that Sophie was gone, burned to a crisp in Monaco. Forever ruined, in every sense of the term.

This Sophie tried to find her spine, and then straightened it.

"You contacted me."

"Is that the game you wish to play, *cara*?" Renzo lifted an indolent shoulder, then dropped it. "You sent me newspaper clippings of your engagement. The wedding of the year, I am to understand. A thousand felicitations, of course. Your fiancé is a lucky man indeed."

Sophie didn't particularly care for the way he looked at her as he said that, but she was too busy reeling to respond to it.

"Newspaper clippings…?"

But even as she asked the question, she knew.

She hadn't sent Renzo anything. It wouldn't have occurred to her, no matter how many times she woke in the night with his taste in her mouth. But she knew someone who would have.

Poppy.

Dear, darling Poppy, Sophie's best friend from their school days. Romantic, dreamy Poppy, who wanted nothing but happiness for Sophie.

And who had never seemed to understand that for all Sophie's advantages, and she knew they were many, *happiness* was never on offer.

"Don't be tiresome, my dear," her mother had sighed years ago, when Sophie, trembling, had dared to ask why her own choices were never given the slightest bit of consideration. "*Choice* is a word that poor people use because they have nothing else. You do. Try being grateful, not greedy."

Sophie had tried. And over the years she'd stopped longing for things she knew she could never have.

That wasn't Poppy's way.

"You demanded I meet you here," Renzo was saying, a different sort of laziness in his voice then. This one had an edge. "And so, naturally, I placed my entire life on hold at such a summons and raced to your side like a well-trained hound."

He made a show of looking around, but there was nothing for miles but fields and hedges. No prying eyes. No concerned relatives who would claim to their dying day they only had Sophie's best interests at heart.

The stately house where her wedding was to be held in the morning was over the next hill and Sophie, who had never sneaked anywhere in her life before that night in Monaco, had felt a sickening combination of daring and scared as she'd crept out of her room and run from the hall tonight.

It was pathetic, really.

How had she lived twenty-six long years and failed to recognize how sad and small her life really was?

Renzo wasn't finished. "Now that we're both caught up, perhaps you can tell me why I've been called upon to take part in this latest episode of what appears to be a rather melodramatic and messy life?"

Sophie swallowed. The words *melodramatic* and *messy* had never applied to her life. Not ever. Not until she'd met him. She opened her mouth to speak, but nothing came out.

That was the real story of her life.

Her heart was beating so loudly she couldn't understand how Renzo didn't hear it.

His mouth moved, then, but she would never call that

a smile. Then he made it worse, reaching over to take her chin in his firm hand, the buttery leather of the gloves he wore only highlighting the intensity of his grip.

And it was the same inside her as it had always been, gloves or no.

Fire.

"What lies will you tell me tonight, I wonder?" he asked, low and dark. Ominous.

"You found me," Sophie said, trying to keep her feet solid beneath her. Trying to ignore the wildfire heat ignited in her. Again. "I... I didn't want..."

She didn't know how to do this.

He had texted her out of nowhere, as far as she'd known.

This is Renzo. You must want to meet.

Now, standing outside on a cool, wet night, Sophie had to ask herself what she thought he had been offering, exactly. Blackmail?

That was what she'd told herself. That was why she'd come.

But she understood, now that he was touching her again, that she'd been lying to herself.

And now she had to lie to him. Again.

The trouble was, Sophie had never told so many lies before in her life. What would be the point? Too many people knew too much about her, and everyone was more than happy to compare notes and then decide what was in her best interest without her input. Therefore, she'd always done exactly what was expected of her. She'd done well at school because her father had made it clear that she was expected to be more than simply an ornament.

"Clever conversation and sparkling wit are not something one is either born with or not, Sophie," her father had told her when she'd been barely thirteen. "They're weapons in an arsenal and I expect you to be an excellent shot."

Sophie had made certain she was. After school, she'd involved herself with only carefully vetted charities, so as never to cause her father or future husband any cause for concern about what she'd done with her time.

Or more to the point, her name.

No carousing. No scandals. Nothing that could be considered a stain.

She'd even agreed to marry a man she thought of as her own, personal brick wall—though far less warm and approachable than any slab of stone—on her eighteenth birthday.

Well. *Agreed* was a strong word.

Randall Grant, the sixth Earl of Langston, had been her father's choice for her since she was in the cradle. Her agreement, such as it was, had never been in doubt.

Dal, as Randall was known to friends and family and the girl he'd been given, had produced the Langston family ring and handed it to her with a few cold words about the joining of their families. Because that was all that mattered.

Not Sophie herself. Not her feelings.

Certainly not love, which Sophie thought no one in either her family or Dal's had believed was real or of any import for at least the last few centuries.

And her reaction—her attempt at defiance—in the face of the life that had been presented to her as a fait accompli had comprised of a single deep breath, which Sophie had held for just a moment longer than she should have as Dal stood there, holding the ring before her.

Just a moment, while she'd imagined what might happen if she refused him—

But that was the thing. She couldn't imagine it. Even thinking about defying her parents and all the plans they'd made for her had made her feel light-headed.

So she had said yes, as if Dal had asked her a question.

As if there had ever been any doubt.

She'd locked the heirloom ring away in her father's safe, murmuring about how she didn't dare flash it about until she was Dal's countess.

All she'd asked for was a long engagement, so she could pretend to have what passed for a normal life for just a little while—

But she hadn't. She hadn't dared. She'd only been marking what time she had left.

Until Renzo.

CHAPTER TWO

"Do it," Renzo growled, snapping Sophie back to her current peril. The dark lane. The powerful man who still held her before him, that hand on her chin. "Tell me another lie to my face. See what happens."

Sophie didn't know how to respond to him. She didn't know how to respond at all. She'd been so certain that his text had been a threat. That he had planned to come here and…do something.

To her.

Did you truly believe it was a threat? asked a small voice inside of her that sounded far too much like her mother. *Or did you imagine that Renzo might save you?*

But that was the trouble, wasn't it? No one could save her.

No one had ever been able to save her.

Sophie tried to pull her chin from his grip, but he didn't let go. And for some reason, that was what got to her. One more man was standing before her, making her do things she didn't want to do. Like the others, Renzo wasn't forcing her into anything. He wasn't brutish or horrible.

He was simply, quietly, unyieldingly exerting his will.

And Sophie was tired of bending, suddenly. She was tired of accepting what was handed to her and making the best of it when she'd never wanted it in the first place.

She'd made her own mistakes. Now she'd figure out how to live with them.

"Why did you come?" she demanded of Renzo then. "I doubt I'm the only woman you've ever spent a night with. Do you chase them all down?"

A flash of white teeth against the night. "Never. But then again, they do not typically furnish me with false names."

"How can you possibly know that if you never seek them out again?"

The look in his eyes changed. Oh, there was still that heat. That simmering temper. But now, suddenly, there was a different kind of awareness.

As if she had challenged him.

She supposed she had.

"I can think of only one reason a woman would wish to meet me the night before her wedding to another man," Renzo said then, his tone cold enough to do her father proud. But his gaze was pure fire. "Is that who you imagine I am? A gigolo on call? You merely lift a finger and here I am, willing and able to attend to your every desire?"

This time when she tipped her head back he released her chin.

"You're here, aren't you?"

"Indeed I am," Renzo said, something blistering and lethal in his voice then. "And never let it be said that I do not know my place."

"I don't know what—"

"I should have known that I was mixing with someone far above my station." His voice was scathing. The look on his face was far worse than a blow could have been, she was certain. "It is no more than we peasants are good for, is it not?"

Sophie's heart kicked so hard she was afraid it might crack a rib. "I have no idea what you're talking about."

"But of course you do. You are so blue-blooded I am surprised you do not drip sapphires wherever you walk. Is that not what you summoned me here to make clear?" He looked around again, as if he could see over the hill to the grand house that had commanded the earldom for centuries. As if he could see her family's own estates to the north. As if he knew every shameful, snobbish thing her parents had said to her over the years. "After all, what am I to you? The bastard son of a Sicilian village woman who raised me on her own, with nothing but shame and censure to ease her path. Oh, yes. And the rich men's washing, which she counted herself lucky to have."

"You don't know anything about me—" she started, determined to defend herself when the truth was, she had no defense for what she'd done. She still couldn't believe she'd actually done it.

"I knew you were a virgin, Sophie," he cut in. She still wasn't used to it, the dark and delicious way he said her name. As if it was a caress, when she remembered his caresses too well. A mirthless smile moved over his sensual mouth, but it failed to make him any less appealing. She doubted anything could. "I suppose I have no one to blame but myself for imagining that also made you an innocent."

"I don't know what you want from me."

"Another lie." Renzo let out a small, hard laugh that was about as amused as that smile. "You know exactly what I want from you."

"Then I'm glad we've had the opportunity to have this conversation at last," Sophie said, somehow managing to sound cool despite the clambering inside of her. "I apologize for not having it with you that night."

"Because you were too busy sneaking off, your tail between your legs, back to your earl and your engagement and your pretty little life in a high-class cage. Is that not so?"

It was such an apt description of Sophie's furtive behavior that morning after in Monaco—filled with the terrible mix of sick shame at her actions and something proud and defiant deep inside of her that simply refused to hate the greatest night of her life, no matter what it made her— that she had to pause for a minute. She had to try to catch her breath.

And when she did, she reminded herself that it didn't matter what he called her or what he thought about her, as painful as it might be to hear. There was a far more important issue to address.

"Renzo," she began, because it didn't matter how little she wanted to tell him what he needed to know. It didn't matter that a single sentence would change both of their lives forever.

Their lives were already altered forever. He just didn't know it yet.

But he didn't look the slightest bit inclined to listen to her.

"What I cannot understand," he seethed at her in that same dark, dangerous way that made the night seem very nearly transparent beside him, "is why you thought you could do nothing more than click your fingers and I would come running."

"I don't know," she said quietly, something she wasn't sure she recognized stampeding through her, like fear. But much more acrid. "But here you are."

Sophie only realized she'd backed away from him when she felt the car behind her. She reached out, flattening her hands against the car's bonnet, sleek and low, a great deal like the only other vehicle she'd seen this man drive.

The stars had come out far above, but she didn't need the light they threw to illuminate the man before her. He would be burned deep into her flesh forever. She saw him when she closed her eyes. He haunted her dreams. The fact that he was standing here before her now, and no matter that he seemed to hate her, was almost too much for her to take in.

She had spent far too much time staring at pictures of him on the internet in the interim, like a lovesick teen girl, but she still remembered him from that night in Monte Carlo. She had walked away from the table of her friends, all gathered together to celebrate her upcoming nuptials at what Poppy had called her *proper hen do*. She had needed the air. A moment to catch her breath, and to stop pretending that marrying Randall filled her with joy. Or filled her with anything at all beyond the same, low-grade dread with which she'd faced every one of her familial obligations thus far.

The good news was, once she provided Dal with the requisite heir and spare, she could look forward to a happy, solitary life of charity and good works. They could live apart, only coming together at certain events annually. Or they could work together as if the family name was a brand and the two of them its ambassadors, just like her own parents.

No one would call her parents unhappy, she'd told herself as she'd tried to find her equanimity again.

But then again, no one was likely to call them happy, either.

Sophie just needed to resign herself to what waited for her. She knew that. She didn't understand why the closer she got to her wedding, the less resigned she felt.

But then she'd looked up, and there he'd been.

Renzo had been dressed in a dark suit, open at the neck, that seemed to do nothing but emphasize the long, sculpted ranginess of a body she knew at a glance was athletic in every sense of the term. His hair was a rich, too-long, dark brown, threaded through with gold, that called to mind the sorts of endless summers in the glorious sun that she had never experienced. He had the face of a poet, a sensual mouth below high cheekbones, and glorious eyes of dark, carnal amber—but he moved like a king.

She had known that he was coming for her from the first glance.

And when she lay awake at night and cataloged her sins, she knew that was the worst one. Because she hadn't turned around or headed back to her friends. She hadn't kept going, pushing her way through the crowd until she could hide herself in a bathroom somewhere. She hadn't assumed her usual mask of careless indifference that the papers she tried her best not to appear in liked to call *haughty*.

Sophie had seen temptation on a collision course with her and she'd…done absolutely nothing to avoid it.

She had stood where she was, rooted to the floor, and while she would never admit this out loud—and especially not to him—the truth was that she hadn't thought she *could* move.

One look at Renzo from across the crowded floor, right there in the grand casino, and her knees had threatened to give out.

And it didn't help, here on a forgotten country lane back home in England, that she knew precisely what he was capable of. She knew that none of her oversize, almost-farcically innocent daydreams were off the mark.

She hadn't been ready for a man of Renzo's skill, much less his uninhibited imagination.

But Sophie had always been a quick learner.

"Why am I here?" Renzo growled again.

He moved closer to her, that same erotic threat a kind of loose promise that hovered in his bones. She could see it all over his face. Worse, she could feel it echo deep within, a kind of fist in her gut and below, nothing but that same bright fire that had already destroyed her.

"There are consequences to actions," she said carefully,

mimicking something her father might say, because she didn't know another way into the subject. "Surely you know that."

"Is this where the threat comes in?" Renzo's laugh was low. And not kind. "You people are all the same. Carrot and stick until you get your way. And you always get your way, don't you, Sophie?"

He was much too close then. Sophie expected him to stop, because she had nowhere to go, backed up into his car the way she was—but he didn't stop.

He kept coming.

And he didn't stop until he'd insinuated himself between her legs and bent her backward so for all intents and purposes, they were sprawled out together over the front of his car.

He was over her but not on her. If she strained to keep her legs apart, he wasn't even touching her. And yet he might as well have scooped her up in his fists and held her fast.

"Let me up," she whispered fiercely.

Desperately.

But if Renzo heard her, he gave no sign.

He didn't claim her mouth in a bruising kiss, as she half expected, the way he had when he'd helped her from the car that night in Monaco. He held himself above her, sprawled over her body to keep her exactly where she was. Pinning her there. If she tried to move, she would be the one to rub her body against his.

And if she did…would she stop? She shuddered at the notion.

"Tell me about these consequences, *cara*," he murmured. "Tell me how you have suffered. Tell me how brave you have been to forge ahead in your gilded, pampered circumstances, feted and celebrated wherever you go, so soon to be the countess of all you survey."

His mouth was at her ear, then down along her neck, and she could feel the heat of him everywhere—but he still wasn't touching her.

Not the way she wanted him to.

And he wasn't done. "Where does your earl imagine you are tonight? Locked away in your virginal bridal suite, perhaps? Dressed in flowing white already, the living, lovely picture of the innocence he purchased?"

It was one thing for Sophie to think of herself as chattel in the privacy of her own head. It was something else entirely to hear Renzo say it, sardonic and mocking.

"He has not purchased me. I'm not a cow."

"Nor are you the virgin he expects."

"I would be shocked if he has any expectations at all."

"When marriage is commerce, *cara*, the contract is signed and sealed in the marital bed. Shall I tell you how?"

A wave of misery threatened to take her over then. Sophie fought it back as best she could. "Not everyone is as...elemental as you are."

"Will you tell him why?" Renzo asked, unsmiling and much too close. "When he comes to claim his bride, will you tell him who else has been between the pale thighs he imagined were his alone to part?"

He shifted his position above her and she sucked in a breath in a messy combination of anticipation and desire, but he only went down on one elbow so he could get his face that much closer to hers.

It made everything that much worse.

Or better, something in her whispered.

"You're disgusting," she told him. "And he won't notice either way."

"I think you underestimate your groom considerably," Renzo murmured. "What purpose is there in being an earl in the first place if not to plant a flag in unclaimed land and call it his?"

Her breath deserted her at that. "I'm not… There's no *flag*—"

But Renzo kept right on. "Why did you bother to remain pure and untouched for so long, if not to gift it to this betrothed of yours who you clearly hold in such high esteem?"

Sophie pressed her fingers hard against the metal of the car beneath her. She tried to pretend she didn't feel that instant wave of shame—but she did. Did it matter how distantly Dal treated her? She'd made a promise and she'd broken it.

Spectacularly.

Over and over again.

And then it had gotten even worse.

"I wanted to wait," she said quietly, fighting to stay calm. Or at least sound calm. "Until I didn't."

"I'm sure that distinction will please him greatly." Renzo's mouth was a scant centimeter from the sweep of her neck and she was sure—*she was sure*—that he could taste her rapid, revealing pulse. "Make sure your confession is vivid. Paint a picture. A man likes to know how many times his woman cries out another man's name and begs him not to stop."

She shoved at him then, no longer caring if that meant she was forced to touch him. She ignored the feel of his broad, sculpted shoulders beneath her palms and focused on all the emotions swirling around inside her, much too close to the surface.

But it didn't matter what she did, because Renzo was immovable. Another brick wall—except there was nothing cold about him. Nothing the least bit reserved. He *blazed* at her and she could feel it as if it was his hand between her legs, breaching her softness and pushing deep inside—

Her breath was ragged. Desperate. "My marriage is none of your business!"

She had the confused sense that she'd walked directly into a trap. Renzo tensed, coiled tight as if he planned to spring at her.

"And yet here I am, right in the middle of it. Where you put me, Sophie. Against my will."

She shoved at him again and again, he didn't move. At all.

"If I put you there then I'll remove you. Consider yourself ejected. With prejudice."

"Why did you order me to meet you?" he asked, and though his voice was deceptively mild, his dark amber eyes gleamed in the dark and made her think of lions. Tigers. Big cats that had no place roaming about the staid English countryside. "Surely you must know you've made a grievous tactical error, *cara*. You've given me the upper hand."

"The upper hand?"

And she recognized that look on his face then. It was pure triumph, and it should have made her blood chill.

But he'd melted her in Monaco and she couldn't seem to get her preferred veneer of ice back, no matter what. Not around him.

"I know who you are," he told her with a certain relish that washed over her like a caress and then hit her in the gut. Hard. "And I have information I must assume your earl would no doubt prefer was not in the peasant hands of a bastard Sicilian."

"…information?"

But Sophie already knew what he would say. And still, there was a vanishingly small part of her that hoped against hope that he was the man she'd imagined he was—

"Exactly what his fiancée got up to one fine night in Monaco, for example," Renzo said, smashing any hopes she might have had. Of his better nature. Of what she needed to do here. Of this entire situation that seemed a bigger mistake with every passing moment. "What do you imagine he would pay to keep your indiscretions quiet? Because I already know the tabloids would throw money at me. I could name any sum I wish and humiliate two of the finest families in England with one sleazy little article. I must tell you, *cara*, I feel drunk with power."

"You…" She could hardly speak. Her worst nightmare kept getting worse and she had no idea how to stop it. Or contain it. Or even get her head around it. "You are—"

"Careful," he growled. "I would advise you not to call me names. You may find that I am far worse than any insults you throw at me."

He pushed himself back, up and off the car and away from her body. Sophie stayed where he'd left her, uncertain what to do next. She was shaking. There was water making her eyes feel too full and too glassy. And worst of all, there was that part of her that wanted him to come back and cover her again.

She was sick. That was the only explanation.

"What I am is mercenary," Renzo told her. He watched her pitilessly as she struggled to sit up. "You know what that word means, I presume?"

"Of course I know what it means." She sat for a moment, more winded than she should have been, and then pushed herself off the car to get her feet back on the ground.

But it didn't make her feel better. Maybe nothing ever would again.

"What it means to you is something derogatory, I am sure," Renzo said, still watching her in that cold, very nearly cruel way. "Everything is mercenary to those who do not need to make their own money."

Sophie understood that was a slap. "I don't—"

He merely lifted a brow and she fell silent, then hated herself for her easy acquiescence.

"Everything I have, everything I am, I created out of nothing," he told her. "I have nothing polite to say about the man who left my mother pregnant to fend for herself. I have only become a better man than he could ever dream of being. And do you know how I did that?"

"Of course I know. You raced cars for years."

"What I did, Sophie, was take every opportunity that presented itself to me. Why should this be any different?" He watched her as she straightened from the car and took a shaky step. "What consequences would you like to speak to me about?"

And she understood then.

She understood her own, treacherous heart, and why it had pushed her out here in the middle of the night to further complicate the situation she had already made untenable with what she'd done. She understood that no matter what she might have told herself about threatening texts and potential blackmail, what she'd wanted was that man she'd made up in her head in Monaco.

The man who had looked at her through a crowd and seen her. Only her. Not her family name or her father's wealth—just her.

The man who had taken her, again and again.

The man who had learned every inch of her in the most naked, carnal, astounding way possible, there in that villa high in the hills with the glittering lights of the city so far below.

The man who had made her laugh, scream, cry, and beg him to do it all over again.

But that had just been a night. Just one night.

And he was just a man, after all. Not the savior she'd made up in her head. Not the answer to a prayer she hadn't known she'd made.

She should never, ever have answered his text. Because this had only made everything worse.

Her hand crept over her belly, because she couldn't seem to help herself.

"I thought…" she started, then stopped herself, blinking back the emotions she desperately wanted to conceal from him. "I wanted…"

"Your cake and to eat it, too. Yes? I'm familiar with the phrase." The curve of his lips was like a razor. "Why give up the bastard for the earl if you can have them both?"

"That wasn't what I wanted at all."

"Of course it was." The razor curl to his lips edged over into outright disgust. "Do you think I don't know your type, Sophie? Cheating fiancées turn into lying wives in the blink of an eye. And bored housewives are all the same, whether their house is a hovel or a grand hall. Trust me when I tell you that Europe is littered with the detritus of broken vows. You are not as special as you might imagine."

She shook at that ruthless character assassination, but the worst part was that she couldn't manage to shove out a single word in her own defense. Of course he believed these things of her. Had she showed him anything different?

What had seemed like sunlight and glory to her had been nothing but tawdry. She had her little accident to prove it. All she had to do was imagine trying to explain her behavior to her fiancé—or worse, her father. She knew the words they would use.

And she would deserve them.

"Renzo," she said, very carefully, lest she jog something inside and send all these terrible, unwieldy things spilling out into the dirt between them. "There's something you need to know."

"I know everything I need to know." His words were terse. His judgment rendered. It only surprised her that she'd imagined he might be different. "What I cannot forgive is that you made me an unwitting part of your dishonesty. A vow means something to me, Sophie, and you made me break one."

She smiled, though it felt brittle. "What vows did you break?"

"I made a promise to myself many years ago that I would never, ever take something that belonged to another," he told her with a kind of arrogant outrage, as if she'd twisted his arm.

"You're right," she said then, because something broke inside of her. She hugged herself as she stepped back, away from him and his car and all these messy emotions she should have been smart enough to leave behind her in Monte Carlo. "I should never have come here tonight."

"These are games children play, Sophie," he told her, fury and condemnation and all that righteousness making his accent more pronounced.

"You're the one making threats," she pointed out.

"You can consider it a courtesy. One you did not extend to me when you decided to entangle me in your sick, sad little marital games."

She could do nothing but nod her head, everything within her swollen painfully and near to bursting—but she couldn't let herself give in. She couldn't show him more of herself. She couldn't allow him to hurt her any more than he already had.

Because the truth was, she didn't think she could survive it. She had been frozen solid all her life. Renzo had melted her, it was true, but Sophie hadn't understood until tonight that the ice had been her armor.

"Marry your earl or do not," Renzo said with dark finality. "But leave me out of it. Or I will assume you are inviting me to share the details of our night in Monaco with the world."

She swallowed, which was hard to do when she felt as if the tears she refused to shed were choking her. "I understand."

He didn't say another word. He stalked around to the

driver's side and climbed into the car with a grace that should not have been possible for a man his size.

And Sophie stood where she was for a long time after he'd gone, driving off with a muscular roar.

She wanted to cry, but didn't allow herself the weakness.

He'd treated her like a naughty child but the truth was, Sophie thought she'd just grown up.

At last.

She already hated herself, so what was a little more fuel to that fire? She would marry Dal tomorrow, as planned. She would carry on with the life that had been so carefully plotted out for her. She would force herself to do her wifely duty and Dal would either do the math or he wouldn't.

Babies were born early all the time.

Her stomach heaved at that, but Sophie shoved the bile back down.

She'd made her bed and now she would have to lie in it. Literally.

Something in her eased at that. There was a freedom in having no good choices, she supposed. If Dal found out, it wasn't as if it would turn a good marriage bad. Their marriage was a business affair, cold and cruel at its best.

If she was lucky, he might even set her free.

That would have to be enough.

The child she carried might not be Dal's. It might never know its real father. But no matter what, no matter what happened, it would be hers.

Hers.

And Sophie vowed she would love her baby enough, with all that she had, so that it would never know the difference.

CHAPTER THREE

RENZO WOKE IN the middle of the night, restless and something like agitated—when he normally slept like the dead.

He had left Sophie behind without a backward glance, roaring off in a cloud of self-righteousness and sweet revenge, delivered exactly as planned. He'd congratulated himself on the entire situation, and the way he'd handled it, all the way back to the suite of rooms he maintained in his Southwark hotel, with its views of the Thames and giddy, crowded London sprawled at his feet.

He would normally top off a satisfying and victorious day with enough strong drink to make him merry and an uninhibited woman to take the edges off. But, unaccountably, he had done neither of those things.

Not because he was *mourning* anything, he'd assured himself. It was nothing to him if a one-night stand who'd lied to him repeatedly was getting married. It was entirely possible every one-night stand he'd ever enjoyed had raced off to marry someone else—why should he care?

He'd sat there in the fine bar on a high floor in his hotel, surrounded by gleaming, beautiful people, none of whom likely knew the first thing about Sophie Carmichael-Jones and her wedding plans, and told himself that he felt nothing at all.

Nothing save triumph, that was.

He had been less able to lie to himself, however, when every image in his head as he'd drifted off to sleep was of Sophie and all the ways he'd had her in Monaco, each more addictive than the last. And a thousand new ways he could avail himself of her lush, remarkably acrobatic loveliness, if she'd been in the vicinity instead of off in a stately house in Hampshire, ready to wed a bloody earl in the morning.

She was a hunger that nothing else could possibly satisfy, and the fact that was so infuriated Renzo.

Still, he had been certain that come the dawn—and with it the inevitability of her high-society wedding, with all its trappings and titles and trumpeting self-regard on the pages of every tabloid rag in Europe—the raging hunger would disappear, to be replaced by his usual indifference toward anything and everything that appeared in his rearview mirror.

But here he was. Wide-awake before dawn.

His body was hot and tight and too many sensations swirled all over him, as if Sophie was beside him in this bed when he knew very well she was not.

He rolled out of the wide platform bed and refused to handle his body's demands on his own. His lips thinned at the thought.

Renzo was not an adolescent boy, all testosterone and infatuation. He would not use his own hands and spill his own seed with the name of an unattainable female on his lips, as if he was fifteen. He hadn't done such things when he'd actually been fifteen, for that matter, loping around the ancient cliffside town where he'd been the no-account bastard son of a shamed whore of a mother—and therefore might as well have been invisible to the village girls.

He wasn't invisible now. The village girls who had snubbed him then were grown now. Married to the men they'd found more appropriate and settled there on the edge of the very cliff that Renzo had imagined throwing himself over, more than once, to escape the realities of a bastard's life in that place. And these days Renzo's illegitimacy was rarely mentioned. He was the local celebrity who had not only gone on to a glorious motor racing career, but had systematically bought and rebuilt every structure in that damned town, then opened a hotel on the next ridge, until there was no doubt in anyone's mind who the king of that tiny little village was.

That was how Renzo handled things. He waited. He bought it.

Then he made it his.

But that wasn't possible in this situation. He padded over to the wall of windows that let in the insistent gleam of one of the world's premiere cities, but he didn't see London Bridge there before him. Or the Shard.

It was as if Sophie was haunting him, though Renzo had never before believed in ghosts.

There, alone in the dark with only London as witness, he no longer felt that sense of triumph.

Instead, he remembered her responses. The catch in her throat. The wonder in her gaze.

The way she'd looped her arms around his neck when he'd lifted her against the wall—directly inside the front door to his villa, because he couldn't wait another moment—and had blushed.

From head to toe, as he'd soon discovered.

He had quickly learned that she was a virgin, and he'd reveled in that fact. That she was entirely his. That he was the only man alive to taste her, touch her, learn how she delighted in every new thing he taught her.

Renzo had never been a possessive man. But Sophie had brought it out in him.

Earlier tonight he'd accused her of being a virgin as a technicality only.

He wanted to believe that, of course. A woman who was meant to be a countess might well keep her hymen intact in preparation for her marriage while involving herself in all manner of other debaucheries. He'd met women like that before—hell, he'd happily participated in the debauchery.

He'd wanted nothing more than to make Sophie pay for thinking that she could pull one over on him. Or perhaps what he had really wanted to make her pay for was the fact that she'd succeeded.

But the truth was, he realized as he stood there and stared out at a city he completely failed to see, it didn't make sense.

Renzo knew any number of mercenary women. They were a lot like him, each and every one of them. They knew what they wanted and they proceeded to go out there and get it. They used everything they had. Status if they had it. Wiles if they did not. Whatever it took to get what they wanted.

He had learned to recognize one of his ilk from afar. Long before they made it into his bed, Renzo knew them for that steel in their gaze and their particular brand of avid keenness. He had never been wrong.

And he'd never been caught by a grifter like himself, either.

Renzo might have convinced himself otherwise since he'd received that newspaper clipping by post, but he hadn't read that kind of sharpness in Sophie.

Not when she'd been calling herself Elizabeth, flowing like sweet honey all over his hands, and charming him within an inch of his life.

Renzo was not easily charmed.

It occurred to him then—high over the Thames in the middle of the night with nothing in his head but the only woman who had ever deceived him—that it was possible he had been hasty.

He had been so busy scoring points, making sure he got in as many digs at her as possible, that he hadn't allowed himself to really listen to the things she said.

And more, the things she hadn't said.

He, of all people, should have known better. After all, he'd spent his entire childhood trying to live up to the fantasy of what he'd imagined he ought to have been and what becoming it would do for him. If he was perfectly well behaved. If he transcended the poverty in which he'd been raised. If he never, ever, allowed what others thought of him or his circumstances to hold him back. If he made his own way in the world, as best he could, whatever that looked like. If he made himself a star in his chosen field and instead of throwing his money away like so many of his peers, used it to build himself a little empire.

If he did all the right things, he'd told himself for far longer than he should have, surely that would gain his father's notice.

But it never had.

Not in the way he wanted, anyway. And when he'd decided to force the issue, it hadn't ended well.

Renzo's idealism, immature and pathetic by any estimation, had been fully beaten out of him in his eighteenth year, courtesy of the very wealthy, very titled prince who had left his mother pregnant with him. Literally beaten it out of him. He'd had relapses since then, it was true, but he'd always learned the same damned lesson in the end.

Meeting his father had taught Renzo that there were no better places or people, as he'd been tempted to imagine. There were no misunderstandings that explained away eighteen years of poverty and shame. There was only reality and in it, people did what suited them with little or no thought to the effect that their actions might have on others.

If it was impossible to conceive of how a person could do something heinous to someone else, a good rule of thumb was to assume that person had been thinking only and ever of themselves.

That lesson had been pounded into Renzo's fool head again and again and again, particularly during that one vile week when he'd been eighteen and stupid and had foolishly imagined his own father would treat him well because of their blood tie. He knew better now.

Still, he'd let this woman throw him.

He knew all about women like Sophie Carmichael-Jones. They thought themselves so high-and-mighty, so far above the peasants—but at the end of the day, they were motivated by money. The same as Renzo's mother had been, desperate to keep a roof over her head by any means possible. The same as Renzo had learned to be, making certain he excelled at whatever he did to pay her bills. The only difference was that the Carmichael-Joneses of the world believed their own scrabbling for cash was more meaningful, somehow, because it was wrapped up in estates and titles, ancient claims and other such things.

Renzo did not share this belief.

A hustler was a hustler, in his estimation.

He couldn't believe he hadn't seen the signs in Sophie, his sad-eyed innocent with the prettiest smile he'd ever beheld.

She'd spoken to him of consequences and he'd thought he'd give her a few—but hours later, he couldn't seem to get that particular word out of his head.

He crossed his arms over his chest and found himself scowling down at the Thames as it wound on, unheeding, the same as it had done for centuries.

It had taken more self-control than he'd imagined it would to be near Sophie again and not take her.

His body had reacted as if they had been lovers for decades. He had been hard and ready the instant he'd seen her come out of the shadows. Even then, when he knew who she really was and had no intention whatsoever of giving her access to him again, his body had made its own wishes known.

He wanted her despite everything. Still. Now.

He hadn't known, from one moment to the next, which one of them he was more furious at. Her, for the lies she had told him and the way she'd made him complicit in her own betrayal of her fiancé. Or him, for wanting her with an edge that bordered on desperation, even then.

Consequences, something in him whispered.

He remembered how she'd stood there before him in the close, wet dark.

Gone was the glowing, carefree woman who'd given herself to him so freely in Monaco. In England, apparently, Sophie was drawn. Agitated.

And had kept holding a hand over her belly, as if her meal had not quite agreed with her…

Consequences, he thought again.

And found himself cursing in a fluid, filthy Sicilian dialect when another possibility altogether occurred to him.

He'd believed he was furious before.

But now…

Renzo thought a far better word to describe his feelings was *volcanic*.

Sophie woke in a confused, hurtling rush and her first thought was that it was much too early to be awake. The light was thin and halting, creeping in between the curtains she'd neglected to close as if uncertain of its reception.

Her second thought was that today was her wedding day.

And that unpleasant reality slapped at her, waking her up even more whether she liked it or not.

"I can see you are not asleep," came a familiar voice from much too close. "It is best to stop pretending, Sophie."

It was voice that should not have been anywhere near her, not here.

Not in Langston House where, in a few short hours, she would become the latest in a long line of unenthused countesses.

She told herself she was dreaming even though her eyes were wide-open.

Sophie took her time turning over in her bed, then sitting up gingerly as if she expected it to hurt, somehow. And still, no matter how long she stared or blinked, she couldn't make Renzo disappear.

He lounged there at the foot of the four-poster bed, here in her bedroom in Langston House as if she'd conjured him up from one of the dreams that had plagued her all night.

"What are you doing here?" she asked, her voice barely more than a whisper.

"It turns out we have more to discuss."

She didn't like the way he said that, dark and something like lethal.

"How did you get in here?" Sophie looked around wildly. She didn't know what she expected to find. Her father bursting through the door, perhaps, assuming Renzo had barged his way into Langston House like some kind of marauder? Or even Poppy, always so concerned, calling out her name?

But it really was early. If she ignored the wild pounding in her chest, there was no sound. Anywhere. No one seemed to be awake but the two of them. Langston House felt still all around.

And Renzo was *here*.

Right *here*, in this bedroom Sophie had been installed in as the future Countess of Langston. It was all tapestries, priceless art, and frothy antique chairs that looked too fragile to sit in, as befitted a room that regularly appeared in guidebooks.

"You can't be here," she managed to say, clutching the bedclothes to her like some kind of security blanket.

"Talk to me some more about the consequences you mentioned, if you please," Renzo said mildly. So mildly it made every hair on her body seem to stand straight up in warning.

He was dressed the way he had been the night before. Dark trousers and boots, sleek and spare, as if to highlight his lean, brooding athleticism. That thick hair of his looked messy, as if he'd spent the hours since she'd last seen him running his fingers through it again and again. The leather jacket he'd worn in the rain last night was open now over the kind of soft, impossibly simple T-shirt that looked as if it was nothing more than a throwaway piece—and yet clung to his sculpted chest, hugging him and exalting him in turn, and likely costing more than some people's mortgages.

If she was a better person, Sophie thought, she wouldn't find him so attractive, even now, when she knew exactly what kind of trouble he'd brought into her life. When she knew that she should have walked away from him that night in Monte Carlo and let him remain nothing but a daydream she might have taken out and sighed over throughout the coming years of her dry, dutiful marriage.

It took a moment for his words to penetrate. And when they did, a kind of icicle formed inside of her, sharp and long and frigid.

"I don't know what you mean," she said, her lips too dry and her throat not much better.

"I think you do." Renzo stood at the foot of her bed, one hand looped around one of the posts in a lazy, easy sort of grip that did absolutely nothing to calm Sophie's nerves. Not when she was sure she could feel that same hard, steady hand wrapped around her neck. Or much, much lower. "I think you came to tell me something last night but let my temper scare you off. Or perhaps it would be more accurate to say you used my temper as an excuse to keep from telling me, would it not?"

Sophie found her hands covering her belly again, there beneath her comforter. Worse, Renzo's dark gaze followed the movement, as if he could see straight through the pile of soft linen to the truth.

"What would be accurate to say is that you took the opportunity last night to make an uncomfortable situation worse," she said, sounding more in control than she felt. She very deliberately removed her hands from her belly and set them on the top of her blankets where Renzo could see them. Where they could be inoffensive and tell him nothing. "That's on you. It has nothing at all to do with me."

"It has everything to do with you, *cara*."

"I would like you to leave," she told him, fighting to keep her voice calm. "You've threatened me already. I don't know what showing up here, hours before I'm meant to marry, could possibly accomplish. Or is this more punishment?"

Renzo's lips quirked into something no sane person would call a smile. He didn't move and yet he seemed to loom there, growing larger by the second and consuming all the air in the bedchamber.

He made it hard to breathe. Or see straight.

Or remember why, exactly, she'd marched back up to Langston House last night filled with new resolve about what she would do and how she would manage her marriage—no matter Dal's reaction to her pregnancy. Assuming she even told him.

She was aware that such concerns made her a terrible person. On some level, she thought she would always hate herself for the things she'd found herself thinking in these awful days. But none of that mattered.

What mattered was keeping her baby safe, one way or another. She couldn't afford to care too much what that looked like.

"We will get to punishments in a moment," Renzo said. His dark amber gaze raked over her, bold and harsh. His sensual mouth, the one she'd felt on every inch of her skin and woke in the night yearning for again, flattened. "First, answer me one question, and do not lie to me. Do not imagine for one millisecond that I will not know if you do, because believe me, I will. And a lie will only make this worse for you."

"That is very hard to imagine."

But he didn't respond to that. His gaze bored into her, so hard and deep she was sure he left marks. "Are you with child, Sophie?"

CHAPTER FOUR

SOPHIE SUCKED IN a shocked, harsh breath that she was instantly afraid announced her guilt in no uncertain terms.

The way Renzo's mouth twisted at the sound, she thought it had.

Her heart was pounding so loud and wild that she was astonished it didn't knock her backward. She sat up straighter as if that could keep such a thing from happening, her throat tight with fear and every muscle in her body tense.

She hadn't slept enough, too busy tossing and turning and looking for solutions to her problem that didn't involve any more deception—or any loveless marriages, for that matter. Her head was too fuzzy as a result and she knew that that was nothing but a liability where Renzo was concerned. He was like a steamroller, for all that he was so beautiful, and the real problem was that there was a small part of her that wanted to make it easy for him.

It was more than a small part of her, if she was honest. All it wanted was to simply lie back, surrender, and let him do with her what he would.

But she reminded herself why he was here. Why she even knew him.

Sophie had stepped out of line exactly once. She'd sneaked out of her cage, thrown caution to the wind, and this was the result.

She'd handed over her innocence to a man who could not possibly understand what it was she'd surrendered to him. And then she'd allowed herself to imagine, like some kind of child, that he could rescue her from this life she'd been born into. That she could see him again the night before her wedding and feel that same sense of impossible homecoming she'd felt in his villa in Monaco. That he would somehow make it all okay.

But he wasn't that man. *That man doesn't exist*, she told herself harshly.

And if last night had taught her anything, it was that throwing away her safe, knowable, perfectly plotted-out life for a taste of passion led to nothing but being left there on the side of a country lane. In the rain.

Pregnant on the side of the road, literally.

Sophie knew she had nobody to blame for that but herself.

"I think that you are carrying a child," Renzo was saying, low and furious, that lazy grip of his on the post… harder. Tighter. "*My* child. And you must understand that if that is so, I cannot permit you to go ahead with this wedding of yours."

"It's not up to you," she managed to say. "Think of all the things you called me last night. What makes you imagine that I would obey you in anything?"

"I have so far been very kind to you, *cara*. I would advise you not test the boundaries of my patience."

"I didn't send you that newspaper clipping." Sophie sat straighter, even though it made her spine ache. "I didn't summon you here. I thought you texted me…" She shook her head. "Why would anyone do such a thing? I assumed it was a threat. And, sure enough, when you appeared, you set about threatening me as soon as possible."

"Did you feel threatened?" Renzo asked softly, that edge in his voice much worse than anything he'd said. "Let me assure you, Sophie, that I have not begun to threaten you. Last night was a game. This, here, this lie you tell with every breath…" He shook his head, though his gaze never left her. "I am no longer playing."

"I think you have me confused with someone who cares whether you are playing games or not," Sophie told him, with tremendous composure she was nowhere near feeling.

Renzo dropped his arm to his side and it was astonishing how much more threatening that was. As if he was no longer bothering to pretend that he was in any way at his ease—something that could only bode ill for Sophie.

"I will ask you one more time," he growled at her, his accent more pronounced, as if to indicate exactly how far south this was headed. Assuming there was a worse place to go than him here, in her bedroom at Langston House, with her and Dal's entire families and wedding parties in residence. "Are you carrying my child? Is that the consequence you dared not tell me about last night?"

Sophie wished she wasn't in bed, her hair everywhere, wearing nothing but a flimsy little sleeping gown. She wished she was wrapped in sheets of armor. Encased in steel. She tried to pretend that she was tough and strong and brave—anything but what she was, a scared twenty-six-year-old in deep over her head with this man, in a situation she'd caused.

That was the part that made her the most panicky. The fact that *she* had done this. No one had done it to her. She could so easily have stayed with her friends that night in Monte Carlo, stayed the virgin she was expected to be, and woken up in the morning prepared to meet her obligations as expected.

Without a brand-new pregnancy that should never have happened in the first place, or the sort of unfortunate connection to a Sicilian race car driver that would send her father into paroxysms of rage.

Oh, the things she wished.

Sophie told herself it didn't matter what she wished or how she felt, it only mattered what she allowed Renzo to see. And even that mattered only insofar as it allowed her to clean up her own mess.

"Here's a hypothetical." She cleared her throat, wishing her mouth wasn't so dry. "Let's say you were, in fact, the father of a child who came about thanks to a one-night stand that should never have happened. That no one must ever suspect happened. What then? What claim do you imagine that gives you?"

"What claim?" He bared his teeth at her. "It gives me the only claim. My child, my claim."

"That might be more meaningful if I was a free woman," Sophie said quietly. "But I am not."

"That sounds a great deal like your problem, not mine. And certainly not my child's."

"You were a mistake," Sophie said, emphasizing that last word. "What right do you imagine you have to barge into my life and change it now? I never promised you anything. And I don't recall you making any pledges yourself."

"I don't think you have the slightest idea what I might have done, since you sneaked off before I woke."

She rolled her eyes. "Which you, in all your years of playing the field in the full glare of the tabloids, never did. Not even once. You preferred to lounge about and spend the mornings with each and every one of your conquests, making affirmations and discussing commitment over breakfast."

"None of them fell pregnant."

"How would you know?" she asked. "Did all the vows you exchanged after your single night in their company extend to them sharing their fertility status with you weeks later?"

"I know because I have never failed to use protection before."

"Until me," Sophie said, and couldn't quite keep her tone as mild as she would have liked. "What luck."

Renzo didn't say anything. And despite herself, Sophie remembered how it had happened. When he'd lifted her against him, right there against the wall. When he'd somehow understood—almost instantly—how little experience she had. He'd laid her down right there on the floor and had taken his time. He'd stripped her as if the act of removing her clothes was a caress.

Then he'd set his mouth between her legs and utterly destroyed her.

And after that, things had only gotten more intense.

But there was no use thinking about any of that now. There was no point and there was certainly no use. She was as trapped as she'd ever been. His presence here didn't change that—it just made what she had to do that much worse.

"In any case," Sophie said when the silence dragged on too long, "this is not my decision to make. After our wedding, I will speak to the earl and see how he wishes to handle things."

"Know this, if nothing else. Your little earl has no authority over my child."

"But what he does have is authority over me," Sophie threw back at him with all the anguish she'd been bottling up inside of her these last weeks. "He will be my husband in a matter of hours and, as perhaps you might have guessed, it is not a modern arrangement. It will be quite traditional, and I imagine the decision—all decisions—will not be mine to make. And if that's the case, believe me, they will certainly not be yours to make, either."

She hardly knew what she was saying. She couldn't imagine Dal asserting his authority over anything—he was far too cold. Remote. He would be far more likely to curl his lip and banish her to a family parcel of land off in the Shetland Islands or somewhere equally far enough away to feel like an appropriate prison.

But she saw no reason to share that with Renzo.

She didn't know what she expected. But it wasn't the laugh that Renzo let out then, loud and long. She might even have thought it was a real laugh if she'd never heard the other.

And if she felt a terrible pang at the thought of his real laughter, spilling over her like light and heat as they sprawled there in his wide bed in Monaco—well. Her entire life was a story of compromises she'd made even before being asked, because that was her role. Sacrifices that only seemed so in retrospect, when she realized what it was she'd missed out on. Obligation over everything, even common sense.

That was what being the Carmichael-Jones heiress meant. That was what it had always meant.

It took precedence over everything, even this. Especially this.

"I will assume that all of this is your roundabout way of telling me that yes, you are indeed pregnant," Renzo said, his voice sounding rougher than usual. Thicker, maybe. Harsher. "You were a virgin when I met you. I can therefore only assume that the baby is mine, as I suspected."

"There is a great deal of debate on that," she told him, tilting her chin up as if she thought he might take a swing at her. As if she wanted him to. "After you, I thought—why not take a tour of Europe? From one bed to the next until I got my fill. As you do. So really, it could be anyone's."

All Renzo did was shift his weight. Or move again without seeming to move at all. She thought his eyes got darker. Or they landed more heavily on her, somehow. All she knew was that the world seemed to shift, then tilt, and all she could seem to do was hold on to the bed beneath her and hope for the best.

He did not dignify her claims of sleeping her way across Europe with a response, which only made her want to provoke him all the more.

She told herself she had no earthly idea why she would do such a thing.

"You should consider your next move very carefully," Renzo told her matter-of-factly. As if he was a general delivering orders to troops whose lives depended on obeying him. "You should bear in mind that I could make a scene now. I could have half the house in this room in the next five minutes, to witness you and me in bed together, mere hours before your wedding. I'd invite you to ask yourself how you think your friends and family would handle such a thing."

Sophie could imagine it all too well. Her father would become apoplectic as his dynastic dreams faded away before his very eyes. Her mother might actually swoon from the shame of it. She even imagined that Dal might allow his expression to frost over into an expression of refined disgust, the deepest feeling she imagined he was capable of experiencing.

Beyond that, Sophie herself would be humiliated, and on a grand scale. The guests would inevitably sell their stories, which Sophie's parents would find almost more unpalatable than the story itself, and which Sophie could expect to haunt her. The wedding would be off, of course. The things that an earl might choose to ignore years into his arranged marriage and after Sophie had dutifully given him children, he would, naturally, be unable to overlook today.

A cheating wife was one thing, especially when they could expect to have little relationship of their own. Or so it seemed with all the people Sophie knew in her claustrophobic circles. But a cheating fiancée with the gall to parade her lover beneath his roof mere hours before the wedding ceremony? That was something else.

If it wasn't, Sophie's father would never have spent all these years lecturing her mercilessly on the value of virtue.

"I'm sure it would be fine," she said now, trying to brazen her way through.

Renzo did not look the least bit impressed with the attempt.

"I'm going to allow you the opportunity to do the right thing," he told her, almost kindly. But she could see his face and she knew that whatever else was motivating him right now, it wasn't *kindness*. "Let us be clear, you and I. You do not deserve this courtesy from me. It is a measure, *cara mia*, of what a forgiving man I am. Charitable unto my soul. If I were you, I would consider flinging yourself at my feet to show your gratitude."

Last night Sophie had been afraid she might cry. This morning, however, that feeling was gone. It had been replaced by this…flashing thing like lightning that swirled around inside of her and made her want nothing more than to land a punch or two. The way he kept doing.

"Charitable. Forgiving." She shook her head. "I think perhaps you're translating the words wrong from Italian, Renzo."

"Is that a dig?" His smile then was so sharp she thought it could have cut steel into tiny shavings. "Be aware, Sophie. I am not your earl. I was not raised with silver spoons stuffed in every orifice, starched and scrubbed within an inch of my life into some cordial automaton. I am not polite. I am not courteous. I was raised with nothing and was forced to make everything that I now possess. And I will do anything to keep what is mine." That smile began to remind her of nothing so much as fangs. "You have no idea what you have done. None at all."

He looked scary and intense, and there was a time—perhaps only a few hours ago—where she would have found that almost too much to bear. But he had said and done these things to her already, and here she still was. She could bear anything.

And the light coming through her heavy curtains was no longer quite so pale or insubstantial. It looked like sunlight.

Her wedding day had arrived, despite her best efforts and no matter that there had been a reappearance of the shockingly beautiful—if wildly overwhelming—Sicilian there before her.

It had been profoundly childish to imagine she could escape this particular noose around her neck. She didn't know how she'd managed to pretend, for even a moment, that she might somehow manage to buck the tremendous weight of two ancient families' expectations. No matter what she'd done.

Sophie made a big show of yawning, complete with a theatrical stretch.

"Oh, I'm so sorry," she murmured, though she kept her gaze locked to his. "Blah-blah-blah. I will pay. I will rue the day. I will cry myself to sleep and your name will be a curse." She sounded so bored she was surprised she could sit upright, and she waved a languid hand to underscore her tone. "This is all very melodramatic and the truth is, you've jumped to a lot of mad, unsubstantiated conclusions. You're lucky I haven't called to have you thrown out of this house. But I will. You have exactly five seconds to go before I do."

"Do you truly wish to test me, Sophie?" Renzo drawled, so soft and deadly it shivered over her skin like its own breeze. "Can you really believe I am a man to be trifled with? I would not have imagined you could be so foolish."

There was some kind of devil in her, needling her. Kicking at her. It made her want to open up her mouth and say something else he wouldn't be able to forgive. It made her want to hurt him, however she could—

She wanted to hurt him the way he'd hurt her last night.

Sophie felt the air go out of her at that. Was that really who she was? She wanted to hurt this man because he wasn't the fantasy she'd built in her head? Could anyone have lived up to that?

Or had she known he couldn't—that no one could?

Did you simply want justification to swan off into the prison of this marriage and get to feel superior and self-righteous? asked a little voice within.

Condemning her thoroughly with a simple question she didn't want to answer.

And as if he could see it, or simply knew it somehow in that way he seemed to know all sorts of things about her he shouldn't, Renzo smiled again.

This time she thought it might cut her in half.

"Do what you must," he told her, with a quiet sort of conviction that made it too hard, suddenly, to sit still. "Have whatever conversations you feel you need to have. I will leave you to it. And I will expect you on that very same lane where you met me last night. You have two hours."

"Or what?" she asked.

Her heart was thumping again, even louder, and so hard she felt vaguely ill. But her voice was barely a whisper.

"You don't want to know *or what*," Renzo assured her. "Trust me on this."

And with that, he turned toward the door.

Sophie couldn't understand what was happening inside of her. There was that lightning flash, urging her on to do things she knew were well-nigh suicidal. There was that reservoir of something thicker, deeper. *Sadder*, something in her whispered. The part of her that remembered him different than this. The part that remembered him generous and like sunshine.

Her brief escape, not a prison all his own.

And more than that she felt something hollow, like an ache that only kept expanding, that wanted things she couldn't seem to make sense of in her own head.

Maybe that was why she was up and on her feet without giving herself a moment to consider it. To think better of it.

But then again, had she really had a wholly coherent thought since the doctor had come back in with the news she hadn't wanted at her physical a few days ago?

Sophie had no time to consider that question now, because she scrabbled to the side of the bed and charged across the floor, chasing that long-legged stride of his. And then she threw herself at him, or close enough.

She grabbed at his arm, which didn't help anything. His leather coat was desperately soft, covering a bicep that appeared to be sculpted from stone. Renzo cast a glance down at her grip, then her face, his sensual mouth flat.

Something hectic glittered in his dark amber eyes like a warning Sophie knew she should heed.

"You can't just come in here and throw all these threats around," she hissed at him.

"I think you will find that I did exactly that," he said in that menacingly soft way of his that should have stopped her dead. And possibly made her cry, too. "Because I can. And more than that, you must understand that these are not idle threats. These are promises. If I were you, I would make peace with that now."

"What do you think is going to happen?" she threw at him, furious and panicked and something else she dared not name. "You are going to ruin my life and why? Just to hurt me? You must know that anything you do to hurt me will hurt this baby, too."

He reached down and put his hand over hers, then peeled her fingers from his arm, demonstrating his superior strength slowly and implacably and without hurting her at all.

Which, of course, made it worse.

"No child of mine will know a moment's want," Renzo told her, something dark she couldn't understand in his voice. "Ever. You, on the other hand, I will maintain only as long as necessary. Why? Do you have a list of demands?"

"I don't want to be 'maintained,'" she hurled at him, as if he'd struck a blow.

She cradled the hand he'd removed from his arm as if his fingers on her skin had left blisters.

"Do you not?" Renzo asked, his dark eyes ablaze. "What, then, do you anticipate your marriage will give you? Or is it that you prefer a certain kind of cage to call your own?"

She shook her head, and opened her mouth to refute him—but he wasn't finished.

"If the bars are pretty and look like the British aristocracy, then why not—is that it?" He was much taller than she remembered when she stood this close to him, and it reminded her that he was entirely too strong, as well. Why was she provoking him? What did she imagine she had to gain from it? "Sadly, Sophie, I'm afraid that you lay down with a dog of the first order. Now you must handle the fleas. The child you carry is a mutt. *My* mutt. And your blue blood turns muddier by the moment." He inclined his head. "You have my condolences."

"I don't understand why, if you think so little of me, you would go to the trouble to disrupt my wedding and—"

"I do not think so little of you," he told her, stern and uncompromising, though that ferocious gleam in his dark eyes told a different story altogether. "I do not think of you at all. All you are to me is a liar who happens to carry within her the only thing I care about in this world."

Sophie felt as if she was swallowing broken glass. She felt as if she was reeling, though she didn't think she'd actually tipped over.

"That's a remarkable amount of pressure to put on child who hasn't even been born yet," she said quietly. "And I didn't sign up to be your brood mare, Renzo."

"Listen to me."

He bent down, putting his face entirely too close to hers, and it wasn't until her back came up hard against the wall behind her that she realized he had moved her all the way across the room. Then he made it worse, placing a hand flat against the wall on either side of her head.

A cage in fact. No longer only in theory.

And Sophie despaired of herself, because her reaction was…fire.

Everywhere.

Renzo leaned in closer. "I am the bastard son of a man so grand and glorious he never condescended to so much as speak my name, much less extend a hand to aid me or the woman who bore me in any way. My mother worked her fingers to the bone—which I am certain is nothing but an expression a person like you might use to be poetic. Descriptive. But when I say it, it is not figurative." Something seemed to vibrate through him, as dark and magnetic as that harsh light in his gaze.

"Her hands were cracked and bleeding. She had wounds that never healed, particularly in the winter. And still she worked. She washed clothes and mended them. She scrubbed floors. If she had pride, she cast it aside and spent eighteen years on her knees so that I might grow and prosper. And all the while, the titled, pampered pig who took his pleasure from her and then cast her aside, lived in luxury far away, where he could pretend neither she nor I existed."

Renzo was breathing hard, as if he'd just run five miles, and that should have terrified her.

Sophie had no idea why instead, all she wanted to do was reach out and try to hold him to her, something she knew—*she knew*—he would never allow.

"This will never occur to a child of mine," he told her, and Sophie understood he wasn't simply saying it. She understood that it was a vow.

"That would never happen." There was a ringing in her head that she couldn't seem to clear, no matter how hard she tried. "I am not penniless. And neither is—"

"You misunderstand me." Renzo's voice was flat, hard. "I would not care if you were next in line to a throne, Sophie. My child will not be illegitimate. He will not only never be treated like a bastard, he will, in fact, never, ever be one."

"My child will not be a bastard," Sophie said, very deliberately. Very carefully, because she was so close she could see the play of his muscles beneath his skin, and all of it washed through her like a warning. "Because I'm getting married in a few hours."

"And even if I were inclined to allow such a thing, which I'm not, how do you imagine that will go down?" Renzo shook his head. "I cannot tell if you're truly this naive or if you're delusional. Your earl will no more take on the by-blow of his new wife's ill-considered affair than he will fly naked over the moon. The fact you imagine otherwise is troubling."

"You have obviously never met the earl. He is not an emotional man." She shrugged, as if she wasn't caged between his arms, up against the wall on the morning of her wedding. "As far as I can tell, he cares about absolutely nothing—least of all me."

"He is a man, Sophie," Renzo said, and he dipped his head, making her more aware of how close he was. "Never forget this."

How he held her there against the wall without having

to put so much as a finger on her. Her hands were at her sides, her fingertips digging into the wall behind her. But she didn't know if it was because she was trying to steady herself, or desperately trying to keep her hands from touching him of their own accord.

"Your groom is a very, very wealthy man, in fact, with a lineage that I am quite certain stretches back to some damp medieval vault somewhere, stacked high with the desiccated corpses of earls just like him. He may not care about you. He may not care about anything on this earth. But here is what I can promise you." Renzo was so close then that Sophie could feel each word like a lick against her neck. "He will care, very much, if you attempt to pass off another man's child as his heir."

Her chest was rising and falling much too fast. She'd thought the urge to cry had left her, drying out forever after what had happened last night out on that deserted road, but she felt the prick of tears again. There behind her eyes, where she could neither blink them away nor control them.

"Renzo—" she began, having no idea what she could possibly say next.

But it didn't matter.

"You are still so beautiful," Renzo said, as if it hurt him. "And yet listen to you. Like all pretty things, you are rotten beneath it, aren't you?"

He murmured that almost like a poem, and somehow, that made it hurt worse. As if he'd reached deep into her, taken great handfuls of her insides and tangled them up before shoving them back haphazardly.

Making certain she would never, ever be the same again.

"I don't want any of this," she whispered.

"Do you not?" he asked, and his gaze seemed darker. Or maybe she was just afraid he could see more deeply inside of her. So deeply she was worried that he saw things she didn't even know were there. "I think you are a liar."

"Of course you do. What a shock."

"I think you lie to yourself all the time," he continued in his relentless way. "What other explanation can there be? You could have stayed right here last night and I would never have been the wiser. You didn't have to come out and speak to me, if you truly believed I was a threat to you. Once you did, you could have steered the conversation away from any hint of *consequence*. But you did not."

He reached over then and traced a faint pattern over her cheekbone, then down the line of her jaw. She felt her hands curl into fists at her side, because this felt like nothing more than a mockery of that beautiful night they had shared. When he had done exactly this, but it had all been so different. His every touch had been a reverence.

When now, it was the opposite.

She couldn't bear it, she thought. She kept thinking it.

And she kept discovering that she could bear almost anything. No matter how it tore her apart inside.

"Is that a tear, Sophie?" Renzo asked with that quiet malice that hurt her. Everywhere. And yet set her alight all the same. "I don't believe that, either."

And then he covered her mouth with his.

Which, Sophie realized in that same blazing instant, was exactly what she'd wanted.

CHAPTER FIVE

HER HEART GAVE a terrific jolt, whether in need or recognition of her own complicity she didn't know, and Sophie's hands came up.

In defense, perhaps. To ward him off or push him away, she told herself—

But all she did was find the soft fabric of his T-shirt, stretched there across his granite-hard abdomen, and then she gripped him, making fists in the material.

And surrendered to the glorious assault of his mouth on hers.His mouth was a punishment. And Sophie was sick—she had to be far sicker than she'd ever imagined possible—because she exulted in it.

It was what she'd wanted last night, out there in the wet dark. It was what she'd wanted when she'd woken up to find him there at the end of her bed.

This—he—was exactly what she wanted.

Because she ached between her legs, in that place only he had ever found. Her breasts felt hard and heavy, as if he didn't need to touch them to make them his. She couldn't seem to help the little noises—of greed, of longing, of total surrender—that she made in the back of her throat.

Renzo made a low, rough sound that was little more than a growl, and knocked around inside of Sophie like a song. He bent, then hauled her up against him, his hands moving to take her thighs and pull her legs around his waist.

And still he kept his mouth on hers, a delicious torment. A bittersweet temptation.

All she wore was the soft, short gown she'd slept in, and Renzo acted as if it wasn't there. He kept his mouth fused to hers, and used the wall behind them to keep her where he wanted her. His trousers were a faint abrasion against the soft expanse of her inner thighs, and it was hard to find purchase against the buttery soft leather of his jacket.

She couldn't help but think of that night in his villa when he'd swung her against the wall, just like this, and had kissed her with this same mad passion—and then had slowed himself down to take her where he wanted to go, but much more carefully.

There was nothing careful about Renzo this morning.

And the only thing Sophie felt about that was a curious sense of...*elation.*

But then Renzo was reaching between them, those long, infinitely sure fingers slipping beneath the little scrap of lace she wore to find her where she was the most soft. Where she was bright and molten and entirely his, no matter what she might have tried to tell herself.

"This is the only part of you that does not lie," he said against her mouth, hard and dark.

And she wanted to protest, but his fingers moved then, parting her and playing with her.

She thrashed against him, feeling that touch of his everywhere. It was fire that grew and grew with every pass of his clever fingers, and a wild, insane need that she'd convinced herself she'd made seem more intense than it really was over these past weeks.

She discovered that if anything, she had seriously downplayed Renzo's effect on her.

"There is not a single thing that comes out of your mouth that I trust," he told her, grim and furious, but even so, the words fell through her like need. Like longing. He reached between them and she heard the sound of his zipper, but could do nothing but shudder. And yearn. "This is the only thing I trust."

She felt the broad head of him against her entrance, and then he was thrusting inside, a deep, thick, irrevocable claim. He had her pinned to the wall, caught between him and a slab of stone—and of the two of them, she thought the stone was more yielding.

Sophie cried out at his intense possession, and his mouth was on hers again.

And then everything got serious.

Scorching need. Searing and wholly mad, and she couldn't seem to care the way she knew she should.

There was only his mouth on hers, a granite, sensual tease. There was only the hardest part of him, slick and deep inside her, rocketing them both into sheer delight with every bone-rattling thrust.

She was nothing but a red-hot, greedy fist of pure sensation.

It was better than she remembered.

He was better.

And she was lost.

It was all she could do to hang on for dear life while he tested that impressive length of his again and again, slamming into her so hard and so deep it was as if he made them both new.

She began to shake. It started deep inside, then fanned out, rolling over her like a wave.

"This is the truth about you, Sophie," he told her, ferocious and cruel and yet she clung to him. She wanted him. God, how she wanted him. "You lie and you cheat and you walk around dressed to shine, blue-blooded and untouchable. But *this*. This is who you really are."

He thrust in once again, harder than before, and she ignited.

The wildfire consumed her. She shook and she clenched. She lost herself in the molten, delirious rush.

And she heard him murmur a word she didn't understand as he followed her over that edge.

She had no idea how long they stood like that, tipped back against the wall with him so deep inside her.

But everything was different now, and so when he recovered himself sufficiently to stand, there was no hint of the Renzo who had taken such care of her in Monaco. That Renzo had carried her to his bath and wiped her gently with a cloth, lest she ache in any way. This Renzo merely set her to the ground and stepped back.

"Two hours," he told her hoarsely. And she did not imagine that the hoarseness in his voice was from the exertion. Not when she could see the dark temper in his eyes. He tucked himself away and zipped himself, and he never shifted that terrible glare from her.

She had lost herself. He had not. She needed to remember that.

"I can't do that," she whispered. "I can't—"

"You will do it," Renzo told her, as if it was a foregone conclusion. "You will call this farce of a wedding off and meet me down in that lane. Or, Sophie, I will teach you a thing or two about consequences."

There were at least two hundred people in the hall, representing almost anyone with any nod toward nobility in all of Europe.

Which was to say, Sophie told herself harshly, these people were not her friends. They weren't here for her. They weren't even here for Dal. This wedding was nothing but a business arrangement, which made the guest list something like…a collection of business associates.

The business they were in was continuing their ancient bloodlines, no matter the cost. And maintaining all the wealth and estates that went with the kind of bloodlines that had been around since the Crusades and in some cases, long before. Standing in the back of the chapel at Langston House, Sophie could pick out any number of couples she'd known forever who had married for similar reasons.

"You will find that our sort of marriages last longer than those predicated on sentiment," her mother had told her when Sophie had failed to entirely hide the emotion on her face at her engagement celebration—a thinly veiled business opportunity for her father and newly minted fiancé. "If you do not give yourself over to false notions of passion and romance, the opiate of the masses and the path to despair if you're not careful, you will discover that a partnership based on shared goals and opportunities is far more secure than any of that other nonsense."

Sophie had been telling herself for years that she believed it.

There was no reason that should claw at her now.

She had waited out those two hours, feeling sicker by the moment. She had done nothing. She had not summoned her father to tell him that things had changed, irrevocably. She hadn't gone to find Dal. She'd run herself a bath and climbed into it, piling her hair on top of her head and letting the steam billow all around her. She'd sunk down deep and sat there so long that if there was water on her face, she couldn't have said whether it was the bath, the heat, or the tears she didn't want to admit she still had it in her to cry.

She thought she might have sat there all day. It felt as if decades had passed. Her skin began to wrinkle and she'd had to run the hot water again and again to keep it warm—but soon enough there was a knock on the door.

Sophie had closed her eyes tight, then opened them. And reminded herself that no one could possibly know that she was faintly swollen and tender between her legs unless she told them—which she obviously wouldn't do. Of course she wouldn't.

The knocking had come again and she'd made herself call out the appropriate reply, bright and happy the way a bride should sound on her wedding day.

Poppy had come in the way she always did. Bustling, optimistic Poppy, who could make the best of anything.

Even this.

She'd dressed in the adjoining room, a bright salon with breakfast waiting, though Sophie hadn't been hungry. She'd sipped at a strong cup of tea while her hair and makeup had been done. Her bridesmaids had trooped in and out. Her mother had even made an appearance, smiling rigidly at the scene and then excusing herself after the photographer suggested one too many mother-daughter shots.

Because Lady Carmichael-Jones was not sentimental. At all.

It had taken Sophie a while to dress. The wedding gown she'd chosen was wide and long, as classic and traditional as everything else today, and took over the whole of one wall in her dressing room. It was a soft, dreamy white, a lovely complement to how she'd dressed Poppy and the rest in a faint pink, as soft as a whisper, to bring out the coloring that her pretty friend believed she didn't possess.

"You are absolutely beautiful," she'd told Poppy when her friend had come in, fully dressed.

"Don't be silly," Poppy demurred, the way she always did, and had run her hands over the dress that actually suited her curves rather than hiding them. "You're the most beautiful woman anyone has ever seen. Even more so today."

Sophie had only smiled, because she felt a great many things that morning and not one of them made her feel beautiful.

The countdown to two hours had long since passed, and nothing had happened. Renzo had not appeared in all his dark fury. No one had come rushing to the room where Sophie was getting ready to tell her that he had turned up and was shouting horrendous, salacious truths in the middle of Langston House. No one had suggested she look up one of the gossip websites, or had brandished a tabloid.

No one had stopped in to let her know that a fairly well-known stranger had appeared, uninvited, and demanded that he speak to Dal.

Or worse, her father.

And it was only when she was stepping into her wedding gown and letting Poppy button her into it as if she was tightening the bars on Sophie's cage that she understood that what she was feeling the most was a kind of... disappointment.

She could still feel Renzo between her legs, sweet and stinging faintly from his intense possession.

Perhaps the truth was that she'd expected that to mean something.

After all this, after everything Renzo had done and she had said to him, she still thought he would rescue her.

There was a lesson in this mess, she thought now as the music started. She was already in place down at the end of the long aisle, standing silently beside her father. She could see Poppy standing up before her, down at the altar where Dal waited, looking for all intents and purposes as if he was waiting for a bus. A bus that might in fact have run late, thus mildly inconveniencing him.

That was her groom.

And this is your life, she reminded herself, before she said or did something that might inspire her father to take it upon himself to say something similar.

There was no escape. She'd been foolhardy to imagine otherwise for even a moment.

Her father took her arm and began the long, slow walk, while Sophie tried not to panic about the fact she would be expected to grow old with a man who held her in the kind of esteem he lavished on a bus.

She would have to sleep with him. *Have sex* with him. How had she never thought of that before?

Sophie had considered it in the abstract, of course. But since that night in Monaco, she'd gone out of her way to avoid thinking about that part of things in any kind of detail. Dal would want heirs, naturally. She knew it was part of her job to provide them. And there was only one way she knew to go about doing that.

She tried to imagine Dal taking Renzo's place in any of the things she'd done with him—

But her stomach lurched.

Everyone was standing and looking at her. There were cameras and phones held aloft.

And Sophie's father was walking her down the aisle toward the duty he'd prepared her for since the cradle.

Whether you like it or not, whether your stomach lurches or not, you are going to have to do your duty, she snapped at herself. Here and in the marital bed.

She told herself it couldn't be that bad. Women had been surrendering their bodies to duty and responsibility for centuries and somehow, the world kept turning. It wouldn't kill her to do her part.

Her parents had said as much today.

They had stood with her in the antechamber before the ceremony, standing side by side, both of them tall and trim and perfectly composed. They never touched, Sophie had noticed, the way she always did. Having now experienced sex herself, she didn't entirely believe that they ever had.

"This is a marvelous day for our family," her father had said, sounding as close to jovial as Sophie had ever heard him. Which was to say, he sounded slightly less wooden and disinterested than usual. "I only wish that the former earl had lived long enough to see us merge the families together like this. It's just as we always planned."

"Oh, happy day," Sophie had replied.

And didn't entirely realize how sharp her voice was until she caught the quelling look her mother threw her.

"Pull yourself together, please," Lady Carmichael-Jones had said coolly. Because she was always so cool she might as well have been sculpted from a block of ice. "It would not do to have the new Countess of Langston mewling and carrying on like a common trollop getting married in the back of a pub, would it?"

That was the sort of cutting comment that would normally slice Sophie into bits and leave her tongue-tied and embarrassed. Her mother's specialty.

But Sophie wasn't the person she had been five weeks ago. Or last night.

Or even this morning when she'd woken up.

Oh, no. Now Sophie was exactly what Renzo had made her. What he'd called her and then what he'd showed her she was. Perhaps this was who she'd been all along.

A dark and greedy thing. Selfish. Base and low and far more of a trollop than her mother could possibly imagine, Sophie was sure.

More to the point, she wasn't afraid of everything the way she'd been before, because the worst had already happened.

It was continuing to happen right now.

"Have you spent a lot of time in the back of pubs, then, Mother?" she'd asked.

The temperature in the antechamber had plummeted.

"Let me be clear, Sophie," her father had said after a moment of silence dragged out into several. Each icier than the last. "My expectation, in case there is some confusion, is that you will acquit yourself appropriately in all things. You were not raised to traipse about the planet, racking up indiscretions and becoming tabloid fodder for housewives in Harrogate to tut over in their local Asda."

"You should consider this an opportunity," her mother had agreed. "To remove yourself from the tiresome social media narrative that seems to have your generation in its claws."

No one waited to see if Sophie was interested in narratives one way or another, she'd noticed. Much less if she'd like to exclude herself from one of them.

Because none of this was about her. None of this was ever about her.

"When in doubt," her father had told her with great satisfaction, "think of your duty. Family and sacrifice is what has made the Carmichael-Jones family great. It will see you through."

"No matter what comes your way," her mother had added, "and no matter how unpleasant, all you need to do is remember who you are."

On her father's arm now, Sophie walked as slowly as possible down the aisle. As slow as she could without looking as if she was dragging her feet—or making her father look as if he was actually dragging her toward her groom.

She was fairly certain that little speech had been her mother's version of instructing her only daughter to lie back and think of England.

But all Sophie could really think about was Renzo. And how, when she was with him, she thought of nothing at all. Not England. Not sacrifice. Not who she was or wasn't.

Because there was only him. There was only that dark, addicting magic he spun with his hands. His mouth.

That hard length of him, surging deep inside of her.

But if there was a less appropriate place to think of such things, Sophie couldn't imagine it.

The faces of the guests were a blur around her. Inside, she was nothing but a scream. Loud, long.

But no one could hear her.

No one could ever hear her.

She was the one in the white dress, walking down the aisle toward the altar, the center of everyone's attention—

But she knew perfectly well that no one saw her. Not really.

Only Renzo ever had.

First in Monaco. But this morning here, too.

The man standing there, waiting for her at the end of the aisle, had never seen her. Not the real her. He saw what she represented. Her father's wealth and lands. But she could have been anyone. If Sophie's father had been in possession of sixteen daughters, she knew perfectly well that Dal would have chosen whoever was most expedient, not necessarily Sophie.

It had nothing to do with *her*.

She understood that it never would.

More than that, she understood with a blinding sort of clarity everything she would have to do if she wanted to keep her baby safe in this particular cage she was walking into.

For all her bold talk to Renzo earlier, she actually agreed with him.

Dal might be more ice sculpture than man, but he was still the Earl of Langston. She could not imagine any scenario in which he would knowingly raise another man's child as his.

That meant it was on Sophie to keep her baby safe.

And *that* meant it was also on Sophie to make certain her marital duty was taken care of as soon as possible. A baby might be a few weeks early, but push it a few months and that was begging for trouble.

She tried to visualize it as she moved. She put one foot in front of the other and she forced herself to imagine it.

They would lie down together in a grand bed somewhere as befit an earl. Assuming she didn't immediately contract hypothermia from a single touch of chilly Dal's hand, how bad could it be?

But there was a sinking sensation inside of her, and Sophie had the unpleasant feeling that it could be very, very bad indeed.

Because even if it was unremarkable and indifferent, it still wouldn't be Renzo.

That harsh little truth sank its claws in deep, and tore at her.

But she kept walking.

Her eyes blurred. Her stomach heaved.

Sophie gripped the flowers in her hands so tight she could feel the moisture from the crushed stems making her palms sticky.

And still she walked.

She set her teeth against her tongue and bit down, so she would not say a word. No sobs. No screams. No trollops in pubs.

Just a dignified silence, no matter if it killed her. This wasn't about her anymore. This was about her baby. She would lie back and think of her baby.

England could burn for all she cared, as long as her baby was safe.

Sophie was three-quarters of the way down the aisle when the doors slammed open behind her.

She saw Dal stand at attention, the blank look on his face sharpening.

Next to him, Poppy jolted, and then her face brightened.

"A thousand apologies," she heard Renzo—because of course it was Renzo—drawl out, louder than all the gasps and muttering. "But I am afraid that there has been a change of plans."

Sophie told herself not to move. To pretend it wasn't happening, even as her father dropped her arm and wheeled around.

But she couldn't help herself. She felt…itchy and wild, or maybe she was afraid that she was hallucinating. She didn't know.

And there, three-quarters of the way down the aisle toward the man she'd been promised to when she was still a child, she turned.

She faced Renzo instead.

Renzo, whose eyes were dark amber and hot with rage. And a deep possessiveness that should have terrified her. It didn't. If anything, she welcomed it.

Renzo, who strode toward her, looking for all the world as if he was out for a quiet, low-key saunter.

Right here in the middle of her wedding.

In the movies, people cried out in moments like these. People leaped up. Everyone reacted, instantly.

But not today. Not here.

Sophie was frozen in place. Her father was beside her, and she could *feel* his scowl, but he didn't move. Around them, lined in all the chapel's pews, there was nothing but shocked silence.

And then Renzo was right there before her.

"I warned you," he murmured.

And then he simply bent, swept Sophie in his arms, and tossed her over his shoulder.

"This is unacceptable!" her father blurted out then.

"This is inevitable," Renzo corrected him, with tremendous calm, as if he wasn't in the middle of abducting a bride from her own wedding. "Accept it now or later, old man. Your choice."

Renzo spun around, making Sophie dizzy, and headed toward the door.

And with every step he took, there was more noise, and not only in Sophie's head.

A voice she thought might belong to her mother, exclaiming, which was something Lady Carmichael-Jones never did, and certainly not in public—

But then Renzo pushed his way through the doors and carried her out into the tremulous summer morning as if he had every right.

He tipped her over again, but only to set her down beside that same low-slung car he'd been driving the night before. He opened the door, then handed her in, and she didn't pretend for a moment that his grip on her arm wasn't anything but an order.

"Do not make me chase you," he told her as he slammed the car door shut.

She was in shock, Sophie thought distantly. Her dress was an impractical layer cake, filling up the interior of the car, flowing over everything. The gearshift. The emergency brake. Most of the console.

She didn't understand until Renzo threw himself into the driver's seat that she could have taken that opportunity to run. To do...*something*. Escape, maybe. Lock him out of his own car, for another. Anything, actually, to indicate that she wasn't on board with being carted out of her own wedding.

But it was too late.

Renzo turned the ignition and the car roared to life.

"I told you what would happen," he bit out.

"So you did."

She didn't sound like herself. But then, if Sophie had learned anything today, it was that she had no idea who she was. Or, to be more accurate, she'd discovered that it was possible she'd never been who she'd imagined herself to be in the first place.

Because surely the proper little heiress, raised from birth to marry the Earl of Langston, would have…fought this.

Struggled, even a little bit.

Instead of what Sophie had done, which was exhale as Renzo had carried her out of that church. As if he'd saved her, after all.

Of course the proper little heiress would likely not have turned up to her own wedding pregnant with another man's child, so there was that.

And now it was done. Even if she tossed herself out of this car at the first turn in the road and ran back to Langston House, the damage was done. There would be no carrying on with the wedding. There would be no pretending this hadn't happened.

There would have to be explanations. And she was still pregnant.

Renzo took a turn too fast on his way out of the Langston estate, exhibiting all the mastery and control that had made him such a star on the racetrack.

He flashed her a look, dark and unreadable, before he took another curve.

And she felt that where she was still tender. She felt it everywhere, inside and out, as if they were connected. As if they were tied up tight to each other with more than just one night in Monaco and an unborn child.

More even than the disrupted wedding of the year.

"Congratulations," Sophie said quietly. "You have well and truly ruined my life."

But Renzo only laughed, that dark shower of sound, male and rough, that made everything worse.

And better, something treacherous whispered inside her.

Because she could feel it.

Sophie could *feel* again, as if that chapel had been antiseptic and gray and this was all sensation and bright color. She didn't know how to process it. She wasn't sure she could.

"I believe I told you I would," Renzo said, and shifted the car into a higher gear, smooth and fast. It felt like a metaphor. And he still had all that laughter in his voice, which was nothing but lightning inside of her, flash after flash. "You are welcome."

CHAPTER SIX

"I HATE TO interrupt this kidnapping," Sophie said mildly when Renzo pulled his sports car onto the tarmac next to his waiting jet at a private airfield outside of London. "But I'm not certain you've thought through the practicalities."

"You will find, *cara*, that I am nothing if not practical. I did not build myself an empire by chance and the liberal application of frothy daydreams."

Renzo didn't wait for her to reply. He was up and out of the car, then moving around the front of it, never taking his eyes off the bridal confection exploding over the front seat of his favorite Bugatti.

It would have helped considerably if Sophie was not *quite* so beautiful, he thought as he moved. Or if, every time he had a taste of her, he didn't simply want more.

More and more, as if she was an addiction.

Renzo had never permitted himself the weakness of addiction, despite the many temptations he'd fielded over the years. Drugs and drink, gambling, women—he'd had a cool head where all were concerned, always. Something spiked and edgy rolled around inside him at the notion that this woman could be what finally changed that.

She's already changed you into a slavering addict, he told himself coldly. *How many other women have you abducted?*

Renzo gritted his teeth, opened the passenger door, and took Sophie's hand to help her climb out of the low, muscular car.

The worst part was, he wasn't immune to the symbolism of the pretty girl in the long white dress, especially as she climbed out of what he had to admit was a particularly masculine sports car. She looked like she should be starring in the wedding he had always assumed he would have one day, if only so he could ensure the legitimacy of the next generation of Crisantis.

No child of his would bear the stigma Renzo had. Not as long as he drew breath.

Of course he had always assumed that he would choose his own bride. Not that she would present herself, already pregnant and dressed for the part.

But if Renzo had learned anything over the course of his determined climb out of the pit of his humble beginnings, it was that nothing ever went as planned. Ever. He'd learned to accept that and more, to lean into the curves life threw at him, long ago.

It was that or crash.

"Where are we going?" Sophie asked.

Renzo hated her composure. It had slipped a bit, there in that chapel at Langston House. He'd seen a sheen of emotion in her gaze when he'd set her down next to the car outside the wedding ceremony. But with every mile he'd driven her away from her stable little life, she'd recovered her equanimity. Her spine had grown straighter against the back of her seat. Meanwhile, her filmy, gauzy gown had been everywhere, filling up the car. Flowing all over his legs, his lap. Reminding Renzo of what he'd done—what he'd set in stone, with no possibility of changing his mind—with every moment.

Not that he was likely to forget.

"We are going to Sicily, of course," he told her as he led

her across the tarmac. He told himself she needed the help, dressed as she was, but he had the lowering suspicion that despite his towering rage at her attempted betrayal, what he really wanted was to just keep touching her. He cast that aside as he glared at her. "Where, pray, did you imagine I would take the mother of my only child?"

She didn't like it when he called her that, he could see. Something flashed in her gaze, making the gold in all that melting brown gleam a little bit harder. But she only lifted her chin.

"I didn't think you would take me at all. As you must have suspected when you found me halfway down the aisle toward a different groom."

"Did you not? A pity."

His temper had cooled, Renzo realized, and he now felt something very like expansive. At his ease, even. It was because he'd solved the issue at hand, whether Sophie was aware of it or not. There was nothing left but the technicalities. Where they would marry to provide his child with legitimacy. When they would accomplish this. And in between their inevitable wedding and the birth of their child? Well. There was a whole host of punishments he could inflict upon the woman who had walked down that aisle, carrying his child, with every intention of pretending it belonged to another man.

Renzo wouldn't be getting over that anytime soon.

"Perhaps, in time, you will learn that I do not make idle threats."

"Will there be more threats then?" She asked the question brightly, and even smiled that razor-edged, polite smile of hers that no doubt cut England's pedigreed hordes into pieces where they stood. It had a far different effect on him, and all of it located where he was hardest. "That certainly gives me something to look forward to."

Renzo ushered her toward the steps of the plane, unfolded before them, and forced himself to let go of her hand. Because he didn't want to let go of it. Or her. And that was unacceptable.

"It cheers me that you can maintain your sense of humor under such trying circumstances, Sophie," he said when they reached the bottom of the steps. He nodded at his waiting staff, then returned his attention to the woman beside him. "It inspires me to imagine that what lies ahead will not set you back at all. I look forward to this…what do you call it? Your British lip?"

She regarded him for a moment. "A stiff upper lip, presumably?"

"Just so." It was Renzo's turn to smile, and he took it, pleased to see her pulse jump in her throat. "I look forward to seeing it in action in the days to come."

"I am desolated, of course, to throw a monkey wrench in the midst of what sounds like some truly delightful plans." Sophie did not look anything like desolate. She treated him to that smile again, that he imagined women of her class were taught in their finishing schools as a matter of course. "And I certainly do not wish to impugn your manhood, but I don't think you're going to be able to simply pick me up and carry me into a foreign country. It generally requires a passport, for a start."

"The passport you left in your bag," Renzo agreed lazily. "Along with the rest of your luggage, carefully packed for your honeymoon as a countess. Alas, that is a trip you will not be taking."

"You have my passport?"

"I would suggest that you stop underestimating me, Sophie. There will come a time where I will only find it insulting."

"You were…in my room? Going through my things?"

She had started to move while she spoke, climbing the stairs as she held her wedding gown in huge bunches on either side. And still it slipped and spilled everywhere, catching every little hint of breeze.

All he wanted to do was peel it off of her, inch by inch. And then burn it, because it represented the great wrong she had attempted to perpetrate upon him. And while the fire raged, feast on what waited beneath all that soft white fabric.

But she wasn't on the menu at the moment, he reminded himself.

Not quite yet.

Renzo waited until they'd cleared the stairs entirely and had moved inside to the lounge area of his plane. He nodded toward one of the deep, cushy seats and Sophie sank into it, aiming her well-bred frown directly at him.

Because he was supposed to apologize, he imagined, for helping himself to her travel documents and what few garments of hers did not look as if she'd purchased them specifically for her new husband.

"Do you expect me to apologize?" he asked when it appeared she intended to stare at him forever, frown locked in place.

"Certainly not," she said in a tone that conveyed the opposite. "Why apologize for pawing through my belongings? Perhaps that's normal where you come from."

"What is normal?" He took his own seat and lounged back in it, keeping his gaze steady on hers. "Is it—to pick an example at random—giving someone a false name and sneaking off in the middle of the night? Is it summoning them for an illicit meeting in the dark on a deserted country road, but failing to mention the most important piece of information? Or, wait. I know." And Renzo smiled at her then, not nicely, until she jerked slightly where she sat. "Normal must be a woman who finds herself pregnant with one man's child, yet chooses to march herself down the aisle toward another."

"I think you'll find that such things are a whole lot more normal than the fragile egos of men may wish to acknowledge," Sophie said drily.

"Is it my fragile ego you think you have damaged here today?" He raised his brows. "Or, perhaps, it is your grasp of human decency that leaves something to be desired."

Renzo thought she looked pale at that, and her eyes glittered. She made a small production out of folding her hands in her lap, and as she did it she sat a bit straighter. As if she was a queen on a throne, not a bride on the run.

He understood that this was the Carmichael-Jones heiress he was seeing before him now. This was the woman Sophie had been raised to become. Quiet, composed. Perfect for the stale, dry duties of a countess and nothing at all like the wild, half-mad, lustful creature she became when his hands were on her.

Something to file away for later. When he could better take advantage of her weakness, as well as his own.

"Do you have any other objections?" he asked her when she only stared back at him as if her gaze alone could shame him. Little did she know that a man raised in shame chose his path early. Either he lived in shame or became immune to it. Renzo had chosen the latter. And along with it, all those other pointless emotions that governed the lives of others. Love, for example. His father had beaten that out of him, too. "Any other obstacles you imagine you can throw in the path of what cannot be avoided? I invite you to try. Give it your best shot. I assure you, I have thought of everything."

She seemed to take a remarkably long time to moisten her lips, and it turned out he was not immune to that. At all. He shifted in his seat, lest she see the power she had over him.

"How long will we be in Sicily?"

"But that is the best part. Did I not mention it?" Renzo

truly enjoyed himself as he let his mouth curve at that. "As long as it takes, Sophie. That is how long we will be in Sicily. As long as it takes."

He wasn't surprised she didn't have much else to say after that. Nor did she ask him to clarify what he meant, because he was certain she didn't want to know.

And he was more than happy to let her stew.

Once the plane was aloft, Sophie excused herself to one of the staterooms. Renzo let her go. He had more than enough business to tend to, as ever, and anyway, he could allow her a little bit of solitude to process what had happened to her this morning. She'd woken to find him right there in her bedroom, confronting her with the scope of her lies and the *consequences*. She'd fought him and then she'd let him take her in a kind of fever, right there against a wall in her fiancé's ancestral home. She'd more than *let* him. She'd been an active, excited participant in that same immolation.

And then she'd gone ahead with her damned wedding anyway. That filled Renzo with pure, unadulterated rage every time he considered it, so he concentrated instead on the part he liked better.

That being when he'd thrown open those chapel doors, strode inside, and taken what was his.

He had never met the Earl of Langston before. Nor any of the well-titled, effortlessly wealthy people who'd attended that wedding. Nonetheless, he'd recognized the type. The big hats and conservative dress of the English peers. The carefully elegant European aristocrats as they'd submitted to another tediously proper ceremony celebrating two of their own. He was vaguely surprised his father wasn't among them in all his princely regalia. By contrast, Renzo was nothing but a beggar at the feast.

But he'd still walked away with the prize.

And there was not one single part of him, the cast-off

bastard son of a man very like the people who'd sat in that chapel and tutted their outrage very quietly indeed, that hadn't enjoyed every moment of that.

An enjoyment that would only get better and deeper with time, he was well aware. Because he hadn't simply stolen the Carmichael-Jones heiress away from her destiny. Oh, no. Anyone could have an affair with a dirty commoner and many people in Sophie's nosebleed-high class did. Repeatedly. But in nine months, Sophie would provide this particular cast-off Sicilian bastard with a child, thereby reminding the entire world of the fact she'd permitted him into her sapphire-blue, aristocratic body.

Thereby polluting her haughty, noble blood.

All he needed to do was marry her first, to add insult to injury and make sure that pollution was entirely legitimate.

He was practically jubilant.

And when Sophie did not emerge from the stateroom in what he considered a reasonable amount of time, Renzo went looking for her.

He found her out of her wedding gown at last and showered, with damp hair dripping on her shoulders. She'd changed into some of the clothes he'd packed for her—a pair of trousers that molded to her shapely legs and a soft, desperately fragile sweater in a shade of pale rose that made her seem to glow as she sat there at the foot of the bed.

That was the trouble with Sophie. She was as beautiful here, now, bedraggled and brown eyes wide, as she had been in that wedding gown. Or even that night in Monaco, gleaming as she had in all the bright lights of Monte Carlo.

"Are you hiding?" Renzo asked.

"Of course I am." She gazed back at him, unsmiling, and he found himself unduly taken with the fact her narrow feet were bare, her toenails painted a glossy red. "Is this the part where you gloat?"

He shrugged. "I prefer to do my gloating naked. Otherwise it is less satisfying, you understand."

"So many things to look forward to. I can hardly contain myself."

He handed her what he'd brought for her and watched her reaction as she took it. She blanched, which surprised him. Then held it gingerly before her, as if she expected it to bite.

"I would have thought you would want your mobile," he said, studying her and her reaction. "Desperately, in fact."

She flipped her mobile phone over and over in her hand. "The thing is, you don't actually know anything about me. So I expect you're going to be in for a great many surprises."

"Every socialite I've ever met is attached to her mobile," Renzo said with a certain quiet menace that even he could feel fill the small, compact room. "But of course, you are a special little unicorn, are you not?"

Sophie tossed the phone onto the bed beside her. And if his sardonic tone bothered her, she didn't show it when she fixed that cool brown gaze of hers on him. Very much as if she was the one in charge here.

"Talk me through how this is going to work," she said. It was an order.

Renzo opted not to take the opportunity to show her how very much he objected to being given orders. That, too, could wait.

"Do what I tell you to do," he said instead. "It is as simple as that."

She did not look as if she appreciated his simplicity.

"You've dramatically, theatrically, kidnapped me from my own wedding," she said. "I can't say that I really mind leaving England while all of the fallout from that happens. I imagine it will get ugly."

"It is already ugly." He nodded at her mobile. "You can see for yourself. It's on all the online gossip sites already."

Sophie didn't even glance at the mobile beside her on the bed. She wrinkled up her nose instead.

"And who is more evil in the retelling? You, for storming Langston House? Or me, for allowing you to carry me off?"

"Opinions are split."

"They won't be for long." Sophie's smile was brittle. "I think you'll find that the woman is always, always at fault in these things. No matter what happens. You can expect to be hailed as a great alpha hero while I will be relegated to the role of just another slut in want of a good shaming."

Renzo assumed that was meant to be a slap at him. What astonished him was that he felt it as such.

"It is not as if you fought to escape me," Renzo pointed out, perhaps a little more harshly than necessary. "You didn't even complain. The truth is that you had no wish to marry that man. I await your expressions of gratitude that I saved you from your fate." His smile felt thin. "Don't flood me with them all at once."

"Whether I wanted to marry him or did not hardly matters."

"It matters to me."

Sophie faltered at that. Then drew herself up. "What matters is that I didn't marry him, after all. The trouble with that is, there were two hundred guests at that wedding and any number of photographers. I'm sure there was a stampede to make it to the tabloids."

"I note that this is your concern." He lounged in the doorway to the stateroom, one shoulder against the doorjamb, as if there wasn't entirely too much of that dark mess he refused to name rumbling around inside him. "I have not heard you mention your earl."

"I am certain that Dal had a moment of concern over the

numerous business enterprises he and my father planned to combine. Just as I'm certain that his first call was to his bank manager."

"This is why I am a romantic," Renzo murmured. "Such love. Such passion. It makes my heart beat faster."

"I don't need you to understand my arrangement with Dal," Sophie said coolly. "What I do need you to understand is that you caused an enormous scandal. That's going to follow both of us." She slid her hand over her belly, which was still the same size Renzo remembered tasting. Repeatedly. It fascinated him that there was a child in there. *His* child. "It will follow this baby around. You understand, don't you? This is something that will never go away."

"And this is a problem…why?"

"Thank you for answering my question, eventually. In a roundabout way." She shook her head. "I'll take all this to mean we'll be staying in Sicily for quite a long time."

"This is not something you need to concern yourself with." Renzo straightened in the doorway. "Your days of merrily skipping around the globe, from this party to that party—"

"I believe you have me confused for some other social-ite," Sophie said drily. "Or perhaps an American reality television star. The future Countess of Langston was not a party girl by any estimation. That would have been very seriously frowned upon. Of course, in retrospect, perhaps a party or two would have been better than running out on my own wedding."

"I warned you not to cross me," Renzo reminded her softly. So softly that she flinched a little bit. He watched the tense way she held herself and told himself that what he felt then was triumph. Not that little prickle of the sort of shame he'd thought he'd exorcised years ago. "You could have met me as I asked. You could have canceled your wedding on your own. You chose to make it into a scene instead."

"I don't think I'm the one who made it a scene."

"I gave you the opportunity to take responsibility for what you had done." His voice was gruff, his gaze hot. It felt a little too much like losing control. "You did not take that opportunity. And as you're so fond of consequences, I am sure you will appreciate that there is a price to be paid for that as well."

"So many prices to be paid around you," Sophie said, though she never dropped his gaze. "I can't imagine why you're still single. But then, who could possibly afford you?"

Renzo did not permit himself to lose control. Ever. He had to take a moment to make certain he was not about to do so here. He had been pushed around by far weightier opponents than Sophie Carmichael-Jones, for God's sake. His own father had taught him entirely too many things about his own breaking points. There was no possible way he could allow this woman to wedge herself any further beneath his skin.

Or at the very least, he couldn't let her see that she'd already done it.

"What I care about is the child," Renzo told her when he was certain he could sound appropriately composed. "I enjoy your body, of course. I think you know that."

He liked turning the tables on her a little too much, perhaps. He liked the spots of color that appeared on her face when he said things like that. He liked the way she let out a shuddery sort of breath.

Most of all, he liked the way she held her tongue, as if she feared that saying something would result in another intense taking, the way it had this morning.

Though perhaps *fear* was not the right word to describe the look in her eyes.

"But I have always had more women than I know what to do with," Renzo continued, and he liked delivering that particular blow most of all. "I cannot imagine any scenario in which I would steal a woman who belongs to another save this one. I would caution you not to read anything personal into it."

"What a shame," she managed to say, her brown eyes glittering with something hectic that he couldn't quite read. "And here I'd planned to start writing you love letters."

"You can make jokes, Sophie. But I know how you sound when you come apart in my hands. I also know that you have never had any man but me. In the days to come, you will likely be tempted to make this something that is not."

"Oh, no," Sophie said, holding his gaze, her own dark with temper. "I don't think that's going to be a problem."

"I'm delighted to hear it. I don't believe in such emotions. And while you are busy not getting the wrong idea about anything because you are so sophisticated, you are free to consider yourself a surrogate. With benefits."

"I hope that by 'with benefits' you do not mean sex," Sophie bit out at him, bristling where she sat. "Because what happened in Langston House will never happen again. That was the absolute last time—"

"Yes, yes." Renzo didn't exactly roll his eyes, as he was not a teenage girl, but he came close. "You will never touch me again. You are a vestal virgin, made new by the force of your outrage. Spare me the puffed up, Puritan melodrama, if you please. I doubt very much you could resist me if you tried."

"I think you'll find I can. Happily and easily and with joy in my heart."

"You have thus far proven otherwise, *cara*. Repeatedly. When all is said and done, you are an inexperienced little thing who has had the very bad luck to imprint on me while attempting to cheat me out of my own child. Don't imagine that I'm above using it. I'm not above using anything it takes to get exactly what I want."

She surged up from the end of the bed then, her hands in fists at her sides. A better man would not have found that arousing.

Renzo thanked god he was not a better man, by any stretch of the imagination.

"I would be careful if I were you, Renzo," Sophie seethed at him. "If you teach someone how to use a weapon, sooner or later, they'll use it on you."

"I will look forward to that sparring match, then," he said, and waved a dismissive hand, right there in front of her face to make sure she felt sufficiently condescended to. "Back to reality, if you please. You will be my surrogate, with benefits, as I said. And I will promise you one thing. You will beg me to take you. That is inevitable." She looked as if she might pop, so flushed with fury was she then. "But that is merely sex. It is hardly worth discussing. The part I want you to pay particular attention to is this. You will live in my home in Sicily. You will be obedient. If you simply do as you are bid, we will get along famously."

She looked mutinous. "If you say so."

"I'm not a quiet, reserved man, like your earl," Renzo told her, his voice mild enough but the steel beneath it impossible to miss. "I do not suffer in silence. In truth, I do not suffer at all. I have created a life for myself where suffering of any kind is expressly outlawed. I will not put up with any of your antics. You *will* obey."

"Because you don't care if I suffer. Only if you do."

He smiled. "Precisely."

"And what does obedience look like in this delightful prison you've prepared for me?" she asked, her voice a little bit scratchy. To match the temper he could see written all over her, he assumed. "I'm going to need you to lay it all out for me."

"You will meet with my family doctor when we arrive," he told her. Stern and uncompromising. "You will follow his recommendations to the letter. You will be pleasant at all times."

He moved from the doorway then and he liked it when he stepped so close to her that she was forced to tip her head back to meet his eyes. He liked the heat he could see there. The truths that heat told no matter what lies spilled from her lips.

"You have spent all these years practicing how to be elegant. That is what I expect. You have the opportunity to be an aristocratic ornament in my home, Sophie. Do you not feel complimented?"

From the look on her face, she was not only not complimented in the least, she would have torn into him with her fingers if she thought she could get away with it.

"So in your imagination, a pregnant woman will flit about your house, decorously. Not lumber about as I grow big and unwieldy. Is that about it?"

"More or less."

"And should morning sickness overtake me, what then? Is there a place where I can be prettily, obediently sick so as not to distress you with such inelegance?"

"I have a large and well-trained staff, of course. I'm not an animal, Sophie. I'm offended you would imagine otherwise."

"Wonderful. So I'll be trotted out before you only when I am fit to be seen." She studied him for a moment. "Is that how you plan to treat your child?"

He reached over and helped himself to a wet, dark chunk of her hair, curling there against her shoulder. He tugged on it, perhaps not as gently as he might have.

But then, she kept landing blows.

"You don't need to concern yourself with how I will treat the child you tried to take from me," he told her softly. Almost sweetly. "If I were you, I would spend some time learning how to resign myself to the future before you. You will not be returning to England anytime soon. You do not have to worry yourself with whatever scandal we've left behind there today. You've just signed yourself up for nine months in my exclusive company. If I were you, I'd spend a little time contemplating what that means."

"Nine months," she repeated, as if it was a death sentence "And then what? Will you toss me out the door as soon as I'm finished with labor?"

"There will be ample time to figure such things out then," he told her, gazing down at her. That pretty face. Those melting brown eyes with hints of gold. He had to remind himself how little she could be trusted. "Visitation rights, for example, because I am certainly not handing you primary custody of my own child. And little things like when and how to divorce so that it damages the child the least, and causes me as little aggravation as possible."

She blinked. Then frowned. "Divorce?"

"Of course," Renzo said. "You cannot imagine that I would wish to be married forever to a woman who once attempted to steal my child from me and hand it to another man to raise as his? Can you be so foolish?"

She actually laughed at that. "Can *you* be so foolish as to imagine I would ever—*ever*—marry you? You seem to keep glossing this over, Renzo, because you think you know something about me because we had sex. But you ruined my life today."

"Oh, Sophie," he said, and even laughed a little himself. "It amuses me that you imagine you will have a choice. You won't. You had your opportunity to make a choice and you made the wrong one. I will not be so benevolent as to allow it again."

He considered putting his hands on her then and there. He could show her just how easy it would be for him to make her beg him to make use of the benefits he mentioned—but he didn't do it. Not because he had turned into a saint in the course of this flight, God knew, but because he wanted her to fret about it. About all of it.

He wanted this to hurt. The problem with sex when it came to Sophie was that he enjoyed bringing her pleasure a little too much for it to be the punishment he wanted. And he wanted her pleasure more than he should have.

Renzo had no intention whatsoever of acknowledging that. And certainly not to her.

"But—" she began, but cut herself off when he shook his head.

"Look at that," he drawled, and very deliberately thrust his hands in his pockets before they started something he would regret. "You can be taught, after all."

CHAPTER SEVEN

SOPHIE EXPECTED RENZO to force her hand from the start. She steeled herself, expecting him to get in her face again and talk some more about *benefits*.

But once they landed in Sicily and were swept off to the village he called his, he left her to her own devices.

It took her at least a week to understand that it was all part of his design. That, like everything having to do with Renzo, it was part of a greater, diabolical plan.

Because he didn't have to do anything to leave her antsy and worried and half out of her mind with what she chose to call restlessness—and no matter that it seemed chiefly located between her legs. She did it to herself.

Day after day after day.

The village was named after an obscure saint and had been built on a hill, centuries ago. It was a tiny little place, filled with old buildings stacked one on top of the next and winding old roads that seemed to tie themselves in knots as they meandered up and down the steep slopes. The highest building in the town was the old church, named after yet another saint. Opposite it, on a steep slope all its own with sweeping views from the Aeolian Islands to the north to Mount Etna to the south, was a castle that had been built centuries ago by the Saracens and was now a painstakingly restored private home.

When Renzo had called this place *his* village, Sophie

discovered, he wasn't being unduly possessive. He'd restored the ancient castle and lived in it like a feudal lord.

The tiny little village that lay at his feet every morning when he woke to gaze down at it was historic, but remote. It was a solid hour and thirty minutes down out of the mountains to Taormina, not that anyone had offered to take Sophie to the only nearby city. Renzo's doctor had been waiting at the castle the day they'd arrived, and had given Sophie a comprehensive physical. He'd pronounced her in excellent health, assured her that the baby was fine, and had promised Renzo—not Sophie, but Renzo—that he would make weekly visits.

"I don't understand what I'm expected to do here," Sophie said after the first week had dragged by.

She had wandered all over the castle. She had walked the twenty minutes into town, down across a narrow little footbridge that spanned the steep ravine separating the castle from the village. She had spent time in the castle library.

Renzo was sitting behind the desk in the office he kept here. It was a vast suite of rooms, all arching ceilings and astonishing art, with a desk facing a wall of windows over the village. He looked up when she walked in and made a great show of putting down his mobile and fixing his attention on Sophie.

"Is that the point?" she asked. "Do you want to bore me into a coma?"

"You say this as if you normally spend your days neck-deep in industry," Renzo said in that *patience-sorely-tried* voice of his. It made her want to scream. And then he smirked, which only made it worse. "And I do not think that is the case. Unless you spent some quality time digging ditches of which I am unaware?"

Sophie ordered herself not to react. Because she was certain that was what he wanted.

She made herself smile instead. "You don't know me at all, as I keep having to point out to you. I've worked at charities since I left school."

"Ah yes. 'Worked.'"

He made quotation marks with his fingers around the word *worked*, and Sophie had to bite her own tongue to make the red haze of her temper ease back a little bit.

Because she refused—she *refused*—to give him what he wanted.

"I understand you find it hard to believe," she managed to say in as cool a tone as she could manage. "But I actually did work. It's one of the reasons Dal and I had such a long engagement. I didn't wish to be relegated to the ranks of the housewives, wealthy or otherwise, who do nothing but go to the charity parties without doing any of the charity work."

"You have sacrificed so much. Truly. And I'm certain your charitable impulses were in no way a delaying tactic to stave off your wedding for as long as possible."

"I'm sure it means nothing to you," she managed to say without snapping and shouting at him the way she wanted to do, especially as his sardonic tone felt like a torch held too close to her skin. Particularly because he was right, damn him. "But I didn't have a choice about who I was born to any more than you did. However, when my father wanted me to marry at eighteen, I declined."

She didn't tell him how hard that had been. How furious her father had been. How they'd forbidden her from leaving the house for a month as they'd tried to work on her, but she'd held firm.

It had been such a hideous ordeal that it stood to reason she'd been leery of signing up for it again.

Or that was what she'd told herself as her wedding had drawn close.

"I'm shocked that was an option." Renzo sat back in his

great leather chair, lounging there with that look on his face that made her hot with something she chose to believe was pure temper. It happened every time he showed how amused he was by her, and how deeply unimpressed. "I was under the impression that you gave your father the mindless obedience you have refused me. That you jumped whenever called."

"I did what I had to do," Sophie said evenly.

She'd walked too far into the room and stood there on the other side of his desk. There were chairs set there behind her, but she didn't take one. She enjoyed the false sense of power she got by standing above him while he sat.

And she had to make her own fun here. With him. Or she feared she would wither away.

"What is your goal here, Renzo?" she asked when it seemed he would be content to simply sit there, watching her as if she was an animal in a zoo. "Do you need me to apologize for every moment of my entire life? I can do that, though I think we both know that that's not actually what you're angry about."

"Perhaps not. But it would make a good start."

"After all," Sophie said, very deliberately, "anyone can see how you suffer. Here in this luxurious castle high on the hill, the lord of all you survey."

Renzo's gaze seemed to light on fire, and Sophie hated that she could feel it *inside* of her. Like flame in her bloodstream and between her legs, a lick of a different fire. He rose from his chair slowly. Deliberately.

And then he was towering above her again, and any advantage she might have imagined she had was lost—but she didn't let herself step back the way she wanted to do. She didn't run.

She held his gaze as if she was daring him to come for her.

Renzo's beautiful mouth hardened. "I lived in squalor. Every day I would walk the streets of this village and dream that one day, I would leave it. As I got older, the dream got more complicated. It wasn't enough to leave this place. I wanted to dominate it."

"I sympathize with the village."

He shook his head at her and the wide desk seemed insufficient, suddenly, to protect her from him. But Sophie ignored that, too.

"I believe you were telling me a very sad story about all you have suffered, were you not?" He looked ready for a fight, sculpted into a dangerous weapon all his own. She didn't know why she imagined she could be the one to give him that fight. "I am prepared to weep openly for you, Sophie. I am certain that any moment now, you will explain to me how your pampered upbringing made the poverty I scrambled about in seem very nearly charming by comparison."

"I was raised for a very specific purpose and that purpose only." Sophie didn't think she was going to convince this man of anything. She didn't know what made her think she ought to try. But she pushed on. "At least you had dreams. I didn't. I was told what my life would be like since I was small."

"Yes, the great tragedy of being raised to become a wealthy, aristocratic countess. My heart bleeds."

"You can mock it all you like," Sophie told him, her voice quiet and her gaze direct. "But that doesn't change it. If I had been a boy, of course, my father would have taught me the family business. But I was a girl, so I was required to marry a man who could handle the business instead."

"You could always have objected. Don't act as if you were helpless." He laughed, in that awful way of his that made everything in her clench tight because she remembered his real laughter. Sunshine and warmth, cascading all over her, making the whole night around them feel like honey, thick and sweet. This laugh just hurt. "A girl like you, everything handed to her on silver platters, is not helpless."

"I'm glad you think so," Sophie threw at him. "If you know so much about my life and how I felt at any given time, why don't you tell me how all this happened? How did I end up here, stranded in a Sicilian castle with a man who hates me? You're the expert, after all."

Renzo laughed again, and it had the same effect on Sophie. But then he moved out from behind the desk and started toward her and that was…worse.

She wanted to stand her ground. She did. But he kept coming, and she found herself backing up. His laugh took on a different note then. Predatory, she thought.

"I'm happy to tell you," Renzo said as he stalked her across the wide floor of his office.

There was something in his dark gaze that made Sophie shake. She had to stop moving to lock her knees against it, but that wasn't any better. That meant he could come much too close.

Then her heart started pounding against her ribs as he began to move around her in a lazy sort of circle, as if he was looking for flaws. And finding them.

"You were born selfish," he murmured, as if these were love words—though he'd told her he didn't believe in such things. Sophie had to fight back a shudder. She concentrated on keeping her fists by her sides. "You were handed advantage after advantage, but never realized how lucky you were. And why would you? You were surrounded by people just like you. I doubt you're even aware that there are people in this world that would kill themselves for an opportunity to face what you consider your problems."

She wondered if he meant people like him—but didn't dare ask. He was behind her then, and she could *feel* him. It was as if he was electrically charged. As if he was his own storm. She could feel her skin shiver into goose bumps because he was there, looking at her. Judging her.

Cutting her down to size.

"Your parents offered you a perfectly acceptable life. You were to be a countess, bathed in even more wealth and status. But that wasn't enough for you, was it?" Was that his breath on her neck? Sophie refused to look. "You needed to create a little excitement for yourself. You needed to make yourself feel better about the life you signed up for with a tiny little rebellion. The one thing you had was your virginity and let me guess—you thought you would seize the opportunity to choose who you would give it to. You thought you would use the only thing that was truly yours."

It was as if he'd been in her head that night, and Sophie felt herself sway on her own feet. How could he know the things she'd told herself? She'd known what he was offering when he'd walked up to her, even before he'd spoken. She'd known that she was expected to keep her virginity for her husband. But she hadn't cared.

Sophie didn't tell him that it wasn't because she'd been hell-bent on a rebellion that night. She hadn't been. By that point, just over a month before her wedding, she'd been nothing if not resigned.

It hadn't been a choose-your-own rebellion. It had been him.

Renzo had looked at her with his face like a fallen angel and she'd decided, in an instant, that he was worth whatever price she would have to pay.

It made her feel light-headed to think of that now. Here. With him circling her like a dangerous feline coming in for the kill.

"After all, as you keep reminding me, yours was a life without choices," Renzo said, soft and lethal. "That every possible choice you could make was showered with trusts and luxury and glorious estates to cushion the blow hardly signifies, I am sure. You decided you would take it upon yourself to use the only thing you had that you could barter. Your body."

"I'm impressed," Sophie managed to say. She'd crossed her arms at some point, and hugged them to her as if that could contain all the buffeting, conflicting things she felt with every circle he made around her. "It's as if you're psychic. Who knew that in addition to driving very quickly, you could also read minds?"

He only laughed, dark and low, stirring things inside her she didn't entirely understand. Or want to understand.

But the bright, throbbing thing between her legs insisted that she was a liar. That she knew full well what he did to her.

And worse, that she craved it.

"I could have been anyone," he said, and she caught her breath at the lethal ferocity in his voice then, so close to her ear. She realized that he'd stopped moving and now stood behind her. Above her. Where he could see her and she had to stand there and…guess. "I assume that was your purpose in Monte Carlo. Find a man, betray the promises you'd made, and then smugly attend your own wedding comfortable in the knowledge that one of the gifts you were expected to give to your husband, you'd given away to someone else. How proud you must be."

Her chest was rising and falling too fast, and Sophie was sure he was well aware of it. The way, it seemed, he was aware of everything she'd thought lived only inside her, secret and safe and hidden from view.

But she fought to keep her voice even when she spoke. "I don't understand why, if I was champing at the bit for a chance to fling my virginity at any man who ventured near, I would wait until I was five weeks out from my wedding. And surrounded by friends who would happily report any indiscretions to my fiancé, had they seen them."

"Time was running out." She was certain that Renzo shrugged then, though she didn't see him do it. She had the sense of him there behind her, like a wall. He was that hard. That immovable. "I have known a great many women like you, Sophie. I know you don't want to believe that. I know that deep down, you really do believe that you're a precious little unicorn. All rainbows and butterflies and desperately unique. But I'm afraid you wealthy women are all the same."

"In the dark?" Sophie managed to ask, her voice sharp. "Or do you mean that in a general sense?"

He laughed. "Both."

Because he was Renzo Crisanti, the man who had abducted her from her own wedding. Of course he couldn't be shamed.

"Here's a reality check," Sophie said, aware that there was too much emotion in her throat and that it bled out into her voice. "Men like you might be completely unable to make it through a day without wasting hours upon hours consumed with base, repulsive sexual fantasies. I assume that's eighty percent of what occupies your thoughts at any given time."

She couldn't bear that he was standing behind her any longer and turned, but that wasn't any better. Because he was just as intimidating when she was facing him. More, in fact. Because when she was looking at him it was entirely too easy to get lost in the way he looked. So beautiful it hurt.

And as out of reach as Mount Etna rising in the distance on the other side of his office windows.

Renzo's dark amber gaze blazed in a way that should have given her pause, but she pushed on before he could comment. "Sex was never a factor for me. There were too many expectations put on my behavior for me to even dare think about it too closely. My mother told me, again and again, that anything I did would directly reflect on the family name. And I believed her." She shook her head, trying to clear it. "I was so concerned with accidentally staining my family with a thoughtless act that yes, I was obedient. It must be easy to stand where you are now and mock that. But then, mockery is always easy, isn't it? You should try obedience to one's parents on for size. It isn't easy at all. But it used to be considered a virtue."

That blaze in his eyes was molten now, and she felt as if he was touching her when she knew he wasn't. "A lecture on virtue. From you, of all people. I admit, I am intrigued against my will at the prospect of such brazen hypocrisy."

"It was you, Renzo," she threw at him, fiercely, not caring that her voice was raised and she was making a spectacle of herself. Not caring about anything but telling him how wrong he was about her—as if that would do any good. "I must have seen a thousand men that weekend, but I didn't notice any of them in particular. It was only you who caught my attention. It was only you who really saw me. My mistake is that I thought it meant something."

"It meant so much that you pretended to be someone else. It meant so much that you went into it already lying to me."

"Because you didn't know who I was," she said, the storm in her passed. There was nothing left but the quiet way she said that. And the helplessness she felt, because nothing she said got through to him. The only time she thought he truly saw her now was when he was deep inside her—but that was far too dangerous. "That had never happened to me before. I wanted to be the woman who would meet a stunning man and go off into a beautiful night with him, just once."

He studied her for a long moment. Then another, while

her pulse beat so hard in her veins she was almost afraid they would rupture.

But he didn't react the way she was afraid he might. Or she'd hoped he might, if she was honest. He didn't put his hands on her. And she couldn't read the darkness in his gaze then.

"You asked me for something to do, did you not?"

She had almost forgotten. She swallowed, hard. "Yes. I've been here a week and I'm already going mad."

"Spend more time in the village," Renzo suggested. "Familiarize yourself with the area. After all, at some point you will have to introduce our child to its many joys."

Something shifted between them at that. Sophie couldn't quite place it—and then she understood. He'd said *our* child. Not *his* child, for once.

As if they were in this together.

"People have managed to keep themselves entertained in this village since the dawn of time. I know it can't hold a candle to the many splendors of the London charity circuit, but I suggest you find something here to occupy your days."

"But—"

"Do not ask me again, Sophie," he gritted out. "Because the suggestions I have I do not think you will like."

That sat there a moment, seeming to shimmer in the sunlight that poured through his windows. Or maybe that was the mask he let slip, showing her all that greed and passion that he'd been hiding behind his stony expression and all his terrible words…

"I thought… You said…" The whole world had narrowed to that need in his gaze, and the cast of his sensual mouth, and she felt as if the air had been knocked out of her. "I thought you refused to touch me until I begged."

But Renzo only laughed again, and this was a new laugh.

This one burned her to a crisp and left scorch marks all over her body, she was certain, though she didn't dare take her eyes off of him to check.

"You will beg, Sophie. Believe me, you will beg." He tilted his head to one side and looked at her the way a predator would eye a meal, and she shuddered. "The only question is whether I will let you come to it on your own or whether I will…move the situation along to suit my purposes."

"I… But you…"

"And the longer you stand here, wasting my time, the less inclined I am to wait."

Sophie stopped pretending that she could stand up to this man. She turned on her heel and bolted from the room, that dark, stirring laughter of his following her down the halls of the castle as she fled.

CHAPTER EIGHT

SOPHIE SPENT THE next week exploring the village, but not because she wanted to one day give her baby a tour of the place. She was looking for a way out.

"There is only one bus in my village," Renzo had told her on the drive from the airfield, down near the sea, the day they'd arrived in Sicily. "It leaves very early in the morning on market days and returns after dark, and that is only when the driver remembers to come all the way up the mountain. You should also know that the driver and his large family live in a house I own."

Sophie had been staring out her window at the sun-drenched landscape, unable to fully process the fact that she'd woken up that morning in Hampshire, prepared to marry Dal, and was now on the far side of Europe with a man she kept sleeping with, who was not Dal. At all.

"Why would I need to know any of that?" she'd asked.

"Because, *cara*," he'd said in that way of his, as if he was creating intimacy every time he looked at her. "One day you will wake up and decide you wish to escape my hospitality. On that day, it will save us all a lot of trouble if you remember these small facts. There is one sporadic bus. Everyone on it will be loyal to me, especially the driver. You will get nowhere."

She'd looked at him then, across the expanse of the

backseat they shared, and had wondered how he managed to be awful at every turn and yet her heart still flipped inside her chest whenever she looked at him. What was *wrong* with her?

Had she really thrown away her whole life for…this?

"Thank you," she'd said stiffly. "I'll be sure to keep that in mind. While walking."

Renzo had smiled, looking something like benevolent, which had been her warning.

"The village is perched on a little stretch of land propped up between many steep ravines," he'd told her. "People fall down them all the time and die, especially in the ice and snow of winter, but they are in many ways more treacherous in the summer. The road is narrow and very curvy. Pedestrians are forever walking on that road and getting struck by vehicles taking the turns too fast. It's also a solid, steep hour's walk to the next little town, assuming you aren't hit by a car on the way. I can't say I recommend it."

Sophie spent her second week in Sicily discovering that nothing Renzo had said to her that day was an exaggeration. The road out of town was terrifying. It shot down from the lowest part of the village in a steep, near-vertical drop, then began to curve this way and that. No matter how many times Sophie girded her loins and determined she would walk it anyway, she stopped the moment she saw a car career up or down, promising certain death.

She wanted to get away from Renzo. But she certainly didn't want to die.

The bus situation was even worse than he'd claimed. The women in the village shrugged and seemed not to know when it might run again. One cited vague "troubles" that Sophie thought might involve the driver's personal life rather than his vehicle, not that anyone appeared to mind that much.

There were no cars for hire. Or no cars for her to hire, anyway.

The locals were friendly. They greeted her with smiles, and happy chatter, but she quickly realized that there was a limit to that friendliness. And that limit was Renzo.

"How much would it cost to get to the airport?" she asked the man with the only taxi she had been able to find in town one warm afternoon.

The man started to quote a number, but then stopped. He eyed her.

Summer in Sicily was hot and sunny all day, then cool at night. The little village had a lovely, sunlit square, with shade trees all around where the old men sat and whiled the days away. And the taxi driver stared at her so long, Sophie was glad they'd stepped out of the direct sunlight.

"Surely *il capo* can take you to the airport when he is ready, no?" the driver asked. That was what they called Renzo here, she'd learned. *The boss.*

"I wasn't planning to ask him," Sophie confessed, and smiled as brightly as she could.

But the driver was unmoved. "I couldn't take you to the airport," he told her, definitively. "Or anywhere. It would not be possible."

"But I can pay you," she assured him. "Double. Triple, even."

The driver shook his head. Then he held up his hands and backed away, as if Sophie was threatening him.

The way the rest of the villagers looked at her, it was as if they thought she really had.

And when she made her way back up the hill and over the ravine—that was a steep shot down so far it made her dizzy to look over the edge of the footbridge—she found Renzo waiting for her in the castle's grand hall.

She didn't say anything. Or couldn't, to be more precise. He was dressed in a dark suit that suggested he'd been conducting video meetings from his office with his employees around the world, and she felt grubby by comparison in the hiking shorts and T-shirt she'd thrown on—selections that had been waiting for her in the closet of her rooms here when she'd arrived. She'd opted not to think too closely about where they'd come from.

"Do you know why there is a castle here?" Renzo asked mildly.

It was the mildness that got her back up. "Because there's a marvelous view?"

"Yes," he agreed. "But back when men roamed the land and built castles, the kinds of views they were looking for were oriented in defense, not leisure. This village is perfectly situated to defend itself against all comers. There is only the one road in and out. It is bordered by cliffs all around. No one can sneak up on this place. Few try."

He didn't say, *And also no one can leave*, but Sophie got his meaning.

"Come," he invited her, in that low way of his that was not an invitation so much as it was an order. "We will sit, you and I. We will have a conversation like civilized people and you will tell me, Sophie, how it is you imagine you can escape me so easily."

His lips curved at her expression of shock, though she'd tried to conceal it.

"The taxi driver you attempted to enlist to betray me called to tell me of your perfidy." Renzo made a *tsk*-ing sound. He might as well have scraped his fingernails down her spine. She glared at him, but that only made his smile deepen. "You will find that betraying me will not come quite so easily as betraying your earl."

"I wasn't trying to betray you," Sophie said tightly. "I was trying to get a ride to the airport. They're not the same thing."

"Where do you imagine you can go?" he asked, almost

as if he really wanted an answer to the question. But then his eyes flashed. "I will find you wherever you run. You must know this."

She cast around for some kind of defense, but she didn't have one. He would view any attempt she made to leave him a betrayal. And she knew that, didn't she? There was no sense pretending she didn't know exactly how he'd react to her leaving. Or even any attempt on her part to leave.

Isn't that what you wanted? something in her asked, wicked and knowing. *Isn't that what you've always wanted from him? His reaction?*

Renzo led her into the library, a glorious room that made Sophie's heart ache a little every time she entered it. Beautiful books lined the walls. There was a fireplace on one side and French doors on the other that opened into a kind of sunroom and then, beyond that, a terrace with views that stretched all the way to the Mediterranean. Inside, there was a great, raised skylight that let the sunlight in and highlighted the many armchairs and couches scattered about, all of which she'd tried at different points during her forced Sicilian holiday.

But this afternoon she followed Renzo to a little cluster of seats before the unlit fireplace, and tried to read his mood as he settled himself across from her.

He usually dressed simply here. A T-shirt and trousers, which should have looked casual but didn't, somehow. It wasn't simply the excellence of the fabrics he chose, though Sophie was certain that played a part. It was Renzo himself. He was not a casual man. Even his casual clothing failed to take away from his intensity in any way.

And today he was not wearing a T-shirt and trousers, like a normal man. He was dressed to emphasize his power rather than dampen it.

It ricocheted inside of Sophie like a bullet, and all he did was sit there.

Looking at him made her palms feel itchy. Sophie rubbed them on her thighs, but then stopped when she saw the way Renzo tracked the movement, as if it was evidence he could use against her.

"You persist in failing to understand your situation," he said after a moment, his tone almost absent, as if he was speaking to a troublesome employee. There was no reason that should slap at her, Sophie told herself, when it was the least of the things he'd done to her. "What about this is confusing?"

"Do you really want to keep me in prison?" she asked, and she had no idea why there was so much emotion in her voice, making it sound so rough. "Am I expected to sit quietly in a room somewhere, staring at the wall?"

"I told you to find something to do in the village. Or is the simplicity of village life too far below a woman of your exalted standards?"

Again, that sardonic tone he used like a lash.

"You don't have to insult me every time we speak," Sophie managed to say without giving in to those emotions that still slopped around inside of her. "Would the world end if you were nice to me for five minutes?"

"There is one way that I'm more than happy to be nice to you," Renzo said, and his voice changed again.

And Sophie caught fire.

"I want you to tell me how it is you think I should spend my time," she said, very deliberately. She wasn't going to touch the sexual innuendo part of the conversation. She had no idea what she might say.

Or worse, *do*.

"You do not, apparently, know how to entertain yourself. Is that what I'm hearing? Again?"

"I'm perfectly capable of entertaining myself," Sophie snapped at him. "I've read a lot of books. I've taken a lot of walks. It's been two weeks and I've seen everything there is to see, twice. What I can't get my head around is what I'm meant to do for the next nine months."

Renzo lounged there in the chair across from her, wicked and angelic at once, mouthwateringly ruthless in all things, and the way he looked at her then was…unfair.

"As it happens," he murmured. "I have an opening."

Something about his tone sneaked down her neck and along her spine, making her too aware of him. All of him. That gleam in his dark eyes and that curve on his hard mouth. The way he sprawled there, his legs thrust out before him. There was something about the way this man's body affected her that made her want to cry. He filled her with despair, wild and huge and overwhelming.

Though Sophie didn't think that was the correct word for the things she felt when she gazed at him.

It was easier to call it *despair* than it was to interrogate the parts of her that pulled tight and greedy, hot and nearly painful, every time he was near.

And there was something about the way he was looking at her this afternoon that made it that much worse than it normally was.

"A position in your business?" she asked.

"My business?" He laughed at that. "You have already told me your résumé, Sophie. I expect you know it is not exactly impressive. You were raised to be a dilettante and lived up to all expectations. What use could I possibly have for that?"

What she would have to sort out later, when she was alone, was why she was always surprised by his sucker punch. He landed it every time. Sophie couldn't blame him—it was clearly just what he did.

Why did she persist in imagining he could ever be the man she'd imagined he was that first night?

"Thank you," she said quietly, after a moment. "For always making certain that I know exactly who you are. That I'm not tempted, for even a minute, to forget."

"I do like to be memorable," Renzo said.

"I'll have to consult the internet when I have a moment," she said, shifting slightly in her seat so she could hold his gaze, her chin tipped up. "But I'm fairly certain your résumé is even less impressive than mine. Car races and a handful of high-profile affairs with actresses in the first rung of their downward spiral, if I remember correctly. And a few hotels and clubs thrown in to diversify your portfolio, of course."

If she thought she could land a similar punch on him, she was mistaken. He only smiled.

Like a wolf.

"Don't worry, the position I have in mind is more firmly in your skill set."

Sophie knew, somehow. It was the way he was looking at her. Less frozen than it had been these last two weeks, for a start. It was the way the air seemed to tighten between them, complex and complicated, thick and textured—and yet very, very simple.

"I'm afraid to ask what you think my skill set is," she said.

"I want you to do what you do best, *cara*." There was something wrong with his voice, then. It was raw. Too dark. It worked its way through her like a roll of thunder. "I am not in need of another secretary. Or an office girl of any description."

"My talent is in running things," she told him, which was true enough, though she doubted he cared. "I have my own support staff."

"I don't require you to run anything," Renzo told her, his dark amber gaze lit with a fire that made her feel lit up and hollow at once. "Or support anything. But in these halcyon days before our inevitable wedding and the birth of our child, I do find myself very interested in a new mistress."

"A new mistress."

Sophie repeated his words as if they were in a language she didn't speak. As if they made no sense to her, when Renzo could see that she understood him perfectly.

He could see it in the flush that worked its way down her neck to flirt with the scoop neck of the casual shirt she wore. He could tell by the way she crossed and uncrossed those long, shapely legs of hers, shown to advantage in the shorts she wore that had him longing to reacquaint himself with every last inch of them.

She was driving him to distraction. And he was tired of talking about it. He was tired of catching her scent in the halls when he least expected it. He was tired of being haunted by her the way he had been all those weeks when she'd disappeared and taken her fake name with her.

And this time, he didn't have to wait for an enraging clipping from a foreign newspaper to find her again. This time, she was right here.

He was tired of pretending he wanted anything but to bury himself inside her until he tired of her, assuming that day ever came.

"Surely you know what mistresses are, Sophie," he said, a little too much aggression in his voice. And that was him trying to control himself. "I would think that in your world, particularly, there are more mistresses than there are wives. If perhaps not all in the same place."

She smiled, but he thought it looked forced. "*Mistress* is such a funny word. Do you mean you just want sex? Is this just how you hit on the women you strand in your castle? You can see why I'm confused. After all, it's not the seventeenth century."

"Of course I want sex, and quite a lot of it," Renzo

said, and the way he said it was deliberate. He wanted her to feel silly. Inexperienced and virginal, and he could see she did in the way she blushed. Then dropped her gaze. "But the role of a mistress is well defined. There are no... unreasonable expectations. Everyone involved knows the terms, and there is no deviation from them."

"That sounds depressingly corporate."

"But that is the point, Sophie. It is not romantic at all. It is an exchange. In your world, I believe engagements from the cradle serve a similar purpose, though they are perhaps less physical. Here, you will get what you want and so will I. No drama. No hurt feelings. No tears."

"You think the word *mistress* is magical enough to prevent all of that?"

"I do," he said. He watched her closely. "Because it's a contract, not a fairy tale."

Much as their marriage would be, given that it was only for the child's legitimacy. He would have no confusion on that score, either—but there was no need to get into that with her now. This was a good first step.

He watched her swallow hard, as if her throat was dry. Her lush lower lip trembled slightly, until she pressed her lips together. She took her time threading her fingers together in front of her, and only then did she raise her gaze to his again.

"What is it you want from a mistress?" she asked. And then, when he let his mouth curve, she hurried on. "Sex, obviously. I'm not sure why, if that's what you want, you have to go to such absurd lengths to make it a transaction."

He forced himself to lounge back against his chair when every part of him was hot. Ready.

"Because I can get sex anywhere," he told her without a shred of conceit. Because it was a fact. "It is thrown at me when I walk down the street. It is everywhere I go."

"My condolences."

He liked when she showed her fangs, and smiled. "But this is the problem, you understand. Simply because a beautiful woman looks at me in a certain way on the street, for example, this doesn't mean that we will suit each other in bed. And let's say that we do suit." Renzo shrugged, though he never shifted his intent gaze from her flushed face. "How do I know she will not make the grave mistake of falling in love with me? Because I do not allow love to pollute my relationships, Sophie. Ever."

"Is that really a concern?" Sophie asked, and her voice was still clipped. Her brown eyes glittered and he thought, whether she knew it or not, his little captive was jealous. "Because I have to tell you, I really don't think that's as much of a factor as you seem to imagine."

"Says the woman who is soaking wet right now, sitting across from me in a library."

He watched her cheeks blaze with heat. She pulled in a sharp breath, and her hands gripped the arms of her chair as if she didn't know whether to run for it or take a swing at him.

And he doubted she was aware that the scent of her arousal hung between them, telling him everything he needed to know.

"I'm not surprised you have a vacancy," she said after a moment, though he was pleased to hear she sounded breathless. "You don't make the position sound very appealing."

Renzo stretched, and enjoyed the way she watched him. As if he was a dessert and she couldn't quite keep herself from taking a little lick. He shifted forward, putting his elbows on his knees and letting his hands dangle in front of him.

The tips of his fingers brushed her bare knees.

Once, then again.

She caught her breath, then let it out in a sigh that sounded a whole lot like surrender.

"Just think, Sophie, if all of this was set aside," he said softly. "The silly games. The outraged posturing. Imagine if all you had to think about was greeting me just as you are, slick between the legs and nipples hard as rocks, with no thought in your head but our mutual satisfaction. Think how quickly these nine months would go if that was your only focus."

For a moment, she imagined it. He could tell by the way her eyes went unfocused. The way her mouth fell open, just slightly. He could see the color on her cheeks and the wild drumming of the pulse in her throat.

He could imagine it too easily. Every day could be like that night in Monaco. She would give herself to him, again and again, and this time, he wouldn't have to worry about losing her every time he went to sleep.

Are you worried about losing her or are you concerned she'll try to call this love? he asked himself. And couldn't seem to find an answer.

Before him, sitting too straight in her chair, Sophie shook herself.

"Don't be silly," she said, sounding particularly British and scolding. He assumed it was as much for her benefit as it was for his. "I can't just…be your sex slave."

"Why not?"

Sophie's pupils dilated. Renzo leaned forward a little more and traced patterns on the bare skin before him. Her knee, again. Then down along the leg she'd crossed over its mate, as if he was drawing patterns on her taut, satiny flesh.

He was so hard it hurt.

"I'm glad this is a joke to you," she said. Weakly.

"I'm not joking at all." Renzo leaned forward and slid his hands onto her lap, relishing the way she bit back a sound at that. It reminded him of the way she came, and he nearly lost his composure. It took him far too much work to pull himself together, but he managed it, though his jaw ached from the way he clenched his teeth. "Here's the problem, *cara*. You can, if you wish, waste your months here traipsing around the village entreating my people to do your bidding. They won't."

"What do you mean, *your people*? This isn't a feudal estate."

He trapped her hands in his and held them, angling himself even closer.

"It might as well be. This village was falling down when I left it at eighteen. No industry to speak of. Goatherds and shopkeepers were the lucky ones. Everyone else was simply trapped here, the way their families have been for generations. But I changed all that."

He turned over one of her hands and examined it, noting the ragged nails that suggested she'd developed her own nervous habits while she'd been here. *Good.* He could only hope he drove her half as crazy as she did him.

"I didn't merely take over all the leases and mortgages I could and fix up all the falling-down buildings. I bought the hotel over the next ridge and I financed it with my own money for the first five years, so it didn't matter if the tourists came or not. But they came." He looked at her other hand and reveled in the deep tremor he could feel go through her. "This village may be sleepy but the hotel is successful, and between it and the connected vineyard, I employ the bulk of the villagers."

"I had no idea you had a single humanitarian bone in your body. I'm shocked."

"What I am trying to tell you, *cara mia*, is that there is not a single person living here who is not aware of the hand that feeds them. They will not cross me. No matter how you smile or bat your eyelashes, you are trapped here. But then, you have been at pains to tell me that you have always been trapped, so perhaps it is not so much of an adjustment."

She worried her lip with her teeth for a moment, then stopped as if she knew how it felt inside him. How it made him ache to test that lip with his own teeth. "I suppose it's good to know that you're capable of kindness, anyway. Even if you feel no particular compunction to show it to me."

"You are the one who asked me for something to do with your time," he reminded her.

Sophie sat a little straighter, and her brown eyes were too dark. "I've never been asked to be someone's mistress before."

"Good," he growled, before he could think better of it.

"I'm fairly certain that the appropriate response is outrage."

What Renzo noticed was that she didn't look outraged at all. And she didn't try to wrestle her hands from his. "What is there to be outraged about?"

"Oh, you know. The stain on my character and how little you must think of me to suggest such a thing. Small, inconsequential things like that."

"Tell the truth," Renzo murmured, dark and urgent. "How often do you wake in the night, wishing I was there beside you? I make you hungry. I make you wet and restless. You torture yourself with memories of how good it is between us. You fall asleep and dream of that night in Monaco and all the ways I filled you and took you and made you mine." She let out a soft little sound, not quite a moan, and it took everything he had not to simply reach over and haul her into his lap. "I see no reason to play these games of make-believe when we both know the truth."

She looked as if she might faint. She tugged on her hands, but when he released them, her expression seemed… crestfallen.

"You can't just go around asking people to be your mistress," she said faintly.

"I'm not asking *people*. I'm asking you."

It occurred to him that he was entirely too invested in her answer, and not only because he was so hard it bordered on pain. And it was that other part that concerned him. He reminded himself who she was. What she'd done.

But when he conjured up visions of Sophie in that filmy confection of a wedding gown, walking down the aisle, it wasn't betrayal he thought of.

In his head, she was making her way down that aisle to him.

That rocked him to his bones. It shook through him like a revelation, dark and terrible. Renzo released her and sat back, then made himself lounge as if he'd never been more relaxed in his life.

"And I'm not really asking you, to be perfectly clear," he heard himself say, cold and impersonal again, the way he should have been all this time. "I'm telling you that the position is open and you can do with that information anything you wish."

Sophie blinked, then went a little pale again. But he didn't let the gnawing thing inside him get to him. He had never been a soft man and he didn't know why there was something in him that wanted nothing more than to bring that color back to her face.

He had the sinking sensation that he was in this much, much deeper than he wanted to admit.

And he had no idea what to do about that.

"Your suite of rooms is directly next to mine," Renzo told her, and he couldn't seem to control his voice anymore. He sounded gruff. He felt…wrecked. "The door is never locked. When you are ready to take on your new role, all you need to do is open that door and walk through it. What could be simpler?"

She regarded him for so long, so quietly, that he started to feel something like panic work its way through him—

Though that was impossible, of course. He was Renzo Crisanti. Lesser men panicked. Renzo conquered.

"What if I never walk through that door?" she asked.

Renzo made himself smile and elected not to notice how difficult it was.

He studied her as she sat there before him. He saw the way she trembled a little bit. The way she kept her mouth shut tight as if she was afraid of the things that might come out of it if she opened it.

At least if this was getting to him, it was getting to her, too.

"It's up to you," he told her. "But as in all things, there are consequences. The longer you take, the more I will demand. It is inevitable."

"Consequences," she whispered. "There are always consequences."

"Always," Renzo agreed.

He thought he was handling himself admirably when he kept his hands to himself. When he only sat there as if he didn't care either way what she chose, when he was rapidly coming to the conclusion that he did. He really did, and he had no place to put that to make any sense of it.

"But the good news for you, Sophie, is that I don't just want to make you pay," he told her, and he had the pleasure of watching those big brown eyes of hers widen, all golden heat, because however hard this was for him, it was harder for her. As it should be. That was why he smiled. "First I want to make you scream."

CHAPTER NINE

It TURNED OUT that having choices was harder, Sophie discovered, and no matter what her mother might once have said about *poor people*. Because she was the only one she'd have to blame once she made them.

Renzo storming into her wedding and carrying her out, tossed over his shoulder as if he was some kind of ancient marauder, was easy because it allowed her to hold him accountable. *She* had intended to marry Dal, as promised. *She* had never meant any of this to happen, so how could she be held responsible for something Renzo had done?

She thought a whole lot about that after Renzo left her there in the library, while she tried—and failed—to catch her breath. Right there, in the chair where he'd left her, that enigmatic look on his dark face and entirely too much carnal promise in his gaze.

Of course she couldn't agree to be his mistress, she told herself stoutly. She was outraged that he'd even suggested such a thing, especially when he kept threatening to marry her in the same breath—

But maybe that was the trouble, she thought a bit later, when she'd showered off her walk and found herself sitting in her bedroom. It was furnished with exquisite antiques and a canopy bed she doubted she'd ever get a good night's sleep in again, after all the images Renzo had put in her head. The sun was beginning to lower in the sky over another day in Sicily, and everything was exactly the same as it had been the day she'd arrived, except her baby was a bit bigger inside of her.

She slid her hands over her belly, imagining that she could already feel a difference. And she wasn't quite as outraged at Renzo's suggestion as she thought she ought to have been.

Sophie had tossed her mobile in the drawer of the bedside table without looking at it the day they'd arrived, and she hadn't touched it since. But the word *responsibility* was dancing around and around in her head tonight, so she went and got it out, frowning down at the thing as she switched it on.

Sophie hadn't wanted to look. She'd spent two weeks with her head thrust firmly in the sand, because she'd been certain that she didn't want to know anything that was happening in the world Renzo had carried her away from.

Which is just another way to avoid taking responsibility for yourself, isn't it? a caustic voice inside her asked.

The truth was that she very much doubted that she had anything to go home to, even if she could manage to escape this remote village.

And when she started going through all the notifications on her mobile, it was as bad as she'd imagined. Worse.

Sophie had too many voice mail messages. Entirely too many texts. Some people she'd called friends for lack of a better term had sent her links to tabloid articles shredding her to pieces, which was helpful, in the long run. Because it reminded her how few real, true friends she'd ever had.

There was only one, by her estimation. Poppy. Sweet, dependable Poppy, who was the only person Sophie wanted to talk to at all. Because she was well aware that she'd left Poppy to deal with Dal, which couldn't have been pleasant—especially since Poppy worked for him.

But she couldn't seem to reach Poppy, which only made her feel worse.

And everything else was character assassination and innuendo. Or outright hostility.

"Don't bother to contact us, Sophie," her father said in the last of the numerous messages he'd left for her, each one more vicious than the one before. "You have tarnished the family name beyond repair. I hope your tawdry affair is worth it."

Sophie knew exactly what lay ahead for her, if she went back to London. She'd seen more than one girl who'd been raised the way she had, complete with a shiny pedestal all her own, who had then fallen straight off. She knew how it went. Some rehabilitated themselves eventually, usually after years of intense publicity campaigns—though that would never satisfy some of the bigger snobs. Some simply made lateral moves into different marriages, though Sophie had always thought privately that said lateral marriages must be even worse than the ones they might have had before.

Because it was one thing to be virtuous and untouched and worthy of one's chilly arranged marriage. It was something else again to be damaged goods.

Just one more concern specific to her exalted position, Sophie knew. Girls without estates attached to their name and trusts that stretched back to the condescension of ancient kings had all kinds of choices. They could do as they pleased. They could marry for love, sow their wild oats as they liked, make their life anything they wanted it to be without concerning themselves with a highly polished family name.

Sophie had never had that choice. She'd never had those options.

But you have a choice now, that same little voice reminded her.

She had no doubt that Renzo would push the legitimacy issue and the marriage he wanted. Her choice was simple—did she want to spend the time before that inevitable marriage and her child's birth the way she'd spent the past two weeks? Or did she want what he was offering instead?

Sophie had made one other decision about the course of her life, and it was what had brought her here. She'd taken one look at Renzo and had wanted him. He was the only thing she could remember wanting—because she'd learned a long time ago that there was no use wanting things she couldn't have.

But she could have him now.

He'd said as much.

All she had to do was walk through that door on the wall nearest her bed that she hadn't realized was only locked on her side...

Mistress. She turned the word over again and again in her head.

He'd called it a practical arrangement. Sophie couldn't help thinking it was begging for trouble. It had been hard enough to walk away from him that night in Monaco. She'd watched him sleep as she'd dressed, feeling as if she was torn into pieces. How could she go back to her black-and-white life, so cold and precisely contoured to other people's specifications? How could she live in all that dark and gloom when she'd finally felt all that sunlight on her face?

But she'd made herself leave anyway, because she'd thought it was the right thing to do.

It had been hard after one night. What did she think it would be like after months? And a child?

Sophie threw her mobile back in the drawer, feeling much more unsettled than she had when she'd picked it up. She didn't bother to call her parents back, because she knew them too well. If she called now, there would be nothing but recriminations. Accusations and harsh words. If she waited, they would retreat into their usual icy hauteur. They always did. And that would be the best time to tell them that they had a grandchild on the way.

Because at the end of the day, her parents were nothing if not practical. The sooner she told him they had a grandchild on the way, the sooner they could start plotting out more dynasties. Which was, as far she could tell, the only time they were ever happy.

Or as close to happy as they ever got.

That night, she lay in her canopied bed, completely unable to sleep.

All she could seem to do was stare at that door on the wall. The only thing she could concentrate on was Renzo lying there, in his bed, just the way she was. Would he be naked? All that sculpted muscle there between his sheets with no other barriers? Was he lying awake just as she was, watching the door? Or was he asleep?

If she slipped through to his rooms, could she make it to the side of his bed before he knew she was there? Would he reach for her?

Or would she crawl over him, and get to revel in another moment of watching him as he slept?

The way she had that morning in Monaco before she'd run back to her life, guilty and ashamed by the things she done and let him do in turn.

"If doing it one night—and one morning—made you feel so guilty and ashamed," she said out loud, her voice sounding strained and strange in the dark room, "why would you do more of it? As an *arrangement*?"

She didn't feel as if she'd slept at all, and when she woke, the light was streaming into her room. It told her she'd stayed in bed much later than she usually did.

When she finally dressed and made her way down to the breakfast room—where there was always coffee, freshly baked pastries, and a soothing view of mountains stretching toward the sea in the distance—she stopped short, because Renzo was there.

"You look as if you didn't get much sleep," he murmured, that damned curve to his mouth and those dark amber eyes all over her. "Whatever could have kept you up? Tossing and turning? Too hot, perhaps?"

"Not at all." She had stopped in the door to the bright little room set over a sweeping balcony and she couldn't seem to make her feet move another inch. So instead, she smiled wide and lied some more. "I'm not sure I've ever had such a deep sleep."

Renzo's gaze lit with amusement. He didn't call her a liar. But then, he didn't have to.

"Have you come to a decision?" he asked instead.

Sophie forced herself to move, then. She walked over to the sideboard where the staff had prepared the usual trays of breakfast treats and selected the traditional Sicilian summer breakfast she'd come to crave each morning, sweet brioche and almond granita, which the locals ate in some form or another to ease into the hot mornings. And an extra strong small cup of espresso, because lord knew she needed that and then some to handle Renzo's unexpected presence after having him in her head all night.

"I love the brioche here," she said, as if that was the decision he'd asked about. "And of course I love it with gelato, but that's a bit heavier than the granita, isn't it?"

"That is, of course, the question I wanted answered. Your breakfast options are an enduring fascination to me. Thank you."

She settled herself across from him at the small table as if that was normal. As if they ate together every day. And she fought to keep her expression bland when she met his too-knowing, too-amused gaze.

Something moved in her then, a little too hot, as she imagined this might be part of the arrangement if she agreed to be his mistress. Instead of having him in her head all night, she would really, truly have him, and then… would they share meals like this? Would he stop treating her with all that barely contained ferocity?

Would he forgive her for what she'd planned to do with their baby?

Will you forgive yourself? a voice from somewhere deep inside asked her then, with a certain quiet savagery that left her reeling.

The question fell through her like a blow. A series of blows, each more brutal than the last. Like shattering glass, leaving marks as it went.

And Sophie didn't know what to do with any of it, so she let her granita melt as she stared at the man across from her.

"I don't understand what makes you think that calling me a mistress would somehow take away all the intimacy of the arrangement," she blurted out. If she'd had the time or capacity to think it through, she wouldn't have said anything and she certainly wouldn't have used that word.

Mistress. It sat there between them like a sexual act. Or maybe that was just how it felt to Sophie. It was so… debauched. Erotic, but wrapped up in such a staid and sturdy little word.

"It is an arrangement that is entirely about sex," Renzo said, and his dark, rich voice didn't help matters. "It is necessarily intimate. What it is not, *cara*, is emotional."

"I don't know why you imagine emotions are something you can order about the way you do everything else," she said, with a little too much of her own feelings on display.

She regretted it instantly. The way she regretted everything that had to do with this man.

Liar, whispered that voice again, and she actually shuddered this time.

Renzo saw, of course. He saw everything. She watched

his gaze shift from that amused heat to something darker. Something unreadable.

"I can't help you with this, Sophie," he told her after a moment. He was not wearing one of his dark king-of-the-universe suits today. That meant she could see far too much of his sculpted biceps beneath the material of his T-shirt. And the strong, golden column of his throat. And entirely too much of his beautiful chest. He was distracting. But he was still talking, and for once he didn't sound ferocious—he simply sounded serious. "You must decide. And then you must convince me. Because when all of this is done, you and I will not play little games of pretend that it was not something you wanted."

"I have no idea what to say to that," she said, which was true, but not for the reasons she thought he might suspect.

"You have no choice whether or not to be here, nor what will happen," Renzo said, his long fingers toying with his espresso cup before him in a way that made Sophie flush. "You will grow ever larger with my child. We will marry to give the child my name. These things cannot be avoided. But how you spend your time here before then? That is up to you."

"One choice," she whispered. "Lucky me."

Renzo looked at her then, and she was convinced he could see straight through her. That he could see every thought, every feeling, every shred of guilt she'd ever entertained. His dark amber gaze inhabited her. It set her on fire and threw gas on the flames.

And he didn't do anything but look.

"I have no doubt in my mind that you will be beneath me, spread out over my bed, begging for my touch," he told her, almost offhandedly. Though there was nothing *offhand* about the way he was looking at her. "Sooner rather than later, in fact. So I do hope that you enjoy this time, *cara mia*. It is the only power you have left."

"And here come those consequences again," she managed to say. She even sounded relatively calm, despite the fact she felt as if he had his hands wrapped tight around her and was wringing her limp. "I was just about to say we should do it. We should jump right in—maybe right here? But you had to be awful, again, and now I just don't know."

His mouth curved. Slowly. Much too slowly.

It was as if he wanted her to imagine those lips all over her naked body—and she did. That was the trouble. She really did.

"Tell yourself whatever lies you require to make yourself at peace with this decision," Renzo told her. "It will all end in the same place."

"You've made my mind up for me," she replied, and let her smile get a little sharper. "I'll just wander the halls for the next nine months like a flesh and blood ghost."

Renzo only laughed.

But Sophie wasn't kidding. She spent the day doing exactly that. She wandered the castle halls. She sat in the library and paged through more books, though she couldn't seem to concentrate on any of the words on the page. She walked down to the village and back. And all she could seem to think about were two words. *Mistress*, still. And *forgiveness*.

She couldn't help but think they were connected.

In the evening, she took her dinner in her room and stared at her mobile again. For a long time.

And then, before she could talk herself out of it, she wrote formal letters of apology to her parents and to Dal, because she owed them at least that much.

Her parents were not warm people, or at least not to her, but they had never wavered in the things they'd wanted and Sophie had meekly gone along with all of them. The only time she'd ever stood up for herself was the matter of her engagement. Her parents had never had the slightest inkling that Sophie wasn't happy. She'd never given them that courtesy.

And of course she knew that they wouldn't have reacted well even if she had told them. But she couldn't worry about their reactions now, she could only do what she felt was right. And running out on her own wedding, leaving them to sort it out in her wake, was a terrible thing to do to anyone.

She took responsibility for that.

Her letter to Dal was harder. She barely knew him, but that didn't change the fact that both of them had expected that they would marry each other, and had agreed to go ahead with it. And the fact he was remote and made entirely of ice, as far as she could tell, didn't change the fact that she'd made a promise to him and then broken it. First in Monaco and then, much more publicly, at Langston House.

When she hadn't fought to escape Renzo. If she was honest, his appearance had been a relief.

She didn't tell Dal any of that. He was a smart man and when her baby arrived, Sophie was certain he'd be more than capable of doing that math. What she did do was apologize for betraying him and humiliating him, then leaving him to pick up the pieces after she'd roared away in Renzo's car.

Sophie couldn't say she wished she'd married him after all, because she didn't. But she could, and did, tell him that she wished she hadn't let the mess of her personal life take center stage like that, and in full view of everyone they knew.

She didn't expect any replies, but when she put her mobile away again, she felt…lighter. Free, almost, in a way she never had before.

Later, she lay in her bed and stared at her canopy again. She thought about Monaco and she thought about her baby.

She thought about that night before her wedding, out on that dark country road, and the deep and utter despair she'd felt when Renzo had driven off and left her there.

She remembered walking down that aisle with her father, her gaze locked on Dal there at the altar. She remembered the misery of each step. Her sheer panic at the prospect of having to give to Dal what she'd so happily and easily handed to Renzo.

And most of all she remembered what she'd felt when the doors had slammed open behind her and Renzo had appeared.

She let out a little gasp, alone in her bed.

Because it hadn't occurred to her until this moment that she was in love with him.

Heedlessly, recklessly, foolishly in love with him. It had happened too fast, right there in Monte Carlo, surrounded on all sides by so much glittering European wealth. It had happened the moment he'd stood there before her and asked why she was sad.

When he'd seen something in her no one else had ever noticed.

She'd told him she didn't believe in immolation and he'd set her on fire anyway.

And then he'd taught her she could feel things she'd had no idea were even possible.

She loved him. She'd never loved anything or anyone in all her life, but she loved Renzo. He was heat and light. He was sunshine. Even his fury excited her on some level— and more, she didn't retreat into frozen affront when he provoked her, the way she did with everything else. She fought back. She lost her cool.

He had thawed her out and she hadn't even realized she was melting, all this time.

And she found she could forgive herself for that. It didn't mean she wasn't accountable for the choices she'd made. She should have called off her wedding. She should have found Renzo the moment she knew she was pregnant and told him he was going to be a father. She never should have forged on with her wedding to Dal, much less tried to imagine ways she could pass her baby off as his.

She would have to live with the knowledge that when pressed, she was the sort of woman who would do all of those things, and had.

The truth was, she'd never been in love before, and it had made her a little crazy. Love wasn't a factor in her world. It wasn't a part of the marriages she'd known all her life. She wasn't surprised, looking back, that she'd reacted to these overwhelming emotions with very little grace.

But she'd apologized. Her parents and Dal could accept her apologies or not—but that was up to them.

Here, now, she had other things to face.

She sat up in her bed and looked at that door that sat there on her wall like a taunt. The truth was, she didn't want to be Renzo's mistress. But she didn't see the point of locking herself away in this room, Rapunzel by her own hand, simply because he refused to offer her the things she really wanted.

When she hadn't even known what she wanted until today.

She'd wanted to be free and he'd set her free, and her reaction to that had been to blame him for it.

She'd wanted to lose her innocence on her own terms and he'd done that—oh, how he'd done that—and she'd blamed him when she'd fallen pregnant. Sophie might have been a virgin, but she wasn't an idiot. She'd known that all those times he'd been inside her that night in Monaco he'd used protection…except that first time. And she hadn't stopped him. She hadn't even tried to stop him.

She seemed to expect Renzo to read her mind and intuit her feelings even when she was a mystery to herself.

Sophie might not know a whole lot about love, but she was fairly certain that wasn't the definition.

And she might not want an arrangement, cold and clinical—but then, Renzo could use any words he liked. She knew how bright and hot he burned. If he was clinical about anything, she'd never seen it.

She could be his mistress, if that was what he wanted. She could love him just as much, and better yet, she could have him while she did. She could explore him every night. She could use these months to get to know the father of her child, the lover who'd blown up her life when she'd least expected it, the only man she'd ever loved or, she imagined, ever would.

All she had to do was walk to that door, pull it open, and surrender.

Renzo heard the door latch and assumed he was dreaming.

After all, he had this dream every night.

Tonight was like every other time he'd dreamed this exact same thing. The door pushed inward, very nearly soundless. And then Sophie appeared, exactly as he wanted to see her. Her thick chestnut hair tumbling down around her shoulders. One of the little gowns she liked to sleep in that he remembered with great fondness from that morning in England. Her long, gorgeous legs were exposed, and the hem of her gown flirted with her thighs as she moved. Even her feet were bare, and he found himself as obsessed as ever.

As if it were this woman's vulnerabilities that got to him the most. As if her beauty was secondary.

He knew the exact moment it dawned on him that this wasn't a dream after all.

It was when she paused there at the foot of his bed, her brown eyes nearly filled with gold then, and more than that—uncertainty.

In his dreams she was bold. Daring.

But it was that uncertainty that had him jackknifing up to sitting position, so he could hold that gaze of hers with his.

"You appear to be lost, *cara mia*."

He hadn't meant to sound like that. But he'd thought this was a dream and so his voice was scratchy with the sleep he needed, though he'd been wide-awake, as usual. Scratchy and gruff and too dark for the occasion, but he didn't take it back.

And she didn't seem to mind.

"I'm not lost," she said softly.

And the thing that rushed in him then wasn't as simple as victory. It was edged with triumph, to be sure, and it seemed to come from different parts of him at once. There was all that longing that he had begun to think would never be assuaged. There was that endless greed for her that made him despair of himself.

But more than that, he wanted his hands on her. As simple as that. It was almost as if he worried that she really was some kind of phantom and if he didn't grip her as hard as he could, she might disappear.

He was already moving when it occurred to him that he had never reacted this way to a woman in all his life. Renzo Crisanti was nothing if not sure of himself, particularly in the bedroom.

But this was Sophie.

And everything with Sophie had been different from the start, loath as he was to admit it to himself.

He rolled to stand beside the bed and then met her at the foot of it, and once there, he indulged himself. He wrapped his hand over the nape of her neck and pulled her even closer.

Renzo knew he could never dream anything as perfect as the feel of Sophie's skin beneath his palm. Or her scent, that soap she preferred and the hint of something muskier that he knew was her. All her.

"I thought you wanted me to beg," she said, those pretty eyes of hers still not as certain as he might have liked, but with a smile on her sweet mouth.

"I insist upon it."

"What does begging entail, then?" Her smile deepened and he could feel it where he was hardest. And neediest. "I assumed it would require I get on my knees."

"That is always a good place to start," he said, expecting her to flinch at his boldness.

But instead, Renzo watched in a kind of stunned amazement as Sophie sank to her knees before him.

CHAPTER TEN

His chest was so tight it made it hard to breathe. And Renzo was so hard he had serious doubts that he would last more than a moment if Sophie actually did what it looked like she was about to do.

Though that didn't seem to matter much as she gazed up at him from where she knelt, that uncertainty in her gaze changing into something a whole lot more like delight.

"What do you know about pleasuring a man this way?" Renzo asked gruffly.

He already knew the answer. But he liked it very much when she responded as he expected.

"Nothing at all," she confessed, almost happily. "We didn't get to that."

He found his hands at her face, his thumbs gently stroking the satiny expanse between her cheeks and her temples.

"A shocking oversight," he murmured. "But I want you too much, I think. I'm not at all certain I can allow you to play with me tonight."

Her delicate hands were on his thighs. She held his gaze as she slid them farther up, waiting until he hissed in a breath to stop.

Renzo had gone to bed naked, as was his custom. He couldn't decide, in this moment, if he regretted that choice or not. Or if, in fact, he was thrilled that she clearly didn't wish to listen to him.

"I'm here as your mistress," Sophie said softly, the glint of something mischievous in her gaze. "It is my duty to serve you, is it not?"

And she didn't wait for him to answer.

She tipped forward, lowered that mouth of hers, and licked him.

And Renzo was only a man. Not a very good one.

He leaned back against the foot of the bed, let his head fall back, and allowed her to do with him as she wished.

That she was inexperienced was immediately evident, but much like that night in Monaco, it only made it better.

Because she treated him like a wondrous discovery. She used her hands. Her mouth, lips, and tongue. And all of that blazed in him, brighter and hotter by the moment to match the sweet heat of her mouth, but what got to him most was her excitement.

The little noises she made, as if taking him this way built the same fires in her as it did in him.

And he didn't have it in him to pull back from the edge when she licked and sucked him straight over it.

But this was Sophie, the woman who seemed to have been put on this earth to match him sexually in every possible way, so all she did was drink him down as he emptied himself into her mouth.

He pulled out, a new and not entirely welcome sensation working its way through his gut.

It was another kick of the sort of shame he'd deny he was capable of feeling, he thought, as he looked down at her and saw only the top of her head. She'd settled back on her heels, one hand at her lips. He didn't understand why she brought these things out in him. These...*feelings*.

"I could have been more gentle," he began, stiffly.

But when she lifted her head again, he saw that she was smiling.

And it was as if something in him simply…broke wide-open.

He hauled her to her feet, then threw her down on his mattress. She laughed as she fell, but then he came down on top of her, and her laughter quickly turned to sheer fire and that wild delight that always arced between them. She wrapped her arms around him, he took her mouth, desperate. Determined.

Addicted.

He couldn't get the gown off of her lush body fast enough. He tossed it aside and discovered that she was even better than he'd remembered. That morning in England had been a taste, and had only whet his appetite for more. For this.

For her.

And while he knew on some level that he had all the time in the world tonight, he couldn't seem to slow himself down. He couldn't seem to control himself.

Instead, Renzo lost himself in her.

She had called herself his mistress. And there was something in him that caught on that, even as the primitive side of him roared its approval.

And either way, he intended to slake his thirst at last.

He took his time, relearning every inch of her body. He lavished attention on her neck, that collarbone that fascinated him, and her delicate, surprisingly capable hands that he couldn't seem to get enough of feeling against his own skin. He focused on her gorgeous breasts, worshipping one hard nipple and then the other. He worked his way down to her abdomen, testing the shallowness of her navel and the faint swell that he knew was his child, and smiled when she squirmed beneath him.

He skirted that part of her he knew was as desperate for him as he was for her, and took his time learning those legs he'd spent far too much time admiring lately. All the way down one leg then up the other, then he flipped her over and tended to her back. The supple length of her spine. The swell of her hips and the endless intrigue of her rounded bottom, and then the dark secrets beneath.

By the time he turned her over again, she was limp.

And better still, she was begging.

Just as he'd promised she would. And in some distant part of his brain, Renzo knew that he'd expected the begging to be different, somehow. That he would feel exalted and she would be humbled.

But it wasn't like that at all.

"Please, Renzo," she whispered. *"Please."*

And he was the one who was humbled that he got to touch her like this. That he alone got to bring her to the brink again and again.

And that he alone ever would, he thought then, fierce and sure.

He settled himself between her legs, and then, finally, licked his way into her molten softness.

And for a while there was nothing but the way she writhed beneath him, lifting her hips to meet his mouth, his tongue, even the edge of his teeth.

When she fell apart, she sobbed.

But Renzo was only just beginning.

He crawled his way back up her body as she lay there, flushed and boneless.

Mine, he thought. *All mine.*

And if there was something in him that whispered that *mistress* wasn't the word he wanted when it came to Sophie—well. It was the word that would do for now. Because it had to do.

Because he'd told her it was what he wanted.

He reached between them and fit himself to her softness at last. As hard and as desperate as if she'd never taken the edge off at all.

Sophie's eyes fluttered open and her gaze met his, and he took that as a sign, sliding himself deep inside her.

He wanted it fast. A wild pounding that would toss them both straight into oblivion, but she shifted beneath him.

Her eyes were brown and entirely too gold. Her mouth was soft and something like vulnerable. She slid her arms around his neck and held him to her, and it wasn't oblivion Renzo wanted.

It was this.

Her.

It was a sweet, hot joining. His deep slide inside of her and the way she clutched at him, as if it could never be enough.

They could never be close enough. He could never be deep enough. She could never take enough.

But for what felt like forever, they tried.

And Renzo knew fire. He knew wild heat and the oblivion it caused.

But there was something secret here, in the dark of his room, with only the sound of their breathing to spur them on.

There was something sacred in the way she held him and the sounds she made, sweet whispers and now and again, his name.

This time, when they reach that edge, it was together.

And there was no oblivion at the end of it.

There was only bliss.

Once Sophie agreed to be his mistress, everything fell into place.

Two weeks later, Renzo stood in the suite of rooms that had been hers when she'd first arrived, impatient and not doing much to hide it.

He had long since had her moved into his bedroom with him, because there was no sense pretending she would ever sleep in another bed but his. Today he waited as the doctor's assistants set up their equipment, turning what had briefly been Sophie's room into a makeshift office.

"You look happy," the doctor said from beside him, in his jovial way. He clapped Renzo on the back. "Just as the proud papa should."

Renzo's first instinct was to deny it. He looked at the doctor, the only man in the village who had ever treated him or his mother with respect back in those dark years, and then he looked back at the bed, where Sophie was lying down. She had an easy smile on her face, and he seemed to be the only one having trouble with the knowledge that she was naked beneath the sheet spread over her lap.

Their days were filled with the hot Sicilian sun and sex, and Renzo could admit that he had never known anything quite like it.

He woke her in the mornings, well before the sky was lit. He took her fiercely then, tossing her from half-asleep into that wildfire they shared with his first deep thrust. They never spoke during those mad sessions. He left her limp and panting when he took his shower, then made his way down to his office to tend to his business concerns spread out across different time zones.

Hours later he met her for her breakfast, if business allowed.

He told her he needed to inspect the growing thickness in her belly, and he did, all over the castle—and then took advantage of the sweetness of his hands on her skin. He knew every part of her better than he knew his own body now, and he liked the taste of hers a good deal more.

Sometimes he knelt on the floor of the shower and licked her until she sobbed. Sometimes Sophie did the kneeling, proving to him what a quick learner she was every time she took him deeper into her mouth.

Other times he lifted her against the nearest wall and

surged inside her, riding them both straight back into that bliss that only seemed to expand every time they reached it, wide and glorious.

It was hard to remember that when she'd arrived they hadn't had their evening meals together. Now Renzo insisted upon it. No matter what time he finished with his various business concerns, stuck on video calls all around the globe, Sophie waited for him. And they sat out on one of the terraces, eating and talking as the night grew deeper blue all around them and the summer sunset painted the sky.

Renzo learned that she was funny. That the poise and elegance she could draw around her like armor was an act, not the truth of her. Sometimes they argued books. Politics. World events and history. She knew proper Italian, so he taught her his Sicilian dialect and the filthy words and phrases he doubted very much anyone else had dared utter in the presence of the excruciatingly correct Carmichael-Jones heiress.

They talked until the stars came out and then he took her to his bed, where he got much more serious.

He was as demanding as he was creative, and Sophie was even better than he'd imagined she was in Monaco, when she had somehow managed to knock his whole world off its axis.

She matched him completely.

And the madness of it was, the more he had her, the more he wanted her.

As if there was no bottom to that hunger, the way there always had been with anything else he'd longed for. She was bottomless.

And she was having his child.

No matter how quickly he divorced her after she gave birth, those things would remain true.

"Impending fatherhood agrees with me," he said to the doctor now.

Because he couldn't quite bring himself to use the word that fit. *Happy.* He'd never imagined it was a word that could be applied to him. He'd never thought much about it either way. He'd survived his childhood. He'd survived his one and only attempt to make sense of how his father had treated his mother and him, but it had been a close call, and not one he cared to repeat.

And his response to his father's harsh welcome had been to make himself rich and famous instead of slinking off into the shadows to die of shame, as he'd clearly been meant to do.

Happiness had never seemed like much of a goal next to all that.

The doctor's assistants prepared Sophie, rolling the machines closer to her. But she was the one who lifted her head and beckoned for Renzo to come near. He did, standing awkwardly by the side of the bed, not knowing where to look.

And then not quite knowing what to do when Sophie took his hand as if it was the most natural thing in the world.

She made it entirely too easy to feel the kinds of things about her that he knew he shouldn't. He *couldn't.*

But he didn't have time, now, to worry about that.

Because there was an image on the monitor. A tiny blob, curled around itself like a marvelous bean.

"Look," Sophie said softly. "It's our child."

Their child.

Renzo found himself holding on to Sophie's hand a little too hard as a hard swell of pure joy threatened to take out his knees.

And he bit his own lip before he called this woman what she was, what he dared not admit even to himself.

Not his mistress. Or not merely his mistress, en route

to being the mother of his child and his wife—if not in that order.

But a miracle.

Sophie had just come back from a rambling walk one late afternoon when one of the castle staff, who largely left her to her own devices, rushed into the master bedroom.

She'd gotten used to it being Renzo who met her here and introduced her to all the delicious things people could do with slick soap and a whole lot of hot water.

She had to force herself to lock up her reaction to the images tumbling through her head and concentrate on the woman before her.

"We must get you ready," she was saying briskly. "*Il capo* is taking you out tonight."

And it didn't occur to Sophie to argue. What *il capo* wanted, *il capo* got—and what Sophie had learned over the course of her time here was that the things Renzo wanted, she tended to love.

She stepped into the gown that was laid out for her when she got out of the shower, a flowing, deep blue affair with a high neck in front and no back. She let the woman craft her hair into a complicated chignon that looked simple and then handled her own cosmetics, using only a bit of mascara to darken her lashes and a slick of color on her lips. She strapped herself into a high, impractical pair of sandals that the woman presented to her, admiring the clean, obviously Milanese craftsmanship.

"You must hurry," her attendant chided her when Sophie spent a little too long looking at herself in her mirror, wondering when she'd started to glow like that. As if she'd been plugged into an outlet. "*Il capo* does not like to be kept waiting."

And Sophie smiled, because she knew that was not entirely true.

She walked out to the grand stairway and began to make her way toward the main floor of the castle. She was halfway down the steps when a man stepped out of the library and moved to the bottom of the stairs. Sophie knew who it was in an instant, of course. She didn't have to see his face.

This man was tattooed deep into her skin and fused deep into her bones. He was a part of her, and not only because their child grew bigger inside of her by the day.

She would recognize that lean, mouthwateringly athletic form anywhere. Renzo wore another one of his dark suits tonight that effortlessly enhanced his already astonishingly beautiful form. He was dark and gorgeous and her blood heated as she moved toward him.

He looked at her as if he already owned her.

Which made Sophie wish that he did. Not as a part of *an arrangement*. Not as a mistress. The trouble with having Renzo at all, which perhaps she'd known from that very first night, was that it was never enough. She wanted everything.

She wanted things she didn't know how to name.

But she knew better than to say such a thing to him. She knew better than to ruin what they had. She knew this man—this beautiful, complicated, proud man—would reject her feelings if she was ever foolish enough to mention them out loud.

She told him with her body, every chance she got. She loved him with her hands and her mouth and the place she burned for him the hottest. She loved him when they slept tangled together, breathing as one. She loved him on those dark, wild mornings when he was inside her as she woke, catapulting her over that deliriously sweet edge before she knew her own name.

She loved him in all the ways she could. The only way she could.

Tonight she loved him with a smile and the way she held on to his hand when he took it in his.

"Where are we going?" she asked.

"Trust me," Renzo said.

And she did.

She wasn't entirely sure when that had happened, either. Maybe it had been right around the time she'd stopped blaming him for doing what she hadn't had the courage to do herself. When she'd accepted that she should have been the one to stop her wedding and leave that life behind if she didn't want it—instead of passive-aggressively waiting for her sins to catch up to her as she walked down the aisle in that chapel.

But she didn't want to think about such things tonight. Not when Renzo was dressed to devastate, that deep fire she loved so much making his dark eyes gleam.

Another sleek, low-slung sports car waited for them out on the drive.

"How many cars do you have?" she asked him, but she was smiling.

Renzo opened her door for her and helped her in. "I like cars."

There was a time when she might have seen a statement like that as proof of his arrogance. But she knew him better now. He had told her stories of growing up in this village, with no heat in the winters. His mother had done whatever domestic work she could find to make ends meet, and Renzo had helped as soon as he was old enough.

She couldn't begrudge a man who'd grown up with a hollow belly every night the things he'd earned with his own hard work. The truth was, she thought as he drove them through the village, was that she couldn't find it in her to begrudge this man anything.

He took the single road out of the village, but instead of turning south toward Taormina, he headed in the opposite direction. It took Sophie a moment to understand that they were headed for the next ridge. And the hotel he'd built high above a sweeping vineyard.

Much like the castle, the hotel clung to the side of a cliff. It was all red roofs and golden light, bright against the evening. Renzo pulled up to the front of the main hotel building, and was greeted by name by the brace of valets waiting there.

But it wasn't only that they knew his name. They appeared to genuinely like him.

The same thing seemed true of every hotel employee they passed when they walked inside. They were deferential, certainly, but Sophie knew the difference between professional courtesy and genuine affection. This was the latter.

If she'd had any doubt that Renzo had done exactly what he claimed to do—that he'd really saved the village and everyone in it, along with himself—she thought this proved it.

Renzo led her through the main part of the hotel, arranged on sumptuous levels to make the most of the views in all directions. Then he ushered her outside again, and up a path scented with night flowers and the distant sea toward a separate villa, higher up on the cliff.

Inside, the rooms were airy and let the mountains in. And dinner had been set for them out on the terrace that ran the length of the building.

Sophie stepped out into the sweet evening and looked out at the village she knew so well now, and beyond that, the castle where she'd lived all these weeks.

It felt like magic, but it paled next to the enchantment of the man who came and joined her at the rail.

"I'm not at all surprised that this hotel is successful," she said. "The village looks like something out of a fairy tale. Complete with a perfect castle."

"I don't believe in fairy tales," Renzo said. There was a set to his jaw that she hadn't seen in a while. Something very nearly belligerent—but in the next moment it was gone, and Sophie wondered if she'd imagined it. Especially when he smiled at her. "But as long as the guests do, that's all that matters."

There was a different charge in the air between them, Sophie thought as they sat at the pretty little table and ate dinner there under the stars. A darker, more insistent kind of electricity, and there was a knot of something like anticipation deep in her belly.

The food was exquisite. The Sicilian summer night was soft and beautiful. And the man across from her was far more stunning than any of their surroundings. Sophie thought she could happily gaze at him forever.

They sipped small cups of strong coffee after the last of the plates had been cleared away. And when she heard the hotel staff close the front door of the villa, Sophie expected Renzo to reach for her.

But he didn't.

Instead, he reached into the interior pocket of his suit jacket, and pulled something out. And before she could identify what it was, he stood from his seat, let his mouth curve into that sensual quirk that still drove her mad, and then pulled her up to stand with him there at the rail.

Her heart stopped beating. Then kicked, so hard it made her dizzy.

"What...what are you doing?"

"I think, *cara*, that you know very well I am not about to break into dance."

His sardonic tone felt like rich chocolate, thick and decadent, pouring all over her.

"I think I'd like to see you dance, now that you mention it."

"Alas, another dream that will never come true," Renzo

murmured. His expression turned serious. "You told me that your engagement to your earl involved the signing of contracts in your father's office, did you not?"

"Yes." Sophie was beyond startled. She was…something else entirely, and she couldn't seem to get a handle on it. She could only answer his questions. "I was called in. Dal was already there and he and my father signed the papers. Then, some weeks later, there was a dinner."

"This is not a contract for your father to sign," Renzo told her then, gruff and serious. "This is a contract you wear yourself."

He presented the box he held to her and cracked it open.

It was a diamond ring that seemed to catch every bit of light and make it brighter. And Sophie hadn't given a lot of thought to the sort of diamond a man like Renzo might prefer, but she knew in an instant that if she had, it would not have been this one.

She would have expected something modern and edgy from him, to match the way he fused history and a contemporary sensibility in places like this hotel or the castle across the way. An emerald cut rectangle, perhaps, to show off the carats and express his domination.

But the ring he held before her looked like all the fairy tales he'd claimed he didn't believe in. Three round diamonds surrounded by pavé and filigree, suitable for princesses and storybooks alike.

It made her heart thud. And more, it told her things about Renzo she was positive he didn't know himself.

Like that intent fierceness in his gaze, as if he didn't know what her answer would be. As if he was in some doubt about this thing between them, though she knew he'd never admit he entertained uncertainty. Not when he'd been so clear about the progression. Mistress. Wife only long enough to provide legitimacy to his child. An engagement, complete with a ring, hadn't been part of it.

But she wasn't entirely sure he knew what she could see in him tonight, and that made her heart kick at her again. Harder than before.

Renzo's mouth was set in that stern line, as if what he expected from her was an argument. Because, she understood then, he had fought for everything he had. Everything.

Even her.

"Marry me," he said, more order than invitation, because that was who he was. The only man Sophie loved, or ever would. "Now."

CHAPTER ELEVEN

RENZO DIDN'T WAIT for Sophie to answer. He pulled the ring from the box and took her hand in his, sliding the astonishingly dreamy piece of jewelry onto her finger.

Where, Sophie couldn't help but notice, it fit perfectly.

As if it was meant to be there. As if *this* was what had been meant to happen all along, no matter what he'd told her.

And for a moment, everything disappeared. The island of Sicily was no more. There was no hotel, no rolling vineyards beneath the stars, no postcard-perfect village in the distance.

There was only this particular moment of communion. Special, sacred. A kind of holy she had only experienced before when he was deep inside her, and she was showing him how much she loved him with every touch.

This was like that. And yet more, somehow.

Sophie felt shaken. But not in a way that left her weak. She felt shaken and strong, somehow.

Right, a voice inside her intoned, like the ringing of a bell. *This is* right.

It was as if everything was finally right, at last. It all made sense. That night in Monte Carlo led straight to this. And every step along the way felt necessary. Important.

Their own kind of perfect.

"Yes, I'll marry you," Sophie said, and smiled to keep her emotions in check, though she wasn't sure she succeeded. "Not that you asked."

"I didn't realize it was a question that needed asking." But there was a curve to Renzo's beautiful mouth. And he still hadn't let go of her hand. "This was always the plan, was it not?"

And she loved him, so she didn't point out that bloodlessly cold arranged marriages rarely began with actual proposals like this one. She loved him, so she only smiled wider. She loved him, so she—

Sophie frowned, as all of his words finally penetrated. "Did you say *now*?"

Renzo kept his eyes on hers. That curve in his mouth became a true smile. And he lifted his free hand.

The staff that Sophie had thought gone reappeared then. And this time, they brought in a man wreathed in smiles who bowed, complimented *il capo* on the happy news, and introduced himself to Sophie as the mayor of the village.

"How is this possible?" she asked Renzo. "I thought weddings in Italy required...?"

"The mayor owes me a favor," Renzo replied, still holding her hand as if he thought she might make a break for it. "I rebuilt his house. In return he issued me a special marriage license, handled the paperwork, and posted the banns over the last weeks."

Sophie found she was breathless, but she couldn't quite bring herself to mind. "When you said *now*, you meant right now."

Renzo only looked at her, his dark amber eyes so fierce and consuming.

And in the end, it wasn't a struggle. Sophie was already in love with him. She was already carrying his baby. As far she was concerned, marrying him was nothing but a technicality.

She remembered what he'd said about their divorce and visitation rights—but she shoved it aside. That had been so long ago, now. She'd seen the look on his face when he'd looked at their baby on the ultrasound monitor. And tonight, as he'd given her the ring she wore.

Renzo might not say he loved her. He might not know that he did. But she was sure—she was more than sure—that there was no way she was in this deep alone.

And this time, there was no aisle to walk down and no second thoughts. They stood on the balcony with all the world sparkling there at their feet, and spoke their vows.

When Sophie promised to love and honor Renzo, she meant it.

And she thought he did, too.

When the simple ceremony was done, the staff made their exit and Renzo finally swept her up and into his arms. For a moment, he simply held her there.

She couldn't keep herself from reaching for him. She laid the hand that now sported the two rings he'd given her against his jaw, and wasn't certain her body could contain all the joy that pulsed in her then.

It was like that light in his eyes, fierce and encompassing.

"You married me," Sophie said softly, and she couldn't seem to stop smiling.

"I told you I would," Renzo replied, his voice low and his dark eyes aglow as he held her high against his chest. "I keep my promises, *cara*. You should know this about me."

"And your vows."

"Always."

He carried her into one of the villa's sumptuous bedchambers. The bed was a high, commanding platform strewn with rose petals, and Renzo carefully laid her down in the middle of them.

And then he worshipped her with his body. There was no other way to describe it.

In a kind of reverent silence, he slipped the shoes from her feet. He set his mouth and his hands to every centimeter of her body, claiming her and exalting her.

It was as if he was imprinting himself…everywhere. By the time he took her dress off, and stripped her down until she was wearing nothing but the rings he'd put on her finger, Sophie felt outside herself.

Almost sick with joy. Heavy with it.

She couldn't touch him enough. She couldn't kiss him, taste him, explore him enough.

She couldn't get *enough*.

Renzo was a man possessed. He ran his hands over her belly and the beginnings of her bump, murmuring praise and devotion to his child the way he always did.

But when it came to the rest of her, he'd clearly set himself the task of taking her apart.

And he did. Over and over and over again.

Sophie lost track of how many times she shattered on his fingers. His mouth.

And when he finally pulled her on top of him, holding her where he wanted her as he surged into her, she was too far gone to be careful. She was lost in the joy of this. The beauty that was this night, this man.

The exquisite wonder that was the light and hope they made between them.

She heard the sound of her voice, repeating something again and again, like a chant.

His hands gripped her hips, almost too hard for comfort, as he set an intense pace.

"Again," he ordered her, ferocious and commanding below her. "I want you to come again."

And when she didn't obey him immediately, he moved his clever fingers to her center, and pressed down hard.

Sophie shattered one more time. She thought she died, it went on so long, and the only thing she was aware of for a very long while was Renzo's hoarse shout as he followed her.

It felt like much later when she came back to herself, slumped on top of him as if he really had broken her.

And it took her longer than it should have to realize that he was not holding her the way he normally did. He was… tense, there below her, still inside her.

She would have said he was angry if they hadn't just—

But that was when she realized what she'd done. What she'd been repeating over and over again while out of her mind, hopped up on their impromptu wedding and these weeks of loving him with everything she had.

Over and over and over again, so there could be no mistake.

She could *hear* it, as if there was an echo in the room, beating her with her own words.

I love you, she'd said, fool that she was. She'd cried it out again and again. *I love you, I love you.*

Renzo, I love you.

She didn't want to open her eyes. She didn't want to face it when she could feel him beneath her, stiff and furious.

But that was the old Sophie. The one who'd walked halfway down an aisle toward a man she could never love and didn't even want because she'd imagined it was easier than causing a scene.

The new Sophie didn't hide from her problems. She didn't go along with things simply to avoid conflict, no matter how much she might want to do just that.

And she had never wanted to do it more than she did just then.

She forced herself to open her eyes and lift her head, facing Renzo straight on.

He was staring back at her, his dark amber eyes like a storm, his expression grim.

And she knew that everything had changed.

Again.

"You do not love me," Renzo bit out at her.

She was soft and much too sweet. He was still deep inside her and all he could feel was that soft heat of hers, making him stir all over again. She was his wife.

His wife.

But that didn't matter. He couldn't let that matter.

Because all he could hear were those damned words. Those terrible, ruinous words.

He expected her to deny it. To wave it away, and the sad part was, he knew he would accept it if she did. He would choose to believe she'd been carried away. They'd had a wedding, after all, and this one hadn't been interrupted. She wore his rings and she'd made her pretty vows, making his child legitimate well before its birth, just as he'd always wanted.

If she told him she'd made a mistake, he would believe her.

He *wanted* to believe her, with a sharp-edged ferocity that made him feel something like dizzy.

But Sophie pushed herself up slowly, still straddling him, as if she could feel him all over her and deep inside her and *in her bones* the way he could feel her.

Her gaze was somber. Almost sad, and he had a terrible inkling—

"I'm sorry if it upsets you," she said, very quietly. Very distinctly. "But I do."

"I told you that was unacceptable from the start. Our arrangement—"

"It turns out that my heart doesn't care what arrangement we made," she replied, much too softly. And with that glowing thing in her melting brown eyes that he didn't want to identify. He didn't want to see it, because he knew it had been there awhile. He didn't want to admit to himself just how long. "And I think yours—"

"No."

He lifted her up and off of him. Then he was rolling out of the bed before he fully understood he meant to move. All he could think about was getting away from her. Getting away from *this*.

His worst nightmare come to life.

"Renzo—"

"You knew the rules. I told you the rules."

He didn't sound like himself. And that was the trouble, wasn't it? He hadn't been acting like himself for weeks. All this…domestic bliss, as if that was a real possibility for a man like him. What had he been playing at?

Renzo pulled his clothes back on in quick, determined jerks. Then he headed for the door, knowing nothing except he needed space. A hell of a lot of space. A continent or two, by his estimation.

He should have known better. He *had* known better. He'd known the moment he'd laid eyes on her in that casino that he should steer clear of her.

The trouble was, he had wanted Sophie too much.

The trouble was, he still did.

There had been so many warning signs and he'd ignored every one. This was supposed to be a punishment, not a love story. Because he could handle one.

The other was nothing but a lie—he knew that better than anyone.

He refused to handle this. He didn't even want to think about it.

He needed to get out of here.

"Renzo, please!"

When he looked over his shoulder, Sophie had pulled

one of the bedsheets around her and was standing there in the center of the villa's spacious main room, her gaze imploring.

And he knew he would live the rest of his life and never manage to get this image of her out of his head. Her gorgeous hair tousled from his hands, hanging all around her. Her beautiful eyes, wide and hurt. That faint trembling he could see on her lips.

His beautiful Sophie. His wife.

"You need to leave Sicily immediately," he growled at her.

"Leave?" She swayed slightly on her feet and he didn't put out a hand to steady her. And he hated himself with a comprehensive ferocity that should have toppled him. And yet didn't. Somehow he was still standing. "Where will I go?"

"I have properties all over Europe. Any one of them will do."

He should never have brought her here in the first place. He understood that now, with the awful clarity of retrospect. There was too much of his old self here. That lonely outcast he'd been. That boy still full up on optimism and hope, in those long, cold years when he'd still imagined things could be different.

And more, that he could change them.

He'd been a fool then. He was a fool now. He should have known that he wouldn't be able to keep the two separate, the way they had been for almost the whole of his adult life. Not with a woman like Sophie.

Her smile was too pretty. It lit up parts of him he'd thought dead for more than a decade.

But Renzo didn't believe in resurrection.

"You said I would stay here for the duration of my pregnancy," she reminded him, clutching at that sheet as if it could save her from this. From him.

But it was too late for that. No one was getting saved here, least of all the woman he'd warned not to do the very thing she'd gone ahead and done.

"Now I'm saying that's unacceptable," he told her, cold and brutal. "You can't stay here another day."

"It doesn't change anything," she threw at him. "I've been in love with you this whole time. Don't you realize that? Do you really believe I would have just gone off with any man who smiled at me that night in Monte Carlo?"

"Stop," he ordered her, though his own voice sounded ragged. "Now."

"Of course not," Sophie said, answering her own question. And there was too much emotion—on her face, in her voice, filling up the villa. Filling up him, too. "It was you, Renzo. Only and ever you. I didn't ask you to love me back. I didn't ask you for anything."

He knew he didn't make a noise, and he didn't understand how, when everything inside him was a roar. A howl.

"You asked for everything," he gritted out at her, hardly knowing what he meant to say. "But I don't have it in me. I don't have anything to give."

"You do."

She stepped closer to him, proving that she was far more courageous than he'd ever given her credit for, and she even reached out as if she meant to touch him. And he wanted that touch. God, how he wanted it—almost as much as he wanted her to never, ever touch him with those hands of hers again, because he didn't think he could bear it.

But she stopped before she made contact.

And Renzo couldn't tell if he was happy about that or if it broke him.

"You do," she said again, more intently. "I know you do. I can feel it."

"Love is a vicious lie," he told her, and the words hurt him as they tore from his throat. "A delusion."

"Renzo—"

But he didn't stop. "I left this place when I was eighteen. You know that. I couldn't wait to go. What you don't know is that I didn't leave here to make money. All I wanted was to take care of my mother, at last. The way she'd always taken care of me."

"I think that's the very definition of love."

"She loved my father," Renzo told her. "She was the chambermaid in his great, grand palace in the Alps, and she loved him. He toyed with her, and she loved him. He brought home a wife, and still she loved him. And he let her because he liked it."

Sophie had dropped her hand back down to her side, but she didn't back away. And she didn't try to interrupt him again.

"Until she fell pregnant, that was, and then he kicked her out. With nothing." Renzo shook his head. "And she still loved him. She made excuses for him. He had duties, you see. Responsibilities. He couldn't help that he was swept up in events and promises beyond his control. Does that sound familiar?"

Sophie blanched at that, and Renzo hated himself all the more for drawing that line between his worthless father and his own, personal miracle.

But he didn't take it back.

"And when I was eighteen and finally a man grown in my estimation, I went to find him. This man who my mother still loved all those years later, when she had done nothing but suffer and raise me, destroying her own health in the process."

"Did you find him?"

Renzo's lips thinned. "My father is not a hard man to find. Access to him is another matter, of course." These were not pleasant memories, but he forced himself to spit them out. This story he had never told another living soul.

"I had to present myself at his gates and petition for an audience. His men escorted me into his exalted presence. And I asked him why, if he'd loved my mother, he'd cast her—and me—aside."

He still remembered that day. Every excruciating detail. The principality his father ruled small and remote and like a little jewel, tucked out of reach. The palace like a fairy tale, high in the Alps.

And the man who'd sat in the desperately ornate hall and smirked when he saw Renzo, because they had the same eyes.

The same damned eyes.

"He laughed at me," Renzo told Sophie with the same old bitterness that had nearly killed him then. Some part of him thought it had. Because he had never been the same. "He laughed and he laughed. He called my mother names that I cannot repeat. And when I took a swing at him, he had his guards beat me."

Sophie only whispered his name, but he felt it like a touch. And he steeled himself to tell her the rest.

"When I was bloody, he told me to kneel," Renzo told her. "I declined. And so this man my mother still loved, my father, threw me into his prison. And left me there for a week."

He found Sophie's face, the only bright thing in the middle of all those dark memories.

But he didn't believe in brightness any more than he believed in love. Or hope.

"They dragged me before him again. And this time, he didn't laugh. He looked me in the eye and he warned me never to return." Renzo shook his head, trying to clear those nasty old memories. The viciousness on the older man's face. His total lack of concern about the things he'd done to his own child. "And when I returned here, some-how, my mother knew."

"What he did to you?"

"No. That I had found him. I never told her what he did." Renzo let out a laugh then, though there was little mirth in it. "And after eighteen years of no contact, do you know what she asked me? She wanted to know how he was. If *he* was okay." He found he still couldn't believe it. "Can you imagine?"

"She loved him," Sophie said simply.

Renzo was glad she did. It reminded him what was at stake here. What was happening when he should have known better than to allow it to come to this.

"I lied to her," Renzo told Sophie then. "I spun her a tale about a man trapped by his duty and unable to do right by her, because that was the story she'd told herself all those years. That was what she needed. And she was a sick old woman who had sacrificed too much for her folly, so she was happy to believe me. But I knew the truth. I knew that man was nothing. Less than nothing. He didn't deserve her love and he certainly didn't return it." He blew out a breath, surprised to find that wounds he'd thought he cauterized years ago still had the power to hurt him. "And I let my own mother die, believing this lie. That is the kind of man I am."

"I'm sure it gave her comfort to believe it," Sophie said with a kind of urgency in her voice, and too much emotion in her gaze. "There's nothing wrong with that."

"Love is a curse," Renzo told her, his voice nearly shaking from the force of his fury, black and terrible. "It is a poison. I told you not to fall in love with me, Sophie. I warned you." He stepped back, because he wanted to step forward and he didn't understand it. But he knew he couldn't allow it. "I warned you."

"Renzo."

She sounded wounded, and he hated it—but there was nothing he could do. He knew what love did. It twisted and corroded. It was nothing but lies and it ended in blood on the floor of a distant jail cell and fairy tales his mother should have known better than to believe. He knew exactly what love was.

"What do you think will happen?" Sophie was asking, sounding as torn up as he was inside. "You can't possibly think—"

"Love is a sickness, nothing more," he threw at her, and it didn't matter how she looked at him. It didn't matter how he felt. What mattered was what he knew. What he'd had proven to him in no uncertain terms all those years ago. "You can love me all you want, Sophie. But you can do it alone."

And he left her there, his rings on her hand and his baby in her belly, because she'd given him no other choice.

Because leaving her might tear at him, more than he would have imagined possible and almost more than he could bear—but it was better than love.

CHAPTER TWELVE

FOR A LONG WHILE, Sophie stood where he had left her.

Right there in the middle of the villa, wearing nothing but a bedsheet. And her wedding rings.

She thought there was likely a joke in there somewhere, though she couldn't quite feel it. Not quite yet. Something about the bride who couldn't make it to the altar and the wife who couldn't make it through her wedding night.

Maybe someday she would find it funny.

She felt like an old woman by the time she finally moved, making her way into the shower though her bones ached and there was that horrible tightness in her chest she was afraid might never go away.

And Sophie stood in the hot spray and let the water course over her for a long, long time, as if it could wash her clean. As if it could rewind this evening to where it had all gone wrong.

As if it could allow her to start over and be a little wiser this time.

She didn't let herself fall apart. She didn't sob into the spray.

What would be the point? Renzo had already left.

When she finally emerged, she toweled herself off and tried not to pay any attention to the parts of her body that still seemed to hum, because longing for Renzo's touch was only going to make this worse.

Assuming it was possible that this could get worse.

She dressed herself in that same blue gown that Renzo had taken off of her so slowly, and swallowed hard against the lump in her throat. She combed her hair with her fingers and then gave it up as a lost cause—but then, she felt like one herself.

And when she stepped out into the main room of the villa again, there were hotel staff there waiting for her.

"*Il capo* has sent a car," the deferential man told her, inclining his head. The woman with him did the same. "If the *signora* would be so kind…"

Sophie tried to smile, but she hardly thought a grotesque twist of her lips did the job. She found she couldn't speak. She could only follow along as Renzo's people ushered her into a car that whisked her down the mountain.

Away from the village. Away from the castle she'd come to feel was like a home.

Away from Renzo.

The car delivered her to the airport in Catania, where a first-class ticket sat waiting for her. A quick flight to Rome tonight and then on to London in the morning.

He was sending her home.

Sophie took the ticket at the counter with fingers gone numb. Her driver had handed her a small folio containing her passport and credit cards when she'd gotten out of the car, as well as a small case. When she made it to her gate, still in a fog, she unzipped it and looked through it. It contained the few clothes Renzo had liberated from her honeymoon luggage back in Langston House, what felt like a lifetime ago, as if he was sending her back with only what she'd had when he'd taken her.

As if none of this had ever happened.

She closed the case and sat back. And then found herself looking at her hands. At the two rings Renzo had slid onto her fingers earlier tonight. The romantic fantasy in diamonds and with it, a platinum eternity band. Bright and shining, no matter what angle she looked at them from.

There was a kind of bubble in her chest, and Sophie was terribly afraid that it was filled with poison. And more, that if it burst it would destroy her.

But the longer she stared at the rings on her finger, the more that bubble…shifted.

Until Sophie was fairly certain it wasn't so much pain in there as a kind of wild fury.

The gate agent started boarding her flight, but Sophie didn't move.

She didn't want to go to back to London. She didn't want to be sent back to her parents' house, or wherever it was Renzo thought she would go once he was rid of her. There was nothing for her but scandal and pity in England, and Sophie very much doubted she'd want to deal with any of that at all, much less in a fashion that would please her family.

Why not just get on the plane? a voice inside asked, sounding caustic and accusatory. *This is what you always do.*

And Sophie didn't disagree. Here she was, sitting in her deep blue wedding dress, her hair still damp and her heart smashed into pieces in her chest. Renzo had raged at her. His eyes had been dark with the past, and she had known without having to ask that he didn't see her—he saw his memories.

And so she had stood there, like that ghost she'd been so sure she was becoming, and she had done nothing but watch him leave.

Then she had simply acquiesced the way she always did.

She'd let them hustle her off that mountain. She'd taken her case and her passport without a word, and she'd obediently marched up to the ticket counter and accepted what amounted to an eviction notice.

The old Sophie would have already boarded the plane and sat there in her seat in a miserable little ball. She would have felt all the same heartache and anger that Sophie did right now, but she would have done what she'd been told to do anyway.

Because she'd always done what she'd been told to do.

But Renzo hadn't married the old Sophie. Renzo had pretty much wrecked the old Sophie. And then he'd gone ahead and married this one.

And *this* Sophie had absolutely no intention of shuffling off quietly into that dark night, simply because Renzo's feelings were hurt. Or because something in his past— even something as truly awful as the story he'd told her— had ruined him and made him think he couldn't feel things or love anyone.

Sophie knew a thing or two about ruin, as it happened. And what she'd learned most of all was that it was entirely up to her how ruined she chose to feel.

"Apologies, *signora*," the gate agent said then, snapping Sophie back to the Catania Airport. To the here and now and the choice she needed to make. "But the plane is fully boarded and ready to depart. If you would take your seat…?"

This time, when Sophie smiled, her lips worked the way they were meant to. She stood, gripping her case so hard in one hand she was surprised that the handle didn't break off.

"Thank you," she told the gate agent. "But I won't be getting on that plane."

She wasn't going to sit around and hope that Renzo came to his senses. She wasn't going to meekly make her way back to England, and spend her life apologizing for something she wasn't all that sorry about to people whose opinions meant nothing to her.

She had told him that she loved him. And Sophie might

not have had a whole lot of experience with love, it was true. But she knew it wasn't leaving when things were rough. She knew it wasn't taking hurtful words as gospel when she knew—*she knew*—that whether he was aware of it or not, Renzo loved her to distraction.

Because love was standing up for what she believed. Love was protecting her little family, the baby inside her and its beautiful, brooding, difficult father—especially when he didn't want her to do anything of the kind.

Renzo might not believe in love, but it was real and good whether he believed in it or not.

Sophie was simply going to have to show him.

When the door to his office in the castle opened, Renzo didn't look up.

He'd been going over reports in a kind of fever since the middle of the night, when he'd stopped pretending that he might get a moment's rest. He'd stared at his ceiling for a while, then decided that it was far better to immerse himself in work than lie in the bed he no longer shared with Sophie, imagining her with him. Beside him and below him.

But the change of venue hadn't helped.

There was no part of this castle he'd restored with his own two hands that didn't remind him of her. There was no escape. She was everywhere. He found himself listening for her step in the hall. He was sure he could still catch her scent in the air. And meanwhile, he felt disfigured by the things he had told her and more, the love she claimed to feel.

I love you, she had said, her head tipped back and her face awash in bliss. *I love you, Renzo. I love you.*

He would rather be in that prison again. He would rather have every bone in his body broken, repeatedly.

He would rather anything but this.

"It is not like you to hide, Renzo. Or to pretend that you are alone in this room when you must know very well you are not."

Sophie.

Renzo took his time raising his head. He wanted to believe that she was nothing but a ghost, but he knew better. She was too alive, there before him. Flushed and fierce, her hair in a glorious tangle and her hands on her hips. She still wore the blue dress he'd had made especially for her, and that nicked something in him.

Like a sharp blade pressed against his flesh.

There were too many things inside of him, then. Something like panic, harsh and suffocating. That same fire that only seemed to grow the longer he knew her, the flames dancing all over him the way her fingers might.

And in and around all of that, fury.

The same fury that had animated him all these lonely years. The fury he'd felt when he'd buried his mother, her ears still ringing from the lies he had told. The fury that had made him famous and then rich, because it had been what fueled him. It had been his favorite companion, down deep beneath the charm he wielded as a distraction or the laziness he assumed as a disguise.

It was the engine that drove him. It was all he'd ever thought he wanted.

Until Sophie had burst over him like a sunrise, making him something other than the weapon he'd made himself into over that long week in his father's prison.

He had been a thing of fury and fire, but she had made him flesh.

Renzo had forgiven her the lies she'd told him, though he hadn't intended to do such a thing. It had happened sometime in these last weeks, a simple shift he'd only noticed after it had happened. He'd even forgiven her that ill-considered walk down an English aisle.

But this was the thing he couldn't—wouldn't—forgive.

"You are meant to be on a plane," he told her, his voice cold. "You should have landed in Rome already."

"It turns out that I don't really care for Rome at this time of year," she told him, and Renzo took an instant dislike to her tone.

She was too calm. Much too composed.

And the hectic glitter he could see in her dark eyes didn't assuage him.

"You have no business here," he said, clipped and chilly. "I told you to leave. I meant it."

"And if I were your mistress, I might obey you." Her gaze met his, bold and defiant, and he hated that it took his breath. Still. "After all, what is a mistress if not a business arrangement? Intimate, perhaps, but never emotional. Isn't that what you told me?"

"You know where the door is."

Sophie's lovely mouth curved. "Unfortunately for you, Renzo, I am not your mistress. I am your wife."

He didn't like that at all. "A situation that can be easily remedied."

"Can it? Not for months, not if you wish your child to be born with your name." She had the gall to let her smile widen when he scowled at her. "Oh, I'm sorry. Did you expect me to simply slink away, tail between my legs, in a shroud of shame for daring to express my feelings?"

Renzo didn't know he'd shot to his feet, but there he was. Standing up, his hands and fists, and this maddening woman right there before him on the other side of his desk. Taunting him. Making him wish—

But no. The mistake he had made was in letting all of this go too far already. He should have sent her off to one of his other hotels in the first place. Somewhere faraway, where he could have had her pregnancy monitored by medical personnel, and never subject himself to this.

This terrible intimacy that felt like some kind of arthritis, making his bones protest.

"I can't imagine what you think this will accomplish," he told her, making a herculean effort to sound at least as calm as she did. "You're not going to argue me into changing my mind. I told you from the start what was between us. I regret that you got the wrong idea." He lifted a shoulder, then dropped it, in an excellent approximation of the ease that had been second nature to him before her. "I did warn you."

"The issue isn't whether or not I love you." Sophie sounded certain of that. "You asked me to be your mistress because you claimed that too many women, if left to their own devices, fell in love with you. That was why we needed the structure. That was why you insisted on our arrangement."

"And you shouldn't have broken the rules."

"I don't think the rules were in place to keep me from falling in love with you," she said gently, as if she was trying to explain astrophysics to a toddler. "You are so certain it was inevitable that you must have expected nothing less. I think you set those rules so that when it happened, you could gently disengage yourself and remind me what we'd agreed." She shook her head, almost as if she was sad. "But instead, you married me. Not as I was heading into childbirth, as threatened. But now."

Renzo didn't like the way that hit him, like some kind of indictment.

"That was always part of the plan. I told you not to read too much into it."

It was Sophie's turn to shrug and it set his teeth on edge.

"It turns out I'm terribly emotional," she said, much too offhandedly for Renzo's taste. "I can't help it. But what about you?"

He felt as if she'd shoved a stake through his heart. Part of him wished she had. It would be simpler. Cleaner.

"I don't know what you mean."

"I would be happy to apologize for the terrible sin of falling in love with you," she said quietly. "But first I want you to admit what we both know is the real truth."

When he only stared at her, she lifted her brows, looking every inch the aristocratic Carmichael-Jones heiress.

His Sophie.

His wife.

"You're in love with me, Renzo," she said.

He was gripped by something he couldn't understand, then. He didn't know its name. It held on to him, like iron fists around his throat, his chest, his gut. It clenched hard, ripping the air from his lungs. Ripping him apart, but not fast enough.

Because he was still standing. He was still breathing.

And worst of all, Sophie was studying him as he stood there, filled with all this rage and need and fury and darkness.

He had the terrible feeling she could see all of it.

That it was possible she always had.

"I am not capable of love," he heard himself say, like rocks scraped together. "It is not in me."

"I know it is."

Her voice was so sure. So offensively *certain*. Renzo wanted to rage at her. He wanted to tear something apart, with his fingers if necessary, but he didn't let himself move. And even so, he felt as if the thing torn most was him.

"Then you have not heard a single thing I have ever told you," he said, through his teeth.

"Renzo." And he told himself he hated the way she said his name. As if it was a part of her. "You told me a story last night. About love."

"I told you a story about doomed, damned men and the

miseries they inflict on everyone around them. If that is not what you heard, then you have too many fairy tales on the brain."

"You told me the story of a boy who was raised on a love story," she corrected him.

"I told you about a boy who was raised on a *lie*, Sophie."

"He had nothing," Sophie continued as if she hadn't heard him. "Except hope. And he took that hope and went to find the truth of the story he'd lived with all those years."

"And that went so well. Hope blooms in prison, of course."

"Your father sounds like an awful man. He beat you, but he didn't break you. You came back here, and you could have passed on the kind of beating he gave you. You could have ripped out your mother's heart and stamped it into the ground." Sophie's eyes were shining in a way that made him…ache. "But you didn't."

"You are telling me a story of weakness," Renzo snarled at her. "Why would anyone want to hear it?"

"You cared so much for her that you let her die believing in that love, when you knew it wasn't true." Sophie lifted her hands in a kind of supplication. "I can't think of a greater love than that. I only hope that you love our child so much, that you would protect it from everything, even itself."

He wanted to rage at that, but he couldn't seem to speak.

"You love me, Renzo, and you love this child," Sophie said, every word a blow. "And I know that you have no desire to be the kind of father yours was. Distant. Damaged. Do you?"

There was that howling thing inside of him, more complicated than simple fury. It was like a hurricane beneath his own skin, tearing him apart from his bones on out.

"You have to go," he managed to grit out.

But she didn't seem to hear him. Or she didn't care. She

certainly didn't turn and leave as commanded. Instead, she moved toward him. Renzo stood as if he was frozen into place as she rounded the desk.

"You love me," she said again, more fervently this time. "You love our child. The only one you don't love, as far as I can tell, is you."

And he was cracking wide-open. He was a hurricane, or he was consumed by one, and he couldn't tell the difference.

The world was a howling thing, desperate and deadly, and Renzo didn't know how to fight it. He was known for his steadiness, and yet he felt rocked straight through. Her melting brown eyes, shot through with gold, were filled with something he didn't want to identify.

He didn't want to feel any of this. He didn't want to *feel*.

Sophie reached over and took his hand in hers. His fingers dwarfed hers, but she held it between the two of hers, and it took him a moment to realize that she was holding the hand where he wore a wedding ring to match hers.

"If you don't love yourself, that's all right," Sophie told him, the faintest tremor in her voice, as if these words were wrenched from her soul. "I can love you until you learn. I can love you forever, Renzo. I feel as if I already have."

And maybe it wasn't her vulnerabilities that he was so obsessed with, he thought in some distant part of his head that was still functioning. Maybe it was that she saw his, and loved him anyway.

Maybe all of this was love.

Maybe it always had been.

And Renzo had learned a long time ago to lean into the curves, the sharper and more treacherous, the better.

He didn't think it through. He'd already thought too much and it had brought him nothing but hurricanes and loneliness, and the truth was, he was tired of both. He shifted so that he held both of her hands.

And then, his gaze locked to hers, he sank to his knees before her.

He had never knelt before anyone or anything. But he knelt before Sophie.

"I don't know how to do this," he told her with every part of his battered, furious heart right there, exposed and open. "I buy things. I wait. I possess them. That is all I know."

She pulled her hands from his, and he felt it like a loss. But she was only moving closer, so she could smooth her palms over his jaw, and sink her fingers into his hair.

"Do you think you are the only one who is new to this?" she demanded, a catch in her throat. "Did you hear a single word I said about the way I was raised? My parents may love something, but it isn't me. And I have never loved anything in all my life except you."

"Ah, Sophie. But I am not a good bet."

"Says the man I met in Monte Carlo," she said, her lips curving into the kind of smile he wanted to take with him and hold forever in his heart.

He shook his head, but her fingers moved as if she was trying to soothe him. As if he truly was a wild beast—but if he was, he saw she loved that, too.

It was written all over her.

"You deserve love, Renzo," she whispered. "You don't have to do anything. You don't have to tell me stories. You don't have to protect me from lies. All you have to do is let me love you. And let yourself love me in return. Everything else will work out."

Renzo wanted to believe it. He wanted it more than he could remember wanting anything, even the father he'd longed to find so long ago.

"How do you know?" he demanded. "How can you possibly know?"

"Because those are the vows we made," she told him

solemnly, her gaze on his. "We promised to love each other, even when it's hard. Especially when it's hard. It's easy to marry for the wrong reasons. It's easy to sign a contract and make it a business venture. It's easy to make arrangements and keep emotions out of things." He was gripping her hips as if he would never let go. And Sophie didn't look away. He wasn't sure she even blinked. "This is the hard stuff, Renzo. This is where the promises really count. Anyone can stay married when they have nothing to lose but a house. Or some money. But this? Loving you means fighting for you. The same way you would fight for me. Even if it hurts. *Especially* when it hurts. Or what's the point?"

Still kneeling before her, Renzo reached up to pull her face closer to his.

"I have never believed in love," he told her, in the way he'd said his wedding vows the night before. Deliberate. Considered. Like a contract signed in blood. "But I believe in you. I've tried so hard to let you go, to make you matter less—but here you are. I've tried and I've tried, but I can't quench my thirst for you. It only grows." Her gaze was too shiny again, and Renzo pushed on. "I want you below me. Beside me. I want you every way I've had you and a thousand ways I have yet to imagine. I want to watch you mother our child. I never know what you'll say, and I still want to hear every word. I want everything, Sophie. *Everything*. I don't know what this is."

"You do," she whispered. "You know you do."

"Promise me," he gritted out. "Promise me that you will always fight for me. For us. Even if you must fight *me* for us. And I will do the same."

"Renzo," she whispered, her lips curving as she spoke. "You tried to send me back to England. But here I am, high on a mountain in Sicily, right where I belong. You couldn't keep me from fighting for you. You can't."

"I will hold you to that," Renzo said, sure he sounded as broken as he felt.

And then he took her mouth with his.

And he was whole.

Renzo hadn't believed in love before he met her, but she did. So he poured the things she'd taught him into his kiss.

All the longing. All the need.

The beauty of her smile that could light up any darkness, even his own heart. The magic of her laughter, that had healed him in ways he hadn't known he was broken.

He kissed her for all the fairy tales he'd never believed in, and the story she'd told him about his own life that made him want to believe in a good tale well told, with a happy ending after all.

Just so long as it was with her.

He would learn to love her if it killed him, he told himself. He suspected he already did.

And either way, she would never spend another moment questioning his devotion to her.

He was Renzo Crisanti. If there was a happy ending to be found, he would find it. And he would give it to Sophie, who had made him believe in forever.

And he was a man who kept his vows.

So that was what he did.

Alceu Cabbrieli Crisanti came into the world as if he was in a race, like his father. On his own schedule, a good two weeks before expected, with all the intensity and fury that Sophie supposed she should have expected from a child made by a man like Renzo.

And she loved him, red faced and angry-fisted, with a kind of ferocity that would have scared her a little, had Renzo not had the same expression on his face every time he looked at the child they'd made.

"My beautiful son," he would murmur, holding the fussing baby when he woke while Sophie prepared herself to feed him. And then, when Alceu latched onto her breast, Renzo would raise that darkly wondering gaze to hers. "My beautiful wife."

"Our family," she would say, as if it was a prayer.

It felt like a benediction.

They had spent a kind of honeymoon together these last months, waiting for Alceu's arrival. For a long time they'd kept the world out, but Sophie had known that was a state of affairs that couldn't last forever. No matter how she wished it could.

"Why can't it?" Renzo asked at the start of her final trimester. He had been lounging beside her in their bed, his hands on her belly to feel the baby kick inside her. "What do we owe the world?"

"This isn't about us," she'd told him, aware that he trusted her more by the day—but that it was still a battle. That his past was always with him.

That some things would take time.

And by the time the baby was born, she'd managed to convince her strong, proud, happily fierce Sicilian husband that it was worth his time to extend an olive branch to her parents. Or to suffer it while she did, more like.

"The truth is that it will cost you nothing," she told him after she'd made the initial phone call. "They will visit rarely, if at all. In the unlikely event they do, it will be as if they are miles away when they're in the same room. None of that matters."

"Then why bother?"

She'd stroked his lean jaw and marveled at the blaze in those dark amber eyes she loved so much. The blaze that was theirs. The blaze that had been there since the moment they'd clapped eyes on each other in Monaco and would be there when they were tottery and old.

Sophie and this man who still considered himself as

solitary as the castle he'd rebuilt himself, even if he'd let her in. This man she was making a family with, making him less solitary by the day.

"Because they are going to be the grandparents of this child," she told him softly. "Whether you like it or not."

"I think it is you who do not like it, *cara*."

"The family business has to be run by someone," she said, raising her brows at him. "You fought for everything you have. Will you insist your son do the same?"

He answered her in his favorite way, with his mouth to hers, stoking that fire that only ever grew between them.

Which was as close to surrender as Renzo ever came.

Though on this particular sparkling day at the start of a Sicilian spring, Sophie thought that there were many different forms of surrender, and most of them looked like love.

Because today was Alceu's christening, in splendid Sicilian fashion. The lovely old church in the village had been ringing its bells all morning, and all that remained was for *il capo* and his little family to walk across the square to begin the mass.

"We will discuss consequences tonight," Renzo told her as they walked. He held his son against his chest the way he liked to do, and Sophie marveled at the way the Sicilian sun made the pair of them glow.

As if love lit them up from all around.

"You do love your consequences," she murmured, laughing at him when he arched one of his king-of-the-universe looks her way. "Unfortunately for you, so do I."

"I believe I deserve sainthood for what I am about to endure. I may take it up with the priest."

"Poppy is my oldest and best friend," Sophie said, the way she had a hundred times already—today alone. "There can be no other possible choice for Alceu's godmother."

"And why that means the man you nearly married

while pregnant with my son must also be involved, I do not know," Renzo retorted.

"Because he's Poppy's husband, as you are well aware." She smiled at him, ignoring his dark expression. "And he was never cruel to me, Renzo. It was quite the opposite."

She could see them up ahead, her best friend and the man Sophie had been supposed to marry. They waited out on the steps of the church, smiling at each other in a way that told Sophie without a single doubt that all of this had been meant to be.

Poppy and Dal never would have found each other in this way if Dal and Sophie had married. This Sophie knew for a fact.

And Sophie knew that she and Dal would never have looked at each other the way Poppy and Dal did. It was as if a warm current wrapped around the two of them and gleamed bright. As if they were connected whether or not they touched.

The fact that they were wildly, madly in love seemed to add an extra glow to the light dancing all over the square.

Not to mention, it made Sophie's heart feel three sizes too big.

Dal had accepted Sophie's apology. Poppy and Sophie had caught up at last—each with quite a story to tell.

And now Poppy and Dal would stand up with Sophie and Renzo and pledge to take care of the precious life they'd all had a hand in making, one way or another. Or maybe it was the other way around—Alceu was the life that had given them the courage or impetus to live the lives they'd been meant to live, not the lives they'd thought they were supposed to live.

Last June, on that bright morning outside of Winchester, could any of them have imagined they'd end up here? Much less so happy?

"Nonetheless," Renzo was saying in that low, dark,

thrilling way of his that still made Sophie shiver in delight, "there will be hell to pay. Naked hell, *cara mia*, I hope it goes without saying. It is because I love you that I must punish you in this way, you understand."

"I love your punishments." She smiled at him. "And you. Always you."

Renzo held the back of his son's head in his hand as if there was nothing on earth more precious, and the smile he aimed at Sophie was filled with too much love to bear and a thousand promises, sex and devotion, honor and beauty, always.

She couldn't wait to live their whole, long, beautiful life together.

Because Sophie was a woman who kept her promises, especially to Renzo.

Each and every promise, as long as they both lived.

So that was precisely what she did.

Forever.

* * * * *

COMING SOON!

We really hope you enjoyed reading this book. If you're looking for more romance, be sure to head to the shops when new books are available on

Thursday
26th July

MILLS & BOON

Coming next month

MARRIAGE MADE IN BLACKMAIL
Michelle Smart

'You want me to move?'

'Yes.'

A gleam pulsed in his eyes. 'Make me.'

Instead of closing her hand into a fist and aiming it at his nose as he deserved, Chloe placed it flat on his cheek.

An unwitting sigh escaped from her lips as she drank in the ruggedly handsome features she had dreamed about for so long. The texture of his skin was so different from her own, smooth but with the bristles of his stubble breaking through…had he not shaved? She had never seen him anything other than clean-shaven.

His face was close enough for her to catch the faint trace of coffee and the more potent scent of his cologne.

Luis was the cause of all this chaos rampaging through her. She hated him so much but the feelings she'd carried for him for all these years were still there, refusing to die, making her doubt herself and what she'd believed to be the truth.

Her lips tingled, yearning to feel his mouth on hers again, all her senses springing to life and waving surrender flags at her.

Just kiss him…

Closing her eyes tightly, Chloe gathered all her wits about her, wriggled out from under him and sat up.

Her lungs didn't want to work properly and she had to force air into them.

She shifted to the side, needing physical distance, suddenly terrified of what would happen if she were to brush against him or touch him in any form again.

Fighting to clear her head of the fog clouding it, she blinked rapidly and said, 'Do I have your word that your feud with Benjamin ends with our marriage?'

Things had gone far enough. It was time to put an end to it.

'*Sí*. Marry me and it ends.'

Continue reading
MARRIAGE MADE IN BLACKMAIL
Michelle Smart

Available next month
www.millsandboon.co.uk

LET'S TALK
Romance

For exclusive extracts, competitions
and special offers, find us online:

f facebook.com/millsandboon

◎ @millsandboonuk

🐦 @millsandboon

Or get in touch on 0844 844 1351*

For all the latest titles coming soon, visit
millsandboon.co.uk/nextmonth